# THIS
# WAY
# TO
# HEAVEN

# THIS
# WAY
# TO
# HEAVEN

———◆———

## TOM FOLEY

A TOM DOHERTY ASSOCIATES BOOK

NEW YORK

This story is fictitious. The characters do not exist. However, while some liberty was taken as to the timing and location of occurrences and atrocities so that they might all be included within the framework of this story, the details of the Bosnian War and the accounts of "ethnic cleansing" are based on historical fact.

THIS WAY TO HEAVEN

Copyright © 2000 by Tom Foley

This book is printed on acid-free paper.

A Forge Book
Published by Tom Doherty Associates, LLC
175 Fifth Avenue
New York, NY 10010

www.tor.com

Forge® is a registered trademark of Tom Doherty Associates, LLC.

Design by Lisa Pifher

ISBN 0-312-87402-2

First Edition: July 2000

Printed in the United States of America

0  9  8  7  6  5  4  3  2  1

# ACKNOWLEDGMENTS

**I WOULD LIKE TO ACKNOWLEDGE** the courage and dedication of the journalists covering the Bosnian War, who by risking their lives exposed the reality of ethnic cleansing in Bosnia—particularly the existence of the camps—to the rest of the world; the efforts of my agent, Carolyn Jenks, who never stopped believing in this book; and Tom Doherty and his outstanding staff at Forge Books, particularly Stephanie Lane, whose talents as an editor made this a much better novel.

I also wish to thank all those in Bosnia who shared their experiences of the war with me, particularly the Mihajlos for their account of the bombing of Dubrovnik; Selma for the role of Medjugorje; Dina for the siege of Sarajevo; Seamus for the refugees; Tina for the Serb perspective; Adem for his experience with smuggling and with the Muslim defenses; and Karlo for the camps. A special thanks goes to Jakobin and his family in Sarajevo, especially little Ilda for staying up all night to translate her neighbor's sometimes graphic accounts. I promised you all that I would tell your story to the people of America. I hope someday you will learn that I tried my best to keep that promise.

# BOSNIA-HERZEGOVINA

0    30    60 km

0    30    60 mi    KRAJINA

VOJVODINA

• Prijedor

• Omarska

• Banja Luka

• Tuzla    SERBIA

• Vukrenica

• Jajce

Travnik •    • Srebrenica •

Zenica

**Sarajêvo** ✪

• Pale

CROATIA

• Split

• Mostar

• Medligorje

YUGOSLAVIA

Ploce

MONTENEGRO

*Adriatic*
*Sea*

Dubrovnik •

# AUTHOR'S NOTE

**THE INCLUSION OF DESCRIPTIONS** of atrocities and violence is, I believe, necessary in order to give a true account of the Bosnian War. While a certain amount of detail is necessary and, I hope, helpful to an understanding of what happened in Bosnia and why, I have tried not to demean the victims or trivialize the suffering of the Bosnian people. If my intent were merely to horrify, there are an endless number of documented atrocities—eyewitness accounts, reports by neutral countries and agencies, testimony and evidence from the international war crimes tribunal—that are more shocking and gruesome than anything depicted here.

# PROLOGUE

September 20, 1992
Dear Maria,

I don't blame you for being disappointed in me. I did everything they said I did. If I go home to stand trial, they'll lock me up for a long, long time.

In fact, I don't even blame you for thinking that for all of these years I had you fooled, that I'm like all those people you try so hard not to be like. People who only care about themselves and about money. I know what kind of person you are. You're the kindest, most compassionate, selfless, most beautiful person I've ever known. I mean, you're probably the only person I've ever met who never did one wrong thing in their whole life. That's one of the reasons why I love you so much.

Look, I'm no saint, but I try—you know I try to be good. I know you don't really believe all those things you said when I called you from Italy You were upset and angry and I can understand that, but I wish you'd given me a chance to explain, because I know I could make you understand what's happening here and then you'd understand why I did it. If being found guilty in a military court makes me a bad person—well, then you can just go on thinking what you're thinking. But I'm doing the right thing, baby. I know I am.

I love you so much, Maria. I want to be with you more than anything, but I can't go back to America because doing the right thing is no defense in a military court. Soldiers are expected to follow orders; nothing more, nothing less. I didn't follow orders so I'm guilty—guilty as charged. They'd throw me in the stockade for sure. That's why going back to America is the one thing that I won't do for you, because it would mean that I'd have to live my life without ever holding you, or kissing you, or touching you again. I'd rather die than live that way.

There's only one solution, Maria. If we're going to be together, you have to come to me. We could still have everything we've always wanted—we could have it here. This war won't last forever. Dubrovnik is beautiful, the people are great—I know I could make you happy here, and you can do what you've always wanted to do. Believe me, with all of the refugees crowding the coastal cities to escape the war, there's not a place in the world that needs a good doctor more than this place.

I know I'm asking a lot, but if you knew what's happening here you'd believe in me and you'd come. I know that it's confusing with all these different peoples you've been reading about in the newspapers killing each other—Bosnian Muslims, Bosnian Serbs, Serbs, Yugoslavs, Croats, Bosnian Croats—it probably just seems like it's a bunch of crazy people killing each other in some senseless war. But this is much worse than a typical war, and the main reason for that is that the Muslims can't defend themselves. They have no weapons to fight back with. That's why I had to help, and that's why I have to stay here to continue to do whatever I can.

If you bear with me, I'll try to explain. It's really very simple as long as you go back far enough to understand where all of these people came from, so that you can understand who they are and why they're fighting now. Once you understand, I know you'll agree I'm doing the right thing. You'll want to come to help the Muslims, too. I know you.

The Muslims in Bosnia are peace-loving Europeans who're caught in the middle of a fight they never wanted, just like Bosnia has been caught in the middle of Eastern and Western powers for centuries. You have to go back a couple thousand years to understand what I mean.

The territory that eventually became the country of Yugoslavia was part of the Roman Empire until about the fifth century, when it was divided into an eastern empire and a western empire. The division of the Roman Empire was made right through the middle of the future boundaries of Yugoslavia. Slovenia and Croatia stayed under Rome's control and were Catholic, while the eastern half— Serbia, Bosnia, Kosovo, Macedonia—came under the authority of Constantinople in the east, which practiced the Eastern Orthodox religion.

By the sixteenth century the Ottoman Turks had invaded from the east and took control of most of the eastern half, including Serbia and Bosnia. The Slavs were permitted to continue to practice their religion but were denied a lot of privileges unless they converted, so a lot of Slavs converted to Islam to make life easier. That's why the three dominant ethnic groups in Bosnia—Muslims, Serbs, and Croats—all look alike: they're all Slavs! The only difference between a Muslim and a Serb or Croat is that people considered Muslims today are descended from Slavs who decided to convert during the hundreds of years of Ottoman occupation. In fact, most Bosnian Muslims don't even actively practice Islam.

Now, at the same time the Serbs and Muslims were dominated by the Ottoman Turks, the Slavs in Croatia (the Croats) were ruled by the Austro-Hungarian empire. After the Ottoman Empire began to lose its power in the late 1800s, most of Bosnia was ceded to the Austro-Hungarian empire. But after centuries of being dominated by the Ottoman Turks, the Bosnians (those Serbs, Muslims, or Croats living in Bosnia) decided that it was about time they were free to govern themselves. Bosnia became very nationalistic in its struggle to be free. In fact, in 1914, a Bosnian Serb (an ethnic Serb who lived in Bosnia) named Gavrilo Princip assassinated the archduke of Austria n Sarajevo. This assassination was one of the causes of World War I.

When the war was over and the Austrians lost along with the Germans, the Allies decided it would be a good idea to just throw all of the southern Slavic people together and make one country for them. So they took the old medieval kingdoms of Serbia, Croatia, Bosnia, Slovenia, Montenegro, Macedonia, Kosovo, and Vojvodina and made one country out of them, which eventually became known as Yugoslavia (which means "southern Slavs"). Despite opposition by the Croats, the Serbs, who were the most powerful of the various ethnic groups, won approval for a highly centralized form of government, which was basically a monarchy under the Serb king.

The Serbs, Croats, Muslims, and the other ethnic groups all got along well enough until just after the Nazis occupied Yugoslavia during World War II. The Nazis set up a fascist puppet government run by the Croats called the Ustasha (which means "uprising" in Serbo-Croatian). There were two Yugoslav resistance groups fighting the Ustasha: the royalist Chetniks, who wanted to return to the prewar Serbian monarchy; and the communist partisans, a multi-ethnic group led by Josip Broz Tito. Although the partisans and Chetniks spent a lot of their time fighting each other, they managed to wage a successful guerrilla war against the Ustasha. The Ustasha fought back with a campaign of extermination, including civilian massacres and concentration camps. With help from the Nazis, the Croat-led Ustasha killed more than six hundred thousand Serbs, Muslims, Jews, and Gypsies. Even the Nazis were shocked at the Ustasha's violence, and they were afraid that the bloodbath would cause even greater resistance. It got so bad that Germany's ally Italy had to occupy some areas of Bosnia just to put a stop to the slaughter.

In the end, Tito's partisans, with help from the Allies, won and took control of the country. Tito abolished the old Serbian monarchy and established the Federal People's Republic of Yugoslavia. He kept ethnic hatreds in check for forty years, but when he died, some leaders started playing on the old ethnic hatreds to gain supporters, which eventually led to the war that's going on right now.

A couple of years ago, when all of those former east bloc countries were breaking free from the Soviet Union, the two most industrialized and westernized Yugoslav republics—Croatia and Slovenia—decided they wanted their own independence. When tiny Slovenia declared independence, there wasn't much of a fight from the Serb-dominated Yugoslav government. But when Croatia tried to do the same, the Yugoslav army, whose senior-officer corps is dominated by Serbs, crossed Croatia's border to take control of an area called the Krajina, which means "miliary frontier."

You see, with all of the shifting of borders over the centuries, a lot of Serbs had settled in southern Croatia along the Krajina.

When Croatia declared independence in 1991, the Serb leaders started bringing up the old stories of the sufferings of Serbs at the hands of the Ustasha during WWII. President Slobodan Milosevic of Serbia, who had risen to power a few years earlier by riling up the Serbs and encouraging a dangerous Serbian nationalism— something Tito had carefully kept in check for forty years—claimed that the only way to protect the Serbs in the Krajina from an independent Croatia was to invade southern Croatia and take over the Krajina.

The war lasted from July 1991 until last January. After six months of brutal fighting, the Krajina was in the hands of Serbia, and a shaky UN-brokered truce was put in place. It wasn't much later that the UN sent in guys like me to help keep the peace and help with the relief missions.

Now, by that time it was pretty clear that Yugoslavia was finished as a country, so Bosnia was the next province to declare its independence. Bosnia had a multiethnic population and planned to establish a multiethnic government. The Muslims, Serbs, and Croats living in Bosnia—which the newspapers back home sometimes call Bosnian Muslims, Bosnian Serbs, and Bosnian Croats—had been living together for centuries, including the last forty years in complete peace under Tito. Bosnia, and especially its capital of Sarajevo, has always been known for its multiethnicity, so there didn't seem to be any reason to think it wouldn't continue that way. Besides, what were they going to do? There are no ethnically pure regions in Bosnia, so you can't just give a third of Bosnia to each of the three sides. Partition is impossible.

So last April, a referendum was taken in Bosnia on whether or not to leave Yugoslavia. The Bosnian Serbs, who were more than happy to remain a part of Yugoslavia, especially now that Croatia had seceded and the increasingly nationalistic Serbs would dominate the Yugoslav government more than ever, boycotted the vote. Ninety-nine percent of the remaining citizens of Bosnia—Muslims and Croats—voted for independence and a multiethnic government. But as the Muslims and Croats were voting, trying to decide the issue democratically, the Serbs were getting ready for war. With guns and money supplied from Serbia and the power of the Yugoslav army backing them, the Serbs went on the offensive.

The Serbs are having an easy time of it now because the Muslims are totally defenseless. The UN has placed the entire former Yugoslavia under an arms embargo—it's illegal to supply arms to anybody in Bosnia. The embargo helps the Serbs because they already have the entire Yugoslav army at their disposal, and because Russia has traditionally been like a big brother to them and is probably supplying them with arms despite the embargo. Even the Bosnian Croats, with their old ties to Germany and with aid from the newly established country of Croatia (whose long coastline makes it pretty easy to smuggle weapons through the embargo), have been able to establish a decent army to protect themselves.

But the Muslims in Bosnia have no army and have no one to help them. They're completely defenseless. Now the Muslims are backed into only a few isolated pockets that are surrounded by the Serbs. The only hope the Muslims have of defending themselves is by getting weapons through the black market, from smugglers who have to run not only the UN blockade in the Adriatic, but also have to get the arms past the Serbs and over the mountain ranges that cover the entire country. That's the Muslims' only chance, Maria. They desperately need guns to defend themselves. Without guns, they'll be slaughtered. They have nobody else to help them.

So now you know why I did it. Everything the army says about me is true. They can call me a criminal. They can call me a deserter. But I don't care about the army anymore. All I care about is you. I only care about what you think.

Please come to me, Maria. Tell me you still want to marry me and I'll make the arrangements right away. We can get married in Venice and, when it's safe here again, you can join me in Dubrovnik, where we can begin our new life together, and where we can do something for people who desperately need our help.

You can reach me through an acquaintance in Italy I work with sometimes. He's expecting your letter and he'll bring it to me:
Robert Jackson
c/o Anthony Brigandi
Piazza Castello 600
Barletta, BA
70051 Italia

Remember when I asked you to be my wife, you said you felt

like you were going to heaven? Please write me back and tell me you still feel that way. Tell me that you'll come to me. I promise you, wherever we are, as long as we're together, it can still be like heaven.

I love you, Maria.

Bobby

1

**A MILE OFF THE SHORE** of Dubrovnik, an old wooden fishing boat peacefully drifted in the Adriatic Sea. Though it was nearly midnight, the running lights had been switched off. Two men sat anxiously in the stern, listening to the waves beating against the side of the boat.

The American was looking westward into the strong wind. He was tall and well built, with black wavy hair and brown eyes. His blue plaid flannel shirt was faded the color of his old jeans, which were slit at the ankles so they could be pulled over his black army boots. He wore a grave expression as he squinted to search the dark horizon. He then looked at the Gypsy, whom he hardly knew, and saw him spit into the water. He watched the Gypsy close his eyes and move his lips without making a sound.

"Are you praying?" the American asked in fluent Serbo-Croatian, the language spoken in the former Yugoslavia.

"Gypsies don't pray. I'm making a wish. If you spit into the Adriatic at night when there is a swelling moon, any wish you make will be granted."

The American looked at the moon and its silver reflection on the sea, then spat into the water.

"What do you wish?" the Gypsy asked.

"I can't tell you. It won't come true."

"Who are you to know this? Are you a Gypsy?"

"Maybe I am," the American answered absently.

"You don't know much about Gypsies, do you, Captain?"

"You don't have to call me captain. And, no, I don't know much about Gypsies."

"There are no Gypsies in America?"

"I suppose there are. I don't really know what a Gypsy is."

"It has different meanings for different people."

"What is a Gypsy to you?" the American asked.

"The government definition is that they are the people of a tribe that came to Europe from the Middle East many hundreds of years ago."

"I didn't ask for the government definition."

The Gypsy smiled, showing a front tooth cracked in half. He was forty years old—fifteen years older than the American—short and thin, fair-skinned, with long, unruly black hair that he was constantly pushing out of his eyes. His brown eyes always seemed to be wide with wonder and he smiled whenever he spoke. He was wearing a worn black leather jacket and loose-fitting gray slacks held up by his gun belt. "To me, a Gypsy is one who has no home."

"Then, yes, we have plenty of Gypsies in America. If that's what a Gypsy is, I'm a Gypsy."

The Gypsy laughed and let out more line on his makeshift fishing rod. He was sitting on a salt-stained wooden chair with his feet kicked up and hanging over the side of the boat. An old carbine rifle he had just cleaned and oiled lay across his lap. He lifted a bottle of slivovitz—plum brandy—to his lips and took a mouthful, making a face as the gum-numbing liquid slid down his throat. He doubled over coughing, pounding his fist against his thigh.

"Good stuff?" the American asked. There were two bottles of whiskey on a shelf next to him but he hadn't opened them yet.

The Gypsy wiped the tears from his cheeks. "It's homemade," he said, handing the bottle over. The American drank and also began to cough.

"You see. We're brothers, my *Amerikanac*-Gypsy friend. Or cousins, at least," the Gypsy joked.

"What are you using for bait, cousin?" the American asked.

"Nothing. No bait. No need for bait. I am fishing Serb-style. When the fish try to flee, I will be waiting for them."

The American smiled and, noticing the glow of a light in the distance, took up his binoculars, focusing on the navigation lights on the bow of a faraway boat. Green light on the left, red light on the right. He returned the binoculars to the floor by his feet.

The Gypsy could see that the American was anxious, and he thought he knew why. "Would you like to know what I wished for?" he asked. "I wished for a beautiful woman, who will love me truly and whose eyes I can look into and know that, whatever tragedy is ready to strike, I have shared real moments with her, and that every morning when we wake, I will know that I'm one of the lucky ones."

The American suddenly lost his smile. "Aleksandar told me you were one of the cheerful ones. What's all this about tragedy and death?"

"I was talking about a woman, not of tragedy and death. Maybe it's the talk of the woman that bothers you? Are you missing someone?"

"I have no one."

"That's not what I was told. I was told the Italian is to bring you a letter from your woman in America."

"Drop it. I said I have no one."

The Gypsy considered the American carefully. "You have no home, and you have no woman?"

"That's right."

"I think you are trying very hard to be a Gypsy."

"I guess so," the American grunted.

"So that is what you're doing here? Learning about Gypsies?"

"Sure."

"And you have come to help your Gypsy brothers?"

"I was with the Blue Helmets," the American sighed, referring to the UN peacekeeping forces, who were identified by the bright blue helmets they wore to differentiate themselves from the warring factions.

"I know," the Gypsy admitted, surprising the American. "Aleksandar told me about you, Captain Robert Jackson."


One year earlier, as a lieutenant in the United States Army, Jackson had volunteered for a tour of duty with the UN Protection

Force in Croatia. He had been fluent in German since high school and had studied Russian in college, so it was not difficult for him to learn to speak Serbo-Croatian. Although he had hated leaving his fiancée, Maria, for an entire year, he had volunteered because the army—desperate for candidates capable of quickly learning to speak Serbo-Croatian to help keep the shaky truce between Croatia and Serbia after the war for the Krajina—offered to end his commitment early if he spent a year with the peacekeepers. Maria was in her third year of medical school in San Francisco, and he had been assigned to Fort Sam Houston in Texas. He took the peacekeeping assignment hoping to hasten his discharge from the army so he could join Maria in California and they could be married. He spent most of his first month as a peacekeeper in the beautiful Croatian capital of Zagreb, where he coordinated relief missions to war-torn areas along the Krajina. But his frustration over the constant hijackings prompted him to soon begin to oversee his relief convoys heading for small towns in southern Croatia.

It had been three months ago that his life had changed forever. His convoy was a day outside of its destination, a decimated village along the Krajina. The UN trucks under his command were parked along the side of the mountain road as most of his men slept. Jackson was walking along the row of trucks, making one last inspection before turning in, when he saw a figure dash out the back of the last truck, running off into the trees.

He pulled his pistol and ran into the dark forest, following the sounds of the thief crashing through the trees, until he came to a clearing where the moonlight illuminated a band of young men. All were unarmed. Standing in the center was a tall, handsome young man about his age, with sharp, dark features. At his feet lay a crate of medical supplies stolen from Jackson's convoy. There were many more crates lying in the clearing.

Jackson aimed his pistol at the tall young man in the center. "You're under arrest," he said in English.

The thief stared back at him.

"You're under arrest," Jackson said again, this time in Serbo-Croatian.

"I understood you the first time," the young man replied in English. He began to laugh. "Never before have I met a Blue Helmet who spoke our language. Or is that the only thing they taught you to say?"

Jackson, wearing his camouflage fatigues and a light blue beret identifying him as a UN peacekeeper, stood uneasily in the clearing. The young man seemed too at ease. Jackson looked over his shoulder, expecting to see someone ready to jump him, but there was nobody there.

The thief took a step toward him. "Maybe they taught you other things to say in our language, too? Did they teach you how to say, 'Yes, we know you're defenseless, but we will give you no guns'? And did they teach you how to say, 'Yes, we know you're starving, but we will give you no food'? Or did they teach you to say, 'We know you're sick, but we can give you no medicine'?"

"You stole from my convoy," Jackson said, even more worried now that he could see that the young man didn't fear him. "These supplies are meant for people who need them, not black marketers. Not criminals, like you."

A couple of the other young men in the clearing who understood English began to laugh.

"Yes, we're criminals," the young man in the center said. "And do you know why? Because we're Muslim. Every Muslim in Croatia is a criminal now."

The other young men laughed again, louder this time.

The thief walked right up to Jackson, his face only inches from the barrel of Jackson's pistol. "Shoot me, lieutenant," he said calmly. "Shoot as many of my men as you can. But you'll run out of bullets before I run out of men. Then they'll be forced to jump you, and if you know what sufferings they and their people have endured while the UN relief passes them by, you'll forgive them for beating you to death with rocks and sticks."

Jackson's hand was sweating, so he readjusted his grip on the gun. "Just leave the crates here and move on. No one will come after you. You have my word. But I won't let you have these supplies. They're needed elsewhere."

"I know better than you do where they're needed. Come with us, lieutenant. Let me show you where we criminals are taking your precious supplies."

Jackson didn't move, but soon the young man in the center,

and then the rest of them, picked up the crates and walked off into
the forest. Jackson hesitated, not knowing what to do. He knew
only that he wouldn't shoot them, so he followed them deep into
the forest, then up the foothills and into the mountains. He was
breathing heavily from the climb and his legs were weary, causing
him to trip over the rocks and roots he couldn't see in the darkness.
Finally they reached a rocky ledge near the top of a mountain. He
smelled smoke. He was waved into a cave, where a fire illuminated
the faces of two dozen children and women.

"I am a Muslim," the handsome young leader told him. "I
didn't even know these people until several weeks ago. I've never
been to their village, but when I learned what was happening to
Muslims here, I came to help. The UN wouldn't protect them. The
UN wouldn't restore them to their homes. Now they have no village
to live in, no village for your UN trucks and your life-saving supplies to be delivered to. So now they're my responsibility. I am
Aleksandar. These are my people."

From then on, Jackson supplied Aleksandar with everything he
needed. Aleksandar and his men would sneak into the airport in
Zagreb at night, where Jackson would be waiting with cases of food
and medical supplies. Each time they met, Jackson would learn
more about Aleksandar, who was almost single-handedly keeping
hundreds of sick and starving Muslims alive. Their arrangement
worked smoothly for several weeks, until the Serbs set their sights
on Bosnia, causing Aleksandar to come to him with another request: guns.

The first time Jackson had tried to divert a few cases of M16's
to Aleksandar, he had been caught and arrested. He was thrown
in the stockade and, having been accused of selling UN guns and
supplies to black marketers, he faced a certain court-martial. It was
an open-and-shut case. Even his military lawyer didn't believe he
was giving the guns away—not that it would be any defense. Pro-
viding guns to foreign nationals in a war zone, especially one in
which the United States was obligated to uphold a UN arms embargo, was a serious offense. He was facing more than ten years in
military prison.

He was being sent back to the states to stand trial when the
truck transporting him to the airport was suddenly surrounded by

a group of armed men in a narrow alley in Zagreb. From the back of the truck Jackson could hear shots being fired, followed by demands to stand down and orders to drop all weapons. In a minute Aleksandar burst through the tarp covering the back of the truck and carried Jackson, whose hands and feet were chained, through the crowded streets and hastily placed him in the back of waiting car. Several hours later they ditched the car and Aleksandar threw Jackson over his shoulder and carried him off into the hills.

"Do you realize the trouble you're in?" Jackson had asked Aleksandar later that night as they sat outside the mouth of the cave. "Why did you do this for me?"

Aleksandar, who was filing through the chains around Jackson's wrists and ankles, did not even look up. "My heart told me it was the right thing to do," Aleksandar had answered simply.

The Gypsy offered Jackson the slivovitz, but Jackson pushed it away. "Yes, Aleksandar told me you were a peacekeeper, but he says that now you're considered a criminal in America and that you can never go home. Is it true what he says, Captain?" the Gypsy asked.

"I never made captain," Jackson corrected him, ignoring the Gypsy's question because he did not want to discuss the fact that he could never return to America, to his family, and most importantly, to Maria. "I was a second lieutenant."

"Aleksandar told me that if you hadn't come to help us, you would be a captain by now in the *Amerikanac* army. So out of respect, I call you captain."

"What do I call you? I'm tired of calling you 'Gypsy.' "

"I am called Zarko," the Gypsy replied proudly.

"Were you a soldier?"

"We are all soldiers now. But, no, I have never been a soldier of any army."

"What did you do before the war?"

"I did what all good Gypsies do," Zarko answered happily. "I avoided work and marriage and family."

Suddenly a bright flash of light burst over the city of Dubrovnik. There was a loud crack as the sound of the flare washed over them, startling them. They stood looking at the green-gray mountains towering over the walled city. Dubrovnik was a city so unique it had been placed under special UN protection as one of the treasures of western civilization. Now, despite the UN designation, tracer fire streaked across the sky, and bombs launched by the Serbs and Montenegrins entrenched in the hills ripped the ancient city apart.

Jackson turned his back on the city and again looked westward. The Gypsy, however, stood transfixed, then tossed his makeshift fishing rod into the sea and cursed at the mountains.

"Is that how the Serbs fish?" Jackson asked.

"I have no stomach for it," Zarko replied angrily. "I've lost my appetite. What kind of Gypsy am I who loses his appetite?" He sat down and shook his head thoughtfully. "I am a false Gypsy," he said sadly. "I am a false Gypsy, and you are a false *Amerikanac*."

"How do you figure that?"

"Because *you* are here, Captain."

Jackson grinned. "Do all Gypsies speak in riddles?"

Zarko smiled again, liking Jackson. "Aleksandar once said that you were not like other *Amerikanacs*. Most *Amerikanacs*, he said, always do whatever is in their own best interests. But Aleksandar says that is not so with you. He says you're a rare *Amerikanac*."

Both men turned to watch as the line from the discarded fishing pole suddenly went taut. Then it skirted through the Adriatic, causing tiny ripples to trail in its wake.

This pleased the Gypsy. He shouted above the noise of the shelling, "Go along, fish. Swim as fast as you can to Italy. Go along, little refugee. I hope they accept you at the border!"

Jackson's eyes followed the departing pole until they caught another glimpse of light on the horizon. He peered through his binoculars at the bow of an oncoming boat. Noticing that the navigation lights had been switched—on this boat the red light was incorrectly on the left and the green light on the right—he tapped the Gypsy on the shoulder and pointed.

"They come!" Zarko agreed excitedly. He eagerly sprang into action and started the engines. "What do your Italian friends bring us, Captain? Do they bring a tank?"

"Stop joking," Jackson told him. "These Italians are not to be joked with. Do you understand?"

"Who's joking?" Zarko asked, feigning indignation. "Why not a tank? We could use a tank."

"The Italians aren't bringing guns or medical supplies tonight, they're bringing a man—an *Amerikanac*—who Aleksandar has agreed to guide north."

"Ah, this sounds like an important mission!" Zarko exclaimed excitedly. "Is this *Amerikanac* coming to kill Milosevic?"

"I don't know exactly what he's coming to do," Jackson admitted. "I don't even know who he is—but don't make jokes with him. His mission could end the war."

Zarko turned completely around. "Now it is you who makes jokes!" the Gypsy exclaimed immediately. "That is impossible!"

"The man who has sent this *Amerikanac* to us is a very important man—a great man," Jackson explained. "I have complete faith in this man. If he says the *Amerikanac* can help end the war, then it's possible."

"In that case," Zarko began, pretending to come to attention like a stiff-backed soldier, then saluting with his left hand, "I hereby pledge my allegiance to this *Amerikanac*."

"I told you no joking."

"I'm sorry, Captain. It's a Gypsy's nature to joke. You better order me—I am the kind of Gypsy who follows orders."

Jackson was readying to throw a line to the other boat. "In that case I order you not to make jokes with the Italians and the *Amerikanac*." He sighed, doubting that the Gypsy was as dependable as Aleksandar had claimed. "All right, Zarko, cut the engines."

"Jackson!" he heard a voice call out from the fast-approaching boat. It was not the voice of his Italian contact. "Robert Jackson!"

"Pull alongside!" Jackson shouted in return, recognizing the boat now, smaller than Jackson's, only twenty-five feet with just a small cabin. The engine had been turned off, and now the boat was gliding toward him, faster than it should. "You better slow it down, Brigandi!"

Suddenly Jackson heard the sound of machine-gun fire and threw himself to the deck of his ship. In a second he was lying face-to-face with the Gypsy, who stared back at him, wide-eyed. "Captain! Are you hit? Are you hit!" Zarko asked frantically.

"Start the engines!" Jackson ordered quickly, his whole body shaking, finding it difficult to think. Despite nearly four years in the army, including taking part in the ground offensive in the Gulf War, he had never before come under enemy fire.

After another brief burst of gunfire, Zarko pulled his carbine off his shoulder and worked it until he could free the action and load it with a single cartridge. Jackson crawled to a storage compartment and pulled out his M16, all the while shouting orders to the Gypsy to head for Dubrovnik at full speed. But by the time he turned to order the Gypsy to cover him, Zarko was standing with his hands in the air, the old carbine lying at his feet.

Jackson could see the dark silhouette of a large man standing at the side of the other boat. "I'm Colonel Samuel West. Are you Jackson?" he heard the unfamiliar voice ask Zarko. When the Gypsy, who couldn't understand English, didn't reply, Colonel West told him, "You can put your goddamned hands down, I wasn't firing at you. I'm coming aboard." He threw his machine gun to Zarko, who, after recovering from his initial fear and surprise, hastily turned the machine gun on him as he came aboard.

As Jackson rose to his feet the stranger landed with a thud on the deck of Jackson's boat. He appeared to be in his late forties, well over six feet tall with a powerful soldier's build and a long, narrow face that was a collage of scars and wrinkles. His graying hair was close-cropped, accentuating his thick neck. Jackson readied his M16, then walked right up to the stranger, squinting to examine the man's camouflage fatigues for any identifying patches or medals. There were none.

"Jesus, you guys are jumpy," Colonel West complained in a deep, gruff voice. "You can put your guns down—Katz sent me."

"Why the hell did you fire at us?" Jackson demanded angrily.

"If I was firing at you, you'd be dead," Colonel West told him matter-of-factly.

"Where's Brigandi?"

"I thought it better to come alone, then sink the boat once I found you. I don't want to leave a trail behind. I was never here, you understand?"

Now Jackson understood, but he was still shaken by the shots and angry that the colonel hadn't provided any warning.

"Call off your man," Colonel West demanded again, nodding toward Zarko, whose hands were shaking as they held the colonel's machine gun.

"It's all right," Jackson told Zarko in Serbo-Croatian. "He wasn't shooting at us, he was shooting out the bottom of the Italian's boat."

The Gypsy did not move.

"Zarko, put the gun down. That's an order. Stand down!"

"Captain, I always obey orders," the Gypsy finally began, his voice trembling as he looked over Jackson's shoulder. "But I must report that . . . I . . . I . . . request that . . ."

Turning toward the Italian boat to see what Zarko was afraid of, Jackson froze when he immediately noticed that the cabin light had suddenly been switched on. The stern was completely submerged with just the bow raised above the water. The boat was now beginning to slide quickly into the sea. Jackson could see a stocky man with tape over his mouth through the small, circular cabin window. Blood was running down the man's face from a gash atop his bald head.

"Brigandi!" Jackson shouted at the boat as the cabin window began to sink beneath the surface. Jackson leaned over the side of his boat and could clearly see the terror revealed in Brigandi's eyes as the powerful Italian man pounded against the glass with his hands, which were bound at the wrists.

Jackson rammed the butt of his M16 against the window once, cracking it, but the boat was sinking quickly now so his next blow landed impotently against the glass as the boat plunged straight down. The light emanating from the cabin momentarily turned the Adriatic a dazzling dark blue as Jackson had one last view of Brigandi, whose wide eyes were pleading for help. It was the first time Jackson had ever watched somebody die before his eyes.

Jackson climbed the railing and prepared to dive in after Brigandi, but Zarko dropped the colonel's machine gun and pulled him down hard, sending them both tumbling to the deck.

"No, Captain, you'll drown!" Zarko cried, trying to hold Jackson down. "The sinking boat will suck you under!"

By the time Jackson wrestled himself free of the Gypsy, the sea was dark, and as calm as Colonel West, who was checking the action of his machine gun. He didn't bother to threaten Jackson with it; he simply slung it over his shoulder.

"No loose ends," Colonel West explained coldly.

"You killed him, murdered him!" Jackson shouted, leveling his M16 at West's chest.

"I can't leave a trail," West replied without emotion.

Jackson's face was red with anger. "Do you know who that was? Brigandi was very important, he has powerful friends!"

Colonel West looked Jackson in the eye and continued emotionlessly, "I don't care about Mafia reprisals. I'm in, I'm out, and nobody knows I was here. You got that?"

"What about me—what about my men. When you're through with us will you kill us, too, to cover your tracks?"

"You're essential to my mission," the colonel told him. "You have nothing to fear from me."

"Mr. Katz wouldn't approve of this. You just murdered a man!"

"The goddamned Jew just paid me and told me what he wants—it's up to me to decide how to do it."

Jackson dropped his M16, balled his fists, and took a step toward the colonel, but suddenly he heard a voice call out over a loudspeaker in Serbo-Croatian.

"Captain!" Zarko cried, shouting above the pounding of the shells exploding in the city. "The false admiral comes! Croat patrol, forward and to the starboard side!"

Jackson rushed to the side of the boat and saw the patrol speeding toward them. It was a large, rusted fishing trawler with the word POLICIJA hastily hand-painted across the sides.

"Croats," Jackson groaned.

West looked at him curiously. "Croats? Are they friends or enemies?"

"Neither. It's Admiral Skopjak."

"What the hell is an admiral doing on that piece of crap?" West asked doubtfully.

"He's not a real admiral; he's the warlord of the sea around Dubrovnik," Jackson explained. "He can call himself whatever he wants." The Croat patrol was a hundred meters away and closing fast. Over a loudspeaker, a stern voice from the patrol ordered them not to move. "They're going to board us."

Colonel West slipped off the safety of his machine gun. "Order your man to get up front; you and I will take up positions in the stern and—"

"Don't give me orders! If it weren't for the fact that Katz sent you, I'd have the Gypsy blow your head off," Jackson said, as if Zarko were a professional hit man, although behind the colonel, Jackson could see Zarko staring at the Croat patrol, hugging his old carbine like a security blanket. "I'll handle Skopjak; just keep your mouth shut."

A minute later the patrol had come about, the Croat seamen lashing themselves to the side of Jackson's boat and flooding it with a spotlight. A dozen Croat seamen stood watch from the trawler with automatic rifles in hand as Admiral Skopjak boarded Jackson's boat.

Skopjak was short and pudgy, which helped him keep his balance at sea even though he had never even set foot on a boat before the war started and he seized the opportunity to effectively regulate the smuggling in and out of Dubrovnik, taking as much as 50 percent of all arms sought to be smuggled inland. He wore a pair of glasses with one lens blackened over his blind eye, and a black police uniform with a black skipper's hat bearing the Iron Cross of the old German army. He held out his black-gloved hands, palms up, and cast a familiar eye on Jackson. "Why isn't my percentage waiting on deck? I have other duties tonight."

"Fighting the Serbs?" Zarko asked dryly, "Or pirating your allies' ships?"

"Even during a war, a nation must enforce its customs laws." He gave Zarko a patronizing grin. "I haven't seen you before. Since you're with Jackson you must be Bosnian. That makes us allies, yes? But you have no coastline, so you must pay duty."

"What an alliance!" Zarko exclaimed. "Will we still be allies when Croatia and Bosnia no longer exist!"

"Lay off, Zarko," Jackson said harshly. He turned to the Croat warlord and said in a conciliatory tone, "I apologize, Admiral Skopjak. It was a wasted night. Our contact never showed up. Sorry for the inconvenience."

"Liar!" Skopjak exploded. "When we first spotted you we saw a boat sink alongside yours! What did you receive from that boat before it went down?"

Jackson held up his hands innocently. "We didn't receive any shipment tonight. We were waiting for our Italian contact when we came upon the other boat you saw. We were able to rescue the passengers just in time."

Skopjak glanced about, laughing at Jackson. "Where are these fortunate passengers?" he asked doubtfully.

Jackson motioned for Skopjak to follow him into the darkness of the cabin, then screwed a lightbulb into an outlet at the end of a wire hanging from the roof. The Croat's skepticism turned to surprise as he looked into the faces of a husband and wife in tattered clothes cramped in the cold, damp cabin, huddling with their three children. They smelled of body odor, their faces were drawn, and they were obviously shaken by the gunfire. They recoiled and shielded their eyes from the light.

Jackson unscrewed the lightbulb and closed the door without saying anything to the refugees in the cabin. He wasn't sure if Skopjak would believe his story, but he needed to show Skopjak the cabin to assure him that no arms or medical supplies had been picked up that night.

"I'll take them back to Dubrovnik until I can arrange another way for them," Jackson said, frowning.

"They look like they've seen enough of Dubrovnik," Skopjak said. The city had been under siege for weeks.

"They'll have to stay at my flat for now," Jackson sighed. "It's right next to one of the walls that surround the old part of the city, so it's safe." As they both knew, the Serbs wouldn't even think about bombing near the old walls of Dubrovnik, which were a national treasure. Napoleon had left the walls alone. The Ottoman Turks hadn't dreamed of harming them. Even the *Nazis* had respected the walls.

Skopjak nodded in agreement as his eyes settled on Colonel West. "I haven't seen this man before, either. He doesn't look like one of your usual peasant friends. Who is he?"

"He's my uncle Sam," Zarko cracked.

"He looks like a soldier," Skopjak said, ignoring the Gypsy.

"He's no threat to your interests, Admiral," Jackson assured the Croat. "He has no money and he brings nothing of value."

"Very well, Jackson," Skopjak said, shrugging, content now that he knew Jackson had not picked up any weapons or medical supplies that night. "I believe that this *Amerikanac* is of no concern to me. I have such limited interests, after all." Skopjak turned to board his ship, but suddenly glanced back at Jackson, grinning. "If you want to sink Mafia boats, that's up to you. But it seems like a very bad business to me." He picked up one of Jackson's bottles of Scotch whiskey, leaving the other. "My percentage," he explained, laughing, and continued to laugh as his boat pulled away, the Croat sailors keeping an eye on Jackson until they were out of sight.

Colonel West folded his arms contentedly. "All right, Jackson, I'm in a hurry to get to Bosnia so—"

Jackson raised his hand in the air, signaling for silence. As he had been watching the Croat patrol heading back to Dubrovnik, he had noticed something different about that night's attack. The sounds of the bombs and rockets had suddenly grown much louder. "We have one stop to make first." He nodded at the city, which was alight under the tracers and the bright flashes of the explosions in the city.

"Jesus Christ," the Gypsy groaned. "The Serbs are bombing the city walls!"

West looked toward Dubrovnik, taken aback at the ferocity of the attack. It was much more than he had expected from what he had mistakenly considered a small conflict amongst equally ill-equipped guerilla factions. "We're not going anywhere near there," he insisted.

"There have been rumors of a Serb offensive—this must be it," Jackson explained. "There isn't a safe place in the city anymore, and one of my men is there. I'm not leaving without him." Jackson turned to the Gypsy and told him in Serbo-Croatian, "We'll pull into the old harbor; I'll jump out and try to get to Franjo. You pull away from the city, give me fifteen minutes to return, then come back and pick me up. If I'm not waiting for you, get the colonel to

Medjugorje. Aleksandar should be waiting there to take him north."

Zarko started toward the wheel, then reconsidered. "Captain, I always obey an order, whether the orders are from you or from Aleksandar. But I beg of you to please reconsider. You know I think Two Faces is an untrustworthy Croat," he continued, referring to Franjo by the nickname Jackson's Muslim men had given him, "but I don't wish him dead. However, it is too dangerous to go to the city now—"

"Aleksandar told me I could count on you," Jackson interrupted.

"If you order it, I'll go to the city myself—even though I think I'll die there. But I will not let you go. Forgive me, but Aleksandar has ordered me to stay with you—to protect you. I would be disobeying his orders if I let you go to Dubrovnik during such an attack as this."

Jackson's eyes narrowed. "That's not why you're here. Aleksandar told me you needed a break from running guns in-country."

"I tell you that Aleksandar sent me here with orders to protect you. If I let you go to the city, I will be disobeying Aleksandar's orders. As I told you, I am a Gypsy who knows how to follow orders."

Jackson looked back at the city, past the smoke and the fires, past the tracers streaking through the sky like lasers in some futuristic apocalypse. He could see only Franjo, buried under the rubble of his flat next to the city walls, or worse, waiting at the old harbor for Jackson to try to rescue him.

"And don't forget the children in the cabin," Zarko pointed out. "You'll be putting them in great danger by sailing into the harbor during such an attack."

Jackson bowed his head, knowing that Zarko was right. In a minute he leaned over the rail and looked at the light of the moon glistening on the water. "Start the engines, Gypsy," Jackson groaned, then spit into the Adriatic.

## 2

**IT WAS JUST AFTER SUNRISE** when they finally docked at the port of Ploče, forty miles up the coast from Dubrovnik. After Jackson found the refugee family a place to stay while they sought another way to Italy, Jackson, Colonel West, and Zarko set out for Bosnia. The morning sun warmed them through the dirty windows of their car, a silver Renault with ill-fitting spoilers that nearly reached the ground. The sky was burning red above the green mountainsides that rose from the sea, their stone peaks blackened by smoke from incendiary bombs.

The Gypsy drove for over a half hour through a wide valley the Neretva River cut through the mountains. Behind them, the dark blue expanse of the Adriatic faded from sight. Jackson turned one last time and looked down the coast, beyond the burned pine forests, to see the smoke hovering over Dubrovnik. He wondered if it would be the last time he would see the city he had come to love, and he wondered if Franjo had survived the night.

He had met Franjo a month earlier, before the Serbs and Montenegrins were firmly entrenched in the hills over Dubrovnik. Jackson's hair was still cut short then, as army regulations dictated. He had just arrived in Dubrovnik to help Aleksandar set up a smuggling operation, and was instantly awed by its charm and beauty. He would take long walks around the ramparts that circled the old city, where it was easy to envision archers and cannoneers from centuries ago, keeping watch over the Adriatic for the invaders who tried unsuccessfully to conquer the city by force. He would shop in the farmers' market for fruits and vegetables—they were still available back then—and he would wander the maze of narrow stone alleys and stairways amongst the tiny villas with red-tiled roofs that made up the interior of the city. Dubrovnik was like a medieval castle, with its residents living in their flats and villas like the king's retainers. He was just beginning to become one of them—the *Amerikanac* arms merchant who came to help fight the Serbs—and everywhere he went the people of the city waved to him or clapped him on the back and called him friend, or even better, *simpatican*— a man of quality. He was like an adopted brother.

He had been sitting in a café along the Placa, the main boulevard in the carless city, where the stones were worn smooth by centuries of foot traffic. It was back in the days when it was relatively safe to walk about as long as he stayed away from the Catholic churches and the Franciscan monastery because they were the favorite targets of the Orthodox Serbs firing mortars from the hills. Jackson had heard the high-pitched whistle before anyone else. He instinctively grabbed his waitress, who was setting down his Turkish coffee, pushed her to the ground, and tried to cover her with his body. The mortar hit twenty meters away. The explosion shook his body and left him temporarily hard-of-hearing. He knew he wasn't hurt, but he feared that everyone else was dead because he didn't hear a sound. Then through the smoke he saw a man running about madly, his hair on fire, waving his arms about wildly, falling over and rolling on the smooth white stones of the Placa.

Jackson couldn't hear the man's screams. He couldn't hear the waitress beside him, now screaming frantically, holding her leg where a piece of stone from the Placa the size of a golf ball had wedged itself. He couldn't hear the cries from the children who had been lifted off their feet and hurled ten meters from the blast. He couldn't hear the calls for help by the others along the Placa, or the café owner rushing about trying to put out the fire. Jackson stood, miraculously untouched—perhaps the only person in the café who had not received a scratch—and looked about at the madness as the smoke lifted, not hearing a sound.

But he could see the man on fire, thrashing about. The fog in his mind lifted as the smoke cleared and he rushed forward, grabbing a tablecloth and falling on the burning man, putting out the flames that had taken half of his hair. He could smell the burning hair and flesh, and he could feel the man's hands beating his own head where Jackson had the tablecloth and was smothering the flames. Then he took the tablecloth away and he saw the most pitiful sight he had ever seen. He saw the man pass out as his skin blistered and smoke rose from the right side of his head and face.

Jackson took the burned man, Franjo, in his arms and carried him up the steep stone steps to his flat next to the city walls. Less than a month later Franjo was back on his feet, keeping the books, helping schedule shipments from Brigandi, sometimes cooking or taking care of the flat. Jackson had suggested to Aleksandar that Franjo could help out by keeping the books until he was healthy enough to run guns in-country, but Aleksandar shook his head disapprovingly.

"As for me, I wouldn't mind," Aleksandar had said. Unlike the others, he was university-educated. "But we're running guns to Muslims. All of our men—other than the Gypsy—are Muslim. They'll never trust a Croat."

"But Muslims and Croats are allies," Jackson had argued naively. "You're both fighting the Serbs."

"You've learned our language, and you know more about us than most *Amerikanacs* will ever know, but there is still much you don't understand."

"Then tell me," Jackson had asked, frustrated.

"It would do no good to simply tell you," Aleksandar said, shrugging. "You're an American. Your country is only two hundred years old. You won't understand unless you stay here long enough to truly care. Only then will you be capable of learning."

"I do care. I could leave now, but I stay because I know what's happening here and I want to change it. How can I help change it if I don't understand?"

It was clear that Aleksandar thought it would do no good, but he also knew that Jackson had proved himself and was deserving of a full explanation. "Very well," Aleksandar sighed. He sat down, crossed his legs, and lit a cigarette. "Our Muslim men will never trust this Croat because each one of them has a parent or grandparent or cousin or brother or sister who was killed by a Croat in

World War II. We've all grown up knowing what the Croats did to us then. When you're told from birth that Croats are Nazis who are planning to rise up again to slaughter all Muslims and also slaughter the Serbs, you cannot fight alongside them. Always, you would be looking over your shoulder."

"But the Muslims and Croats do fight together, as allies, against the Serbs," Jackson interrupted.

"Muslims and Croats have agreed not to fight each other, but that's not the same thing as being allies. The only reason the Croats don't attack us is because they need our help against the Serbs. If the Croats could hold the Serbs off on their own, they would be killing us now, just as the Serbs are doing. It's only a matter of time before either the Serbs wipe us out or the Croats turn on us. Either way, we Muslims are doomed."

"But you said you would welcome Franjo. Why are *you* above it all?"

Aleksandar exhaled a mouthful of smoke and carefully considered his answer. "In truth, my head tells me not to trust Franjo. But as with all important questions, the true answer lies in the heart. In my heart, I know that trust must begin somewhere, peace must begin somewhere. So in my heart I know that I must welcome him. But when Franjo turns on us—as my head tells me he will someday do—I'll kill him."


Fearing the snipers who shot out of roadside cafés or from the houses in the hills, Zarko drove as fast as he dared through the valley. Soon they passed through a town devastated by fighting, weaving in and out of the wrecked cars and fallen trees that clogged the streets. Then they were out of the town, climbing steadily into the hills on a winding road with very little traffic. When they neared the top of the mountain pass, Zarko stopped the car on the side of a cliff where there had been a scenic rest stop for tourists before the war.

"Give me your weapons, Colonel," Jackson said.

"Like hell I will."

"Fine. Keep them. But the Gypsy assures me that the Serbs at the roadblock just ahead confiscate them."

"The Gypsy assures you? You mean you've never been through the roadblock before?"

"I work out of Dubrovnik. Aleksandar, the man who will guide you, handles the shipments in-country."

"Why are you going to Bosnia now?"

"You saw Dubrovnik. Aleksandar won't go there to meet us now. Medjugorje is where we'll find him." Jackson got out of the car. "Zarko has excellent forged papers that say he's a Serb, so they won't bother to search the car. You'll get your weapons back after we cross the border into Bosnia."

West grudgingly turned over his pistol, rifle, and two knives. He thought for a moment before also producing an envelope from the inside breast pocket of his olive jacket. He handed the envelope to Jackson. "Give this to the Gypsy until we get through the road-block," he told Jackson. "Tell him if he opens it I'll slit his god-damned throat."

"What is it?"

"Don't be so curious," West warned him. "Your Italian friend regrets his curiosity."

Jackson glared at him, clenching his jaw, then handed Zarko the envelope and said in Serbo-Croatian, "The colonel asks you to protect this important document until we're through the road-block."

"What is it?"

"I don't know. But it's very important, so keep it somewhere safe."

"It must have something to do with why he's here!" Zarko exclaimed excitedly. "I'll read it while I wait and I will report to you the contents—"

"No. You're not to open it."

"But how—"

"I said not to open the *Amerikanac*'s envelope," Jackson told him, harshly now. "Just hide it somewhere safe until we get through the roadblock."

"I have a great interest in this *Amerikanac*'s mission to end the war, but I will do anything you order," Zarko grudgingly agreed. "Even a Gypsy understands the necessity of following orders during times such as these."

"Then I make it an order," Jackson said seriously.

After securing the weapons in a compartment bolted to the bottom of the car, they drove on until reaching a large tractor-trailer parked sideways across the road, blocking their way. Flying from the radio antenna was a flag with four crossed Cs back-to-back in each corner, representing the Serb saying, "Only gathering can save the Serbs." There were several black crows perched atop an abandoned tavern just off the road.

Jackson's heart began to race as the soldiers in black uniforms unslung their rifles. He could tell by their long, square black beards and long, unkempt hair that they were Chetniks—Serb paramilitaries styled after Serbian guerrilla outfits formed as long ago as the 1800s to carry out murders for which the regular army would otherwise be blamed. The Chetniks were best known for their brutality during World War II, when they battled for control of Yugoslavia against both the Nazi Ustasha puppet regime and the communist partisans led by Tito.

"Papers!" the Chetnik demanded. He was a large man who looked to be in his forties, with a long black beard and hair hanging out from a black beret. He had a flattened nose, upturned like a boar's. A compact AK-47 assault rifle hung by a strap from his shoulder. He held out his hand, which was fat and stubby, like a paw, covered by a black leather glove.

"I am a countryman," Zarko replied, digging into his pocket for the papers he always carried with him that identified him as a Serb. The papers were flawless, so the Chetnik only looked at them briefly before handing them back.

"Papers!" he grunted, looking at Jackson and Colonel West.

"We're *Amerikanac* journalists," Jackson lied, "on our way to Sarajevo."

The Chetnik considered him closely. "Show me your credentials."

Jackson tried to look annoyed. "I wish I could, but just down the road, a band of armed Serbs stole our car and our equipment. This man," he went on, looking at Zarko, "was passing by and offered us a ride."

"You must be mistaken?" the Chetnik said innocently, speaking directly to Jackson and Colonel West. "Serbs are peace-loving.

I assure you it must have been the pigs." *Pig* was a favorite Serb insult for Muslims—ironic since strict Muslims do not eat pork. "Only pigs would do such a thing. Haven't you heard that they murder innocent Serbs and sacrifice Serb babies to their god and burn our churches? They are to blame for this war. It was the traitorous Slovenes and Croats who stole Yugoslav land, and the Bosnian Turks, too, when they turned to traitors." Jackson knew that it was a common Serb insult to refer to Bosnian Muslims as Turks.

"I'll decide for myself when I get to Sarajevo," Jackson said arrogantly, confident that the Gypsy's plan was working.

"Ah! You are new to Serbia?" The Chetnik seemed to forget that Sarajevo was in Bosnia. "Come with me. I will give you proof that the Turks are to blame, proof that you can show on your *Amerikanac* televisions!"

"Brother," Zarko said suddenly, and smiled at the Chetnik, showing his cracked tooth. "We don't have time. I must get to Mostar. I am in a great hurry."

"You'll wait here until I say you may go!" the Chetnik growled. "You'll wait here until I'm through with these *Amerikanac* journalists, who must learn that the Turks are slaughtering our brothers!"

Jackson and Colonel West had little choice but to follow the Chetnik behind the roadside tavern, which served as the guard station for the roadblock.

"Stand here," the Chetnik ordered before setting off up a path through the pine trees. The black crows perched atop the tavern suddenly flew away, their harsh calls echoing through the hills. They noticed that the back wall of the tavern was covered with bloodstains, and bullets had chipped the cement away.

Colonel West knelt and brushed his fingertips through the red-stained dirt. "What the hell did you say to the soldier?"

"I told him we're reporters," Jackson explained. "The Serbs are terrified that the U.S. will help the Croats and Muslims against them. They realize how important the press is in affecting public opinion back home, so the Gypsy knew they wouldn't dare mistreat us if they thought we were reporters. Besides, I needed another excuse to get through without having the car searched. We've got a couple of cases of rifles bolted to the bottom of the car."

"You and that Gypsy better know what you're doing," West snarled, wiping the dirt and blood off his fingertips.

Just then another Chetnik appeared from the path in the woods carrying a rifle. He wore a tall, fur winter cap adorned with a medallion of the Serb double-headed eagle. The Chetnik looked at them for a long moment, then pointed his rifle at them, motioning with it to follow him.

"Hurry up!" he barked.

After following him up the short path to a stone house, they found themselves in a small, smoke-filled den where several Chetniks were drinking and shouting obscenities at each other. Two fought over a pack of cigarettes. One pointed his gun at the other.

"Enough!" a Chetnik at a small desk told them. He had been flipping through a pornographic magazine. He had the customary long black beard, and his long black hair was tied back in a ponytail. He was the only Chetnik not wearing the black uniform. He had on a cheap black suit with wide pinstripes, like an old Chicago gangster. "I told you, no drinking on duty."

"But look at you," the Chetnik with the fur cap said, pointing to the bottle of slivovitz the man in the suit had been drinking from at his desk.

"Yes, but I know that when I'm drunk I won't shoot someone's head off." The Chetnik in the suit looked up at Jackson and Colonel West. "So, *Amerikanac* reporters, eh?" He stood and shook hands with both of them. "I am Captain Arkanic. I understand you wish to see proof of Muslim brutalities? Well, follow me. I'll show you much you can write about. The *Amerikanac* people should be very interested."

Captain Arkanic led them to a small room in the back of the house and invited them to sit on an old, musty couch. After producing a jug of slivovitz he stayed with them to watch the first film, entitled, "Muslims Slaughtering Whole Villages." He added his own commentary and told them of the time he visited the Genocide Museum in his home city of Belgrade, where he saw the bones and teeth of Serbs exterminated in Bosnia. Irrefutable proof, he claimed, that Muslims and Croats were slaughtering Serbs.

Captain Arkanic refilled their shot glasses and excused himself after hearing his men calling for him to join them at the roadblock.

On the screen was a picture of rows of dead bodies. On each corpse's forehead was a number written in black ink. It was not explained what the numbers meant. The English-speaking narrator only explained that Muslims had set fire to an Eastern Orthodox church and, using machine guns, had mowed down the defenseless Serbs when they tried to flee.

Colonel West ignored the film and stood up immediately, looking out the windows and then inspecting the room. He noticed two videotapes on top of the television. One was entitled, "Muslims Raping Serb Women," the other, "Mujahideen Torturing Serb Prisoners." Mujahideen, West knew, were fundamentalist Islamic warriors, mostly from countries such as Iran, Libya, and Syria, who vowed to give their lives for Allah in jihad—Islamic holy war.

He walked over to a map on the wall of the six republics and two provinces of the former country of Yugoslavia: the boomerang-shaped Croatia and its long Dalmatian coastline; Serbia, making up most of Yugoslavia's eastern border with Romania and Bulgaria; tiny Slovenia, bordering Italy and Austria; Montenegro and Macedonia in the south; and the two Serb-dominated provinces, Vojvodina and Kosovo.

Then there was multiethnic Bosnia and Herzegovina, more commonly referred to simply as Bosnia. It was roughly the shape of South Carolina, but only two-thirds of its size, landlocked between Croatia and Serbia. The statistics printed at the bottom of the map stated that the population in Bosnia was 45 percent Muslim, 34 percent Serb, and 17 percent Croat.

"What route am I taking into northern Bosnia?" Colonel West asked.

"There's a road that goes through Citluk and Suica that's safe enough," Jackson answered, glad to take his attention from the gory propaganda video. "Before you get to Kupres, Aleksandar will ditch the car. There's scattered fighting just north of there. You'll have to hike through the mountains until you pick up the Sana River, which you'll follow through more mountains to Sanski Most. Then it depends on where you need to go. I apologize for the long stretches on foot, but the roads in the north aren't safe and Mr. Katz said it's important you make it there quietly."

West nodded. "It's even more important that I make it *out* quietly."

Jackson paused, then said, "If my men are going to help you, you're going to have to tell them what this mission is all about."

"I know," West replied. "But not until we reach our destination. Those are Katz's orders. If we're caught along the way he doesn't want the Serbs to . . . to extract . . . the information from your men. Katz knows I'll never talk."

"Did you meet Mr. Katz personally?" Jackson asked.

"I already told you—don't be so curious."

"I only ask you because I did, and it was a great honor. He's an amazing man—a Holocaust survivor, you know?" The colonel offered no reply. Jackson was sure he wouldn't be able to get the colonel talking about it, so he simply asked flat out, "Look, I need to know what my men are risking their lives for."

"Same thing I am—Katz's money."

"We're not getting paid."

Colonel West turned to face Jackson. "I thought you worked for him."

"I've never worked for Mr. Katz before. This is the first time," Jackson explained. "All he told me when I met him a few weeks ago in Venice was that your mission was confidential. He's an Israeli diplomat; his career and all of the programs he helps fund around the world depend on his good name. He explained that he can't be linked to some mission sending a soldier into a sovereign nation."

"If you're not doing it for money, why would you agree to help?" West asked incredulously.

"Mr. Katz said that this mission, if successful, could end the war."

West laughed, shaking his head doubtfully. "Yeah, that's what he tells me, but I think he's wrong. I'll complete the goddamned mission all right, but I doubt Katz will get the results he's hoping for. He overestimates the importance of his plan." West looked out the window again, noticing several Chetniks walking drunkenly back toward the road. "So that's it? You're an idealist, like Katz? You don't stand to benefit personally by helping me?"

"He suggested that he'd provide food and medical supplies I could smuggle in-country if my men helped you," Jackson admitted.

"I hope for your sake you got that in writing."

"I trust Mr. Katz completely," Jackson said without hesitation. "Besides, I had already agreed to guide you for free. I'd do anything to help end this war. I've been to refugee camps in Croatia—all the stories you've heard are true. I went with relief missions and spoke to the victims myself. They were defenseless civilians who were driven from their homes by the Serbs. I saw their scars. I saw men and women and children with missing limbs. I spoke with girls who'd been—"

"What do you expect from these people—they're all animals," West interrupted. "Besides, I've heard the stories about attacks on civilians, and I'm telling you, it's simply not true. Refugees always claim they were intentionally attacked when in reality any civilian deaths or injuries are nothing more than collateral damage. Armies don't bother with civilians. The purpose of war is to defeat the opposing *army* so you can impose your will on your enemy's people. An army doesn't waste its time—or even ammunition—on civilians. It doesn't make sense."

Jackson was about to disagree when the crack of a single gunshot, then the sounds of a woman screaming and a child crying, interrupted him. There was one more shot, then silence. He jumped to his feet and went for the door. Before he made it there, West blocked his path.

"It's none of our business," West told him.

"Are you kidding me? I heard a woman and a child."

"Guerrillas," West said.

"I'm going out there."

"What do you think *you* can do about it?" West challenged him.

Jackson, who was unarmed and obviously outnumbered, suddenly felt helpless. "They think we're reporters," he tried, thinking aloud. "Maybe there are more people out there about to be executed. They won't shoot them if we're there to witness it."

West smirked. "It's more likely that they'd just shoot the witnesses, too. Don't be naive, Jackson. You don't understand. You weren't in 'Nam. All the gooks were guerrillas. Women, kids, old people, sick people."

"They're innocent civilians and you know it!"

West shrugged. "What do I care what these savages do to each other?"

Jackson had to fight to control his anger. "Then what are you doing here, West? Don't you realize that Mr. Katz is helping the Muslims too?"

"I'm only here to achieve the objective of my employer. As far as helping anyone—that's Katz's concern. What the hell do I care if these goddamned savages slaughter themselves."

"I can't believe Katz would send *you*! You don't even care about what's happening here!"

West laughed at him. "You're the worst kind of fool, Jackson— an idealistic fool. And a war zone is no place for an idealistic fool."

"Think what you want about me, West, but you better understand one thing. If you turn on any of my men like you turned on Brigandi, I'll kill you. I swear to God I'll forget this whole fucking war and I'll come after you!"

They stared at each other for a long moment, neither man blinking, until West returned to the couch and watched the propaganda film silently.

Jackson looked out the window, feeling angry and helpless, thinking again of the gunshots he heard, of the woman screaming and the crying child. He tried to picture how it went with them. First, a shot out of the blue. That had probably been a Chetnik shooting the husband. He had probably been pleading for the life of his child and his wife. They were probably hoping to make it to the coast, then out of the country, to safety. After the first gunshot he had heard the scream and the cries. He imagined the mother screaming as she dropped to her knees, the child still in her arms as she knelt and pressed her face against her husband's face. In his mind's eye he could see the Serb paramilitary, like an animal in his black uniform and long black hair and long black beard, smiling with crooked yellow teeth as the woman begged for her child's life. The Chetnik probably put his gun against the child's head and pulled the trigger, killing both the mother and child with one shot.

In the space of ten seconds an entire family had ceased to exist.

But then Jackson realized that what had happened was over now, and West had been right. There was nothing he could do. He returned to the couch and fell into it, suddenly exhausted, and closed his eyes.

"I recognize that picture," West said suddenly, rubbing the gray stubble on his cheeks with one hand as he considered the pictures on the television. "Those aren't Serb victims, they're Vietnamese. That's My Lai."

Jackson listened as the narrator explained that Muslims had overrun a Serb town in the north and massacred every Serb in it. On the screen was a picture of rows of dead bodies. The narrator claimed that Muslims had bombed a school filled with Serb children.

Jackson looked again at the rows of corpses lying in the blood-stained dirt. "How can you be so sure that's My Lai? You've seen these pictures before?"

"I don't need to see pictures," Colonel West said. "I was there."

"You're a liar," Jackson insisted. "They don't make you a colonel in the U.S. Army after taking part in a massacre like My Lai."

"I never said I was a colonel in the U.S. Army."

Jackson's eyes narrowed. *So, West is one of those,* he thought. *He's not a real colonel at all.*

"Impaled," West said almost absentmindedly, reacting again to the video. "You know how they do that?"

"It doesn't take a genius to figure it out," Jackson said, looking away.

"You don't understand. It's much more than just ramming a spear through a man," West explained. "If the spear is greased and it's done right, no organs will be pierced and it could take all day for the man to die."

Jackson gaped at the television. "You mean they do that to a man when he's alive?"

"Of course. That's the whole point."

"I wonder what the Geneva convention says about that."

"Geneva convention, my ass," West scoffed. "You can't try to legislate a civilized war. There are no rules in war."

Just then, a Chetnik abruptly came in and grunted that they

were free to go. They were led past Captain Arkanic's empty desk, past the group of drunken Chetniks, and down the trail through the forest. When they reached the back of the roadside café, they came upon the small pool of wet blood. They couldn't walk around it. The Chetnik walked through it as if it weren't there. West stepped over it with his long strides.

Jackson looked down as if in a daze, slowing to see it clearly, to see it running off where the ground sloped, to see how it seeped into the earth, to smell it. He put his right foot into it, feeling his boot slip a little. His stomach heaved and he was almost sick. He stepped out of the blood and watched his right foot as he put his boot down in the dirt. When he lifted it again to take another step, he saw the bloody footprint his boot made on the ground, but with each step he took away from the place where the family had been murdered, the blood from his footprint became fainter and fainter, until finally there was no trace of it at all.

## 3

AFTER PAYING A "road repair toll" of fifty deutsche marks, Jackson and Colonel West rejoined Zarko, who was waiting for them in the car. They began their descent into a fertile valley of chestnut trees and vineyards, where there was a sudden increase in traffic as they neared the town of Medjugorje.

In 1981, six children were in the mountains near the then-tiny village when they saw a vision of a beautiful woman with black curly hair, blue eyes, and a glowing face. When they asked who she was, the woman replied, "I am the Blessed Virgin Mary." Ever since, religious pilgrims poured in every day by the hundreds and even thousands. Catholics from Ireland and America spent their life savings to make the long trip to Medjugorje. A beautiful new church, pale yellow with two towers, was built in the center of the suddenly thriving town, where the Mother of God was said to continue to appear daily to the six children, who were now in their twenties.

But during the war, Medjugorje also became a black-market junction. Strategically located between the port of Ploče and the inland city of Mostar, its abundance of hotel rooms and restaurants originally built to serve the religious pilgrims were now occupied by smugglers, black-market dealers, and highway pirates.

They pulled onto the main strip, passing the gift shops with their rows of religious statuettes and multicolored rosary beads dangling from display stands. "Who would bomb a town with such

religious significance as this?" Jackson asked absently, looking at
the skeleton frames of houses and hotels.

"It must have been the goddamned Muslims," West said.

Jackson asked Zarko which side bombed the town.

"Those buildings weren't bombed," Zarko explained. "They're
in the process of being built. This is a town from your *Amerikanac*
cowboy movies. How do you say? Gold rush? Boomtown? They
are building more hotels and restaurants and souvenir shops every
day. The war hasn't touched Medjugorje, although at night you can
see the rockets fired at Mostar."

Zarko left the main drag and drove very slowly as the low-
hanging spoilers and the guns beneath the car scraped along an
uneven dirt driveway. He parked in the rear of the newly built Our
Lady of Medjugorje Hotel.

"Watch the car," Jackson told Zarko, getting out.

Jackson and West walked past the children in the lobby of the
hotel. Jackson found the main desk and asked a young girl flipping
through a fashion magazine where he could find Zinna. Without
looking up, the girl pointed to the small gift shop down the hall.
West followed him. "Wait here," Jackson told him. "Zinna is—well,
Zinna may be a little unpredictable."

"Don't tell me what to do," West warned. "I want to meet this
guy."

"Zinna's a woman, and that's her first name, not her last. You
should always address people here by their first name only now,
West. Most Bosnians haven't used their last names since the war
began, to protect themselves and their families in case they say
something to offend one side or another. It's become very bad man-
ners to ask someone their last name. The fact that I even have to
tell you this should explain why I'm not taking you to meet Zinna.
Now wait here."

Zinna was in her midthirties, a red-haired, pale-skinned Irish
woman with hard, wary eyes. Aleksandar had once explained to
Jackson that Zinna had left her husband and children to come to
Medjugorje years ago to visit the site where the Virgin Mary had
appeared, hoping to cure a lifelong psychological disorder she simply referred to as her "troubles." When her troubles disappeared
immediately after she claimed to have seen the Mother of God on

Apparition Hill, Zinna vowed never to leave Medjugorje. She tended bar for a few years in an Irish pub on the main strip, saving enough to buy the struggling little hotel. Unfortunately, as the number of religious pilgrims visiting Medjugorje from around the world declined due to the war, she was forced to cater to gunrunners in order to pay her bills. She soon earned the smugglers' trust and, after her initial reluctance, Zinna began brokering deals for them. The money was so easy she soon turned her attention full-time to the black market. The hotel was now merely a front.

"You have a very eclectic inventory," Jackson told her, noticing a stack of ashtrays with the swastika emblazoned on them displayed right next to several statuettes of the Virgin Mary.

Zinna was standing behind a counter going over her books with the help of an old adding machine. "A lot of Croats stay here," she nearly growled in a rough Irish brogue, apparently thinking that he was accusing her of something. She sized him up as she lit a cigarette. "You know how the Ustasha are."

Jackson nodded. He knew that the Ustasha—the name of the Nazi puppet government set up after the Nazis overran Yugoslavia during World War II—had been fascist Croats who carried out their own primitive genocide against Serbs, Muslims, Gypsies, Jews, and even dissident Croats. They had used axes and sickles while the Nazis had used gas chambers. Now there were once again groups of Croats paramilitaries roaming the countryside calling themselves Ustasha.

"You're American," she said suspiciously. "We don't have any vacancies."

"I'm Robert Jackson."

Suddenly Zinna smiled, unable to hide her surprise. She seemed to transform before his eyes. She snubbed out her cigarette and waved the smoke away, then reached out to shake his hand. "Aleksandar talks about you all the time. He says you're the only American he's ever met who he couldn't figure out. He says that most Americans—"

"That most Americans always do what's in their own self-interest," Jackson finished for her. "Aleks has told me a lot about you, too, Zinna."

"I heard the news about the offensive," she told him, referring to the attack on Dubrovnik. "I thought you'd probably end up here. It seems everyone eventually ends up in Medjugorje." She motioned with her head to follow her into her office in the back and closed the door. They sat on folding chairs on either side of an old dinner table that now served as her desk. "What have you got? I got a guy who'll pay anything for a few French Milan antitank missiles."

"No, no missiles," he replied, trying not to laugh. Aleksandar had told Jackson that he did not think Zinna was completely cured of her "troubles" and that she often appeared to suffer from delusions of grandeur. "I have six cases of heroin," he told her.

"Too bad," she said, frowning. "That's very hard to sell these days. The market has been flooded since the Hungarians moved in. You would have been much better off selling it in Ploče, but I'll see what I can get for you."

Jackson shrugged. "I'll take whatever I can get. I want to buy some guns. About four cases."

"Oh, that will cost you," she warned. "Guns are going at twice the usual rate."

"Twice the usual rate?" Jackson smiled at her. "It's funny, Zinna, but whenever my men show up with heroin, the price is down. Whenever they show up with guns, the price for guns is down."

Zinna glared at him, realizing she was beaten. "You have guns, don't you? Four cases?"

Jackson nodded. "I'll take cash only—but no dinars. Deutsche marks or American dollars only. What's the exchange rate today?"

"Hard to say," she grumbled, visibly upset with herself for blowing the chance for a greater profit. "It changes every hour. But I have no dollars, so it will have to be marks." With the war came hyperinflation, rendering the Yugoslav dinar virtually worthless. The German mark was now the favored currency.

"Fine. I'll have the Gypsy bring the guns around." He started to get up, but Zinna suddenly put her hands on his.

"You're not very popular with the other smugglers around here, you know," she told him, lowering her voice as if someone might hear. "They don't like the way that you just give arms away. You force the other smugglers to keep their prices down—you're hurting their profit margins."

"That's their problem."

"It's my problem too, Robert. There's a lot of pressure on me to stop helping you guys out."

"You always get your standard cut," Jackson pointed out. "If you don't want our business, I'll find someone else." He stood to leave.

"Look, I have a proposition for you," she said, guiding him back to his chair and then pulling her chair right next to his. "I'm through with just being an intermediary. There's a fortune to be made here, but I need help. Aleksandar tells me that you've got contacts in Italy. I need those contacts to bring in heavy arms, and I need your help moving them in-country."

"You know we don't do this for profit," Jackson told her. "Why should we help *you* get rich?"

"Because with my help you can move more arms than you've ever dreamed of. I'm not talking about a few cases of guns, I'm talking about heavy artillery—missiles, helicopters, tanks—"

"Tanks!" Jackson repeated incredulously. He was beginning to think that Aleksandar had been right—Zinna was crazy. The Muslims had only two tanks to the Serbs' three hundred.

"Tanks are possible!" she insisted. "East bloc nations are practically giving them away, but I need you to get them here. Think about it. The profit would be enormous. The Muslims will pay anything for a few tanks!"

Jackson looked into her dull and lifeless green eyes. They reminded him of the painted eyes on one of the religious statuettes on the main strip.

"Do me a favor, Zinna," he said, unable to suppress a smile. "Don't mention this idea of yours to the Gypsy. If he finds out you want us to smuggle tanks, I'll never hear the end of it."

"You think I'm crazy, don't you?" she accused him. "Aleksandar thinks I am, too. Don't deny it. I know he thinks I'm insane. Everybody here thinks I'm nuts, but they're wrong, you have to believe me. Tanks, missiles, rockets—together we could do it. Stop thinking small. Don't be a fool."

"How many others did you go to with this opportunity, Zinna? There are others here with more men, more resources. You're only coming to me because everyone else turned you down."

"They're all fools. They don't realize what an opportunity they're missing."

Jackson tried to explain without upsetting her. "It's one thing for them to stay in your hotel, or to come to you to set them up with a buyer or a seller. But this is a dangerous business—nobody's going to become partners with someone who claims to have seen the Mother of God on that hill."

She bit her lip, suddenly very serious. Her eyes grew wide and she again glanced about to make sure no one else was listening. "It happened again," she confided. "Last night, something made me go there again, and it happened just like the first time. I had a vision of Mary."

"Zinna," he said as gently as he could, taking her hand. "You should go home. Go back to your family."

She pulled her hand away from his. "I swear I saw our Lady with my own eyes! I'm not crazy! It was a miracle!"

He felt so sorry for her. "Your troubles are back, aren't they?" he guessed.

She looked at him blankly, then put her face in her hands and began to cry. "I'd be fine if I hadn't lost my faith," Zinna sobbed. "I can't explain it. How can I believe in God when every day I hear of the terrible things happening in the north? I mean, you'd have to be crazy to believe that there's a God with everything that's going on up there. But then something happens, like last night, and I don't know what to believe. I swear to you, I saw *her!*"

Jackson leaned across the table. "Zinna, have you ever considered that you never witnessed a miracle? Maybe the cure for your problems is all in your head," he suggested. "Think about it. You were a devout Catholic and you heard about a hill where miracles occurred and people were sometimes healed. When you climbed that hill and prayed for a miracle, you had so much faith it would happen that in your own mind you convinced yourself that you had a vision—a miracle—and you believed that God had cured you. It's all in your head, Zinna. That's why, when you lost your faith, you lost your belief that God could cure you, so you're sick again."

She began shaking her head violently. "Have you ever been up Apparition Hill?" she asked without looking up.

"It wouldn't do any good," he told her.

Zinna took her hands away from her face and looked at him, suddenly remembering something. "That's right. Aleksandar told me that you and I have something in common. He says you used to go to church every Sunday when he first met you, but now you claim there's no God. He thinks the war has caused you to lose your faith as well."

Jackson folded his arms. "Like you said, Zinna. With everything going on here, you'd have to be crazy to believe in God."

**4**

**THE ROOM ALEKSANDAR KEPT** in Zinna's hotel was dark and appeared empty. On the walls were posters of U2, Pearl Jam, and John Lennon. On the back wall was a huge "Don't Tread on Me" flag with a coiled snake ready to strike. A poster of a beautiful woman in a bikini was taped to the ceiling. An electric guitar lay at the foot of the bed. At first the room appeared empty, but upon closer inspection, Jackson saw a figure tucked away on the floor in a corner.

"Aleks?"

The huddled figure turned slowly. "Robert?" The young man immediately made the sign of the cross in a hurried way.

Jackson rushed forward and grabbed him by the shoulders. "Emir! What are you ... are you all right?"

"Yes, Robert." Emir backed away and made the sign of the cross twice, very quickly.

"How long have you been here?"

"Things are ... things are very bad in the north," Emir said in a shaky voice. He was a boyish-looking twenty-one-year-old with straight brown hair and light blue eyes. He wore a loose-fitting green flannel shirt over his slight frame, a red down vest, and brown wool pants. A long scar began at his Adam's apple and sliced halfway across his neck, then turned sharply up his jaw, stopping near his right eye. "Roads that are supposed to be under UN control are blockaded by the Serbs. Chetnik pirates and local Mafia are stealing from smugglers and UN relief trucks. I have been traveling through the mountains for four days. I got here . . . yesterday . . . I think." He crossed himself. "I don't know about the others."

"What happened?" Jackson said, crouching next to Emir on the floor. "Tell me everything."

"We delivered the medical equipment to Sarajevo, as you ordered," Emir began. He crossed himself three times in succession. "We made it through the Serb lines in an armored Volkswagen van, down a steep mountain road under the Serb guns. Snipers lined the roads, but Aleksandar drove with much skill, so we made it through. Unfortunately, it was impossible to take the mountain road out because we would be traveling uphill, and therefore very slowly. We would have been easy targets for the Serbs. We were trying to arrange a safe way out of the city when we learned that the Serbs had just attacked Jajce, which is Aleksandar's home. He was in such a hurry to get out and try to help his family that he decided to risk sneaking past the Serbs by cutting through the airport.

"The airport is somewhat under control of the Blue Helmets," Emir went on. "The Serbs control the two narrow ends of the airport. The Muslims and Croats in Sarajevo hold one side of the runway, with freedom on the other. We waited for darkness to start sneaking across the tarmac. Suddenly, we were lit up by a searchlight. It was the Blue Helmets. Then Serbs began shooting at us from both ends of the runway."

"The peacekeepers must have shut off the lights once the shooting started," Jackson interrupted.

Emir shook his head, crossing himself again. "The Blue Helmets did not shut off the lights. I saw Aleksandar sprinting across the runway for freedom, but there was much firing that way so Adem and I ran back toward the Bosnian side. I made it, but Adem was shot. He went down, but still the Blue Helmets lit him up, so the Serbs kept shooting. There was nothing I could do."

"No," Jackson agreed solemnly, swallowing hard. "What about Aleksandar?"

"I didn't see him get hit, but the Serbs began shelling the other side of the runway after the UN lights went out. Then a UN truck came and searched for Adem's body in the dark." Emir made the sign of the cross very deliberately, waited a few seconds, and then crossed himself again. "I waited in Sarajevo for three days for my chance to get out through a sewer that runs under the airport. I had to crawl the entire five hundred meters."

Jackson put his arm around Emir and sat thinking for a moment. "If Aleksandar made it out, where would he go?"

"First to Jajce, but he should have brought his family to Medjugorje by now."

Jackson sat on the bed and put his head in his hands. *You can't worry about Aleks,* he told himself. *You have responsibilities; you have to think coldly, without emotion, the way they taught you in the army.*

"Emir, can you guide us north?" Jackson asked, realizing that since West didn't speak Serbo-Croatian, he had no choice but to help guide West north.

Emir crossed himself. "To Mostar the roads are safe enough, but to the north there are many roadblocks and the Serbs are everywhere. However, most of our men either quit or were killed before we made it to Sarajevo. It's only you and me now. It would be dangerous for two men to go alone, especially without Aleksandar."

"Zarko is with me. We need to get an *Amerikanac* north, then back to the coast. Can you guide us?"

"I know the way. But it will be very dangerous. Perhaps we can go to Jajce first, to find Aleksandar. He can take the *Amerikanac* the rest of the way."

Jackson hadn't thought of that. "Do you think there's a chance Aleksandar made it there?"

"If it were anyone other than Aleksandar, I would say no. But, it is Aleksandar."

Jackson looked at the young shepherd, forcing a smile and telling him gently, "I'm very happy you made it back, Emir." He stood and helped Emir to his feet. "You go get some sleep. Be ready to leave at sunrise."

"As you wish," Emir said. Then he crossed himself twice and said, "But without Aleksandar to lead us, I don't think I will sleep tonight."

**5**

**JACKSON FOUND ZARKO IN** a bar along the main strip. From their table in a corner, they could hear the rosary service being played over a loudspeaker outside the church down the street, so that the whole town could share in the evening prayers, even those who were working and could not attend. One of the original six visionaries who had seen the apparition on the hill would say the first half of a Hail Mary, then the congregation would finish it. Then, at the same time she appeared every evening, the Virgin Mary would appear to the six in the church choir to give her message of peace.

Jackson was already drunk from the wine he had found in Aleksandar's room He switched to whiskey now because wine made him think of Maria, who grew up in California's wine country. Thinking of Maria reminded Jackson that, after what West had done to Brigandi, it would be a long time before he could receive word from her.

The war had made delivery of the mail impossible and had knocked out all telephone service. Brigandi, who had been his only link to the rest of the world, was supposed to be carrying Maria's answer to his last, desperate letter. Jackson was beginning to get that weak, hopeless feeling and the emptiness in his chest that he always felt when he began thinking that it was possible he might never see her again.

*Now Maria's letter is at the bottom of the Adriatic,* he thought. *I'm sorry you're dead, Brigandi. I liked you, even though you were a crook. But more than anything, I wish you'd lived long enough to give me that letter.*

The Gypsy was sitting with his feet kicked up on another chair, his eyes closed. Jackson could tell he wasn't sleeping because he could see the Gypsy's lips moving. He put his bottle of whiskey on the table next to Zarko's nearly empty bottle of slivovitz and leaned forward. "I thought Gypsies didn't pray," Jackson said over the sound of the prayers being read over the church loudspeaker.

The Gypsy suddenly opened his eyes and sat upright. "I wasn't praying," he replied defensively. "You're mistaken. But surely you are an *Amerikanac* Gypsy, because you read my mind. I was thinking about religion."

"You were praying," Jackson insisted. "I saw you."

"No, Gypsies don't pray, but I was thinking about those kids who claim to have seen the Virgin Mary on the hill. It is very curious, don't you think? Many claim to have seen her."

"You're drunk," Jackson accused him. "Nobody saw anything. I bet those kids were late coming home for dinner one night, so as an excuse they told their parents they saw a vision of Mary. They were just kids; they didn't realize what they would start. All they cared about was not getting into trouble for being late. What could they say when their parents brought in priests, who brought in bishops, then cardinals? The whole town, the whole country, probably heard of it within a few weeks. How could these kids go back on their story after all that? A year later, the whole town's economy revolved around their story, so they went along with it. Now, instead of farming or raising livestock, they're worshipped almost like gods themselves. Instead of living in a rickety little house, they probably own their own hotels, so they perpetuate their own lie. Visions of Mary, my ass."

"I should find myself a hill and have visions." Zarko laughed. "Then I will live like a god, too. You really don't believe in these visions, Captain?"

Jackson shook his head. "I don't even think I believe in God."

"What do you believe in then? Nothing? How can you not believe in something?"

"What do Gypsies believe in?"

"Haven't you heard? We believe in food, drink, women, and

music. And we believe in laughter. You say you are an *Amerikanac* Gypsy. Do you believe in those things?"

"Sure."

Zarko nodded thoughtfully. "Always it is sadness with you. It's even worse now that you are drunk."

"I'm not drunk."

"It's not like a Gypsy to deny his drunkenness, my *Amerikanac* Gypsy friend. I am very drunk," Zarko proudly announced. But when Jackson remained silent, Zarko became serious again. "Always it is the sadness with you. It is the part about women again, eh? I can arrange a woman for you if you want. There is always Zinna. I think she likes you."

"She's nuts."

"You don't know her like I do. She's very clever. Besides, she's beautiful, and eager to please in bed."

Jackson smiled at the Gypsy. "You and Zinna?"

"Only sometimes. I'm in love with her, but it's hopeless. She doesn't take me seriously because I'm only a Gypsy."

"You're too good for her," Jackson said sincerely.

"I see. You want someone special, like your *Amerikanac* girlfriend that Aleksandar told me about."

Jackson looked annoyed.

"He only told me because he thinks it's important for me to understand certain things about you, since I am to watch over you."

"I don't need anyone to watch over me."

"Please don't be angry with me," Zarko pleaded. "We are becoming friends, yes?"

"Yes."

"Then tell me about your *Amerikanac* girlfriend. Was she very beautiful?"

Jackson stared at the whiskey bottle. "I don't want to talk about her."

"Yes, you do. Was she a beautiful blonde with a big chest?"

"No," Jackson said, smiling, picturing Maria now. "She has black hair and she's very thin."

"Does she have white skin that glows like a ghost, like all *Amerikanac* actresses have?"

"Her mother was Mexican-American, so her skin isn't pale; it's my color. But, yes, her face glows. Especially when she smiles. And she has very uncommon eyes for someone who's part Mexican."

"Tell me about these eyes!" Zarko exclaimed excitedly to urge him on.

"Did you see, when Brigandi's boat sank last night, how the cabin light lit up the Adriatic? Remember how blue the water was, dark, but with a glow underneath that made the surface sparkle? That's the color of her eyes."

Zarko whistled. "You must truly be in love, Captain," he said. "What a time to think of your woman."

"I think of her every second of every day," Jackson admitted, then downed another shot. "Even as Brigandi was going down, a part of me was thinking about Maria."

Zarko rolled his eyes. "How can a woman's eyes be such a color? I think every time you see something that is beautiful and blue you imagine it to be her eyes."

"No," Jackson insisted. "That really is the color of her eyes."

"What about her hair? Is it soft and light to the touch, and does it bounce about her face when she runs to you with her arms outstretched?" Zarko teased.

"Are you a Gypsy or a bad poet?"

"You don't think of her the way poets write about their true love? I thought all men who are in love think such thoughts."

"What about you? You said you love Zinna."

"Perhaps it isn't love that I feel for her," Zarko said sadly. "But I admire her greatly."

"You should be happy you're not in love."

"After listening to you, I'm glad all I have to think about is the war." Zarko laughed, but when Jackson began staring into his whiskey bottle, Zarko became serious again. "Captain?" he asked. "Would you do it again if you could go back, if you knew that you could never return to America if you were caught giving us supplies? If you knew that your woman would refuse to leave America to be with you?"

Jackson suddenly slammed his shot glass on the ground, shattering it. "That's not true!" he shouted at the Gypsy. The bartender looked up, concerned, but Zarko signaled to him that everything was all right, that he'd take care of it. "That's not true! She'll come.

I just need to make her understand what's happening here, make her understand that I was only trying to do what she would have done if she'd been in my position. You don't know her. She's a saint! She's going to medical school so she can help people who can't afford doctors. Believe me, if I only had the chance to sit down with her and explain everything to her, she'd want to be here, too. She'd want to help."

"Please, I don't want to upset you. I only meant to suggest that perhaps she isn't worthy of your sadness," Zarko said soothingly. "You are my captain. If you say she's worthy—I believe she's worthy."

"She's worthy," Jackson insisted. "It's just that nobody in America understands. If Maria knew what was going on here, she'd be here helping me."

"Why don't you explain things to her?"

"I've tried," Jackson replied, the frustration in his voice obvious. "I telephoned her the first chance I got—a few weeks ago when I was in Venice. She wants to believe me, but she says that if I didn't do anything wrong I should come home and face the court-martial. She told me she'd wait for me even if I were convicted. But I can't go home now—I'd get life. I'm a deserter now as well as a black marketer."

"She assumed you were guilty? This woman who claims to love you?"

"I am guilty," Jackson pointed out. "In my country it's a serious crime to help Bosnia."

"What has Bosnia done to America?"

"Nothing. I'm talking about the arms embargo."

Zarko nodded. "Yes."

"So here's what I finally did," Jackson said, his hopes rising now as he told the Gypsy. "I wrote her a letter explaining everything. Aleksandar helped me write it. I explained about the history of this place, explained who the Croats, Serbs, and Muslims are and why they're fighting, and how the Muslims are defenseless and have nobody to help them. How can she not understand what I did after reading my letter? Believe me, you don't know how wonderful she is. She'll come. She'll leave America to be with me. She'll want to help."

Zarko frowned as he poured the last of his slivovitz. "I am very glad I am not in love."

"Let's talk about something else," Jackson mumbled, pouring another shot. "Aleksandar said you'd be cheerful."

Zarko didn't have his customary smile now. "Why don't you go up that hill? Maybe you'll experience something."

"Stop joking," Jackson said, downing his drink. "Here, have some whiskey with me. Put that poison away." Jackson poured Zarko a shot of whiskey, but he refused it.

"During the Second Great War the Chetniks used to commit their murders after getting drunk on slivovitz," Zarko explained. "I don't enjoy the taste, but I've decided that to beat the Chetniks I must fight like the Chetniks."

Jackson pushed the shot of whiskey in front of the Gypsy again. "You said we're cousins. Share a drink with me, cousin. A drink between Gypsies." Jackson was smiling.

Zarko grinned, nodding, and drank the shot. "This is much better," he admitted.

"It's not very good whiskey," Jackson told him. He downed a final shot. "Now, go get some sleep, Gypsy. But first, make sure the car is ready to go."

"What use have we for the car?" Zarko said sadly. "Without Aleksandar to lead, the *Amerikanac* can't go north. Only Aleksandar can speak English, and besides, I'm only a Gypsy—I'm no guide."

"We can get him there. Emir will guide us."

"You go north? No, no. Aleksandar ordered me not to let you go north. I cannot disobey an order."

"I'm *ordering* you to get the car ready. We leave at sunrise."

"But—but Aleksandar ordered me to. . . ."

Jackson almost felt sorry for the Gypsy, who seemed genuinely upset and confused, especially in his drunken condition.

"No matter what I do, I will disobey an order."

"What are you worried about? A court-martial?" Jackson paid the Gypsy's bill and stood. "Did you ever see anything on that hill?"

"I saw the sun dance."

"Did you have as much to drink then as we've had tonight?"

Zarko laughed. "More."

"How long does it take? To witness a miracle, I mean."

"For some, even those with great faith, their miracle never comes."

"I'll give it fifteen minutes," Jackson said "I'll give God fifteen minutes to prove he exists. Not a second more." He began stumbling for the door. "If I see her, I'll tell her you said hello."

"Captain," Zarko called after him. Jackson turned to see the Gypsy holding up the whiskey. "I would take this. Sometimes it helps you see the visions."

**6**

**THE NEXT MORNING JACKSON,** West, Zarko, and Emir drove off through the mountains of southern Bosnia for over an hour. When the roads became impassable due to craters, overturned trees, and the imminent Serb roadblocks, they hid the car just off the road in the forest where Aleksandar had shown them, covering it with branches and leaves as best they could.

They set off on foot through a valley surrounded by cornfields and freshly whitewashed farmhouses. As they began climbing, the cornfields became green foothills where sheep were grazing. Then they were in a forest of huge oak trees, which gave way to hornbeams and beeches as they reached higher altitudes, until they passed through the pines near the rocky tops of the mountains. They left the road and trudged through the dense pine forest until they found a narrow trail along the edge of a deep gorge. They could hear the sound of rushing water as it poured through a hydroelectric power station downriver.

"This can't be the best way," West complained.

"Emir knows what he's doing," Jackson insisted. He wore his pistol in a shoulder holster and had an M16 slung over his back, like West. "He's done this plenty of times with Aleksandar."

West shot a look at Emir, who carried a compact machine gun in his left hand. With his right hand he was making the sign of the cross over and over.

"That kid is our guide?" West asked doubtfully. "I thought the

Gypsy was guiding us." Jackson shook his head. "What is he, a priest or something?"

"He was a shepherd before the war," Jackson explained "He knows these mountains. He's been herding sheep and goats through the hills in central Bosnia since he was a boy."

"Why does he keep crossing himself?"

"I think it's some sort of obsessive-compulsive habit or something. He's all right though. He's been in a few tight spots with Aleksandar, that's all. He's just nervous. Don't let his crossing himself worry you."

"I don't like relying on all these Muslim bastards."

"What is it that the colonel says, Captain?" Zarko asked. The Gypsy was overloaded, carrying his carbine in his hands, an automatic rifle on his back, two pistols in crisscrossing holsters around his waist, and a heavy brown canvas pack full of spare clips. There were several grenades clipped to his gun belts, which also held a few spare shells for the carbine. Jackson wondered how such a small man managed to carry so much through the mountains.

"Stop calling me captain," Jackson said irritably. He had a terrible hangover. "And he's not a colonel."

"But he calls himself—"

"He's a liar."

"He is a false colonel?" Zarko asked.

"He's an *Amerikanac* Chetnik," Jackson explained.

"They have Chetniks in America?" Emir asked.

"Yes. They're called militias."

Zarko looked over his shoulder at West struggling up the steep mountain trail. "What's keeping us from leaving this *Amerikanac* Chetnik? Let us complete his mission without him."

"We don't know what his mission is."

"Captain," Zarko began, as if he had a confession to make. "Yesterday, while you and the false colonel were with the Chetniks, I held his envelope up to the sun. I saw many names, and next to each name was a figure and, most importantly, a dollar sign."

"I *ordered* you to leave the colonel's letter alone!"

"What do you expect? I do my best to follow orders, but I'm a Gypsy, not a soldier," Zarko said, shrugging. "I thought about this a great deal last night and concluded that the *Amerikanac* must be an assassin."

Jackson looked at Zarko out of the corner of his eye. "I'm surprised you remember anything from last night, Gypsy."

"I don't drink to forget," Zarko told him seriously. "I did at first, but I never forget anymore. It's unfortunate."

"The man who sent the *Amerikanac* wouldn't send an assassin," Jackson told him. "He's a peace-loving man."

"The peace-loving man might have sent this colonel to assassinate Milosevic," Emir suggested.

"The president isn't in northern Bosnia. He lives like a king in a palace in Belgrade," Zarko told him, laughing. "And haven't you been listening? Captain Jackson just told us that the *Amerikanac* isn't a colonel."

"Stop calling me captain!"

Zarko pretended to zip his mouth shut, but he was still smiling.

"Forget about this mission for now," Jackson told them. "When we reach our destination, the *Amerikanac* will tell us." Jackson was going to warn them that West could be dangerous once he no longer needed them, but there was no need to alarm them yet. West would need them at least until they reached their destination in the north, and probably until they guided him back to the coast. Jackson planned to take precautions well before that time.

Zarko sighed. "If only I was the kind of Gypsy who sees the future."

Suddenly there was a rustling from the woods alongside the trail. The four men dropped and lay flat in the pine needles that covered the forest floor.

"Someone's there," Emir said in a timid voice.

"I think there's more than one," Zarko whispered. He checked the action of his old carbine, forgetting about the automatic rifle strapped to his back.

"Do you see anyone?" Jackson asked West.

"Nothing."

"Zarko? Emir? Can you see any men?"

Before either man could answer, the quiet of the forest was broken by three long bursts of gunfire. They all pushed their faces into the dirt. Jackson finally looked up to see West firing high into the forest. He hated the sound of gunfire when it was this close—it was so loud he could hear the sound of metal against metal when the trigger clicked and the action snapped back into place and bullets dropped into chambers, reminding him that guns were nothing more than mechanical killing machines.

"Hold your fire!" Jackson shouted.

"Don't shoot!" a thin voice cried out from the woods. "Don't shoot, we're unarmed!" A small man came out of the woods with his hands up, looking frightened. "We are not soldiers! We are unarmed!"

"Hold your fire!" Jackson again shouted to West, who had his M16 trained on the little man. "He's surrendering! Hold your fire!"

Jackson ran down the trail as the others covered him. There was indeed more than one in the woods. He could see an old woman holding a child.

"The rest of you, come out!" Jackson ordered. Then, much to his surprise, nearly a hundred people trickled out of the woods, each carrying a large pack on their back and bundles in their arms. Men, women, and children.

"Who are you?" Jackson demanded.

"I am Karlo," the little man said timidly, taking off his peasant's wool cap. "I'm the mayor of a town in the Drina River valley. These are the people of my town."

"What were you doing in the woods?"

"Our scouts saw that men with guns were coming," Karlo explained. "We don't want trouble. We are farmers. We are unarmed."

"What are you doing in these mountains?"

The mayor reached into his pocket. West immediately covered him, but Jackson waved him off. He had little fear that the mayor was reaching for a weapon.

The mayor fished out a torn piece of newspaper and handed it to Jackson. It was an advertisement for a "Town for Trade," boasting of thirty houses, paved roads, a school, and a gymnasium.

The mayor kept his eyes lowered as he spoke. "We are Croats who have traded our town for a Serb town advertised in the newspaper. It's near the Croatian border. We're on our way there."

"You traded your town?" Jackson asked incredulously.

"Yes. We're mostly Croats. Chetniks in our area would soon have taken our town from us. The Serbs we trade with would have soon lost their town to the Ustasha. Hopefully, now all will live in peace."

"What's he saying?" West demanded.

Jackson ignored him and spoke kindly to the mayor. "I'm sorry if we scared you."

"You are soldiers?" the mayor asked.

"We're just trying to get north."

"To fight Milosevic?" Muslims and Croats often referred to the Serb army and the Chetniks as Milosevic.

"Yes, we're against that devil," Zarko told the Croat mayor. "What's it to you?"

"I don't mean to pry, nor do I wish to talk politics. I ask you because there is one among us who doesn't belong—a boy we found along the trail two days ago. He was trying to find his way home but he was starving and too weak to go on. Many times today he has tried to get away, but we won't let him go because surely he'll die on his own. He doesn't know his way."

"Where is he?" Jackson asked.

The mayor called for the boy. Two men escorted him forward, standing on either side of him, holding his upper arms so he wouldn't run away.

He was a tall, thin boy of sixteen, with dark brown hair and blue eyes. His face was extremely thin, with sunken cheeks and eyes and pale skin. He wore brown peasant trousers and a home-made brown denim jacket. His shoes were worn and muddy.

"What's your name?" Jackson asked him.

The boy struggled against the men holding him and did not reply.

"His name is JuJu. It's written inside his jacket. Also, he has this," the mayor said, reaching into the boy's jacket pocket and taking out a velvet pouch. He dumped out a large emerald. Everyone who could see it gasped at its size.

"My name is Jusuf," the boy said angrily. "And that belongs to my family!"

Jackson stood directly in front of the boy and smiled at him. "Where are you in such a rush to go?"

"Vukrenica," the boy told him.

"It's on the way, Robert," Emir said. "It is where Aleksandar stops to rest and to pick up provisions for the second leg of the trip."

"What's going on?" West demanded, losing patience.

"This Muslim boy is trying to find his way home," Jackson said in English, still looking at the boy. "It's on our way."

"Not another goddamned Muslim. It's bad enough we've got him," West said, and pointed at Emir, who crossed himself nervously when he saw West point at him.

"We'll get him there," Jackson told the mayor. He put out his hand. "Give me the emerald."

The mayor hesitated.

"If I wanted it, I could take it from you," Jackson pointed out. "If I carry the emerald, he won't run off."

The mayor replaced the emerald in the velvet pouch and handed it to Jackson, who handed it to Zarko with orders to take care of it.

"You better be on your way," Jackson said to the mayor. "It'll be dark soon. I hope everything works out for you."

"I believe it will," the mayor said. "We're told they have good farms in our new town."

The Croats sent their scouts ahead and resumed their journey. As they walked away, West swore under his breath.

"Now the Muslims outnumber us," he said. "Why did you agree to take another one?"

"He's just a boy. Besides, we need to stop in his town to pick up provisions."

Zarko stood next to Jackson and watched the displaced Croat women of the town walk away, tall and thin, many with black turtleneck sweaters and tight, black denim pants.

"Beautiful girls," Zarko said, admiring them. "Not a fat one in the bunch."

Jackson nodded. Actually, he had been thinking the same thing.

"They are starving," the boy, JuJu, told them angrily, over-hearing Zarko. "And can't you see they wear black because they're in mourning?"

## 7

**THE NEXT DAY, JACKSON** and the others quit the trail by the gorge and started off into the untracked wilderness in the mountains. Emir proved a capable guide. They were all content to follow him through the evergreen forests, up steep ascents, and over narrow rock crevices to avoid the occasional gunfire they could hear coming from down in the valley.

They had hoped to reach JuJu's town on the Sana River in two days, but darkness had fallen on the second day and they had had at least another two-hour hike down through the mountains. With no discernible path, the descent would have been too treacherous in the dark.

That night, they huddled in a small clearing, where the pines shone like Christmas trees in the silver moonlight. It was cold in the mountains but they made no campfire. They had no food left to cook, but more importantly, they didn't want to draw the attention of the Serb units in the valley. They tried to keep warm and sleep through the pounding of the Serbs guns they could hear in the distance.

In the middle of the night, Jackson nearly leaped off the ground when he was awakened suddenly.

"Robert," he heard a voice whisper. "Come with me."

Jackson shook himself out of sleep and followed silently behind the shepherd. They hurried down a steep slope, crossed a dirt road very carefully, then continued down until they reached a plateau.

Two ravens called to each other from the pines overhead.

"I smelled a campfire so I came to see who it was," Emir explained. "Be very quiet."

They crawled now on the pine needles. Soon Jackson could hear voices. Emir sidled up beside a large pine tree and Jackson crouched next to him. They were looking down on a group of fifteen paramilitary soldiers, their black berets, long black beards, black uniforms, and heavy arms clearly visible in the firelight.

"Chetniks," Jackson groaned.

They could hear a Chetnik in a long black leather overcoat calling off names. "Sefer Sehic. Toni Hasenovic. Fikret Ganic. . . ."

"What are they doing, Robert?"

"Sounds like roll call."

"But those aren't Serb names," Emir told him. "They're Muslim." They listened as the Chetniks read off a few more names.

Jackson didn't want to wait around to try to figure it out. "Let's go."

They slowly backed off a few feet, but lay flat on the ground again when the Chetniks began shouting. Through a break in the trees, they could see that a pig was being carried into the Chetnik camp. The Chetniks began yelling at the pig, then formed a circle around it and taunted it with cries of, "Die, Turk!" or "Where is your daughter, pig!" or "Pray to Allah, Turks!" Soon they began kicking the pig. This continued until a Chetnik threw a knife next to the feet of another, the youngest-looking of them all. The young soldier looked at the others. They were all shouting at him, encouraging him. He picked up the knife and stared at it as he made a fist around the thick handle.

"Come on, Sasha!" the Chetnik leader shouted at the young Chetnik. "We have taught you how it's to be done. Show us your patriotism!"

Sasha, who had only been with the Chetniks for a week, was pushed into the middle of the circle. He was short and fat and only nineteen years old. He was trying to grow a Chetnik beard, but he had only a few whiskers on his chin and along his jaw. He wore the black Chetnik uniform and had a Kalashnikov strapped on his back.

Sasha looked at the pig. It was running about wildly in the

middle of the circle of Chetniks, panicked and trying to find a way out. The Chetniks kicked it back into the center every time it tried to escape. Sasha felt nervous because he was the new man. He knew the others had all proved their courage and patriotism many times before on previous campaigns, and they were all watching him now. He didn't want to let them down.

Sasha chased after the pig, finally grabbing it in an awkward hug. He wrestled with it until he had the pig's head pinned over a fallen tree trunk. Then, taking a deep breath, he drew the knife's blade across the pig's neck. The pig let out a horrible shriek, like an eagle's cry. The sound echoed ominously through the mountains as blood poured out from the pig's neck and covered Sasha's hands and arms. The other Chetniks began to cheer. Sasha stood and delighted in these cheers, knowing he had done well.

He was so eager to impress the others he dove back to his knees and sawed at the pig's throat until he had cut all the way through it. He hoisted the pig's head into the air and paraded it around the clearing. The pig's blood dripped down onto his head and shoulders. Sasha was smiling. He began to shout Chetnik slogans and signaled to the others to follow him. The Chetniks fell in behind him, singing a Chetnik song. Sasha led them over to where the mountain sloped steeply away. He threw the pig's head out as far as he could. They all came close to watch it tumble down into a rocky creek. The Chetniks drew tremendous delight from this and clapped Sasha on the back and saluted him.

Sasha smiled and accepted the congratulations. For the first time since he had been recruited from his town in eastern Serbia two weeks earlier, he felt like he was one of them.

Jackson and Emir had been watching the young Chetnik from their place up in the pine trees.

"Why did they kill the pig in such a way, Robert?"

"They're just drunken lunatics. Come on. Let's wake the others and get out of here."

They were across the dirt road and climbing up the rocky hill again through the pines.

"Robert, you haven't yet told me where we're going when we get further north," Emir said. "Are we bringing the *Amerikanac* where he needs to go, or are we going to Jajce first to find Aleksandar?"

"What do you think we should do?"

"I would put off looking for Aleksandar until after we help the *Amerikanac* complete his mission. That's what Aleksandar would do."

"Yes, that's what he'd do. But I'm surprised that's what you'd do."

"I love Aleksandar like a brother."

"I know. He says the same about you."

"But to end the war is much more important than one man. Even if it is Aleksandar."

They climbed silently for a few minutes, until Jackson had to stop to rest.

"Robert, is it true what the *Amerikanac* says? That his mission will end the war?"

"A great man sent the *Amerikanac*. If he says it's possible, we have to do whatever we can to help."

"But what do you believe in your heart? Do you truly believe this *Amerikanac* could end the war?"

Jackson closed his eyes and sighed, knowing that it made no sense to him but telling himself, for the thousandth time, to have faith in Abram Katz. "Let's just worry about getting into that town. I don't like the fact that Chetniks are so close by."

"Perhaps we should not go to the town."

That was exactly what Jackson had been thinking. "We have a couple more days to hike before reaching another town. We need provisions. I'm starving. Aren't you hungry?"

Emir nodded. "I bet the Chetniks will cook that pig down in the clearing. They will have a feast."

"But you're Muslim. I thought Muslims don't eat pork."

"Forgive me for saying this, Robert. I know you are a friend to my people. But that was a very *Amerikanac* thing to say."

"What do you mean?"

"Muslims in Bosnia are not typical Muslims. Before the war, maybe three Muslims in one hundred prayed at a mosque. My mother was the only Muslim I knew who prayed. We gladly eat pork and drink wine. We take vacations over the Christmas holiday and exchange presents. We don't want to die for Allah. We're not mujahideen warriors; we don't want help from the Arab world."

"I realize you're not Arabs, but—"

"We're Slavs, like the Croats and Serbs. We speak Serbo-Croatian, not Turkish. We're Europeans, not Arabs. Don't we look and dress like any other European?"

Jackson was struck by how far the quiet shepherd had come in the last couple of months. Emir was an uneducated young man from the hills of central Bosnia who had volunteered to bring back food and medicine to his starving town during the first days of the war. He made it to Mostar and came back with a horse-drawn cart full of provisions. But by then, the Chetniks had burned his village to the ground. His family had disappeared.

Jackson remembered the first time he and Aleksandar met Emir. They were staying in a small garage in Ploče that Aleksandar had conned a Croat out of, just two weeks after Aleksandar and his men had rescued Jackson from the peacekeepers. He and Aleksandar had put the word out that they were looking for men to help smuggle arms. All day long, men came to see them, thinking it was a paid position.

"This isn't a typical job," Aleksandar would tell them. "We're looking for men who are strong and brave and are willing to fight for a united Bosnia. There are no wages. Sometimes, there may be no food. Many will die at the hands of the Chetniks and the Yugoslav army."

Emir came in timidly, barely lifting his head. Jackson could not even see his face. Aleksandar gave him the speech, but Emir was still interested. He was the first man who had not immediately walked out on them.

"What are you?" Jackson had asked. "Serb, Muslim, or Croat?"

"I am a Muslim," Emir replied. He reached down into his shirt and fiddled for a moment, then pulled out a silver crescent and star medallion.

They were looking for men who could prove themselves to be above the ethnic hatreds that consumed the country. Aleksandar, who was also a Muslim, tested Emir.

"Muslims are pigs! We don't want swine where we're going!"

Emir had fidgeted nervously in his seat, then reached his hand down into his shirt collar again, fiddling with something. When he brought back his hand, he was holding a Roman Catholic crucifix. "I am a Croat," he said softly. "I was only joking about being a Muslim."

Jackson and Aleksandar looked at each other in wonder. "We don't want Croats. We hate those Nazi worshippers. We're looking for Serbs," Jackson said to Emir.

Emir reached down into his shirt a third time. This time he pulled out an Orthodox cross.

Aleksandar reached across the table and pulled the chain out from under Emir's shirt. "What is this for?" he asked, seeing that the chain held all three icons—the Muslim crescent and star, the Roman Catholic crucifix, and the Orthodox cross.

"I practice no religion," Emir explained nervously. "I am whatever I need to be to get through the day. When a Croat policeman harasses me in the middle of the night, I show him the crucifix. When I try to go to a town and a Serb sticks a gun in my face, I show the Orthodox cross."

"And the crescent and star medallion? What's that for?"

"That is to show my mother, when I find her."

Jackson and Aleksandar were silent. In a moment, Emir began crying. He didn't yet have the long scar across his neck and up his right cheek, but his face was a mixture of nervous ticks and twitches. Emir went on weeping and looking at them as though he didn't realize what was happening to his face.

Jackson didn't want to take him, but Aleksandar had insisted. "Who in their right mind wouldn't be affected by what's happening in this war?" Aleksandar would say to Jackson later. "We should be concerned when we find men who are not made nervous and are not upset by this war. This boy has a heart. He's lost his family. We're taking him."

So Aleksandar took Emir under his wing, and Emir proved to be the most loyal and dependable man they had. Anytime Aleksandar went in-country with arms to smuggle, Emir always went, even if it wasn't his turn to go, no matter how dangerous it might be.

"Emir, tell me the truth," Jackson said as they continued hiking back to their camp high in the mountains. "You've been in the north. What we're doing here—running guns. We're not spinning our wheels, are we?"

"I do not understand that of the wheels," Emir said. "But I can tell you that without smuggled guns, my people are defenseless."

"It seems to me if you're defenseless, you have to surrender."

"To surrender would mean certain slaughter," Emir insisted. "Besides, if this was happening in your country, Robert, what would you do?"

"This could never happen in America." Jackson said, laughing.

"No? What if the black *Amerikanacs* and white *Amerikanacs* and Hispanic *Amerikanacs* began fighting for America?"

"It could never happen. You've learned a lot about my country, but that could never happen."

"I've studied much about America, but I have much more to learn," Emir admitted. "It is my dream to go there, and Aleksandar's as well. After the war, can we go with you? To America?"

"I can't go back."

"Aleksandar told me you would say that. He also says a woman tore out your heart, jumped up and down on it, and spat on it before throwing it into a fire."

Jackson couldn't help laughing. "The way he puts it, it doesn't sound that bad."

"Tell me, Robert. I have never loved a woman, but I have heard from others that a broken heart feels like your insides are ripped out of your body, leaving an emptiness. But then I have also heard that it feels like someone hit you over the head with the back of an ax, and you are left in a daze, unable to smile. Which is it, Robert? Which does it feel more like?"

"It feels like both at the same time," Jackson told him.

Emir stopped hiking and turned to face Jackson. "You are my friend. I want to help you. Perhaps there is a way we can smuggle you back to America so you can be with your woman."

"I'll be arrested. I'm a criminal there now."

"But I'll go with you, and Aleksandar as well. We'll live in your mountains and hide from your police."

"You'll have to go without me."

Emir frowned. "It is such a large country. We wouldn't know where to go."

"Go to California," Jackson told the shepherd as they resumed their climb.

"Are there mountains there?"

"Yes, but if I know Aleksandar, he's going to want to live near the beach."

"I would prefer to live in the mountains."

"There are places where you can live in the mountains, but still be very close to the ocean."

"It's like that in some places in Croatia," Emir said. "But to have that in America, where nothing bad ever happens—it is my dream. Are you sure you can't come?"

"Yes," Jackson said flatly.

"When we get to America, Aleksandar and I will find your girlfriend and tell her that you're a hero, and we'll tell her where you are so she can come to you. I promise you, Robert. And she will be safe because I'll give her my silver chain with the three medallions to protect her. I won't need my chain in America."

"No. You won't."

"No, not in America. How good it would be to live in a country where people don't care about religion."

Jackson laughed. "What's stopping you from going now?"

Emir had been smiling, but his smile turned to a look of concern. "I can't go there until the war is over," Emir said seriously. "But that shouldn't be long. We can't hold out much longer. Even you know it, don't you, Robert? That is why you asked me this of the spinning wheels?"

"I shouldn't have said anything. I don't like this kind of talk."

"I don't ordinarily speak in such a manner," Emir said. "But it's necessary sometimes to say what's on your mind. I'd like to have someone I could confide in." He stopped and faced Jackson. "I don't want *Amerikanac* boys to die," he said truthfully. "But I don't understand—why does the West blockade us and prevent us from obtaining guns and tanks and rockets so that we can defend ourselves?"

"There are people in America who think that if we arm the Muslims, it'll lead to more killing."

"*Amerikanacs* are fortunate that the world didn't think that way in 1776 during the American War for Independence. It's a good thing Lafayette didn't think in such a manner."

"Lafayette? Most *Amerikanacs* don't even know about Lafayette. You've learned a lot about my country." Jackson could not help but laugh again at the shepherd. "Let's not give up hope, Emir, not now. Remember, the peace-loving man thinks the *Amerikanac*'s mission could lead to an end to the war," he added, although he did not see how it was possible.

"Yes. And there is always the chance for a miracle," Emir agreed. "Sometimes miracles just take a little time."

**8**

**JUST BEFORE SUNUP THEY** were all following JuJu down the mountainside, keeping as quiet as possible in case there were more Chetnik bands in the hills. JuJu was guiding them now because the boy had worked after school for the lumber works in town, so he knew the hills even better than Emir did.

They were within sight of the town when they came across an upland pasture. Every man froze at the sight of a tank.

When he first saw the Serb mountain battery, Jackson thought a bomb had exploded there. The soldiers, who all wore the uniform of the Yugoslav army, the third largest army in Europe and now under the control of the Serbs, were sprawled everywhere, some even sleeping on top of each other. Several were passed out atop a T-72 tank that bore the red star of the Yugoslav army. Many more lay on the ground next to spent bottles of slivovitz. Fortunately, the soldier on watch that morning had been drunk the night before with the rest of them and had fallen asleep.

Jackson grabbed JuJu's shoulder and jerked his thumb backward. JuJu led them away. When it was safe enough to talk, Zarko whispered, "Did you see it, Captain! A tank!"

"Keep your voice down," Jackson told him.

"With that tank they will make me a general!"

"No more about tanks. That's an order."

West pulled Jackson close. "The town might be surrounded."

"We can avoid the town and these hills, but we need food and water," Jackson said. "It's another three days in the hills before we reach friendly territory. Besides, what about the boy? We can't just leave him here in the hills. That's his town down there."

"Not for long."

"We can turn back. Take the boy with us."

"That's not an option," West told him. "You're taking me north."

Neither spoke for a minute. All of the men seemed to stare into the forest, wondering how many more Serbs might be encamped in the hills above the town.

"Look," Jackson said to West after speaking with JuJu. "The boy says we can be in and out in twenty minutes, with all the provisions we can carry."

West thought for another long moment, then reluctantly told him, "If we hurry we should be able to get out before sunrise. But if we encounter any more troops, we'll have to move on."

JuJu and the others backtracked for a minute to avoid the Serb unit, then followed an old logging trail and eventually slid down the last muddy hill. They trekked through the damp underbrush until they came to a road that led into town. They stayed low and to the side of the road. As the early morning light began to turn the blackness of night of gray, they sprinted across the small bridge over the Sana River, then ducked behind a wall that had been blown in half by a Serb shell.

Nearly all the red-tiled roofs had been blown off the buildings. Serb shells had gutted many of the whitewashed homes. The lumber mill, the lifeblood of the town, had been turned to rubble.

As they walked through the plum orchards and fruit trees on the edge of town, they could see shadowlike figures hurrying about. Nobody stopped to speak to one another. Once in the besieged town, only an old woman sweeping away the rubble with a broom remained in the street long enough to be spoken to.

"*Majka,*" JuJu said. "Do you remember me? I am Jusuf Feric. I worked with your son with the loggers. I'm looking for my family. Do you know of my mother, Kadira Feric, who had her own table at the farmer's market? Or my sisters, Martina and Selma? Are they well?"

The old woman with the broom did not reply. The boy repeated his question, but again she did not answer.

"Where is this?" the old woman with the broom finally asked, looking around as if she had just awakened from nightmare.

"Looks like hell," Zarko replied.

"I knew it," the old woman said, still looking about. She walked away, still sweeping.

JuJu led the others to his family's neighborhood at the base of one of the surrounding mountains. When they neared his house, JuJu set off running. Suddenly a high-pitched whistle rang out and a mortar exploded a few hundred meters north of them. JuJu dove to the road, covering his head. Soon bombs were dropping all over the town. The men started running. When they reached JuJu, Jackson pulled at his shirt collar until JuJu was running along with them.

"No! This way!" JuJu cried. They darted down side streets, past burned-out cars and the skeletal remains of houses. A mortar exploded fifty meters away and knocked them to the ground, but they were up again in an instant, sprinting down the street.

JuJu finally ran into his yard. There was a crater the size of a swimming pool in front of the single-story house. The windows were boarded up with plywood. JuJu ran to the door and knocked furiously, calling out for his mother. Another bomb exploded down the street, causing West to push JuJu aside. "We don't have time!" he shouted, taking aim at the door with his machine gun.

Just then the doorknob turned slightly. Emir grabbed the muzzle of West's gun and pointed it at the ground.

The door opened a crack. A female voice cried out, "JuJu! Are you out there! Is that you?"

Beaming, JuJu pushed the door open. He embraced a pretty girl perhaps a year older than himself, but more bombs prompted the other men to rush at the door. They fell over themselves rushing to get in before someone slammed the door shut.

Zarko was breathing more heavily than the others due to the small arsenal he had strapped to his body. He groaned with the effort as he picked himself up off the floor.

"Grandfather, these men brought me to you," JuJu said excitedly.

Behind the girl stood an old man. He was short, balding, in his late sixties, with a carpenter's rough hands. Chetniks had nearly beaten him to death when he tried to smuggle food into his city at the start of the war. They shattered his nose and fractured his cheekbone, causing damage to his tear ducts, so now he needed to wipe tears from his eyes with a handkerchief every minute. When fighting resumed in his home city two weeks ago, he fled and came to live with his daughter and her children in what was then a peaceful mill town.

"Welcome, oh, welcome, friends, to our home! I am Ado, JuJu's grandfather. Welcome to you and your blessed guns," he said, and began inspecting each man's gun. He ran his fingers over Zarko's old carbine. Zarko jerked it away from him. "They are a gift from Allah. You're all a gift from Allah!"

JuJu's mother, a thin woman with a long neck, pale skin, and hard, strong hands, rushed in from another room. She hugged and kissed her son furiously. When she was sure he was all right, she greeted the men and introduced herself as Kadira. She thanked them and begged to know each of their names. When she knew them all she greeted them individually and thanked them again.

They followed Kadira into the living room, which had been made into a bunker. Floorboards and furniture from other rooms had been nailed to the walls as extra protection against Serb shells. The family dining table, an old, sturdy oak, sat in the middle of the room. Under it JuJu's younger sister huddled silently, oblivious to her brother's return. JuJu scrambled underneath and held her but she hardly moved and didn't even look at him.

Finally, JuJu's mother could contain herself no longer. "Your father, JuJu. Where is he?" She went to the door and looked outside. "Isn't he coming? Where is he, son?"

"Father is dead," JuJu said softly. He came out from under the table and held his mother as she began to wail. "He was killed on the way into Mostar."

Jackson glanced under the table. The younger girl had no reaction at all to the news. The older girl, Martina, covered her mouth and turned away.

Ado was wiping the ever-streaming tears from his eyes. "JuJu," the old man called to the boy. "Are these the only guns you've brought, these that are on the backs of our comrades? Come on, boy. Surely that emerald purchased more guns than just these. It was a precious heirloom."

"Didn't you hear what I said? My father is dead!"

"Yes, but your mother and your sisters are still alive. And so am I, your grandfather, who is ready to fight the men who killed your father, who was like a son to me. There is no time to mourn your father properly. So, tell me. Where are the guns you and your father were sent to purchase? Tell me quickly. Stop acting like a child."

JuJu stood up straight and told the old man, "I have brought you no guns. There are no guns for sale. Not even in Mostar."

The old man's face was red with anger. "It is the embargo!" he shouted. He wrung his hands for a moment, but then composed himself and said, "It's not your fault, boy. You were brave to try. What news is there from Mostar?"

JuJu glared at his grandfather, brushing away the last of his tears. His mother was still weeping, clinging to him.

"It's very bad there now," JuJu said. "The Muslims and Croats succeeded in driving away the Serbs, as you know. But it's still a divided city. The Croats are on the west side of the river, the Muslims on the east. Only the Stari Most connects us now."

Jackson knew that the words *stari most* meant "old bridge." "If there's going to be trouble between the Muslims and Croats, they better mine the bridge," he told the old man.

Ado looked at him and shook his head violently. "I would rather lose the city," the old man said, wiping more tears from his eyes, "than destroy the Stari Most."

Jackson followed West into the kitchen. The roof had been blown away. Most of the rubble had been swept out the back door. West opened every cabinet in the kitchen, but there wasn't a scrap of food. The refrigerator wasn't working. There was no food in it anyway, just an empty milk bottle with a half-inch of cloudy water.

"So much for provisions," West said. "You're a hell of a guide, Jackson. If one of those mortars hits this house, we're done."

Martina came into the kitchen. She had long black hair, blue eyes, and thin, red lips. She was skinny in the way of teenaged girls who haven't grown into their bodies yet. Martina was wearing tan slacks that had not been washed for a week, with a white turtleneck under a black knitted sweater. Jackson didn't know what to say to her. There was an awkward silence until she spoke.

"You're hungry, it's easy to see that," she said in English. "But we have no food. The bombing has gone on for five days now. The Serbs cut the electricity and the phones on the first day. I'm sorry. I should have something to offer you, but I have nothing."

Jackson swore under his breath. He was starving, and he was trying hard not to show his fear each time a shell exploded. "Of course we didn't expect anything. We only came to see that your brother made it here safely."

The girl tried very hard not to cry. "I have been preparing myself for the worst. At least my brother has come back to us."

A shell exploded nearby, causing everyone to cringe and close their eyes. And cover their heads with their arms.

"Does the old man speak English, too?" West asked the girl.

"No. Only I do. I learned in school. JuJu chose to learn Italian, and Selma, my sister, is learning French."

"It must be a mistake," West said, referring to the bombing. "This is a residential area. It has no military significance."

"They bomb us every day," Martina said.

"How long will it last?"

"Until we are all dead."

"No. I mean they couldn't have been bombing you all night long. When will they stop tonight?"

"They bomb all day and all night, until the early morning hours."

West turned to Jackson. "We're leaving."

"Now? Isn't that too risky?" Jackson asked. He felt helpless in the house as the bombing continued, but remaining there still seemed better than trying to make it through the Serb lines in the hills now that the sun was coming up. "Look, it was a mistake to come here, but don't you think it would be better to find some cover—the basement maybe—and wait for darkness—"

"It's only a matter of time before this place takes a direct hit," West said, clearly losing patience. Now that they were in what amounted to a combat situation, West expected the others to follow his orders. "You want to be in the basement when this place collapses?" He didn't wait for an answer. "We're going. Now!"

"I would suggest waiting until after midnight, when the Serbs are sleeping," the girl, Martina, told them. "It's the only time they don't bomb us."

Almost as soon as she said it, the bombs stopped falling. Nobody moved. They hardly breathed, waiting for the bombing to resume.

"Oh shit," West said, breaking the silence. Jackson followed him back to the living room.

"I don't understand it," Ado said to Jackson as he wiped the ever-streaming tears from his eyes. "For three days the bombs have kept up all day long. This is like the first day. They bombed us for an hour, until everyone had found shelter. Suddenly it stopped. Then, when people came out of their homes and gathered in the streets, they bombed us in the streets."

"Tell everybody to stay here," West told Jackson. He went to the front door and walked out to the front step to survey the area. One by one, people in nearby houses opened their doors and squinted in the growing sunlight. Nobody spoke. They all listened for the sound of more bombs.

"What do you make of it?" Jackson half-whispered, coming to the door.

West signaled for silence. He cupped his hands behind his ears. He sniffed the air. He saw a raven land on top of a telephone pole. He looked up and down the street. Then he thought he heard something. The raven flew away suddenly.

"We're leaving," he said. "Right now."

Just then the sounds of vehicles and machine-gun fire could be heard rolling toward them from every side. Shouts and shrill cries could be heard coming from every direction. People all along the street retreated into their houses in a panicked rush. JuJu's mother hurried under the table with her daughters.

"God help us," West muttered. "Back inside!"

"What is it?"

"Back inside. Now!"

•       •       •

West closed the front door and locked it. "The refrigerator. Have your men carry it in here. Put it against the door. Then wedge some chairs between the refrigerator and the stairs to make it hold firm." He picked up his machine gun and, conserving bullets as best he could, shot two gun ports out of the plywood nailed over the windows. He began relaying orders to Jackson to translate.

"Here," Jackson said to JuJu, grabbing one of Zarko's pistols and handing it to the boy. "Do the same to the other window and stand watch over the street. Zarko, you stay here, too, with West and the boy. Emir, cover the back door." Emir rushed to the kitchen.

"What about me?" the old man asked excitedly. "Have you a gun for me?"

Jackson looked at Ado for moment, considering him. "Zarko, give me your carbine," he said, holding his hand out to the Gypsy.

"Captain, please don't order me to part with my uncle's rifle," Zarko pleaded. "He took it from a German officer in the Second Great War and killed many Nazis with it. I'm a marksman of the highest caliber with this rifle."

"Don't be ridiculous. You're using the automatic rifle."

"As you wish. But please, Captain, don't take my carbine. I wouldn't trade my uncle's old rifle for even a tank!"

Jackson reluctantly pulled out Zarko's remaining pistol and handed it to the old man, whose eyes lit up when he held the pistol in his hands. "You stay next to JuJu at this window," he told Ado.

Zarko squeezed off a few rounds to make a gun port for himself in the plywood. "Are they invading, Captain?"

Jackson stood next to West, trying to contain his fear in the presence of the combat veteran, who seemed completely focused and concerned, but not at all afraid. "What is it? Is the army attacking?"

"If I'm right, we're going to wish it was the army," West replied.

"Just be ready for anything," Jackson told the Gypsy. He went off quickly, filled with nervous energy, to inspect the rest of the house. When he returned, he asked the old man if Kadira could shoot.

"She has never even seen a gun before," Ado said.

Jackson pulled his pistol from his shoulder holster. On West's orders, he showed Kadira how to use it, then stationed her and the girls in a bedroom. The only window looked out the side of the house, where he didn't expect any trouble. When he was sure they understood his directions, he looked down at the little girl's blank expression. "Is she all right?" he asked, brushing his hand through Selma's blond hair.

"She hasn't spoken since the bombing began days ago," Kadira said.

"I think they call it shell shock," Martina added.

Jackson nodded. "Stay in this room. You should be safe here— the gunfire will come from the front and the back. If anyone tries to break in through the windows, come back to the living room, but keep low," he warned as he was returning to the others.

In the kitchen, looking out into the backyard, Jackson crouched anxiously next to Emir. "How goes it?"

"Not good. I want to be sick. I've heard the way things are here in the north. This could be very bad."

Jackson nodded.

"Robert, please, if I am to be captured . . . please don't let them take me. I—"

"We won't be captured," Jackson interrupted.

"Yes, I know. But still, in case something unforeseen happens, I would not like what I understand happens to captured Muslims to happen to me."

Jackson kept his attention on the backyard as he spoke. "We're going to find a way out. I promise you we won't die in this town. Stay with me, Emir. We'll be all right." Jackson doubted that he sounded convincing. His voice was trembling.

"Yes, I know. But still, it would make me feel better if I knew you wouldn't let them capture me if something does go wrong. Dying would not be so bad, but I'm afraid to be left alive to suffer."

"Fine. If it comes to it, I won't let them capture you alive."

"Would you like for me to do the same for you?"

"Look, just . . . just keep your eye out for soldiers."

Emir looked back outside. "It will comfort me to know that I won't be captured. It would be terrible to be wounded, unable to run, with no gun and no way to kill myself. They leave you alive just so they can—"

"Are you going to talk this much before you shoot me?" Jackson snapped.

Emir shook his head solemnly. "I will do it quickly and you won't feel a thing."

"You're a good friend."

"Now you are joking," Emir said. "It isn't out of fear of dying that I speak this way. I'm not scared, Robert. I will fight them. It's not fighting or dying that I worry about, it is only the pain. I have a great fear of the pain they can cause if they choose to do so. It's only if the worst happens—"

"Shut up!" Jackson demanded. He regretted saying it so harshly, especially to the young shepherd, but it was his own fear that made him speak that way to his friend and he couldn't help it. "Please, Emir. I'm thinking."

Emir was quiet for a minute. "I am not scared," he repeated, crossing himself twice in rapid succession.

Jackson heard West calling his name, so he rushed back to the living room to translate West's orders. "Don't shoot until the other *Amerikanac* shoots," he told Zarko, JuJu, and Ado. "They may just pass us by, but if they come up to the house, duck down, don't let them see you. If they try to get in, or if they start firing, fire back in short bursts. Don't leave your finger on the trigger. Conserve your bullets—short bursts at a specific target."

"Where's my mother?" JuJu asked. "Where are my sisters?"

"They're safe in the bedroom."

"I want to be with them," JuJu said, his voice cracking.

Ado wiped the tears that were streaming down his wrinkled old face, turned to the boy, and looked at him clearly in the eyes. "They will be safer in the other room. We need you here. You're a man. The other room is for women." The boy shook from fright. Ado put a hand on his shoulder. "You will do just fine. Believe me, I know how it is for you. But like me, someday you will tell your children and grandchildren that you fought to keep the Serbs away from your home. That they came into your town one day, and since it was mostly a Muslim town, you had no army, no defenses, and very few guns. You will tell how you and your people stood up to the Chetniks and from your living room you fought them back. And you will tell them that an old man fought by your side, an old man who fought with Tito's partisans against the Chetniks and the Ustasha in the Second Great War when he was your age. You will tell them the old man's name was Ado Begovic, their great-grandfather, and that he wasn't afraid of the Chetniks because when he was a boy he had killed Chetniks when they came to his town, and he grew to be an old man so that he could fight them again. You, too, will grow to be an old man. You will tell your children about me. Won't you, Jusuf?"

JuJu gritted his teeth and looked at the old fighter whose eyes were always filled with tears. "Yes, Grandfather. I'll tell them about this day. And as Allah is my God, I will name my first son for you."

"That would be an immense honor," Ado said formally. "Thank you, Jusuf."

The boy turned back to the street, where there was the sound of approaching gunfire. "I will tell my first son about how we killed many Chetniks together."

Zarko and West were staring intently out the window when Jackson joined them. "Look, West, don't fire unless they try to storm the house. If we're lucky, they'll pass us by."

"Don't give me orders," West snarled. "What the hell do you know?"

"I know a thing or two. I went through the training."

"Have you ever killed a man before?" West asked.

"Sure," Jackson lied.

West looked back at him, grinning. "What about him?"

Jackson asked the Gypsy in Serbo-Croatian.

Zarko nodded. "With a grenade. I didn't see the motherless sons-of-whores die, but there can be no question I killed them."

"Chetniks?"

"They were highwaymen—Montenegrins, I think—very skilled mountain fighters. They'd opened fire on the others and me when Aleksandar was leading us north. We were delivering penicillin to a suburb near Karlovac in the first days of the war, even before Aleksandar met you, Captain. When a truck stopped in front of us in the road and fired on us, we all ran into the woods, but more highwaymen were waiting in the woods for us and they opened fire. It was an ambush. They were fighting for the Serbs.

"I was so scared I didn't even think to fire back at them. But by the time I found cover, Aleksandar—he is a rare man—was sitting in the highwaymen's truck, firing their mounted machine gun. There were several dead Montenegrins lying at Aleksandar's feet. I and another who survived the initial attack ran back to the road. Aleksandar covered us by shooting over our heads, but the Montenegrins in the woods began shooting at us again. The other— whose name was Marijo—pointed to the woods and shouted to Aleksandar. He couldn't hear Marijo, but he understood and fired into the woods. He couldn't see the Montenegrins at first because the woods were so dense, but you know how a mounted machine gun is."

"I've heard."

"In no time, Aleksandar had cut down the woods and then the highwaymen with the mounted machine gun. But during that time, more Montenegrins turned up in a second truck. When they saw Aleksandar at the great gun, they tried to retreat, but Aleksandar opened fire on them and they drove their truck into a ditch and flipped over. Marijo was wounded, so Aleksandar ran to him. Then a shot rang out from the overturned truck. At least one Montenegrin was still alive, maybe more. Aleksandar was going to finish them off, but Marijo was in great pain and hanging on to Aleksandar. Marijo knew he was dying. He loved Aleksandar and wouldn't let go of him. So Aleksandar ordered me to take my carbine and finish the Montenegrins off.

"I circled around to the rear of the truck so I wouldn't be shot. The roof had collapsed and they could not have much room to move. Still, I was afraid to get too close and stick my nose in there in case they could shoot me. So I threw my grenade in and ran back toward Aleksandar, who had Marijo over his shoulder and was taking him back to our car. The truck blew up. I didn't look back, but surely they all died."

"What did Aleksandar say about it? About using a grenade instead of shooting them?"

"Nothing. He never mentioned it to me."

"What happened to the other man?"

"Nothing," the shepherd replied, crossing himself three times.

"Well, get ready." Jackson rushed back to his place in the front of the house. "The *Amerikanac* says to be ready to fire when he fires," he said to all of them, pointing his M16 out of the hole in the plywood. Ado nodded to the boy and they both placed their guns in the holes they had made in the plywood. Zarko began shouting a long string of obscenities, which was cut short by the sound of West's machine gun. Then they were all firing.

Emir burst in. "What is it!"

"Get back there!" Jackson cried without turning around. Emir hesitated, watching them all firing out the windows. Soon there was return fire that blew through the boards nailed over the windows. Emir hit the floor and crawled back to the kitchen, where there was suddenly much firing from the backyard.

Sasha was following three other Chetniks to the back of JuJu's house. This would be his first battle against the Muslims.

The first two houses they had stormed that morning were easily taken. He believed the reason that there had been no resistance until now was because it was a surprise attack. They had rushed the houses, firing madly because they had ammunition to spare. Once inside the houses, their enemies were summarily shot, or if there were women who could bear children, they were raped. In the last house, Sasha had raped a woman while her three children looked on. He had been a virgin before that first time and had actually been looking forward to it. He had been told that it would be expected of him and he was nervous because it was something he had never done before. He was proud that he had performed well, and the other Chetniks were proud of him, too, but he found that he didn't enjoy it. The woman screamed and fought the entire time. It was his duty, and he was proud that he had performed it well, but he did not enjoy it.

Later, as they were firing at the man with the hunting rifle, he and his comrades had been ambushed from behind. He had been warned that the Muslims were treacherous. Several of his comrades had been shot in the back, which he felt was a cowardly thing for the Muslims to do to them. Captain Šešelj, the clean-shaven leader of all Chetnik forces in the area, who was trained in Belgrade and had very important political connections there, rallied the Chetniks and sent Sasha and three others to the back of the house, to try to take the Turks from behind by surprise.

As they ran into the backyard, two of the Chetniks running next to him were suddenly knocked off their feet by machine-gun fire. If he hadn't been so slow as to lag behind, Sasha would have been cut down with them. Sasha dropped his Kalashnikov and dove to the ground. There was still much machine-gun fire and he would have been shot, but his Chetnik comrade pulled him to his feet and together they scrambled for cover in the trees. Sasha and the other Chetnik, who had a full Chetnik beard, crawled behind a couple of oak trees and were lying a few feet away from each other on the fallen leaves. The other Chetnik started firing at the back of the house.

"Maravic!" the other Chetnik cried, calling Sasha by his last name. "Where is your gun?"

Sasha was too frightened to reply. The fanatics inside the house were still firing into the woods. He pressed his head into the dirt and leaves, keeping low, terrified of the Muslim warriors. He had learned all about them when he was recruited from his town in eastern Serbia, when the men came with the films that showed the Muslim atrocities against Serbs in Bosnia. Then, on the march through the mountains, and also during the last few days while the army bombed the town, the older Chetniks were constantly telling horrifying stories of Muslim brutalities and tortures. He could picture the fanatics in the house, who had been preparing for this Islamic insurrection for forty years, wearing turbans and robes, with hook-bladed knives and guns from Iran and Libya. He could imagine them shouting out Islamic war cries to Allah as they tried to kill him.

"Maravic," the other Chetnik said after firing another clip at the house, "take out your pistol. We must fire on the Turks so they'll have to reinforce the back of the house. That way, our brothers in the street will have less resistance in the front and can storm the house."

But Sasha did not move. He stayed low and watched the flashes of light from the machine gun in the house.

The Chetnik put his pistol to Sasha's temple. "I said to pick up your gun! Kill the pigs the way you killed the pig last night!"

Sasha was afraid of the Chetnik next to him, who was one of the more vocal and brutal of the Chetniks he had met. But he was more afraid of the Muslims in the house.

"Coward! You're nothing but a fat, useless boy! I'll show you what it is to be a soldier!" The Chetnik readied his gun, popped his head out from behind the tree, and fired off a long burst of gunfire. He shouted madly at the house, "Pray to Allah, pigs! You will soon be joining him!" He did this several times, each time shouting a different insult at those he tried to kill. Finally he stuck his head out from behind the tree and was shot in the head, dying instantly.

Sasha looked over at the Chetnik, at his blood staining the red and yellow leaves. He closed his eyes and prayed, his lips trembling as he mouthed the prayer. In a minute there was no more shooting from the fanatics in the back of the house, but Sasha didn't dare to move. He hugged the ground with his eyes closed, praying.

Jackson had joined Emir in the kitchen just after Emir had picked off two Chetniks who carelessly ran into the open. The other two dove to the ground before scrambling for cover in the trees. Emir was holding down his trigger and firing haphazardly, madly. He nodded out the sign of the cross with his head as he fired. He couldn't use the sights of his gun because his head jerked up, down, back, and forth. But he stood his ground and didn't shrink away, not even when the return fire came very close.

Jackson came to the kitchen to help. As the plywood in place of the windows was splintering away, he moved from hole to hole so the enemy couldn't pinpoint his location. Emir continued to fire at nothing in particular, but Jackson waited, wanting to pick his targets more carefully, as West had instructed. Finally he set his sights on a location in the bushes where every ten or twenty seconds he saw the flash from a gun. He saw a Chetnik poke his head out just a bit. If Jackson had not hesitated he could have killed him. The Chetnik shouted something and fired, then ducked out of sight. Jackson took a deep breath and aimed again at the spot. Again, the Chetnik with the long black beard stuck his head out and shouted, firing at the house. Jackson could see him clearly in his sights. The crosshairs were trained on the center of the Chetnik's forehead. But again, he did not fire.

"Emir," he shouted as he crawled over to the shepherd. "Emir, stop. Stop for a second." Emir finally took his finger off the trigger. He was hyperventilating, sweating, and shaking.

"Look, there. One meter up the first oak tree, just to the right of the bushes where there's a dead branch." Suddenly the Chetnik poked his head out, shouted, and fired. "Did you see it! Aim there. He'll show himself again in a minute."

Jackson watched Emir slam another clip into his Uzi, lie on his stomach, and take aim. Then Jackson watched the woods, and when the Chetnik poked his head out, Emir shot him dead in the center of his forehead. They saw the Chetnik's head jerk back in an explosion of blood. They waited several minutes, but there was no more return fire.

"*Dobro,* Emir! Now wait here and keep watch. I'm going out front. There's still a lot of firing there."

"Robert," Emir said in a shaky voice as he crossed himself with his left hand. "I'm almost out of ammunition."

Jackson frowned and handed Emir his M16 and spare clips. He took Emir's Uzi and cautioned Emir to squeeze off short bursts. When Emir nodded that he understood, Jackson went to the living room.

"All clear out back, but I need ammunition!"

The men in the front of the house were using up their ammunition very quickly—even the dozens of clips in Zarko's pack. There were a dozen Chetniks entrenched out front.

"Get the pistol from the woman!" West told him.

JuJu came forward with his machine gun. "I'll get the pistol," he cried. He handed his machine gun to Jackson, his hands shaking.

Suddenly a jeep with a mounted machine gun skidded to a halt on the other side of the road. It opened fire on the house across the street, blowing the front to pieces. The Chetniks rushed inside the house, where their machine-gun fire lasted for an entire minute.

"Shoot out the gunner!" West said, and aimed at the jeep. But now the Chetniks regrouped, and with the confidence that the mounted machine gun gave them, they resumed firing at JuJu's house. Wood fragments were flying in all directions. The driver of the jeep pulled out a grenade.

"Everybody out the back!" Jackson ordered as soon as West turned and ran.

West was the first one to reach the kitchen, followed by Zarko, who had used up all of his ammunition for the automatic rifle and now held only his old carbine. Ado rushed into the bedroom to get the woman and the girls. "Let's go!" Jackson shouted. West led Emir and Zarko out the back door. A grenade suddenly landed in the center of the living room, where Jackson was waiting for Ado and the others. Jackson ran and dove out the back door. Soon he heard the explosion and felt the shock wave. After a moment he picked himself off the grass, looking back to see bullets ripping through the front of the house, and rushed for the woods.

JuJu was firing a pistol out of the bedroom window. Martina did the same after wresting the pistol from her mother, who was petrified.

"Come on!" Ado shouted. "We have to run!"

The old man was the first one into the hallway. The grenade had blown apart most of the front of the living room. What remained was flooded with light as wood and stone fragments flew like shrapnel from the bullets tearing through what remained of the front of the house.

Ado realized that there was no escape. They couldn't pass through the living room to get to the kitchen and out the back. Bullets began pouring in through the bedroom window. JuJu and Martina fired back until they were out of ammunition.

"The basement!" Martina screamed. She pulled the door open and they all rushed down the stairs, with Ado firing off the last of his ammunition to buy the time they needed.

# 9

---

**JACKSON AND ZARKO RAN** down a street several blocks from JuJu's house. They had to hide several times as Chetniks in jeeps with the Yugoslav red star painted on the sides roared past them. With every passing minute it seemed there was more shooting, more jeeps roaming by, more cries for help.

They were running hunched over behind a row of hedges when Zarko suddenly stopped and pointed. Jackson followed his eyes and saw the words "THIS IS A SERB HOUSE" painted in large red letters across the front of a two-story home. He looked about, hearing the Chetniks but not yet seeing them. The two men looked at each other. Jackson nodded.

They ran to the front of the house. Zarko pounded on the door, but there was no answer. Just then, they heard the first Chetnik band enter the street about two hundred meters away. Jackson instinctively reached for the pistol he had given to Kadira, but his holster was empty. He had dropped Emir's Uzi running from JuJu's house. Zarko had only a few shells left for his carbine and only one grenade. His other grenades had been used to cover their escape from JuJu's house.

Zarko put his shoulder into the door several times until it crashed in. He lay sprawled across the floor for a moment, dazed. When he looked up he could see the Serb family huddled in a corner, staring at him wide-eyed. His carbine rifle was slung over his shoulder, but he could see he would not need it.

He closed the door quickly. "Couldn't you hear me!" the Gypsy yelled at them, but realizing their fear, he didn't scream again.

"You are not Serbs?" the wife asked, holding her two young sons.

"What if we aren't? Would you turn us over to the Chetniks?"

The husband stood suddenly. Zarko quickly turned his gun on him. The husband raised his hands, then waved for Zarko to follow him. He led Zarko and Jackson to the basement door. Zarko kept looking over his shoulder, half-expecting the Serb woman to shoot him in the back, but she only sat there holding her sons.

They followed the man down the stairs and were immediately overcome by the smell of human body odor. Before they were even halfway down the steps Jackson could tell the basement was crammed with people.

"These are our neighbors," the Serb said simply. "They are Muslims. We hide them from the Chetniks. With luck, the Chetniks will leave our house alone. You are welcome to stay."

*A Chetnik with a Kalashnikov and a few pans of ammunition will have a field day if he comes down here,* Jackson thought. He looked at the sad, scared faces. There were men, women, children, elderly, and infants. They all sat on the floor silently, staring at him.

"What's your name?" Zarko asked the Serb man.

"Petar."

"Thank you, Petar. We will stay."

Petar nodded, then rushed back upstairs. He didn't bother to lock the door. If the Chetniks decided to search the basement, Petar knew he could not stop them.

There was no room to sit on the floor. The bottom steps were also taken, so they sat in the middle of the staircase, looking in silence at the faces that stared back at them. Then Zarko realized they weren't staring at him, but at his gun.

"I am sorry to bring this weapon into your presence," he said to the crowd. "I use it only in defense against Chetniks. I don't mean to worry you. I'll keep it safely away."

A woman seated on the floor next to the staircase stood and touched the rifle gently, almost caressing it. "If only we had more like this, we wouldn't need to hide in our neighbor's house," the woman said dreamily. "We could fight the invaders and keep our homes and our families safe. I would give my life for ten like this to give to my people." When she touched the barrel, she noticed it was hot. She smiled up at Zarko.

"Are you Muslim, too?" a man on the floor whispered.

Zarko hesitated. "I am a Gypsy."

"You're welcome here, Gypsy."

Zarko nodded his thanks, but the peace was soon interrupted by several high-pitched howls from upstairs. Jackson and Zarko looked at each other but didn't even try to hide their alarm. A pack of Chetniks had entered the house.


West stumbled against the side of the old stone church. He had been running for over a half hour. Unlike the others, he hadn't run away from the Chetniks but had climbed a tree and waited for them to pass. Then he had run back into the center of town, which the initial stampede had already trampled over. He still had to be careful, because there were many smaller herds of Chetniks roving about, looting stores and searching for Muslims.

He made his way to this church because it was the only building that looked untouched, both from the bombing and from the Serb irregulars. West didn't realize that this was an Eastern Orthodox church. It was a Serb church.

He checked the doors but they were locked. He scaled the intricate sculpture carved into a corner of the building until he reached the roof, which sloped at severe angles. He could be seen, he realized, if anyone were looking, so he scrambled to the top and fell over into the small bell tower.

From this perch he could look out over the entire town. In the square below him, Chetniks in cars and jeeps drove about with their loot—televisions, small appliances, jewelry—even many of the cars belonged to local Muslims. Many of them were shooting their guns off into the air. On the outskirts of town he saw houses with blown-out fronts or caved-in roofs, a couple on fire, only a few untouched. Further out from town, he could just barely see the Chetnik swarm buzzing madly from house to house.

He watched as the Chetniks piled dynamite around a house that was flying a white sheet from a second-floor window. The house was soon blown to pieces. Chetniks came running out of other houses with all sorts of plunder. Then, as a sign to other Chetniks that the house had been stripped of anything of value, the Chetniks would lob grenades into the houses when they were done looting them.

He saw many things that were much worse than even he could have imagined, and he had seen many very bad things before. But never to a town like this.

He was amazed at how this town resembled his home of northern Idaho. The people were Muslim, he knew, but they didn't look the way he had thought they would. Without the red Venetian roofs, the town could easily be mistaken for small-town America. There were grocery stores and clothing stores, a sporting goods store, restaurants, bars, a school, playing fields, basketball courts, tennis courts, traffic lights, sidewalks, paved roads.

From above, he watched as Chetniks forced a man to paint a cross on the side of the mosque. West didn't know that the man was the imam of the mosque, the leader of the prayers. The Chetniks then forced him to eat pork. Next they brought a young Muslim girl to him and stripped her and tried to force him to rape her. When he refused, they beat him to death with the butts of their guns.

West tried to figure out the Chetnik strategy. He couldn't make sense of what he saw, but that was because he was thinking militarily. What he saw made no military sense.

He thought of Vietnam, and compared it to what was happening here. The Viet Cong were Orientals, not blue-eyed whites like himself and the people in this town. He told himself that what he had done in Vietnam was nothing like this. They were two completely different things, killing these Muslims, who looked European, if not American, and killing Vietnamese, who to a racist like West were better dead than alive because they were an inferior race that he considered barely human.

Then there were the Serbs. They, too, looked European or American. They weren't some African tribal warriors brutally killing each other, or native-looking Central or South Americans who could neither read nor write. The Serbs—except for the Chetniks with the long black beards, he thought—looked like they, too, could be his neighbors back home. They were *normal*-looking to him. Even in the twisted, racist logic of his mind, West couldn't understand how things could have become this way between these civilized-looking people.

He looked up into the hills that surrounded the town and could just make out the gun emplacements of the Yugoslav army. Occasionally he could see the soldiers from behind their mortars and heavy guns, looking down on the Chetnik frenzy. The hills and the valley created a perfect amphitheater from which the Yugoslav army could watch, like watching the Christians being fed to the lions. Several soldiers were sunning themselves in the hills on top of a tank. The soldiers sat and watched as the Chetniks ignored the scores of white sheets that hung from the windows of Muslim homes as makeshift flags of surrender. The white flags only made it easier for the Chetniks to locate them. They might as well have hung Bosnian flags from their windows.

The Yugoslav army watched all day long as the horrors continued. It was as if they had an open alliance with the Serb irregulars, West thought. Who could have given the army such orders?

Down in the basement, the Chetniks' footsteps sounded like hooves clopping against a cobblestone road. All eyes in the basement looked to the ceiling. Zarko, who was the only armed man in the basement, tiptoed up to the door and listened. Jackson followed closely behind. They could hear a Chetnik march across the floor and stand in the middle of the room.

"Hurry, little man. Can't you see I'm busy?" the paramilitary said to Petar.

"Yes, yes. I can see you are a very important man. Here, here it is—my driver's license. And look there—at the Orthodox cross on the wall. I swear I'm a Serb. My father's family is from Belgrade, and my mother's from Pranjani." Petar went to the wall and kissed the Orthodox cross.

"We will see about that." The Chetnik took a few steps and crouched next to one of Petar's little boys. He was five years old. "Tell me, boy, who do you fear?"

Petar and his wife gasped simultaneously. The boy looked to his mother, then his father.

On the staircase, Zarko readied his carbine. Jackson could feel the sweat running down his back.

The Chetnik had his hand on the boy's shoulder, next to his neck. The boy began to speak, stopped, then finally said, "The Turks." Jackson, Zarko, and the boy's parents breathed again.

The Chetnik smiled. "That's right, boy. Someday, when you're older, you will have to fight them, too." The Chetnik walked up to Petar and snatched the driver's license from Petar's hand. The Chetnik slipped the driver's license into a pouch in the front of his black jacket. "Why don't you fight the Turks like the rest of us?" he said to Petar. "How can you live in this town with those fanatics? Are you a Muslim sympathizer?"

"No," Petar lied. "It's just that I'm afraid. This town has so many Muslims. We Serbs were outnumbered. Even after the army arrived it was too dangerous for my family to try to leave because of the bombing, so we waited here," he explained, adding, "Thank you for coming to liberate us, sir."

In the basement, Jackson could sense Petar saluting the Chetnik or shaking his hand. *You're doing very well, Petar,* Jackson thought.

"If you weren't a coward I would give you a gun and you would help us liberate your neighbors' houses. But I promise you, man, you will participate in this victory whether you want to or not. I'm keeping your driver's license. If you're not at the bridge by the mill tomorrow at dawn, I'll come back here and put a leash around your neck and drag you to the bridge myself. If I break your neck on the way, I'll have to come back to this house and get your wife, or your sons, and they'll stand in for you. Somebody from this house will be at the bridge at dawn to take part in this great victory we have achieved here today over the Turks. Do you understand?"

Petar's voice cracked. "Yes, sir."

Jackson and the Gypsy could hear the Chetniks stomping away.

In a minute, Petar opened the basement door. He was surprised to see Zarko aiming the carbine at him.

"You're a brave man," Zarko said, pointing his old rifle at the floor.

Petar broke down and began to weep. "I was so scared for my family. And . . . and for all the others downstairs. . . ."

"You did very well," Jackson assured him. "You're a very brave man."

"No, I am a coward," Petar admitted without shame. "I'm afraid. You are a soldier," he said to the Gypsy, who was trying unsuccessfully to release the jammed spring-action on his old carbine. "Why do you think they want me at the bridge?"

Zarko didn't look up from his work on the old gun. "I don't know, friend, but they don't mean to kill you. They could have done that here."

"I'm afraid to go."

"Not going would be very bad," Zarko said, finally ramming the action back into place. "Unless you plan to leave tonight."

"But this is my home. How can I leave? I own a bakery. It's all I have, that and my house and my family."

"Then you must go to the bridge."

Petar knew Zarko was right. He put his head in his hands and sobbed.

Jackson and Zarko watched him in silence. When Petar looked up again a minute later, Zarko told him, "My friend and I must leave here."

Petar reached out and pleaded, "No. You mustn't."

"We have to—"

"No! If they see you leave, they'll come back to search the house."

"They won't see us," Zarko promised.

"Please! You must not leave!" Petar cried.

"Now that the plague has passed your door, it will be safe for us to go."

Petar looked at Zarko without understanding.

"Look, it's not the Hotel Bosna down there," Zarko said, forcing a smile. "Besides, we have important things to do," he added seriously.

"Please, wait until dark. If you must leave, do it tonight. Many lives are at stake in this house. Please wait, soldier—"

"That's the second time you've called me that. I'm not a soldier."

"But you carry a gun."

Zarko smiled, showing his cracked tooth. "So what? Soon, if we're lucky, many Muslims will be carrying guns. It will be the latest fad, just in time for the holidays. You'll see."

Petar did not smile back at the Gypsy, but finally Jackson extended his hand. "All right. We'll wait until dark."

Petar shook Jackson's hand and thanked both of them, then closed the door and returned to his family. Jackson and Zarko returned to their place in the middle of the stairs. The Muslim man just below Zarko on the steps tapped him on the knee.

"Where did you get your gun?"

"Out of a cereal box," the Gypsy said.

"I would like to know what kind of cereal this is. I would buy every box in the market."

"It's an *Amerikanac* cereal. They have so many guns in America they give them away as trinkets in cereal boxes. They are plentiful there."

"You make jokes. That's easy for you, because you have a gun. If I had a gun I would feel like a man and I would be content to fight the Serbs and try to save my town and my home. If I had your gun I'd feel that we have a chance, and perhaps I'd feel like joking, too."

Zarko lowered his voice. "What I tell you now, you must not repeat." The man drew closer, eager to hear. "We have come to this town with a soldier—an *Amerikanac* soldier—who will bring an early end to this war."

"How?" the Muslim gasped.

"I cannot tell you. It's a secret—strictly confidential—for my ears only. I will go out tonight and find this *Amerikanac* so that I can help him."

"You are a rare Gypsy," the man said.

"Just because I'm a Gypsy, people don't think I care about anything but music and drink and laughter. But this war has taken much laughter from me. Many times I have wanted to run—it's a Gypsy's nature to run, I am told. But how can I run? Even a Gypsy can't stand for what is happening. So I stay, and I will help the *Amerikanac* achieve his mission."

"There is a mission?"

"You make me talk too much. Yes, it is a mission. What else could it be? But don't ask me more questions, man. I cannot tell you any more."

"Can this *Amerikanac* get us out of our town?"

"His mission is too important. You understand?"

"Yes. But what about you? Could you get us out? Many here have money and jewels. We could pay you."

Jackson overheard the man talking about money and jewels, which reminded him that Zarko was still carrying JuJu's emerald. He thought of JuJu and his family, his sisters and mother, and the old man, causing a great feeling of guilt to overcome him. He could have stayed with JuJu's family, or fought the Chetniks from the woods in the backyard. He probably would have died, and he thought he had convinced himself that he was prepared to die, but when the time came, he didn't stay and fight. The guilt hung heavily on him and he shut his eyes tightly, hardly hearing the Gypsy talking to the man in the basement.

"I don't care about money," Zarko was saying. "I must help the *Amerikanac,* but I will promise you this: I'll return here someday with a tank and I'll drive the Serbs from these hills."

"You are a rare Gypsy!" the man said again in admiration.

"I am a false Gypsy," Zarko corrected him, smiling.


Hours later, just as the light from the small windows high up on the basement walls was fading, Zarko jerked awake. He had forgotten where he was, and had to squint in the last of the gray light before recognizing Jackson, standing in the center of the floor in the basement, holding off several angry men who were shouting at a short, fat man with a handlebar mustache.

"You Croats always think you know what's best!" one of the Muslim men was shouting at the man with the mustache. "You Croats think you're so smart and so Western in your ideas. But how long have you run your pharmacy and still you live in that tiny house by the mill? If you were so smart you would be police chief. But I am the police chief, and I will lead!"

"It's your fault we're in this situation!" the Croat with the mustache shouted at the police chief, who was tall and thin with a full head of curly gray hair. "You should have surrendered to the Serbs days ago to spare us this horror."

"Fool!" the police chief shouted. He lunged at the Croat, but was held back by Jackson. "The Serbs never asked for our surrender! They bombed us and now have invaded us and never once offered any terms for surrender. Of course I would surrender to them. How can we fight them without guns? But they didn't want that. They have no intention of letting us stay. Has one shot been fired at them until today? How many guns are there in this town? Maybe twenty hunting rifles. They know we can't fight back. They could have had our surrender, but they didn't want it!"

"You should have gone to the hills yourself to negotiate," the Croat insisted. "They would have listened. They would be reasonable if you had gone to them. They're soldiers; they understand surrender. Why would they fight when they could save their bullets and bombs? If I were leader of this town, I would have gone into the hills myself. You lead us? Ha! I would rather follow a pig!"

The word "pig" hung over all of them. After the insult, Jackson didn't think he could hold all of them back.

"Kill the Croat!" an angry voice shouted from the rear of the basement.

"Break his neck," another man suggested.

"Cut out his tongue!" a third called out.

"Please, no more arguing," Jackson begged them, even though he could see his words were having no effect and the crowd, which was becoming a mob, closed in and began reaching for and punching the Croat. "There are no Croats here, no Muslims. We're all—"

"What are we?" Zarko suddenly called out. All eyes were on him now as he stood, towering over the crowd from his place on the stairs, the carbine slung over his shoulder, the single grenade dangling from his gun belt. "Aren't we Yugoslavians? No, sorry, I forgot. There is no more Yugoslavia. What are we then? Aren't we 'former Yugoslavians?' No, that makes us sound like we're dead. When we're dead, certainly then we are 'former Yugoslavians,' so when we're alive during this war we must be 'soon-to-be-former Yugoslavians.' So, when we finally become 'former Yugoslavians' we are also corpses. Therefore, I think what we all are is 'soon-to-be corpses.' There. Does that satisfy you? We are all 'soon-to-be corpses.' " He jumped down off the steps. The crowd parted and allowed him to make his way to the Croat and the police chief.

"What logic," the Croat with the handlebar mustache groaned, but he was relieved that the Gypsy had helped calm the others.

Jackson frowned. "Don't talk that way, Gypsy. You may prove to be prophetic."

Zarko smiled his cracked-tooth smile. "No. I'm not that kind of Gypsy."

The police chief looked down in disgust. "You are right, stranger. We're all Bosnians. Anyone who believes in a Bosnia the way it was before, with Muslims, Croats, and Serbs living together peacefully, is a Bosnian. Our enemies are the ones outside, the ones who bomb us day and night and now ride through our town killing and looting."

"I'm sorry I questioned you," the Croat with the handlebar mustache said. "It's not your fault we're here. It's Milosevic's fault."

Everyone in the basement groaned in agreement.

Soon the Bosnians in the basement took their places once again on the floor and it was dead quiet again. Jackson and Zarko returned to their places on the stairs.

"I believe you have a future as a diplomat," the Gypsy joked.

Jackson exhaled in relief. "They would have killed that man if you didn't wake up. It wasn't anything I did that stopped them; it was the sight of your gun. When it was remembered that there was only one armed man in this basement, and that you were my friend—only then did they listen."

"I still say you would be a worthy diplomat." Zarko laughed, adding with a wink, "Especially if I stand behind you with my gun."

Jackson closed his eyes and rested his head against the wall, thinking back to his first day in Zagreb. He had been ordered to the Hotel Esplanade to brief a group of generals and diplomats about his plan to route UN relief convoys through the Serb-and Croat-held territories in southern Croatia, along the Krajina. He had stayed up all night preparing his presentation, but when he arrived in the palatial conference room, he realized he had forgotten his map.

Hiding his embarrassment as best he could, Jackson had asked the distinguished men if any had a map. He would never forget their response. The men who held the lives of so many defenseless civilians in their hands, who were the only hope for millions of defenseless people, burst out laughing.

Soon each general, each ambassador, each negotiator, each aide, doubled over in laughter, holding their generous bellies, with tears streaming down their cheeks. Then, one by one, through their fits of laughter, the men who were the last hope for Bosnia pulled open the drawers in front of their seats at the huge conference table, or reached into their leather briefcases, and pulled out map upon map upon map. They tossed them haphazardly all over the table. Maps of the former Yugoslavia, of Croatia, Serbia, and Bosnia. Maps of cities like Sarajevo and Mostar and Tuzla and Jajce and Bihać and Dubrovnik. Jackson was red with embarrassment as he looked down on these maps, all marked up, with arrows pointing to shaded areas in black that read, "Proposed annexed land to Serbia" or "Proposed Croatian annexed territories" or "Bosnian enclave." The maps kept coming and the men who were Bosnia's last chance laughed themselves silly. He remembered looking at them, dumbfounded, until his eyes fell upon the only other man in the room without a smile on his face. That man was Abram Katz.

Now he was stuck in a basement in some miserable little lumber town along some trickle of water in the mountains that they called the Sana River. He wondered whom the diplomats were proposing to give the town on the Sana River to on their precious maps?

*Well, if it's the Muslims or Croats, they're a little late,* he thought, and tried to make himself laugh, but he couldn't.

**HIGH OVER THE TOWN** on the Sana River, Samuel West watched from the bell tower as the sun began to set. There were even more fires now than before, veiling the bloodred sky with black smoke. There were the same shouts and cries as earlier. Every so often there would be a new horror to watch: a sixteen-year-old girl tied naked to the front of a car and driven through the town; men and women taken to the soccer field and shot: a headless corpse tossed out of a second-story window. As he observed the terror from the safety of his eagle's nest, it seemed unreal to him, as if he were watching it on television from the comfort of his own living room.

A commotion caught his attention on the road leading into the town from the south. He saw a Chetnik jeep swerving violently down the road. Upon closer inspection, he could see that there was a man standing behind the driver with a rope around the driver's neck. Then as the jeep came closer, West could see that it wasn't a man, it was JuJu. He was trying to strangle the driver.

The driver was a Chetnik with a long black beard. JuJu pulled him right out of his seat with the rope and appeared to be killing him, but the driver suddenly jerked the wheel violently, causing the jeep to roll over. JuJu tumbled to the ground thirty feet away.

By the time he was able to get to his feet, a Chetnik from up the road who had seen what happened opened fire on him. JuJu darted down a side street, then climbed a gutter to the roof of a store. He ran along the roof in West's direction as the Chetnik ran the opposite way on the street below. JuJu made a magnificent leap to another building and appeared to be safe, but suddenly a sniper from atop the minaret of the town mosque opened fire on him. JuJu scrambled through a trapdoor that led down into the building and disappeared from West's sight.

JuJu was breathing heavily, searching the farm equipment store for something he could use as a weapon. The boy chose a long-handled scythe with a crescent-shaped blade. He crept up next to the shattered storefront window and stood there with the scythe in his hands, waiting for one of the Chetniks to come in after him.

"Oh, come quickly, you cowards," he said aloud. He could feel his hands trembling as he held the wooden handle tightly.

The waiting, he realized, was harder than the killing. The Chetnik he had killed that day at the bus station had been easy because he had come upon him by mistake and suddenly found himself fighting for his life. It was easy not to be scared when you were fighting for your life, he thought.

*But I must not be scared now, either,* he told himself. *I am a man now, the man of the family. No, not the man of the family. I have no family anymore. What about Grandfather? Yes, there is still Grandfather, but I don't wish to see him again. He's a coward.*

Thinking of his grandfather made him remember the last summer before the war, when his parents sent him to stay with Ado in Mostar. He remembered being very unhappy away from home for the first time. He had no friends in Mostar, so one day, bored and with nothing better to do, he decided to go down for a look at the Stari Most—the old Turkish bridge that he had heard so much about since he was a little boy.

Every child growing up in Yugoslavia had been told the story of the Stari Most. Many architects had tried and failed to put a bridge across the Neretva River. Then, in 1566, an architect named Hajrudin had the idea to build a stone bridge with no supports, using iron clamps instead of stone or cement for support. The sultan promised Hajrudin he would be put to death if he failed. On the day the scaffolding was to be taken down, Hajrudin, frightened that the bridge would fall into the river, fled into the hills. He was found later that day, digging his own grave. Those who found him had to drag him back to Mostar, where he was sure he would lose his head. To Hajrudin's surprise, a banquet had been arranged in his honor. The bridge had stood, and stood even now, four centuries later.

*He built a good bridge,* JuJu thought, *but it was cowardly of Hajrudin to flee to the hills. I could have run into the hills, but I'm not a coward. Not that I'm brave, but I am certainly not a coward.*

The boys at the bridge thought he was brave. That day, when he went down to the Stari Most for the first time, a group of local boys dared him to jump off. He was too frightened, so they laughed at him and taunted him. Then the girls came, and they also laughed at him and dared him to jump. So JuJu climbed on top of the stone wall of the bridge and did not just jump, he dove headfirst into the rushing emerald waters far below. He didn't know it at the time, but none of the other kids had ever jumped off the bridge, and certainly none had ever dreamed of diving headfirst. It was just a cruel joke, to single someone out and dare him to jump, then ridicule him when he wouldn't do it. The other kids didn't think he would actually jump.

He felt like he fell forever, and he remembered wanting to pray to Allah on the way down, but he didn't know any prayers.

After that, the boys on the bridge became his friends. He would hang out on the Stari Most with them, smoking cigarettes and flirting with the girls. Every once in a while, someone would recount the story of JuJu's spectacular dive off the bridge. They admired his bravery very much.

JuJu didn't consider himself to be brave. He remembered how scared he had been when he dove from the bridge. He knew you weren't brave if you simply did something you felt you had no choice but to do. If that was bravery, every Muslim in Bosnia would have to be considered brave. Muslims all over Bosnia were cornered, just as he was now. Most were trapped in cities and towns, surrounded by Serbs with modern weaponry. They defended themselves the best they could with hunting rifles and a few mortars or grenades smuggled through the Serb lines, or they walked day and night through the mountains to get their families to safety, or they went a week without eating in order to have enough to feed the sick and wounded, or they hid in basements in Sarajevo for months

at a time rather than surrender. Was that bravery? If that was bravery, he didn't consider it to be very special because everybody he
knew was doing it.

To JuJu, the Muslims were simply reacting to a false hope, like
a man lost in a desert who keeps crawling forward because he
thinks he sees water but it's really just a mirage. Or they were like
the religious pilgrims who traveled halfway around the globe to
climb Apparition Hill in hopes of seeing visions of Mary. Or maybe
it was desperation, or just something to do while they waited to
die. Perhaps it was honorable, for what that's worth, to never give
up, to die fighting. But was it brave?

JuJu could have glorified himself in his last moments and been
proud that he would take some Serbs with him before he died, but
killing a few of the Chetniks outside would have absolutely no effect on the war and he knew it. He wouldn't romanticize it. He had
seen enough war to know not to romanticize it. He had seen enough
war to know that you don't need to be brave to die.

JuJu was not afraid to die, but he was sad that he would die
because he would miss certain things. His family, of course, but
they were gone now anyway. He would miss the soccer games on
television and his mother's spicy meatballs, going to movies, the
smell of sawdust in the high timber after he felled a tree with the
other lumberjacks. He would miss going to the pizzeria on Friday
nights with Ilda, the girl with the curly brown hair who used to live
next door to him, whose family fled to Germany to escape the war.
He had always thought that he would marry her. He had even told
her—last year, when he was still just a boy—that he wanted to
marry her. Ilda had teased him and called him silly, but she had
been blushing and he knew she liked him as much as he liked her.
He would miss her a lot, much more than the other things. He
wondered what she would think of him if she could see him now,
killing Serbs.

He wondered if he looked different now that he had killed. He
knew he felt different. He had never thought of killing a person,
even a Chetnik, before the war, but recently he had been thinking
about it a great deal. Now that he had done it, he didn't mind it as
much as he thought he would. The Serbs made him do it. They
invaded his town, destroyed his home, and raped his sister. They

killed his mother, and they killed his father when he fought at Mostar. They made him kill, and now he learned that he didn't mind the killing because they gave him no choice. But he felt different now that he had killed. He didn't feel so young anymore.

"I only regret that I will die today and I won't be able to kill many more Chetniks," he said aloud, but he said it matter-of-factly, not in a way that romanticized the killing. That was his only regret. That, and knowing he would never see Ilda again.

*I would very much like to see her one more time,* he thought, and it made him suddenly very sad.

He checked the street outside, where he saw a Chetnik running straight toward the store. JuJu raised the scythe in his hands. As he was swinging the scythe in a wide, crescent-shaped arc, he was still thinking of Ilda, the girl who used to live next door.

West was standing now in the bell tower of the Eastern Orthodox church. One of the Chetniks had just run into the store where JuJu was hiding. A minute later, JuJu ran out with a scythe in his hands, blood dripping along the length of the blade onto the sidewalk. The Chetnik who had run in after JuJu never came out. Then another Chetnik ran around the corner, but he wasn't ready and before he had a chance to aim his gun, JuJu swung the scythe at the Chetnik's neck. The Chetnik raised his arm instinctively and JuJu nearly sliced it off. The Chetnik fell with the scythe still buried in the bone of his upper arm. JuJu pulled it out and brought it straight down on the Chetnik's head, leaving it buried in his skull.

*My God!* thought West.

Now the others had spotted JuJu, so he sprinted across the street into a pizzeria. The Chetniks soon surrounded it, but all were afraid to be the one to go in to get him. For five minutes they debated what to do. They couldn't throw a grenade into the pizzeria, because a Serb owned it.

Before they came to a decision, a Molotov cocktail came flying out of the door of the pizzeria and exploded in a Chetnik jeep. The two Chetniks crouching behind the jeep dropped their guns and ran. Soon the engine caught fire and all of the Chetniks ran for cover. The jeep exploded, scattering the Chetniks.

West saw JuJu use the diversion to climb out a side window and run down the alley, where he couldn't see the Chetnik waiting in the town square. He watched as JuJu came sprinting into the open space and the Chetnik spotted him and hastily opened fire. JuJu was hit and went down. The Chetnik kept firing as JuJu, on his hands and knees now, struggled to reach the cover of the large stone memorial in the middle of the square.

West had to walk out onto the roof of the church now to see what was happening. He didn't forget that he, too, was in danger, but he simply had to see what would become of the Muslim boy. He was drawn to the courage of JuJu, who was fighting the Chetniks all alone, and with no weapons.

*If he had come close enough, I might have thrown him my gun,* West thought. *Imagine what that little Muslim could do if he were armed?*

Sasha Maravic moved carefully toward the memorial, his finger still on the trigger of his Kalashnikov, following the blood marks on the pavement. Though there was a great deal of blood, he wasn't sure if he had killed the Muslim boy. When he reached JuJu, who was lying now at the foot of the memorial, he kicked him hard with his steel-toed boot. JuJu did not move. Sasha, still with his gun trained on JuJu, rolled him over.

*I've finally done my duty, and done it well,* Sasha thought, looking into JuJu's lifeless eyes. Now Sasha was over the shame he felt after his failure at JuJu's house, when he was too frightened to fight. He looked at JuJu and spat on him, then began searching his pockets, as he had been taught.

He found nothing of value, and was about to stand and walk away when he noticed a thin cloud rising from JuJu's body. It shocked him because he didn't realize what it really was. He thought it was JuJu's soul, or perhaps a ghost rising from JuJu's corpse. He was terrified at the sight, but he couldn't take his eyes away.

When the steam leaving JuJu's body stopped floating up into the cool air, Sasha found himself looking directly at the bronze plaque on the town memorial. The inscription, now stained with JuJu's blood, read, "In Tribute To The Courage Of The Brave Fighters Of The Partisan Cause, Who Fought And Died For A Free And United Yugoslavia."

The town on the Sana River was a Serb town now.

**11**

NIGHT HAD FINALLY COME to the valley. Jackson and Zarko carefully made their way toward the center of town, sliding along the sides of buildings, keeping in the shadows thrown by the moonlight, until they reached the library. Jackson could not see any flashlights or torches in the building, so with the butt of Zarko's rifle he smashed a basement window and crawled through it, then watched as Zarko let himself down.

"We'll stay here until a few hours before dawn," Jackson said. "That'll be the safest time to get out through the army in the hills."

"Yes, Captain, that sounds very smart."

They walked through the stacks of books on the bottom floor of the library, trying to find a defensible position to spend the next few hours.

"How about over here, Captain?" Zarko suggested.

It was a small study room, glass-enclosed with a waist-high concrete wall over which they could shoot if the Chetniks came.

"All right. You stay here, check out the basement. Make sure there's nobody here, friend or enemy. I'll check upstairs."

Jackson walked through the maze of bookshelves, then up the stairs and into a spacious main lobby. He checked in the librarians' desks for food, but found nothing. He wandered until he came to a couple of old vending machines. One had the standard American candy bars, the other Pepsi. He had no change, but he tipped the machine over, sending it crashing against the marble floor. The candy machine broke open, but he found that it was empty. Next he tried the soda machine, but it, too, was empty. He slammed the door shut in frustration.

He noticed the candy bars in the display windows next to the selection levers. Smashing the glass with the heel of his boot, he pulled out the six candy bars. He did the same with the soda cans in the other machine, but the cans were empty. He put the candy in his pockets.

Just before walking down the stairs, he noticed a large map hanging in the lobby. It was a population map of Bosnia and Herzegovina, from the days before the war when it was still just a province of Yugoslavia. The interior of the Bosnian borders were a leopard skin of colors, each color representing the dominant ethnic group in a region. The map was displayed there proudly, as if to remind the people of the town that Bosnia had successfully survived for hundreds of years as a multiethnic society.

He returned to the study room in the basement, where he and Zarko hastily unwrapped the candy bars and tried to bite into them. They were as hard as rocks. They tried cutting them with Zarko's switchblade, but the candy bars had probably been in the display windows of the vending machine for years.

"We have to find food," Jackson groaned. He could not remember ever being so hungry before. "It's been two days. We have to eat before trying to escape this town. It seems quiet enough now in this area; we'll split up and check some of the nearby buildings. Meet back here in one hour. And don't do anything stupid."

"Captain, you shouldn't go unarmed."

"I'm not planning on running into anybody."

"You never do," Zarko said. He reached into his pocket and pulled out his switchblade. He flipped it in the air and caught it, then slapped it into Jackson's hand.

Jackson pocketed the knife and climbed out the window into the chill night. He crouched there and signaled for Zarko to come up. They nodded to each other and set off in opposite directions. Jackson was careful to take his time and not be seen as he made his way back to the center of town.

He crouched at the corner of the Orthodox church, looking across the square, where there was a pizzeria with a broken window in the front. He knew that others must have broken in before him, perhaps also looking for food, but right now it was his best bet. However, it was a long way across the square, and though it was quiet and there were no Chetniks in sight, he didn't like the idea of sprinting across the entire open space of the square. He would have to circle along the rear of the buildings around the square and approach the pizzeria from the rear.

Suddenly he heard shuffling feet behind him. He turned and saw a figure approaching. It was a man, carrying a gun. He was stumbling though, and appeared too weak to raise the gun. Jackson rose slowly, his back to the church, and waited as the man approached him.

"What happened to you!" Jackson asked, his voice filled with concern as he recognized the figure. He felt both relief and concern upon seeing the shepherd.

"I was shot escaping the house," Emir replied. Jackson unbuttoned Emir's brown wool jacket and lifted his shirt to see the wound in his right side that was staining his jacket. "I made it over there, to that car, where I have been hiding. I planned to wait until darkness and try to get to the hills, but now. . . ." His knees buckled. Jackson caught him before he fell, and eased him to the ground.

"What about the others? JuJu and his family?"

"I never saw them."

"West?"

Emir shook his head.

"Zarko is with me. I'm meeting him in an hour. Then we're heading for the hills."

"I cannot make it," Emir said weakly.

"Sure you will," Jackson told him, trying to hide his concern. "I'll see if I can find any first aid, maybe some sewing supplies. We're going to have to stitch your wound."

"There is first aid in the car," Emir said. "I tried to patch myself, but I passed out. I am unable to look at my own blood."

Jackson hoisted Emir over his shoulder as gently as possible and carried him to the broken window of the library. He eased him through the window and hurried down after him. He carried Emir to the study carrel and propped him up against the back wall.

He then went back and retrieved the first-aid kit from the car that Emir had pointed out. He returned to find Emir with his eyes closed, weakly making the sign of the cross over and over. He didn't stop crossing himself until Jackson finished stitching and bandaging his side.

Emir opened his eyes and inspected the bandage. "It is a good field dressing. Robert. Were you a doctor in the United States of America?"

"I was a soldier."

"You should be a doctor."

"Maria is going to be a doctor."

"Is that the girl who Aleksandar says makes you unhappy?"

"She makes me very happy."

"You haven't seemed happy."

"That's because I'm not with her." Jackson could see that Emir was confused, but he didn't know if it was because Emir was too weak to concentrate or because he was too young to understand what it was like to be in love. In any case, he needed to keep Emir talking, keep him awake until Zarko returned and they could try to make it to the hills. "Maria was my fiancée. She's studying to be a doctor. She wants to help the migrant workers in California who can't afford doctors."

"She sounds like a good person."

"She's a saint," Jackson said quickly "All she ever wanted to do was be a doctor so she could help people."

"You should be a doctor, too."

"I should be in Italy right now."

"You should be a doctor in Italy then." Emir tried to stand, but Jackson held him down gently. "Why did you want to become a soldier instead of a doctor?" Emir asked.

"I didn't exactly want to be a soldier. I had to serve in the army to get my country to pay for college."

"I would rather be ignorant," Emir said, "then to have to be a soldier."

"It's funny, but even after four years in the army I never really considered myself a soldier. You see, from the very start I've been in supply—I requested supply from the start. My father was a truck driver. I drove cross-country with him once, when I was about six-teen, right after my mother died. I wanted to be a truck driver until that trip." Jackson laughed, remembering it so clearly now. "I had some romantic notion of owning my own rig, dreaming about all of the interesting places I'd go. I never would have thought you could drive on an interstate from L.A. to New York without seeing a damn thing.

"Anyway, that took care of the trucking bug, but I still used to help my dad out, arranging schedules and things. He was an independent, but he started talking about us building a trucking empire together. I'd go to college, and after graduation I'd help him start our own company and run it with him. Of course, as usual, he took off for a couple years and by the time I ran into him again he'd lost his license—he's an alcoholic. Still, I guess I never got the thought of having my own company out of my mind, so I put in for supply to learn what I needed to know to start my own shipping business after I fulfilled my commitment with the army. I thought it would be an easy four years. I never thought I'd end up like this, fighting like a real soldier."

"But you fought in Iraq—Aleksandar has told me so. You were wonderful there. I watched it on the television in my village. How terrible of Hussein to try to take over a peace-loving nation. It was right of the United States to help Kuwait get their country back. Were you very proud?"

"I was proud that I lived," Jackson said. "But I didn't really fight—I helped supply the frontline troops."

"Ah, but without supplies an army is nothing! I'm sure you were a hero!"

"Some say we were heroes," Jackson said absently.

"I say you were heroes." Emir smiled. "I've seen *Amerikanacs* amongst the Blue Helmets. They are heroes as well, though what they do, I can't tell you."

"They aren't allowed to do much of anything."

"It's hard to imagine you as a Blue Helmet. Why did you leave them?"

"Aleksandar never told you?"

Emir shook his head.

Jackson stared thoughtfully into space. "There was no peace to keep."

Emir thought about that. "Maybe the Blue Helmets should

fight the Serbs. When you get back to America, you tell your people that we have oil here."

"There's no oil here."

"If you tell them, they'll help us take our country back, too."

"You can tell them," Jackson said, smiling wearily. "You can tell them when you get to America."

Emir smiled at the thought of it. "How wonderful it would be to live in a country where no one remembers the past. Do they raise sheep and goats in America?"

"Yes. But the real money is in cattle."

"I like sheep and goats though. I would like to live in America to raise sheep and goats in the mountains of California. And I will holiday at the ocean with my friend Aleksandar." Emir smiled contentedly. "Heaven must be like these mountains of California."

Jackson picked up the M16 by the strap and placed it in the shepherd's hands. Emir was suddenly very serious again.

"Robert. Do things like this happen in America?"

"Not like this," Jackson said. He thought of the L.A. riots, but they were insignificant compared with what was happening in Bosnia, or even to this one little town. "Listen to me, Emir. I'm going out for a little while. I think I saw a place where I might find food, or at least water. Stay here and rest, but don't fall asleep—in case the Chetniks come. And be careful not to shoot Zarko and me when we come back. Do you understand?"

Emir pulled off his chain. The cross, crucifix, and crescent and star medallions clanged against each other as he reached up and pulled it over Jackson's head.

"That is for protection," Emir told him. "If a Chetnik stops you, show him the Orthodox cross."

Jackson felt the smooth cross with his fingertips, then stuffed the icons down his shirt. He suddenly wondered what Maria—a devout Catholic—would think of him wearing a necklace with the Muslim and Orthodox icons on either side of the crucifix.

*She'd say it's blasphemy,* Jackson thought. *Well, maybe in America it's blasphemy. But in Bosnia, you can't afford to worry about blasphemy.*

Emir tugged on Jackson's blue jeans. "Robert, remember what

you said at the house? About the service you would perform for me in case we are in danger of being captured?"

"We aren't at that point, Emir," Jackson tried unsuccessfully to say with confidence.

"But you have not forgotten?"

Only now that he could see the pain etched into his friend's face could Jackson understand truly how much it meant to him. He didn't avoid saying it now. "I'll kill you if it comes to it. I'll do it quickly. You won't feel a thing."

## 12

**THE MOSQUE IN THE TOWN** on the Sana River was built in 1463, just after the Ottomans conquered central Bosnia. It took six years to construct. It had been the architectural pride of the town for centuries, built from rock from the same quarry that was used to build the famous mosque in Sarajevo. All who had seen both agreed that this mosque was more beautiful. Despite its beauty, the mosque did not attract large crowds in the town—until this day.

Ado was walking through the mosque calling JuJu's name over and over, but there was no sign of the boy. There were a couple hundred Muslims in the mosque, which was just across the town square from the Orthodox church. All day long, and now into the evening, Muslims whose homes and businesses had been destroyed fled to safety in the hills or in neighbors' homes. Others fled to the mosque. For many Muslims of the town, it was the first time in years they had come there.

Ado did not know why so many Muslims had fled to the mosque. The Serbs had no reservations about destroying a religious building. Over the past few days the mosque had been one of the main targets of Serb rocket attacks. Whether because the army was not accurate enough to hit the right places or because the mosque was five hundred years old and strong, it had so far stood defiantly erect, welcoming its prodigal sons and daughters

Ado had a feeling that the Serbs were happy to have them there.

He had spent a dangerous afternoon looking for JuJu, but since he was only an old man, the few times he came across a Chetnik patrol, he received little more than a punch or kick. The Chetniks would call him names and spit on him and be on their way. Finally he came to the mosque, where there was still no sign of his grandson.

He sat down against the wall and rested his tired legs, trying not to think of the horror his family had endured in the basement.

It had been dark and damp and cool in the basement.

"Hide the girls! Hide the girls!" Kadira, JuJu's mother, screamed.

Martina pulled a small table away from the wall. Behind it was a crawl space where the wood had rotted, an old hiding place the children used to play in when they were younger. There was just enough room for Kadira and the two girls to fit. Ado replaced the table in front.

With no ammunition left, Ado and JuJu searched for a place to hide. The only option was behind the rusty old water heater in a corner of the room. Ado smashed the lightbulb hanging from the ceiling before they squeezed behind the water heater, forgetting that the electricity had been cut days ago.

The shooting outside suddenly stopped and in a minute the sound of many boots rushing over the floor above filled the basement. Dust fell from the ceiling.

Within seconds, five Chetniks tentatively came halfway down the stairs. "All Muslim pigs come out!" one of the Chetniks demanded. There was a long pause. Ado could barely hear them whispering before they shouted. "We're throwing a grenade down there in five seconds! Any Turks that wish to join their beloved Allah can stay where they are! But those who wish to live, come out now! We will not harm you!"

Ado could hear no sound in the basement. Kadira and the girls were obviously waiting for him to decide what to do. Ado noticed that JuJu was now looking at him, waiting for him to make the decision for all of them. Ado did not know any better than the rest of them what was best, but he knew that he was too frightened to willingly surrender himself and his family to the Chetniks.

Five seconds passed, then ten, and then a full minute before Ado heard the stairs creaking, and saw the beam of light. Soon he could see four Chetniks, all armed with machine guns, following a fifth Chetnik with a flashlight down the stairs. The Chetnik with the flashlight, whose beard was much longer than the others', began searching as the others looked suspiciously about the basement, covering him.

Suddenly the long-bearded Chetnik with the flashlight stopped. Ado gasped when he saw that he had not replaced the table in exactly the same spot that he had found it. The Chetnik crouched now to inspect the dusty floor and the marks where the table legs had stood probably for years.

"Over here," the Chetnik said to the others "Vlade, help me with this table."

JuJu shifted just a bit, as if readying himself to charge the Chetniks, but Ado motioned to him to stay down.

Ado looked out from behind the water heater and watched the Chetniks move the table, exposing the hole in the wall.

"Fall back!" one of the Chetniks shouted, and they all retreated, diving for cover. Soon they all had their guns trained on the hole in the wall. "Come out, pigs! Throw out your weapons or we'll open fire!"

"No!" Ado heard Kadira shout. Ado had to cover JuJu's mouth with his hand to stop him, too, from screaming. When the boy tried to get up, Ado wrapped his other arm around JuJu's neck and pulled him down. The boy began to thrash with his legs, but he could not be heard by now because seven more Chetniks came down into the basement and all were screaming at the hole in the wall.

Among them was their clean-shaven leader, Captain Šešelj

Ado, who could no longer see the Chetniks because he was behind the water heater struggling to control JuJu, could hear Kadira's screams as the Chetniks dragged her out into the basement.

"Ah! Good! A woman!" one of the Chetniks exclaimed.

"Maybe there are more," another shouted hopefully.

"You, bring them out," Ado heard Captain Šešelj order one of the Chetniks. In a few seconds Ado could hear Martina screaming and Selma crying.

"Where are the others, woman?" Captain Šešelj demanded. Kadira must have been too frightened to speak, because he asked again in a louder voice. Once again he received no reply. The next sound Ado heard was the sound of a long hunting knife quickly pulled from its sheath.

Ado had already determined that the boy had no weapons. He strained his neck to look down at his hip. A single grenade Zarko had clipped onto his belt was still there.

"Tell us, woman!" Captain Šešelj demanded again.

"What others, sir?" Ado heard Martina answer for her mother.

"Those with machine guns who killed my men, who shot them in the back like cowards! Where are those pigs who ambushed my men?"

"They're gone, sir," Martina said in a timid voice. "They ran away. They left us here."

JuJu was crying by now and began to moan, but Ado applied more pressure to the boy's neck so his sobs could not be heard. Tears were streaming down Ado's cheeks, but he did not have a free hand to wipe them away. If he let go of the boy, Ado had no doubt that they would all die.

"Obviously, the men saved themselves and left their women behind," Captain Šešelj said, and now Ado could hear several of the Chetniks climbing the stairs. "Lieutenant, you know what to do."

As soon as Captain Šešelj and his men had gone, slamming the basement door closed behind them, Ado heard the Chetnik with the longest beard tell two of his men to put down their weapons. "You," he then said to Martina. "Take off your clothes."

Martina cried as Kadira pleaded incoherently. JuJu began to struggle even more.

"Listen, child. We do not want to do this," the Chetnik with the longest beard explained. "But it is our duty and we have to do it. If you do not struggle, it will all be over soon."

JuJu continued to struggle to free himself from Ado's arms.

If Ado threw the grenade, he knew the Chetniks would die—

but so would the woman and the girls and possibly he and the boy as well. He didn't care about his own life, but he cared for the boy's life very much. The boy could fight, if he could live to see another day. The old man considered the boy to be a valuable Muslim commodity.

Ado looked again toward the grenade on his belt. He could no longer see it. The tears were blurring his vision.

"Please, sir, take me, not my daughter," Kadira cried.

"Shut up, woman!" one of the Chetniks demanded, slapping her.

Ado could hear them tearing the clothes off of Martina's body. Martina was screaming as they threw her down on an old table.

"Hold her down!" one of the Chetniks said.

"Stop struggling, pig!" another ordered.

"Hurry up," another demanded. "We don't have all day, and I want to have a turn with this one!"

"Give me a minute!" the Chetnik raping Martina replied. "I am planting the seeds of Serbia in Bosnia!"

After they had all had a turn, Martina was still screaming so loudly that one of the Chetniks dragged her upstairs. "I will take her with me," he said. "I have many friends who will enjoy her tonight."

Ado could hear the Chetnik climbing the stairs, dragging Martina. Soon the basement doors closed, muffling the girl's screams.

"Now the little one," a Chetnik growled.

"What about the old one?" another asked.

"You can have the old one."

"I don't think we have to bother with her. I think only the young ones," the one with the longest beard said.

"Let's bring them both out for the others."

"No. Let's do them ourselves."

"There are plenty more houses," the Chetnik with the longest beard said. "Let's leave these pigs alone. This one is too young and the other is too old."

"I'm taking the young one with me."

"The other one is not too old. I'll take her," another said.

"She is beyond childbearing years," the Chetnik with the longest beard argued.

"I say we kill her."

"Kill both of them right now," the most rabid Chetnik said.

"No, just kill the mother. I want the little one."

Ado tried to blink away the tears that were inhibiting his sight and running down his face. The boy was struggling so hard that Ado was losing his grip on him.

"Let's have them now, then kill them."

"Kill the old one, but not the little one. Let's take her with us."

"There are plenty more houses," the Chetnik with the longest beard repeated. "Leave these for now. They will be here when our work is done. Where can they go?"

Kadira was begging now. "Please, take me, even kill me. Please don't take my daughters. They're so young. They've done nothing. Please leave them—"

"I don't like listening to her," one of the Chetniks said.

"I'm going to kill her."

"No, you won't! There are plenty more houses!" the Chetnik with the longest beard said for the third time, this time raising his voice in anger. "I'm in charge here. Do as I say!"

Suddenly a shot rang out.

"You imbecile!" Ado heard a Chetnik cry. "You got Turk blood all over me!"

"I told you not to kill her! Those were not our orders!"

"Don't kill the little one. I will take her with me."

"Look at the old one. She bleeds like a pig."

"Finish her."

"You might as well now," the Chetnik with the longest beard said, exasperated.

"No. Let's just let her lie there while we take the daughter."

Ado could stand it no more. He released his grip on JuJu, who, once free, let out an agonized scream. A second later the Chetniks were firing at the water heater. Ado wiped his eyes with his sleeve and quickly grabbed the grenade. He pulled the pin, and with his free hand he pulled JuJu back down behind the water heater. The Chetniks were still firing. Ado waited as long as he dared before throwing the grenade into the middle of the basement. The Chetniks scattered, running for cover as the grenade rolled up against Selma, who was slouched on the floor with her back against the wall. Ado saw her look at the grenade. In the last second of her life, she managed a slight smile before her world exploded.

After the grenade went off, JuJu was the first one on his feet. Without checking to see how his grandfather was, he rushed out from behind the water heater. When he saw the sight of his mother and sister, he screamed again at the top of his lungs.

Ado was quickly behind him, putting his arm on his shoulder and trying to lead the boy upstairs. "Come on, son. Do not look. Their pain is over."

"Why did you wait!" JuJu screamed at him through his tears.

"Please, don't blame me," Ado said, and now he was sobbing and he knew the tears running down his cheeks were real tears. "I thought the Chetniks would leave them alone when it was over. They said they would."

"Why didn't you pull the pin and threaten to blow us all up? You could have forced them to drop their weapons!"

Ado's mouth dropped.

"You coward!" JuJu screamed. "You let my sister have the unspeakable done to her! I should kill you myself right now!"

Ado found that he was scared of the hysterical boy—his own grandson. "You're right to blame me," the old man said, wiping his eyes. "I did not think of a standoff."

"Yes, I blame you! You held me down!"

Ado put his head in his hands helplessly. "I thought I was giving our family their only chance."

"You're a coward! How could you just throw the grenade and kill my sister and mother along with the Chetniks, instead of trying to save them first?"

"I thought it best not to let them suffer any longer," Ado whispered.

JuJu suddenly pushed the old man to the floor. "You have no courage! You don't know how to fight! But I will fight the Chetniks and die like a man!"

The steps had been blown apart, but the boy climbed out of the basement with the practiced ease of a child climbing a tree. Ado called after him, but JuJu ran out of the house.

*The boy was right,* Ado said to himself minutes later, still in the basement. He had been reliving the moment over and over in his mind. *I could have made it a standoff.*

*I am not a coward, though,* Ado told himself. *The boy was wrong about that.*

Ado finally took a deep breath, trying unsuccessfully to forget for a moment about his granddaughters and daughter. *Now I must go and find the boy,* he thought, wiping his eyes dry with his sleeve so he could survey the area that used to be the stairs. He knew it would be impossible for him to climb. Sighing, he began the laborious task of constructing a makeshift stairway with broken furniture and other debris.

As a younger man Ado had fought many times, but he was not a professional soldier or even a policeman who might know what to do in such a situation. He was merely an old man who tried his best to fight for his family.


A great explosion rocked one corner of the mosque. The ancient building shook from the blast. Dust flew and people held their breath, but the mosque held strong once again.

When the people settled down, Ado heard sobbing coming from under one of the many rugs that worshippers knelt on when they prayed, bowing toward Mecca. Wiping his eyes on his sleeve, Ado crawled forward to see who was there. He found a little boy, much younger than JuJu.

"Are you hurt?" Ado asked. The boy continued to sob but did not reply, so Ado lifted the rug and lay next to him. When the boy rolled over, Ado could see he was clutching a puppy to his chest. "What's his name?" Ado asked nicely, propping his head up with one arm.

"Muhammad," the boy said timidly.

"Ah! After the great prophet?"

The boy shook his head. "After the great prizefighter."

"May I pet him?"

"Uh-huh."

Ado stroked the puppy gently. "Is he sleeping?"

"Yes."

"Where are your mother and father?"

"Sleeping."

"Where?"

"At our house." The boy looked up at Ado's face. "Why are you crying?"

Ado ignored the question, petting the dog. "Can I hold your puppy for a minute?" he asked.

"Why?"

"Because I like puppies, too."

The boy slid out from under the rug and knelt, as did Ado. Ado could see now that the puppy had been shot in its side. The boy began to hand the puppy to Ado, but the blood from the wound caused it to stick to the boy's shirt. Ado pealed the stiff puppy off and now confirmed what he had feared. The boy had been hit in the arm by the same bullet that passed through the puppy.

"Yes, now I can see that he is asleep. You say your parents are asleep, too?"

"Uh-huh."

"I am just going to put the puppy down for a minute, because I would like to see the cut on your arm."

"I got shot."

"I see. Does it hurt?"

"Uh-huh."

Ado examined the boy's wound, which was fairly clean, since the bullet had passed right through his muscle. *If the bullet passed through the puppy and then the boy, he must have been shot at very close range,* Ado thought.

"So, what do you want to do when you grow up?" Ado asked, hoping to take the boy's mind off his wound.

"I want to go home," the boy replied.

"What's your name?"

The boy's reply was cut off by the sound of a bullet slamming into the great wooden door of the mosque.

"Why does the mosque bleed?" the little boy asked, looking at the old wooden door.

Ado turned and squinted, trying to see through the tears building up in his eyes. He couldn't explain the blood he saw running down the inside of the great wooden door. He thought, perhaps, that it was a miracle. "It bleeds for all of us," the old man whispered.

## 13

**A WIND BLEW INTO** the valley and made the church spire unbearably cold. West had noticed a trapdoor in the floor earlier. He opened it now, revealing a ladder descending into the darkness. He took the ladder to a small landing, then followed the stairs into the great expanse of the church. It was empty, so he walked through it without worry and admired its beauty. It was an old church, with colorful stained-glass windows, carved pillars, centuries-old frescoes, and a painted ceiling. He marveled at how it had been left untouched. He assumed the Serbs would not dare harm such an architectural treasure, but of course he did not know their plans for the mosque. He walked across the altar to the priest's quarters in the back.

Searching for food, he thanked God when he found several bottles of wine. He opened one with his knife and found some stale bread that he cut into small pieces. He lifted a piece of bread to his mouth, but caught himself and put it down.

He closed his eyes, clasped his hands under his chin, and prayed quickly without hearing the words. "Bless me oh Lord and these thy gifts which I am about to receive through thy bounty through Christ our Lord Amen."

As he ate the bread and drank the wine, West lamented the current state of his mission. It was certainly not going the way he had planned it. It was supposed to be easy. If Jackson and his men had known what they were doing, he thought, he could be on his way out of the country by now. He hated working with amateurs, but that was the way it had been ever since he had been discharged from the army.

He still got angry when he thought about the shame of being told he could no longer serve his country, that he could no longer do what he knew he was born to do. He was put on earth to be a soldier, and he was a damned good one, he thought. Anyone who knew anything about soldiering would know that. It was the bureaucrats in Washington, the liberals from those watchdog groups who ended it for him. Sure, he was at My Lai, and sure, he was alongside the lieutenant when they went in with their guns blazing and finished off everyone in the village.

*But hell, we were told they were Viet Cong. The lieutenant was just following orders, like every good soldier does. He was a good man, and a damned fine officer. He knew you couldn't fuck around with the Viet Cong. He did what any good soldier would do, but when they needed a scapegoat, they pinned it all on the lieutenant. The poor bastard's life was ruined. He was court-martialed.*

*The lieutenant was a patriot,* West thought. *He deserved a medal—and so did I. When they came to me and wanted me to rat him out, I wouldn't do it. When they offered to let me stay in the army if I admitted I made a mistake, if I admitted that I followed illegal orders to massacre everyone in that village, I refused. It was a question of honor. I am a patriot.*

He sat in the church eating the bread and wine, certain that he had done the right thing in Vietnam.

*What I saw in this town today only proves my point,* he thought. *You can't have rules for war.*

When West was done eating, he lay down in the priest's bed. He put his hands behind his head and closed his eyes contentedly. He thought of his mission—of Katz, who had hired him.

*That old fool sure as hell couldn't come over here. He made a point to tell me how much he despised me and loathed what I had done at My Lai, but he hired me because, when it comes time to go to war, men like him need men like me.*

# 14

A HALF HOUR AFTER HE had left Emir, Jackson was returning to the library. He couldn't find a scrap of food, but dozens of Chetniks had suddenly returned to the center of town, so he, Emir, and Zarko would have to get out and head for the hills now, with or without food.

When he got close to the library, his hunger was quickly forgotten. There was a bonfire out front. Chetniks were burning books by the hundreds. They were singing Chetnik patriotic songs, firing their guns into the air, and passing around bottles of slivovitz.

Jackson felt his stomach drop. Where was Emir?

He circled a few buildings so he could come upon the library from the rear, then quickly slid down through the window he had broken earlier. He was horrified to see that the basement had already been ravaged—every bookcase was overturned and books were scattered everywhere. He picked his way through the mess until he came to the bodies of two Chetniks crumpled behind a fallen bookcase.

As soon as he was over the shock of seeing the bodies, Jackson rushed to the study carrel where he had left Emir. The glass had been shot out. Dozens of bullet marks scarred the concrete wall. He took a deep breath and turned the corner.

He had expected to see Emir's body, but all he found was Emir's gun and a great deal of blood. There was no ammunition left in the gun.

*He must have fought them until he ran out of bullets,* Jackson thought. *But then what? What would they do to him—*

Suddenly Jackson's chest tightened and he couldn't breathe. He dropped to his knees, then fell in a heap where he had left Emir only a half hour earlier. He wept uncontrollably when he realized that Emir must still be alive. The Chetniks would not have left their comrade's bodies but taken Emir's unless the shepherd was still alive.

In a few minutes Jackson stood, his blue flannel shirt and blue jeans now stained with Emir's blood. Still sobbing, he followed a trail of blood on unsteady legs to the stairway. He began walking up the stairs, but shouts from above kept him from going much further.

He could hear a Serb voice booming above the others on the main floor, urging them to find the Turkish books. "Six centuries of Ottoman rule will cease to exist after tonight, brothers! We will wipe the Turks from our history books and cleanse our libraries of their memories. Their culture will disappear because of the patriotic work we do tonight. Find those books, brothers. Tonight, we rewrite history!"

A loud chorus of approval echoed throughout the library as the crazed Chetniks scrambled about, looking for any books concerning the six hundred years of Ottoman rule or anything to do with the Bosnian Muslims that had lived in the town for centuries.

Jackson stood at the bottom of the stairway, desperately wishing he had the courage to climb it. He wanted to keep his promise to Emir, but he knew if he climbed those stairs he would die, and he wasn't prepared to die.

## 15

**EMIR LAY BLEEDING IN** the dirt. He was in a small park just off the town square, lying near a campfire. The Chetniks had been beating him repeatedly since midnight. Now it was nearly three in the morning. He had just regained consciousness and could hear the Chetniks playing a game where they tossed a bayoneted rifle into the air, flipping it so that it made several revolutions, then tried to catch the butt of the rifle. The first drunken Chetnik Emir saw try it missed, grasping the bayonet by mistake, slitting his hand open. The others laughed at him and drank slivovitz as he howled in pain and held his bloody hand to his chest.

Then another tried, but he was afraid so he let it fall. Two more did it this way, until another, a small man with deep-set eyes, tried it and was successful. They all congratulated him. He was told the boots were his.

That was when Emir first noticed his boots had been taken from his feet. The little Chetnik was putting them on. They were clearly too big for him and the others teased him, but he kept them on nonetheless. The little Chetnik with Emir's boots noticed that Emir was conscious.

"Now we'll have some more fun," one of the Chetniks called out, pulling Emir up by the hair. The wound in Emir's side had reopened and he had glass cuts from the study carrel all along his forehead. They made him stand right next to the fire, where the heat burned his legs.

"Let's make the Turk eat pork," one of them called out.

"Let's make him cut off his own penis," another suggested.

One of them came forward and poured slivovitz into the wound in Emir's side, causing his legs to wobble as he nearly passed out again. Emir began making the sign of the cross over and over and over. He could not help himself. At first the Chetniks laughed at him, but soon they became furious. He was crossing himself from left shoulder to right shoulder with one finger, the way Roman Catholics crossed themselves.

"See how he mocks us," one of them said. "I beg of you to let me kill him now with my own hands."

"Maybe he's a Croat," another said.

"Croat or Muslim, it's clear he is no Serb."

"Surely such a display warrants a particularly painful death," another said, walking right up to Emir.

"Let's impale him," the small one with Emir's boots called out. One of the Chetniks pushed him to the ground and unsheathed a large Bowie knife, but the Chetnik who wanted to castrate Emir stopped him.

Finally, unable to agree, the Chetniks left the decision to their leader, the strongest of the group. He was a veteran of the Yugoslav army and, though he did not yet have a full black beard, wore the traditional black of the Chetniks.

"Leave him to die," the leader said in a deep voice. "He hasn't long to live."

But the other Chetniks disagreed and began arguing all over again. Occasionally they shouted at the leader and cursed him, questioning his loyalty. They demanded an appropriate punishment for the Turk who had killed their comrades in the basement of the library.

The Chetnik leader was washing his hands in a bucket of water. "Very well," he announced finally, knowing the others wouldn't be satisfied until a severe punishment was meted out. "I will decide what to do to him." After drying his hands, he walked over to Emir and ordered him to stand.

With a great effort, Emir was able to push himself to his feet. Then, as much as he tried to stop his hand, he made the sign of the cross right in the largest Chetnik's face.

•        •        •

Zarko moved through the town very carefully, waiting until there were absolutely no people about before dashing across streets or through yards. He tried to blend into shadows cast by the moonlight and slink along the sides of buildings like a phantom. It was slow going and required great patience, because everywhere he went there were Chetniks running about, shooting guns into the air and shouting drunken war cries.

He turned and saw a dog running by with a human arm in its mouth. The hand seemed to beckon to Zarko.

*If I were a true Gypsy,* Zarko thought, *I would take that as a bad omen.*

He could hear Serb propaganda being played from the minaret at the mosque now. He made his way back to the town square and hid inside a looted pharmacy. He was over two hours late in returning to meet Jackson, but the library was on the far side of the square, with more and more Chetniks pouring in every minute. Every time he tried to find a way to the library, he ran into Chetniks, who shot at him twice.

He watched as the Chetniks tied a man to the front seat of a car. The car was then filled with explosives and a brick was dropped on the gas pedal. The vehicle sped toward the mosque. It ran a little off center and slammed into the corner of the five-hundred-year-old building, causing a mighty explosion that took a chunk out of the corner. A little white Yugo went speeding by with four Chetniks in it, their guns sticking out of the windows. The Chetniks fired into the air and shouted their approval and called for the Chetniks responsible for the explosion to do it again.

That was when Zarko first noticed Emir.

Sasha Maravic was in the town square with the other Chetniks and dozens of Serbs from the town. Many of the Serbs were carrying torches, which lit up the square. He watched and cheered when a Muslim was tied up and put in a car filled with explosives and sent barreling into the mosque. He sang Chetnik songs with the others as they passed bottles of slivovitz to each other. He had had wine once before, at a wedding, but never slivovitz, so he had drunk far too quickly and was very drunk now.

He had had very much to drink because it had been a long day, and he had killed several Muslims, and was not sure whether he liked the killing. Other than the one house that he had tried to attack from the rear, and other than the young fanatic he had killed at the partisan memorial, the Muslims he had encountered had not fought back. He had raped a Turk girl that day, and he had destroyed several houses with grenades, so now he was glad to be drunk because all that was forgotten and he enjoyed being congratulated by the Serb townspeople that he had helped to liberate.

Suddenly he heard a group of Chetniks calling out above the singing. They were leading a naked Turk who was bleeding from his head and his side. The Chetniks wanted everyone to watch as they paraded the Turk through the square.

"Yes! Yes! Kill the Turk!" Sasha cried. Someone passed him a bottle of slivovitz. He took a drink and raised the bottle. "Kill all the Turks!"

The Chetniks were marching Emir around the square, but he was very weak and dropped to his knees. The Chetniks pulled him to his feet and marched him around the square again, but in a minute he collapsed. They picked him up and resumed the procession, but when Emir fell for a third time, a Chetnik pulled Sasha out of the crowd.

"The Turk must make it to the mosque," the Chetnik, who was toothless and had a large mole under his right eye, explained. "You will help him."

Sasha shook his head furiously and refused. "No, brother, not me. Find another. I would not touch a Turk except to kill him!"

The Chetnik grabbed Sasha by the hair and jerked his head back. "You will aid the Turk or you will join him."

Sasha was pushed right next to Emir, who was now struggling to get to his feet. Sasha reluctantly bent to help him up, using all of his strength to lift him, because Emir was very weak. He put his arm around Emir and reluctantly set off toward the mosque.

There were Chetniks and Serb townspeople now in two lines facing each other, creating a narrow corridor to the steps of the mosque. Sasha helped Emir through the lines, where they were punched and kicked and insulted. Sasha cursed the Chetniks and Serbs, crying out that he was a loyal Serb and was helping the Turk against his will. The Serbs and Chetniks did not intend to spit on him or to punch and kick him, and they were not directing their insults at him, but walking next to Emir he felt as if he were the object of their hate. He could not understand why they would hate him. He had never done anything to deserve such treatment. It was a long, slow walk to the steps of the mosque.

As they neared the steps, Sasha looked at Emir. His light blue eyes were barely open and his brown hair was matted with blood.

"Thank you," Emir groaned weakly.

That startled Sasha, who looked more closely at Emir.

*He looks nothing like a pig,* Sasha thought. *Even in this condition, he does not even smell like a pig.*

Sasha was supporting almost all of Emir's weight by the time they arrived at the stone steps of the mosque. The entire crowd had assembled there, waving their torches and passing their bottles of slivovitz and cursing Emir. Finally they were standing before the great wooden door of the mosque. There was a dead Muslim lying on each side of the door. Sasha let Emir down gently, and the group of Chetniks who had led Emir into the square fell upon him. Sasha looked at Emir one last time, then fought his way through the crowd until he was alone on the edge of the square.

One of the Chetniks ran from the steps of the mosque to the farm equipment store next to the pharmacy where Zarko was hiding. He returned a minute later, waving a hammer over his head.

The Chetniks converged on Emir. Zarko could not see what they were doing to him, but he could hear Emir's screams above the Chetniks' singing. Then he could hear a loud banging against the great wooden door of the mosque. By now the entire crowd had gathered there. When the Chetniks were done and stepped away, a great cheer went up. Emir had been nailed to the door of the mosque, his arms outstretched, blood streaming from his hands and feet, from the wound in his side and from the glass cuts on his forehead. A couple of extra spikes had been nailed under his collarbone to support his weight. He was clearly in agony. The Serb townspeople began insulting him, running up the steps of the mosque and spitting on him.

Zarko clenched his teeth in anger, then had to gasp for breath as he tried to control his sobbing. He left his hiding place and climbed atop a mailbox on the edge of the square. There was no danger of being seen—all the Serbs, including the Chetniks, were crowded around Emir. He quickly rammed his final cartridge into the chamber and aimed his carbine over the crowd at Emir, who continued to writhe in pain, to the delight of the Serbs who jeered him. This was Zarko's last bullet so he took careful aim, trying to steady his shaking hands.

Suddenly he heard someone near him to his left.

Zarko turned his head and saw a short, fat Chetnik with a few whiskers on his chin kneeling in the gutter, throwing up. Sasha looked up to see Zarko atop the mailbox, his carbine still pointed toward the mosque.

They looked at each other for a long moment, then Sasha looked where Zarko was aiming. He looked back at Zarko before disappearing into the shadows.

Zarko turned back to Emir, closed his right eye, and through the old, crooked sights of his carbine, aimed for Emir's heart. His eyes began to fill with tears, but not because he was about to try to kill his friend; rather, he knew in his heart that, despite bragging that he was a marksman with his uncle's rifle, he was a terrible shot.

*But the shepherd's heart is a very considerable target,* Zarko thought hopefully.

Zarko had to readjust his aim because his hands were shaking. Then, once again, he concentrated on lining up Emir in the uneven sights of his carbine as the Serbs in the square delighted in his friend's suffering.

Finally the rusty trigger creaked as the Gypsy squeezed it slowly, careful not to upset his aim. A single tear ran down Zarko's cheek.

The Gypsy's aim was true, but he had to wait until he could see the blood coming from Emir's chest before he would believe it. As he sat staring at his friend's body nailed to the door of the mosque, one of the Chetniks pointed him out to the others. The entire mob rushed forward to shoot at the Gypsy, but he slid off the back of the mailbox, which deflected most of the shots. Then he was around the corner and running for his life.

It seemed that every Chetnik in the square was chasing him. He took his last grenade, pulled the pin, and threw it back over his shoulder. In a few seconds he heard it explode. He looked back to see a cloud of smoke, but nobody in sight. Ahead, he saw a refrigerated meat truck. He tried to open the heavy steel door on the side of the truck, but it was locked. He rammed the butt of his carbine against the lock until it finally broke open, then climbed inside and held the heavy door closed.

In a minute he could hear the mob running by. In time they came back and began searching the buildings for him. *The murderous Turk with the gun,* the Serbs were calling him.

He waited there holding the door of the meat truck closed for hours, until he finally drifted off to sleep.

The door only slipped open a little.

## 16

**WEST SLEPT PEACEFULLY THROUGH THE** night. He woke only after the morning sun shone through a stained-glass window, drenching him in multicolored light. Still groggy with sleep, he walked through the empty church and climbed back to his perch in the bell tower to look down at the town below. It was hard to believe that this was the same town he had come to just the morning before.

Most of the fires had burned themselves out, leaving only the blackened remains of homes and businesses. There were many bloodstains on the pavement and walls, many bodies still lying where they had fallen. He could even make out the bloody spot at the partisan memorial where JuJu had died.

He looked over at the mosque, where a great deal of activity was taking place. A bloody, naked corpse was hanging nailed to the huge wooden door. Chetniks had just finished surrounding the old building with loads of dynamite and were now backing away. A Chetnik came forward with a bullhorn.

"Muslims inside the mosque, this is Captain Šešelj. I am the law!" the young, lean, short-haired, and clean-shaven Chetnik leader announced melodramatically. "This town is officially liberated!" He didn't say from what, but a huge cheer rose up from the Chetniks and the Serb townspeople gathered in the square. "I must warn you that I have been ordered to remove your mosque. But first I will give you an opportunity to come out and give yourselves up. When you come out, you will have several options. If you wish to leave this town, I will provide transportation. If, however, for some reason you wish to stay, I will permit you to stay. But only under certain conditions:

"All Muslims will be forbidden to move about after dark, and no Muslims will be permitted to gather in public places in groups of more than two men. No Muslim will be permitted to fish in the river. No Muslim will be permitted to sell real estate except through official channels. No Muslim will be permitted to contact anyone outside the town. Finally, no Muslim may show contempt for the struggle of the Serb nation. Oh, and no Serb will be permitted to visit a non-Serb without permission.

"The mosque will be dynamited in five minutes. All Muslims must be out by then or you will be blown up. It is not my wish to hurt any Muslim civilians."

With that the Chetnik captain returned to the library, which now had a huge hand-painted sign hanging from it which read: "Bureau for Population Resettlement and Exchange of Material Goods."

The Muslims filed out of the mosque. They joined the line at the library steps if they wished transportation out of the town, or the line outside the post office if they wished to stay. In a few minutes, all but twelve people had lined up at the library.

A Chetnik and a local Serb walked up and down the line in front of the library. The local Serb pointed out certain people, whom the Chetnik would then pull out of line and order to wait at the post office. As they passed, those in line noticed that those chosen were many of the town leaders, the educated, the most successful businessmen, and the best athletes. Surely they were to be given special treatment. Ado was among those chosen, because the Serb mistook him for a teacher from the school.

"Can I take my grandson?" Ado asked the Chetnik who was pushing him toward the post office. Many of the others singled out had begged for their wives or children to remain with them and had been granted permission.

"What do I care?" the Chetnik replied, looking down at the little boy, who had finally put down his puppy.

The chosen ones were led to the post office. There were now forty men, women, and a few children standing there.

West had noticed Ado and watched him, but now he turned his attention to the Bureau for Population Resettlement and Exchange of Material Goods. He knew that he needed to get out of this town and complete his mission. He could try to wait out a couple more nights in the church until the army would no doubt leave the hills and move on to the next town, but if it was reasonably possible to get out now, it would be the much more sensible thing to do. He paid close attention to the library after noticing several buses parked next to a side door.

He couldn't see the soldiers behind the buses sewing Red Cross patches on civilian clothes. These soldiers then took their positions at the doors to the buses and waited.

The sound of a massive explosion woke Zarko. He had fallen asleep in the refrigerated meat truck a couple of hours earlier. He was about to look outside, but he could hear men coming down the sidewalk.

"That must have been the mosque," one of the Chetniks said.

"Of course it was. What else could it be?" the other Chetnik replied.

"Hey, how about this one?"

Zarko heard them open the driver's-side door of the truck. He scurried to the back and lay down flat in a corner. In a minute, the truck engine started.

"What about this door? It's broken." The side door of the refrigerated compartment opened. Zarko could see the shadow of one of them looking in.

"Get some rope, we can tie it shut. This truck is perfect."

"Where will I get rope?"

"Don't be stupid. Find a dead Muslim and take his shoelaces."

"I am driving the truck. You find the shoelaces."

The other Chetnik slapped him. A brief fight ensued. "You're weaker than a Turk!" the one who slapped the other said.

"Leave me alone."

"Get the shoelaces!"

"Ah! Stop biting me!"

They separated and the weaker man went off. In a minute he

came back and tied the lock shut. The truck began to roll down the street.

They only drove a short distance before the truck stopped and the door was untied and opened. Zarko's heart beat fast with fear as he crouched in a corner. He still had his carbine, but he had no shells.

In a minute he heard a thump which shook the truck, followed by another. He looked up to see two bodies lying near the opening to the back of the truck. Then another and another, and then a child's body.

"This is the part I hate the most," the stronger Chetnik said.

The truck moved about a block before more bodies were tossed in. Soon the Chetniks argued about moving the bodies to the back of the truck, since they were crowding the door. Zarko, realizing one of them would have to jump into the back of the truck to move the bodies, rolled up against the stacked corpses and played dead. One of the Chetniks jumped in, grabbed Zarko by an arm and leg and dragged him to the back, then began piling bodies on top of him and all around him.

Zarko had no choice but to lie in the back of the truck at the bottom of the pile. He pulled his shirt around his mouth and nose. He closed his eyes and rolled his head toward the wall.

After spending the night in the library basement waiting in vain for Zarko to return, Jackson had climbed a back stairway in the library and was watching from the second-floor landing as the Muslims began filing in. Each Muslim would be directed to the long librarian's desk, where they would be asked if there was any property in the town held in their name. If there was, they would have a form thrust in front of them stating that, without coercion or duress, of their own free will, they were signing over their property to the local authorities, "for good and valuable consideration." They were ordered to sign. If they did not sign, they could not leave on a bus, and neither could any member of their family. The person behind them on line would witness the document. Anyone not willing to sign the document was told they would be led to the river. They did not know what that meant, but from the way it was said there could be no mistaking that it was not somewhere they should want to go.

Then they were directed to the next line, where they joined those who owned no real estate. They were to list all motor vehicles, valuables, businesses, and sign them away, also to the local authorities, "for good and valuable consideration." The person behind them in line would witness the document. If they did not wish to sign, they would be led to the river.

Next they would line up to sign a form that stated they wished to be sent to Croatia—again, of their own free will. If they did not wish to sign, they were led to the river.

Finally they were directed to a line where they were asked if they had any overdue library books. If they did, they would be forced to pay for them on the spot. If they could not pay, they were led to the river.

Those who signed all the necessary papers were led out a side door, where they were told to stand in line alongside the buses. Before they could get on a bus, Chetniks searched each person. Few weapons were ever found, but any money or valuables were taken as "bus fare" out of town.

Jackson was about to return to the basement when he noticed the population map from the night before. The interior of Bosnia had been painted completely red. Across the top of the map, someone had painted the words THIS IS SERBIA.

Jackson climbed down the back staircase to the basement. From a telephone booth there, he could hear a Serb officer shouting into the phone. He didn't know that it was Captain Šešelj.

"I don't care what Belgrade says! Tell the president we need more buses!"

Jackson made his way to the broken window he had used the night before and stuck his head out. Red Cross workers were directing the Muslims to form orderly lines alongside the buses. He scrambled out of the basement, circled the first two buses, and squeezed into line. Ten minutes later, he heard a familiar voice.

"You're not thinking of deserting me, too, are you, Jackson?"

"Where have you—"

West lowered his voice. "The church. I was deciding whether or not to try to get on one of these buses when I saw you climb out of the library."

"Have you seen any of the others? Have you seen Zarko?"

"The boy is dead. I saw the old man over by the post office. I haven't seen anyone else."

As difficult as it was for Jackson to think about it, he knew that Emir must be dead by now. But he hadn't known about JuJu. "After we realized the town was surrounded, we never should have brought the boy here."

"You're guiding *me;* it was your decision," West said, but when he saw that Jackson already felt responsible, he changed his tone. "If you saw him fight, you wouldn't still be calling him a boy."

In a minute Jackson asked, "Do you think we could signal to the old man?"

"When I left the church and came around the back of the library, I noticed he and some others were walking away, toward the river."

"I suppose he knows what he's doing," Jackson muttered absently. "I guess it's every man for himself now."

"Not between you and me," West insisted. "You're still guiding me north."

**17**

**ADO HELD THE BOY'S HAND** as he and the others were finally led away from the post office by a group of Chetniks. They walked down a blood-stained street swept clean of bodies, past burned-out businesses. They were herded behind the stores and through a back parking lot onto a trail that began behind a large trash container.

The Muslims began looking around in surprise. Instead of being allowed to return to their homes, they were being led through the woods toward the river. Once they reached the river they walked along its banks toward the lumber mill, where they could see the small bridge into town.

They were ordered to stop just before walking onto the bridge. There were many more Chetniks waiting there. The Chetniks formed a half circle around the forty Muslims and waited for further instruction. A rock as big as a church pew had been placed in the middle of the bridge. Several Chetniks waited next to the rock.

The first man on line was a short, squat Muslim who stood with his wife behind him. He was a local bureaucrat whose primary duty was collecting taxes. He was called forward and told to walk to the center of the bridge. He began to pray, but was pushed along by a Chetnik and then strode forward on his own with short, suspicious steps. The Chetniks watched in silence. Finally, the Muslim man reached the rock, where several Chetniks were waiting.

From his place in line near the entrance to the bridge, Ado saw the tax collector directed by a Chetnik to stand in front of the rock.

Looking terrified, the man did so. He was then told to crouch. As he did, the Chetniks threw him backward over the rock and held him down. A Chetnik with a long black beard came forward and held a butcher knife over his head.

As he leaned over the tax collector, his Serb brothers cheered him on.

"Oh Lord!" the man next to Ado cried when it was over. "The river is taking his body!"

The group of Muslims, no longer holding any illusions about why they had been brought to the river, began screaming and wailing. Several men and women tried to run off into the woods, but each was mowed down by the Chetniks with machine guns, making it no further than ten or fifteen feet. Others dashed for the river, but they were shot and their bodies toppled down the steep banks, piling atop each other at the bottom of the riverbank.

Ado grabbed the boy and held him closely when the boy instinctively tried to run. The Chetnik nearest him had his gun on the boy, and if Ado had not held him, the boy would have been shot. Ado's first thought was to plead for the boy's life, but if they had let him come this far, they meant to kill him, too. Instead, he held the boy and soothed the Chetnik.

"All right. We will not run. It is all right."

Now the Chetniks called for another. The wife of the tax collector had been shot and killed when she tried to run to him. Next was a handsome young man with long sideburns. He had been a university student before the war. He tried to put on a brave face, walking as straight and tall as he could, stepping over the body of the tax collector's wife, looking the Chetniks in the eye.

All of the Muslims waiting their turn desperately wanted to run, but they knew they would only be shot. They could do nothing but watch the university student walk bravely to the center of the bridge, when suddenly he turned around and called back to them.

"Allah is good! Allah is great! I am a Bosnian!"

Those who were waiting their turns to die were greatly surprised, because none of them could ever remember seeing him at the mosque. He was better known for his drinking. He drove a motorcycle, and usually he could be found on a street corner wearing a black leather jacket, smoking American cigarettes.

As the university student continued to shout, the Chetniks wrestled him down like a pig. Then they called forward one of the many Serb townspeople who had been brought to the bridge to watch. They chose Petar, the Serb who had been summoned to the bridge the day before as Jackson and Zarko hid in his basement. The Chetniks placed a butcher knife in Petar's hand. As Petar stood over him, the university student was still screaming out, "Allah is great! I am a Bosnian!"

"Come on, Petar!" the university student shouted. He knew Petar well. He had gone to school with Petar's youngest sister. "Come on and finish your brother's work!"

Petar came close and knelt next to the university student, whom he knew was named Tomo, his sister's good friend. Petar began to sob and mumble an apology, but Tomo spat in his face. Petar didn't turn away. Trembling, he put the butcher knife to Tomo's throat as Tomo screamed at him and spat in his face again.

"Do it while you can!" Tomo shouted at him loud enough so that the Muslims waiting their turn could hear. "Your time will come, Petar! Allah will protect my people! Your time will come!"

Petar looked up again at the Chetnik standing over him. "Please, sir," he pleaded, offering the butcher knife to the Chetnik.

"Hurry!" the Chetnik demanded, folding his arms, refusing to accept the knife. "There are many Turks to kill."

Petar was weeping now as he once again placed the long blade on Tomo's throat. Tomo was shouting, "Allah is great!" as Petar closed his eyes tightly and ripped the blade over Tomo's throat, silencing him.

A cheer went up from the Chetniks. Two of them came forward to toss Tomo's body into the Sana River. One of the Chetniks shouted above the cheers, "Go to Allah, Turk!"

Petar was soon forgotten by the Chetniks, who chose another Serb from the town to kill the next Muslim in line. Petar staggered back to the group of Serb townspeople who waited to be called forward.

The next Muslim, a policeman, went in tears. He had to be carried the last ten feet because his knees had buckled and he could not get up. Then came a doctor, followed by the town judge. One by one the Serb townspeople were called to take part in the killing.

In the beginning they had to be forced to participate, but soon several of the Serb townspeople volunteered, and then they were fighting over who would go next. Some took more than one turn. Several Muslims ran from the line to avoid the knife. Their bodies began to pile up at the bottom of the riverbank.

"There will be many bodies in the Sana if we continue to throw them down there," one of the Chetniks near Ado said to another.

"Yes," agreed the other. "But fish must eat, too."

Ado decided he would not walk helplessly to his death on the bridge. Better to be shot in the back, unarmed and betrayed, than to allow his death to be made a spectacle. He was Ado Begovic, partisan, fighter of Nazis and the fascist Ustasha and the savage Chetniks, father, husband, and carpenter. He would not die like a pig.

"Boy, listen to me," Ado whispered in the boy's ear. The boy was clutching Ado's leg, unable to understand how these men with the long beards, some of whom had helped his father harvest the fields the previous autumn, could slit their neighbors' throats. He couldn't take his eyes off the bridge as Ado whispered his directions. "Do you understand, son? Don't move a muscle."

The boy nodded his head up and down almost imperceptibly. Ado waited until the Chetniks were absorbed in watching the first woman go to the rock in the middle of the bridge, then he clutched the boy and ran for the riverbank. Just as he reached it he heard the shots. As he threw the boy forward and saw him tumble down the bank, Ado felt the bullets rip into his back, then felt himself tumbling after the boy. When he finally stopped he was lying right next to him.

"Stay down," Ado groaned through his pain without moving his lips. "Don't move. Are you shot?"

"No," the boy whispered in a trembling voice.

"Don't move." The boy was crying softly. Ado could feel his blood rushing out of the wounds in his back. It was a struggle for him not to writhe in pain. The tears building up in his eyes began to blur his vision. "You must play dead. Have you ever played that you were dead before?"

"Yes."

"You must do that now, for as long as it takes. You must do it even if they come down here and start shooting some more. You must do it even if they throw you in the river. You must float on the top of the water on your back so you can breath. You must not let them know that you are alive. Can you swim?"

"Yes."

"Let the river take you until you are out of sight of any of those men with the beards, and also the soldiers of the army. You must not let them see you are alive. Do you know the way to another town?"

"No."

"Walk downriver at nighttime, when you cannot be seen. Eventually you will come to a town. When you get there, find the mosque. If there is no longer a mosque there, you must walk to the next town. Do you understand?"

"Yes."

Suddenly another body rolled down upon them. The man who had just been shot tried to get up. A Chetnik atop the riverbank saw him and fired, killing him.

The boy had instinctively moved to cover up at the sound of the bullets. One of the Chetniks on the bridge shouted to those on top of the bank, "I saw someone move down there!"

The Chetnik at the top of the riverbank waved in understanding and began to fire into the bodies piling up by the river.

With all the strength that remained in him, Ado stood and stumbled forward, away from the boy. This attracted the gunfire. He was weak and about to fall, so he dove away from the boy. He was hit again in the back and also in the legs and his hand. He tried to get up again, but he could not. Ado stretched out his bloody hand, reaching for the river.

"Make sure you kill them next time!" one of the Chetniks from the bridge shouted at his colleagues standing at the top of the riverbank.

Ado opened his eyes. The tears had filled his eyes and were running down his cheeks, so he couldn't see his bloody hand dangling in the river, but he could feel the cold water rushing through his fingers. In a moment he could no longer feel the coldness of the water. Then the pain from his wounds subsided and he lay there not feeling anything as tears continued to run down his face, and as his blood mixed with the blood of those who had died with him on the banks of the Sana River.

## 18

**THE BACK OF THE TRUCK** was filled with corpses now, and Zarko was on the bottom in the back. The truck had not stopped for close to ten minutes, so he was fairly certain the Chetniks were no longer looking for bodies. They were going someplace to get rid of them.

Zarko opened his eyes and forced himself to turn. He was inches from a dead man's wide-opened eyes, which were magnified in their horror by the glasses stretched crookedly over the gray face. Zarko let out a gasp, then began pushing bodies away frantically, keeping his eyes closed and swimming his way through the sea of corpses to the top.

He crawled across them to the door. The door banged, as the shoelace used to tie it had some slack. He looked out of the crack and could see trees and bushes and the potholed road going by. He tried pushing the door, but it was tied securely. He pushed more forcefully and then even kicked at it, risking being heard by the driver, but the door wouldn't budge. He remembered his switchblade and reached for it, but it was gone. Panicking, he began pushing at the door repeatedly. He grunted and threw his shoulder into the door and kicked some more, but the door would not open.

Then he remembered the first corpse, the one that had been lying right next to him. He pulled himself together, took a deep breath, and grimaced as he crawled back across the bodies. He pulled bodies up and out of his way until he reached the corpse with the glasses. The glasses were covered with blood because the man who had worn them had been shot directly between the eyes. Zarko pocketed the glasses and also pulled out his carbine, then returned to the door.

Pulling out the glasses, he snapped out one of the lenses from the frame. The edge of the lens was not very sharp, so he put it in the crack of the doorway and pulled the door closed as hard as he could, breaking it in half.

Zarko squeezed his hand through the door and began sawing at the shoelace with the broken lens. He could not know that the driver's-side mirror reflected perfectly on the door and the lock where the shoelace was tied. He was close to the whole way through when suddenly he heard the driver shout.

The truck immediately skidded to a halt. Zarko kicked the door, which crashed open now. He jumped out with his carbine, tumbled once, and came up kneeling, aiming his rifle at the driver, who looked familiar to him, standing with one foot out of the door of the truck.

"Don't move!" Zarko shouted almost hysterically, noticing a pistol in the driver's holster. "Drop the gun on the ground, you motherless turd!" The driver dropped his pistol and put his hands in the air. "Where's the other one! Where's the other motherless son-of-a-whore!"

"He's right here!" Sasha Maravic said in a terrified voice, motioning with his head.

Zarko was worried that his knees might buckle, but he managed to take a few careful steps and look into the cab. The other Chetnik was standing outside the truck on the other side. Zarko couldn't see his hands, but he was sure the Chetnik must have a gun.

"Put your God-cursed hands up! Put them up or I'll blow his motherless head off! Put them up! Put them up!" Zarko shoved the barrel of his rifle into Sasha's mouth. "I'll blow his head off! I'll do it! Put up your motherless hands!"

"Fuck you!" the other Chetnik shouted back. He was clearly as scared as Zarko.

"I'll do it! By God I'll do it!"

"Fuck you!" the Chetnik with the gun shouted again.

Zarko bent to the ground and grabbed Sasha's pistol. As soon

as Zarko moved, the Chetnik on the other side of the truck ran
away. Zarko dropped his rifle and hit the ground, rolling away from
Sasha. Looking under the truck now, Zarko could see the Chetnik
with the gun running into the woods. He fired off three shots, then
the pistol clicked impotently.

He turned to see Sasha aiming the carbine at his head.

"Go ahead!" Zarko shouted. "Shoot me, motherless Chetnik!
Come on! Go ahead! Try to shoot me! Shoot me!"

Zarko knew that there was no ammunition left in the rifle.
Smiling, he crawled over to Sasha and knelt in front of him and
put the barrel of the rifle to his forehead.

Sasha looked at the crazed man before him, the long, brown
hair, the pale skin, and the cracked tooth that was visible whenever
the man shouted at him. He was terrified of this man, and he knew
that he could kill him easily with the rifle, the man's head resting
there right against the barrel.

But when he looked into the man's eyes, he knew he wasn't
looking at a pig. He didn't want to kill any more men.

Sasha dropped the carbine. Once Zarko got over his surprise,
he hastened to his feet.

The two men stared at each other, both sweating in the cool,
early morning air. They began circling each other slowly, warily.

"We could fight until one of us is dead," Sasha said finally.

Zarko grunted. He was breathing heavily and his heart was
pounding.

"Or you could let me get into the truck and drive away, and I
could let you run off into the trees and escape."

"Now that we're on equal footing, you're not so eager to fight,"
Zarko taunted the young Serb, the adrenaline rushing through the
Gypsy's body.

"I would rather we both go on our way. I don't want to fight
anymore. I wish only to go home."

Zarko grinned at young Sasha, showing the cracked tooth a
Chetnik had given him only weeks before when Zarko was defenseless at a roadblock.

*I finally have a fair fight with a Chetnik bastard,* the Gypsy
thought. *He's much younger than I am, but I could kill him. I know
I could kill him. He's short and fat, probably slower than a mule. I*

*would batter his face with my fists until he fell to the ground. Then I would kick him in the head with my boots until he was unconscious. Then I would kneel behind him, take his head in my arms and snap his neck. I could do it. Yes, now that I have a fair fight, I could easily kill him.*

"All right," Zarko said, letting down his guard. "Go."


Night had just begun to fall over the town on the Sana River. The Chetniks had a great celebration that night, joined by the Yugoslav army units as they came down from the hills after the Chetniks had finished their work.

In the foothills, the Muslims who had fled were hiding in caves. Still more Muslims were in basements of their Serb neighbors who were ashamed at what other Serbs had done to their town. They were beginning to second-guess their good intentions, however, when they saw what happened to other families who were caught trying to hide Muslims.

Down by the Sana River, the little boy finally raised his head from the center of a stream of corpses. He sat up and looked for the old man but could not see him right away. He stood and walked about until he found the old man, lying with his liver-spotted hand resting in the rushing water.

The boy looked at the old man for a long time. He neither spoke a word nor made a sound. He did not want to touch the old man or get too close to him—with the puppy it was all right to hold him and pet him when he was sleeping, but now that the old man was sleeping that strange sleep, well, he figured that was something he should not get involved with.

Then the boy remembered what the old man had said. He was supposed to walk down the riverside until he found a town with a mosque. He did not know why, but he knew that if he found a town and it did not have a mosque, it was a bad town. He should run back to the river and try another town, and keep trying until he found a town with a mosque.

## 19

**THE BUS HAD BEEN ROLLING** along for over five hours. The countryside went by in all of its beauty—lush forests, green valleys, and golden wheat fields. The men, if they talked at all, talked in whispers.

Chetniks had confiscated the knife and pistol West had tried to conceal in his boots in the town before they boarded the bus. Jackson had surrendered Zarko's switchblade and the Chetniks had taken his wallet, but not before he removed the pictures of Maria. He received a slap from a Chetnik for keeping him waiting while removing the pictures.

Jackson looked at the picture of Maria taken at Heavenly Valley, her long black hair tied back, ski goggles on her head, red ski parka and tight black ski pants, a view of Lake Tahoe in the background. Then he looked at the one with the Golden Gate Bridge in the background. She was wearing bicycle shorts and a tank top. He was behind her, hugging her and smiling.

They had grown up together and had dated since high school. They went to the same college, and when the army stationed him in Georgia after graduation, Maria came with him. They lived together in a house in the country with a small duck pond in the back. Those were happy times that both wished could go on forever, but then he was sent to the Persian Gulf. By the time he came back and was stationed in Texas, she was in medical school in California. They saw each other whenever they could, and rather than growing apart for the next two years, they were engaged just before he left for his peacekeeping tour in Croatia. They had planned to marry as soon as he returned to California.

Looking at her picture now, Jackson was afraid he might never see her again.

At first he thought that she just needed time to understand why he tried to supply guns to Muslims. He called her when he went to Venice to meet with Katz, and she told him she still wore his engagement ring, but he knew that he was losing her because she never gave him the chance to explain. He didn't blame her. Maria was the most honest person he had ever known—how could he expect her to blindly believe in him after he was arrested and faced a certain court-martial for dealing with Muslim black marketers, which is what the army had considered Aleksandar and his men? How could he expect her to understand what he was doing there— nobody in America seemed to understand what was happening in Bosnia. That was why he had spent an entire week writing and rewriting a letter that he was sure would change her mind. He told her everything he knew about the history of the people of the Balkans, who the Muslims were and why they were now defenseless, so she would understand why he had helped them, and why he felt so strongly that he had to continue to help them.

Jackson knew that his letter would convince her not to give up on him. He was convinced that Maria would finally understand what he was fighting for and she would come to him. He wasn't profiting as a black marketer, or helping Muslim fanatics slaughter Christians. He was simply trying to do the right thing, to do what Maria herself would have done if she had been in his position. He knew Maria would come to help and to be with him. There was no doubt in his mind that Brigandi must have been carrying a letter from her telling him so.

*Once I make it back to the coast, somehow I'll get through to you, Maria,* he thought. *I'll make a special trip to Italy to telephone you so we can make arrangements for you to meet me there. You can fly into Venice and we'll get married and spend a week there before coming back here to . . . to. . . .*

That was where his fantasy always ended because, despite what he told others and what he tried to tell himself, he was afraid that he might never see Maria again.

*Do you honestly think that she's going to leave America to come here just to be with you?* he asked himself. *You sure expect an awful lot from her.*

"Your girlfriend?" West asked Jackson, looking over his shoulder. "Pretty. What is she, Italian? Greek?"

"Leave me alone." Jackson carefully put Maria's picture back in the chest pocket of his flannel shirt.

"You from San Francisco?" West asked. "I spent some time in California. I hated it though. All those niggers and Mexicans."

"You're a real asshole, you know that," Jackson told him. "After everything you've seen here, you haven't learned a thing, have you? Don't you see what's tearing this country apart? It's like a fucking race war. It's genocide."

West rolled his eyes. "I forgot you're an idealist. Let's drop it. Just get me where I have to go, then you can go fuck a nigger for all I care."

"Fuck you. Find your own way."

West wasn't very surprised. He knew plenty of men like Jackson. They would back any cause and could even sound sincere, as if they truly cared. But they were such hypocrites. When things got tough, when it was time to fight, to pay with blood and the lives of young men, they were gone. America was filled with men like Jackson. *I am a man of honor,* Samuel West thought. He placed himself well above Jackson and his phony ideals.

West smiled. "You're gonna desert the Muslims the same way you deserted the UN peacekeepers. Where will you go? To America? You'll be arrested. You'll spend your life in prison."

When Jackson made no reply, West laughed at him. "You're crazy. The answer has been right under your nose. *Katz.* He's powerful, and very connected. If you help me complete my job, he'll do whatever you ask."

"He doesn't have any pull in the States."

The bus began to slow, then came to a halt at a roadblock before Yugoslav army soldiers waved it through.

"Look, even if Katz couldn't help you out of your trouble, he's ready to break the bank," West tried. "He'd set you up real good somewhere in Europe—you could live like a king. It's that important to him."

"I don't care."

West refused to put the issue to rest. He had to find a way to convince Jackson to help him. "By helping me you can really help the Bosnian cause. It could be the Bosnians' only chance, if the Jew is right."

Jackson had concluded, along with Zarko, that West was an assassin. He couldn't think of a single person in northern Bosnia who was so important that their assassination could change a thing.

"Go home, West."

"All you have to do is take me to a town—Brčko, Omarska, Banja Luka, Prijedor—whichever is closest."

"The north is Serb-held territory now," Jackson told him. "You won't be up against just the Yugoslav army and the Chetniks. Every Serb who can carry an ax will be our sworn enemy."

Jackson shook his head and looked out the window, where many of the men were staring with a sudden interest. He could see what looked like an old factory, with several large buildings and a muddy field like a courtyard surrounded by numerous sheds. The bus was pulling up to the industrial complex. A ten-foot-high barbed-wire fence surrounded the compound.

West suddenly broke the silence in a voice that for the first time had a trace of fear in it. "Well, Jackson, it looks like I won't be needing you after all."

The bus stopped at the main gate until the Chetniks waved it through. Above the gate was a sign in big black letters that read OMARSKA DETENTION CENTER.

"God help us if the Jew was right," West said.

# 20

---

AS THE BUS PULLED THROUGH the gate at Omarska Detention Center, Jackson and West noticed scores of old women pressed up against the guard shack. The women were calling out names of men, and many were crying. The guards either ignored the old women or laughed at them.

When the bus stopped in the center of the compound, the men inside were told to get out. They formed a motley group as they waited in the mud. They were told to take off their boots. Jackson was reluctant, but did so, knowing from his experience in the town that the Serbs would not tolerate disobedience. West, however, did not move.

West was not noticed right away because the guards were arguing over where to take the men. It was clear that none of the guards knew where they should go. They insulted and threatened each other as they argued. Finally, as their disagreement became very heated, a man stormed out of a two-story brown wooden building.

He was short but very solidly built, like a boar, with oily gray hair, pasty white skin, and a long, sharp nose. He rarely moved his head; rather, his eyes would shift back and forth ceaselessly. Yet for all their movement, his eyes lacked any trace of empathy or compassion.

His name was Ratko Stonisic, the commander of the guard at Omarska. He was both feared and adored by his guards. They all fell silent when they saw him approaching with short, high-kneed steps, staring straight at them with his cold, shifting eyes.

"What is the problem here?" he demanded curtly.

The guards who had been arguing were not exactly at attention, but they were quiet now and seemed to cower in the presence of this man. "A bus just came in. We were not told where the prisoners should go," one of the guards said.

"For this you disturb my sleep?" It was late afternoon.

"Well, I thought they should go in the pit, but Vladimir thinks the cages would be better for this group because they have had it easy. I told him the cages are full, but he says—"

"I don't want to hear any more. Who cares where they go? Just get them somewhere and don't disturb me further. Why must I command such fools?" The commander of the guard began to walk away, but his roving eyes fell on West. "Why does this man still wear boots?" he demanded.

West could see that they were talking about him. He was about to tell them that he was an American, that he did not belong there, but the two guards rushed forward and tackled him to the ground, kicking him hard with their steel-toed boots.

"Not in the face," the commander of the guard said. "The chief investigator will want to interview this big one."

They kicked West in the back, the stomach, chest, arms, and legs. Occasionally he was kicked in the face by mistake. Blood flowed from a cut opened over his eye and from his nose. When the guards stopped kicking him, they untied his boots and pulled them off.

Jackson's first instinct was to rush to West's defense, but the reality of his situation suddenly hit him hard. This was no mistake— he was a prisoner of the Bosnian Serbs. He had seen what they did to defenseless towns, to the elderly and children and young women. He was well aware that one mistake in judgment could cost him his life—or worse.

When West's beating was over, Jackson expected the important Serb to make a speech. He expected to be told that insolence will not be tolerated, that they were prisoners of war and if they wanted to live quietly and stay out of trouble they could sit out the rest of the war as comfortably as reasonably possible. But there was no such speech. The important man marched back to the wooden house and slammed the door.

As the guards talked among each other, Jackson looked at the various sheds and the large warehouse abutting the courtyard. He noticed a door to a red shed open fifty meters away. There was a large dump truck next to the shed. Several girls, most of them teenagers, came out of the red shed. One, in particular, stood out.

She had blond hair pulled tightly back in a long ponytail. She was taller than the others were and thin, but not sickly thin like the other girls. She wore a spotless white nurse's uniform and was leading the others to a nearby white shed, where she held the door and waited for them to enter. Jackson didn't take his eyes off her. She paused to look back at the new men and noticed him staring at her. She met his gaze for a moment, then quickly ran her eyes over him before disappearing into the white shed.

The guards herded the prisoners toward a large, rusted-metal, hangarlike shed that they referred to as "the pavilion." Jackson had to help West walk. The shed door was unlocked and the guards pushed them inside. Looking around, Jackson couldn't believe his eyes.

Inside the huge, rusty metal shed were three large steel cages stacked on top of each other. Separating each of the cages was a metal grate. Jackson later learned that the cages were used in the process of mining ore in peacetime. Each cage was about seven hundred square feet, and all three cages were filled with Muslims and Croats.

They were dirty, emaciated men, most with shaved heads. The ones in the front were bruised and feverish, shivering and scratching their sores. Many were smiling when they saw that new men were being brought in. Their toothy smiles seemed out of proportion to their drawn, sickly faces. They hardly made a sound as the new men were herded into the shed.

After some debate between the guards, it was decided to squeeze all the new prisoners into the bottom cage, which required less effort than the two cages on top. Jackson, who was supporting West, was pushed into the cage along with the others. They fell upon some men sitting in the dirt, and the cage was locked behind them.

"Sorry," Jackson said to the men whom he and West had fallen on. Most of them only grumbled and pushed him away, toward the door. One man moved away a little from the door of the cage and made a bit of a space and told him to sit there. There was only enough room to kneel.

"Thank you," Jackson said.

"No, thank you," the man said in return. He was even taller than West, but must have weighed one hundred pounds less. His shirt was unbuttoned and was now several sizes too large for him, revealing ribs that showed clearly through his skin. The teeth he still had were black, and he stank, like the rest of them. He appeared to be covered with mud.

"Why thank me?" Jackson asked him.

The man seemed to have trouble speaking because his lip had been recently split open. "Because now I am further from the door. Every time a man is taken out of the cage, you will see everyone moves back as far as possible from the door. It is not a good place to be."

"Why not?"

"You will see."

"I'd like for you to tell me, old man."

"Don't call me 'old man.' I'm thirty-five."

Jackson couldn't believe it. "I'm sorry. It must be the mud on your face—"

"It is not mud. It's shit."

"What?"

"Where do you think the men above us go to the toilet?"

Jackson felt his stomach turn, but it had been so long since he last ate he had nothing left in his stomach to vomit. "My name is . . . Emir," Jackson said, not sure if it was wise to let it be known that he was an American.

"I'm Haris."

"How long have you been here, Haris?"

"I'm not sure. Four months, maybe. I have been here longer than any I know of. I had a good place at the back of the cage and was able to hide back there for a long time. But two days ago they came with their flashlights and picked me. They pulled me from the back and beat me, so now I am at the front of the cage again. I will not live much longer here in the front."

Jackson felt ill again. "Why is the front of the cage so bad?"

"Because every day they pick men to beat and torture in front of us. Usually they take the men at the front of the cage because it is easier for them to drag us out. Some men are beaten for days in a row because they cannot get far enough back. Some men are tortured and killed, especially late at night because they come then, too. At night they call us out by name. If your name is called you never come back. They might kill you in the daytime, but usually you're just beaten or tortured. If you're lucky enough to be returned to the cage, you must try to fight your way to the back. I have no energy left to fight. I will stay here in the front until I'm dead."

"When will they come to pick those to be beaten?" Jackson asked.

"Soon."

"How will they pick the men?"

"They point at you with a flashlight and you stand and they ask your occupation. Then, depending on your occupation, they either order you out or they pass over you and ask another man."

The solution seemed simple to Jackson. "It's easy to lie about your occupation," he told Haris. "What occupations do they want to punish, and which do they let go?"

Haris shrugged his bony shoulders. "That is a mystery, Emir. I've tried to solve it since I have been here, but the answer escapes me. Perhaps it's because I'm hungry and can't think straight. Some men say they are farmers, and they are chosen. Some men say they are lawyers, and they are chosen. Others say they are businessmen and are not chosen, but I am a computer-parts salesman, and I was chosen. A man who was unemployed was chosen, but a man who was fired from his job was not chosen. I have long wondered at their method, but there is madness in it and I can't figure it out. All I know is, the next time I'm chosen I'll run so that hopefully they'll just shoot me and I'll die quickly. I cannot take any more."

Jackson considered the man's words carefully, wondering what occupation he would give when his turn came.

"Do they feed you?" Jackson asked after some time had passed. Oddly, no one else in the cage had spoken since he arrived.

"A loaf of bread a day for everyone in the cage to share. Every three days we are given hot water with a few beans. You are new, so they will not give you beans and water for a week. Some men went on a hunger strike once in protest. The guards only laughed at them. One day, an old woman came with food for a prisoner here. The young man was brought out. The woman was his grandmother. The guards beat the young man in front of her, then took the food and ate it themselves in front of both of them."

Jackson could see his life depended on learning as much about the camp as soon as he could, and Haris seemed to know a great deal.

"When we were outside, I saw women walk from one shed to another. Are they prisoners, too?" he asked.

"Yes. They are Muslim and Croat girls stolen from their towns."

"Why are they here? They can't be soldiers."

Haris laughed without smiling. "None of us are soldiers, Emir."

"Then how can they hold us prisoner?"

"Because this is Serbia."

"No. Omarska is in Bosnia."

"You have not seen a Serb map lately."

Jackson nodded, understanding. "There was one girl in particular, dressed all in white. She was going into the white shed on the other side of the camp."

"Ah, yes, I believe I know who you speak of. There are many pretty girls here, but she was the kind of girl that all men dream of?"

"Yes. That's her. Is she with the Red Cross? Her uniform makes me think so."

Haris shook his head, his eyes growing large with barely controlled anger. "That is Sabina. She's a traitor. She works as the camp nurse to save her skin. Did you not notice that she is pregnant?"

"No."

"She is the commandant's whore."

That wasn't what Jackson had hoped to hear. "She's a Muslim or Croat though?"

"She is Muslim, but she has willingly chosen to be his whore. The other women are kept here against their will to be raped. We often hear their screams in the night. They are raped for weeks until they become pregnant, then they're shoved out of the camp gates and sent away to have Serb babies."

"You're crazy," Jackson insisted, meaning it.

"Maybe. But I have been here long enough to figure that much out. When their stomachs begin to show, the guards throw them out. Only Sabina stays. She is the commandant's woman. She is always clean and well fed and wears white, and every night she goes to bed with the commandant. You see that window?"

"Yes," Jackson replied, noticing the window in the shed that was adjacent to their cage, allowing them to see out into a small portion of the camp.

"We are lucky to be in this bottom cage, because we get to look out that window. From that window we can see a little of the world. It is not a pretty view, but it is the only one in this shed. I have had two months to look out that window. I have learned very much of this camp by now."

West stirred and mumbled something that Jackson couldn't understand. Haris reached out to wipe some of the blood from West's face and dab it on his own face so it looked like he was bleeding. "Your friend is waking," Haris said.

"Yeah," Jackson said, preoccupied. "You said the woman is a nurse. Then there's a hospital?"

Haris shrugged. "I have heard that a hospital exists, but no man who has gone there has ever returned. I know there are no doctors. There was a veterinarian once who cared for the girls, but when he objected to their treatment he was locked in a car with a starving dog and eaten alive."

"What?" Jackson cried, thinking once again that Haris might be crazy.

"Oh, yes," Haris said almost casually. "I saw it from the window. We all heard the screams."

"That's insane!"

"It is certainly not logical. You would think there is nothing more important in a place such as this than doctors."

*That's certainly true,* Jackson thought.

"The commandant," he asked Haris suddenly. "Is he a short, stocky man with shifty eyes?"

"That is the Vulture, Ratko Stonisic, the commander of the guard."

"Why is the commander of the guard called the Vulture?"

"Because when he comes near there is almost certainly soon to be a death, or at least a beating. And he looks like a vulture, don't you think?"

"But why would he allow—"

Just then the shed door opened. Several guards walked in, stood quietly, and waited. The tension inside the cages was unmistakable. Jackson felt a man's urine drizzle down onto his shoulder from the cage above. He shifted away in disgust just as the stocky figure of the Vulture high-stepped through the door.


One of the guards hurried to unlock the bottom cage for the commander of the guard. When the commander of the guard looked at a prisoner, the guard pointed his flashlight at him.

"Get to your feet, Turk!" the guard demanded.

It was a young man who had been sitting near the front of the cage. Jackson remembered that the young man had been on the same bus as he and West, so he came from the town on the Sana River. The young man stood, shakily. Jackson wondered whether he had overheard Haris explaining things about the camp.

"What was your occupation?" the guard demanded.

At first the young man's mouth moved, but no words came out. Finally he managed to say, in a whisper, "I am a mechanic."

The guard looked at the commander of the guard, who nodded.

"Out!" the guard ordered the mechanic.

When he reached the gate, the mechanic was thrown to the ground. Then the guard directed his flashlight on another man the commander of the guard was looking at.

"What was your occupation?" the guard asked.

This man was also from the same bus and the same town that

Jackson and West had come from. He was short but muscular and stood bravely before the commander of the guard. He said proudly, "I am a chicken farmer!"

The commander of the guard nodded yes immediately, and this man, too, was dragged out and kicked and left to wait. A third man, this man not from the town on the Sana, was asked his occupation.

He was small and dirty and had been there for several weeks. It was clear that he had been beaten recently and his bruises had not yet healed. He picked himself up off the filthy floor with great difficulty, looking as though he had not eaten for weeks. "I was a football player," the man said weakly. The guards all laughed at him because now he hardly had the strength to lift a soccer ball.

The commander of the guard did not make any indication right away, then let his gaze fall on another man. The football player collapsed to his feet, nearly fainting from the relief of being passed over.

This drill was repeated several more times. Soon a grocery clerk, a business executive, and a painter were all dragged from the cage and made to wait. Then the commander of the guard began surveying Jackson's side of the cage.

"Don't look him in the eye," Haris whispered as he looked down at his lap.

Jackson looked the commander of the guard square in the eye, knowing he would be picked. He could see that they were looking for the strongest and healthiest prisoners. The question of occupations was just an excuse to have each man stand, so that the commander of the guard could determine his physical well-being.

Sure enough, the eyes of the Vulture settled on Jackson and the guard flashed the light on him. When Jackson didn't move, the guard stepped in, grabbed him by the ear, and pulled him to his feet. "What occupation were you?"

All eyes turned to Jackson, who didn't answer.

"What was your occupation!" the guard demanded again.

"I am a doctor," Jackson said quietly.

The commander of the guard examined Jackson curiously, then uttered his first words since entering the shed. "What kind of doctor?" he asked.

"A gynecologist," Jackson replied.

The commander of the guard considered him for almost a half a minute before making his decision.

"That one, Dusko," he finally said to the guard, looking at a man sitting next to Jackson.

Jackson was still shaking when he sat back down, not taking his eyes off the commander of the guard. The Vulture looked back at him for a long moment before looking away. His eyes settled on West for a few seconds, but West was freshly beaten and was spared this time.

The commander of the guard was then elevated by a forklift, and he repeated the process in the cages above Jackson's. The chosen men were forced to jump from the cage, and then were gathered in a group and told to stand in a line.

For the next half hour, the chosen ones were put through the basest tortures as the rest of the prisoners were forced to sing Serb patriotic songs.

The torture was nearly over when the chicken farmer refused to eat his own ear, which one of the guards had sliced off with a bowie knife. As a punishment for his refusal, Dusko suggested that they make the chicken farmer bite off the mechanic's testicles. Even most of the guards did not want Dusko to be given permission to force the chicken farmer to do it.

"Go ahead, Dusko," the commander of the guard said. "But take them outside. I don't want to see it."

Dusko, who was plain-looking, of average height and build, with an ordinary face and apparently average intelligence, smiled back at the commander of the guard. He dragged the mechanic, who had already been beaten unconscious, outside and then came back for the chicken farmer.

Jackson could see Dusko outside the shed, standing in front of the window. He was shouting, and every time he stopped shouting he clubbed the chicken farmer a few times with a stick the size of a small baseball bat. In a minute, Jackson saw Dusko cross his arms, finally satisfied, and smile.

As it was happening and the chicken farmer's cries were soon joined by the mechanic's screams, many of the prisoners held their hands over their ears. Even some of the guards looked uncomfortable and turned away.

But outside, Dusko looked on, feeling the anger inside him grow. Like many Serbs that served as guards at the camp, he firmly believed that no torture was bad enough for his Muslim and Croat enemies. When he heard the word *Croat,* he automatically associated it with the Ustasha and would remember all of the terrible crimes done to the Serbs during World War II at the hands of the Nazi collaborators. When he heard the word *Muslim,* immediately he thought of the mujahideen and could recite a dozen horrifying stories he had heard in Serbia when the war broke out.

When the war against Croatia began, it was not just a war against the generations of Croats born since World War II. It was the continuation of a war the Serb people had been fighting for centuries, against numerous enemies. The Serb motto, Only Gathering Can Save the Serbs, reflected an attitude that had been handed down for generations and was not easily forgotten. So when President Slobodan Milosevic of Serbia sought a share of the Krajina, he had thousands of men like Dusko who had been indoctrinated practically since birth into his nationalistic cause. All they needed was someone to bring it out of them again, to stir up the nationalism stewing in so many Serbs. It was all too easy to find men like Dusko.

As he stood there and watched the mechanic and the chicken farmer with one ear, Dusko felt no remorse. He was absolutely sure that, sometime in the annals of Balkan history, a Serb had been forced to do the same thing by a Muslim or a Croat. Dusko knew that he was acting honorably, avenging the fate of so many Serbs throughout the centuries, as if it were the chicken farmer or the mechanic themselves who had slaughtered Serbs so many years before.

## 21

**DARKNESS FELL OVER THE CAMP,** leaving the men inside the shed unable to see their hands in front of their faces. Jackson had spent the whole day and much of the night trying to work out the details of a plan he had already put in motion, but now he was tired of concentrating on his situation, tired of worrying that his plan might fail and that soon he would be beaten and starved and, eventually, too weak to even consider escape.

Wanting to talk, he began telling Haris how he got to the camp, though he told him he was originally from the town on the Sana River and did not tell him that he was an American. Then Haris, who Jackson learned was a Croat, told his story.

"My town was terrorized like the town you were in, Emir," Haris began with little emotion, having been drained of emotion in the past four months. "They killed many. They raped our wives and daughters. But they did not take us all away—some of us stayed. There were many rules for Muslims and Croats, but I decided it was better to stay in the town rather than lose my home and all that I had worked for my entire life. Things were very difficult for us. My wife, who had worked in an asylum just outside of town, told me that even the patients there thought the Serbs were crazy. It got so bad the Serb police chief was murdered by hard-liners of his own people.

"For three weeks we went on like this, until the Chetniks came back. They rounded up our daughters first and took them away.

They arrested the town leaders, the politicians, the teachers, the athletes. Anyone who could lead us. Those who fought back were either killed or taken away by the Chetniks. They used the minaret of the mosque as a sniper's nest and picked off Muslims for sport. I hid in the caves in the hills with many others that did not want to leave the town while our daughters were with the Chetniks. But there was nothing we could do to prevent it. We had no weapons to fight with."

Jackson was amazed how similar the events in Haris's town were to what occurred in the town on the Sana River. It was as if Serbs all over Bosnia had read the same instruction manual on how to create ethnically pure towns.

*Either that, he thought, or they all received their orders from the same authority.*

"Finally I came down to the town one early morning to find food," Haris went on. "A Serb neighbor of mine spotted me. I went up to him, for he was always a very good friend of mine. I asked him for news of the town, and news of my little girl, who was used as a whore for the Serbs in the gymnasium. I also asked him for some food. He told me to wait in his garage, he would get food and bring it to me. When he came back, he had a Chetnik with him, who beat me and brought me to the soccer field where they were keeping many men.

"I was put on a bus. First I was brought to a center near Brčko. It was bad there, too. It used to be an animal feed plant before the war. They have ovens there, and some days the smoke from the furnaces smelled strangely. Fortunately, I did not stay long enough to find out what they were doing with the ovens. I was transferred here and at first was kept in a huge open pit where they used to mine the iron ore. Others are housed in the earth-moving equipment hangar, and some are left to stand all day outdoors. But at least they have grass to eat."

"So there are more men here than just us?" Jackson asked.

"Thousands."

Jackson could only shake his head in fascinated disgust at the extent to which the Serbs were willing to go. He reminded himself for the millionth time how lucky he was to have been born in America.

*God, when I die, please let me be reincarnated as an American again, he thought. Oh, that's a good one. Your first prayer in months and you talk about reincarnation. That's blasphemy. It's a good thing there's no God.*

*Do you really believe that?* he asked himself.

He remembered how he had put God to the test in Medjugorje. It was only a few days ago, though it seemed like a lifetime since he had left Zarko at the bar and walked through the town square in the early morning, joining the other pilgrims walking to Apparition Hill, where the Mother of God had appeared to the six children.

*Allegedly appeared,* he corrected himself. *Oh, this isn't a goddamned trial; you can say she appeared. You're not saying you believe it happened. It was only out of curiosity that you walked up there with your whiskey, where the souvenir vendors were setting up, displaying their rosary beads and religious statuettes.*

It was a rocky path and he was drunk so he had to walk carefully. He was worried about turning his ankle, even in his army boots. The believers, however, walked atop the jagged rocks in bare feet. He hurried past them as they kneeled at the ten or twelve or however many sculpted bronze slabs there were on the way up, wanting only to get to the spot where she appeared.

There were a couple dozen pilgrims wearing name tags that identified the tour they were with. Many knelt on the rocks. It was completely silent, other than the sound of a cock crowing in the valley below. The pilgrims either looked extremely happy or very somber, but the one thing they all had in common was that they all looked like they were waiting for something. It bothered him because he couldn't figure out what they could be waiting for.

*But now you know, don't you?* he asked himself. *They were waiting for a miracle. They were waiting for her to appear. They prayed for a sign, something to give their life meaning, or proof that God existed. I just sat there and shook my head at them and drank from my bottle. I thought they were fools, fanatics.*

To Jackson—who had renounced religion after seeing with his own eyes the suffering of the refugees fleeing Bosnia, unable to understand how God, if God existed, could allow such things to happen—it was a strange scene, made even stranger when he con-

sidered that just ten miles north of Medjugorje, Catholic Croats and
Orthodox Serbs and Bosnian Muslims were slaughtering each other
in Mostar.

Then he began to think, as he often did despite himself, *It
would be nice to believe in God right now. But how can I believe in
God when so many people are killing each other in the name of
religion, disguised as ethnic hatred? Or is it ethnic hatred disguised
as religion?*

He had given God one last chance. He waited at the top of
Apparition Hill and gave God fifteen minutes to send him a sign,
but none appeared. He had no vision of Mary. Instead, he stood
atop the hill in the darkness, drinking his whiskey, with nothing to
look at but the glow from fires raging in Mostar, where Muslims
and Croats, once allies in the ancient city, were now fighting each
other.

*What did the people doing the fighting think they would gain
from it?* he wondered. *Instead of being governed by corrupt politicians from a multiethnic government, they fought so that they could
be governed by corrupt politicians of their own religion? Oh, what
does it matter? For some reason they started fighting and look at you
now, stuck in the middle of it.*

In the blackness of the shed, he turned to Haris, who was
scratching the lice from his eyebrows. "Why do you think they're
doing it?"

Haris misunderstood the question. He did not have the luxury
of thinking about the big picture. He only knew that he would soon
die in the camp. The camp was the extent of his world now.

"Terror," Haris said. "Death of their enemies. They say we are
soldiers and spies and that is why they keep us here, but they know
it is a lie. The chief investigator knows it, too, but still he insists on
questioning and torturing all of us until we sign confessions saying
we are Islamic soldiers rebelling against Yugoslavia. Eventually,
every man signs just so he will be left alone."

"Chief investigator?"

"All new men go to him. You will, too. He will question you
and insist you are a soldier. He will demand to know about troop
movements and how many weapons we have and where they are
stored and what missions we are to complete. I told him, 'I am not

a soldier, and I know of no Muslim troops. I also know nothing of guns or attacks or defenses.' But then he will douse you with gasoline and light a match, and you will make things up just to stay alive. Unless he is a fool—or just plain mad—he must know we are making it up. But then he lets us go, as if he has broken us into confessing the truth. If he thinks you are a spy you will be tortured and killed. Of course, there are no spies here, but he has killed many men he insists are spies. He must be a madman. No man here that lives will forget their interview with the chief investigator."

The door at the end of the shed suddenly opened. Jackson sat quietly in his space in the dung and urine. He could see a guard with a flashlight approaching the cages. The guard began calling out for the gynecologist to stand up and come forward.

"West," Jackson demanded as the guard continued to call out for the gynecologist. West had been slipping in and out of consciousness for the last two hours. "West, wake up."

"What . . . ?" West groaned.

"I'm getting out of here."

"You can't leave me."

"I'll try to get you out. But there's one thing you have to remember—"

"Where is the gynecologist! The commander of the guard demands that you come forward!"

"Don't tell them you're an American."

"You can't leave me here," West pleaded.

The guard had been shining the light in the prisoners' faces. He stopped when he recognized Jackson. The guard unlocked the cage and dragged him out.

"Don't tell them!" Jackson demanded in English, surprising the guard, who understood. "Don't tell the chief investigator!"

"Remember why I came," West said, also in English. "Remember Katz's mission."

The guard made a note of West's face, then led Jackson out of the shed, to the commandant's quarters.


Jackson was taken to the camp administration building, the brown wooden building that the commander of the guard had appeared

from earlier that day. He was pushed down a corridor into the
commandant's quarters and was brought directly to the office,
where the commandant was waiting for him.

The commandant was a short, husky man with gray hair
trimmed until it stood on its ends, like a porcupine's quills. He had
elephant ears, a long, hawked nose, and lifeless shark eyes that
seemed to look through you without seeing you, almost as if he
were blind. He was constantly smoking cigarettes, exhaling the
smoke out of his nose like a dragon.

"Good evening, Doctor," the commandant said loudly in a
deep, intimidating voice. "I am Slobodan Princip. And you are?"

Jackson lowered his eyes to the floor. "Emir Bosnic," he lied,
using Emir's full name.

"Dr. Bosnic, I am very pleased to meet you. I wish to speak
with you, but this office is so dreary." The commandant stood and
walked out from behind his desk. "Shall we get more comfortable?"

With a gesture of his hand, the commandant directed Jackson
to a small but comfortable living room, where there was a dining
table set for three, with candles and a bottle of bourbon.

"We are having chicken this evening. I thought you might wish
to join us. Are you hungry?"

Jackson could only stare at the commandant.

"Perhaps you would like a shower and clean clothes first?"

"Yes, Commandant. Please."

"When we are not in front of any prisoners you may call me
Slobodan. Please, follow that man. He will take you to a shower
and give you clean clothes."

Jackson followed the guard out of the building, where there
was a hose lying in the mud. He was given a bar of soap and was
hosed down. He was then handed a pair of Yugoslav army olive
green pants, and a black cotton shirt that a Chetnik might wear.
He was also given a pair of peasant's shoes that were too small.

When he was returned to the commandant's quarters, Slobodan
Princip was seated at the head of the table. To his left was the
beautiful young nurse Jackson had noticed when he was first
brought to the camp.

Now, up close, he could see that she was young but not a teen-
ager, and she was more than just pretty—she was seductive, like a

European model. She had green eyes and olive skin, with blond hair that glowed in the candlelight. Her nose was small and sharp, slightly upturned, and dotted with tiny brown freckles. Her skin was smooth, not bruised, and her eyes were not puffy, the way they might be if she were being beaten or disciplined. She sat up straight in her chair and hardly moved. But when she put her hands on the table he noticed her long fingers were not smooth and blemishless like her face. There were cuts, the skin looked dry and wrinkled, and her nails were short and uneven, not the long, painted nails he might have expected. She was looking at him very closely, at his eyes first, but then she seemed to be concentrating on his mouth.

"Dr. Emir Bosnic, this is Sabina Cehajic," the commandant introduced them. Jackson wanted to look at her longer, but he made himself lower his eyes and nod his head. He had been careful not to stare at her, for fear of offending the commandant, but he also sensed that the commandant had her there to show her off, so he was sure to at least look at her and nod respectfully to her. He did not see the woman nod back and smile at him. "Please sit, Doctor."

The food was brought in immediately by a young girl who did not look at the commandant, but stole a few glances at Jackson. There was chicken, vegetables from the camp garden, and a fruity wine from the Mostar region—it was all that the commandant could muster because of the war, he explained as though he owed Jackson an apology.

They ate in near silence. Occasionally the commandant tried to be charming, but he failed miserably. Jackson would only nod and continue eating. He ate everything they put on the table, drinking more wine than he should have. Throughout the meal, he could sense Sabina staring at him from across the table, but he didn't look at her.

Finally, when they finished eating, the pretty young girl brought out a bowl of fruit for dessert. Jackson helped himself to a peach as the girl spooned thick Turkish coffee into three tiny cups. The commandant offered Jackson one of the cups of Turkish coffee, making a point to call it Serbian coffee.

"Dr. Bosnic, you may be wondering why I have brought you here and have treated you so well," the commandant said, lighting another cigarette, which he smoked from a carved, Turkish cigarette holder. "I understand that you just arrived, but already you can probably see that this is a very unpleasant place to be a prisoner. I wish things did not have to be this way, but it is war, after all. I cannot say that I enjoy what goes on here, but it is wholly necessary for the Republic of Serbia to achieve our military objectives. The running of this transit center is my responsibility, and I take that responsibility very seriously.

"It's not as easy as it might appear to run this center." He never called it a camp, always a center. "The guards here are not paid. Most Serbs fighting in Serbia are not paid. Like the glorious Serb fighters of history, they fight for the spoils they can take. But what can my guards take from these Muslims and Croats that are brought here with nothing but the clothes on their backs? I have thousands of prisoners here, most of whom would like nothing more than to escape to Bosnia." He seemed to forget that Omarska was in Bosnia. "What makes the guards stay?

"I have been given a very unique type of man to help run this collection center. They stay mainly to fulfill their duty, which they inherit by birth into the great Serb nation. However, men cannot live on nationalistic spirit alone. They must be fed and cared for, given time to sleep and, most importantly, perhaps, they need recreation. These men that I have been given are a special breed. Torture is their recreation, Dr. Bosnic. I do not turn a blind eye to what is going on. I am not afraid to admit it. I know torture takes place in this camp. I myself do not take part in it, so I have a clear conscience. There is no blood on these hands," he said, smiling, holding up his hands in front of his face and turning them in the candlelight.

"My men also want women. That is not difficult to provide, since it is nothing to have women delivered here regularly by . . . by a higher authority. These women are given the privilege of carrying the Serb soldiers of tomorrow. They are impregnated here. It provides recreation for the men, and at the same time it advances other Serb interests. And it is quite natural for Muslim girls, who, everyone knows, breed like rabbits."

Again Jackson could sense Sabina's eyes on him, but he did not change the blank, scared expression on his face.

"The problem is, I have been directed not to let the girls leave until they are several months pregnant. And sometimes, as I think you can understand, in the situation my men find themselves in, they can get a little rough with the girls. It is a great power for these men to have control over pretty young Muslim girls, girls who in peacetime would not give them a second look. Sometimes the girls require medical assistance.

"That is why I brought you here. That is why I am offering to save you from pain and hunger and filth, and, sadly, perhaps even death. I want you to work in the camp hospital with Sabina. She does what she can to care for the girls, nursing them back to health when the men get carried away. She also checks them weekly for diseases and gives pregnancy tests. She has even tried to operate several times in emergencies. Also, the men can play rough with each other. Sometimes they require medical assistance. In short, I am offering you a job. You will be given three meals a day, a clean bed and clothes, and an occasional girl of your choice. It really is an offer you cannot refuse. Normally I would give someone time to think it over, but in this case—"

"No," Jackson said, interrupting the commandant.

"What did you say?"

"No."

The commandant leaned back in his chair. Behind his head, against the wall, hung a large pair of bull horns. From Jackson's point of view, the horns appeared to be coming out of the commandant's head.

"You will regret that decision," the commandant said simply.

"I am a doctor, Commandant—"

"I said to call me Slobodan."

"I've been trained to help the sick and give them care. I won't treat your men so they can torture more prisoners and rape more helpless girls. Unlike this nurse here," and now Jackson looked at Sabina briefly, "I will not put those little girls back together again only to be raped some more. I will not be your mad doctor. What's more, I must protest the treatment of these prisoners. There is no sanitation in this camp, no exercise. The prisoners are starving to death. I would be very interested to hear what the Red Cross would have to say about this camp."

Jackson could tell that the woman, Sabina, who had been silent and demure all evening, was shocked by his refusal.

"The Serbian Red Cross gave this center a clean bill of health," the commandant told him evenly.

"And the International Red Cross?" Jackson asked.

"This is a center, not a camp. Therefore we are not required to have the International Red Cross in for inspections."

"You have my answer. It's unforgivable what you're doing here."

"You are a fool!" the commandant shouted, jumping out of his seat and pointing a finger at Jackson. His face turned dark red and veins in his forehead bulged and throbbed visibly.

"I was born in Jasenovac, Dr. Bosnic!" He was referring to the World War II Ustasha concentration camp, where as many as one hundred thousand people, many of them Serbs, were executed. "Both of my parents committed suicide when I was a boy because they could not live with the memories of the things the Ustasha put them through. My father was an Orthodox priest, yet he committed suicide—a mortal sin! Can you imagine what they must have done to him? Do you think I should show mercy today after what they did to my people? I will show no mercy, Doctor! Our enemies will never do such things to us again! Never again will anyone defeat us! You may rejoin your people and die with them if that is your wish! But do not preach to me! I will not be preached to!"

The same man who had played the perfect host only minutes before had now shown the monster within. In a minute, however, he was the same reserved, would-be-charming man he had been during the meal.

Slobodan Princip spoke perfectly calmly now. "There are many things I could do to change your mind, Doctor. Things you would not find so pleasant. I had another doctor here before, and he spoke as you did. He did not work out very well for us. It was unfortunate, because we really do need a doctor. But you will die in this center if you refuse my offer one more time."

Jackson took a few moments to pretend to think. "Perhaps we can make a deal, Slobodan."

The commandant's eyes narrowed momentarily in anger, but then he smiled and waited.

"There is a man in the cage I would have brought out to assist me."

"Is he a doctor?"

"Well . . . no."

"Then why do you need his assistance? You will have Sabina to help. She has run the hospital on her own for several weeks."

"He was beaten badly yesterday when we first arrived, and requires treatment." Jackson leaned forward and met the commandant's gaze now. "I promise that if you bring him out of the cage, my hand will never slip while operating on a Serb, or on a prized Muslim or Croat girl."

The commandant looked away and roared with laughter. "Doctor, you know so little about the way things are here. No, you cannot have your friend brought out. How do you like that? Now let me tell you something, Doctor. If you so much as nick one of my men, or even one of those whores, I will have you hung by your ankles and castrated." He laughed some more. "How is that for negotiating?"

After pausing as long as he dared, Jackson said, "You leave me little choice."

"Good. Sabina will show you the hospital in the morning. A guard will take you to your new quarters." The commandant stood to leave. "By the way, Doctor, what is the name of the man you wished to have brought out?"

Suddenly there was hope. "His name is—" But Jackson stopped himself. An American might be treated better or even released, but then again he might be killed on the spot for fear that he might bring stories of the camp to America. It was not a chance he was willing to take for himself, so he would not risk West's life, either. "He won't answer to his name—he was beaten badly when we first arrived for refusing to take off his boots. The guards will remember him."

The commandant nodded. "I hope you have a good night's sleep, Doctor." He held his hand in front of the young woman's face. She glanced at Jackson out of the corner of her eye, then gave her hand to the commandant and stood.

"One more thing, Slobodan? If it's not too much trouble, could my boots be returned to me? These shoes are too small."

The commandant ordered the guard to take Jackson to find his boots. "You see, I can be quite reasonable." He smiled. "Good night, Dr. Bosnic."

Jackson watched as they walked away together, the beautiful young woman sneaking a peek at him as she left.

## 22

MANY OF THE MEN from the town on the Sana River were called from their cage that night. Some were brought to the "red house," which they would never leave alive, but most went to the "white house," where they were tortured. Samuel West was a special case. He was brought to the administration building for his interview with the camp's chief investigator.

Radovan Meakic was a bear of a man, with mounds of scruffy gray hair atop his large head, and fleshy jowls that shook when he spoke. He was tall, he slouched when he walked, and he wore bifocals that made him look older than he was. He was the only Serb in the camp who did not wear a uniform. Instead, he always wore the same gray suit, perfectly pressed, with a white shirt and one of his many Italian designer ties. He looked at West's bruised face and said in perfect English, "Can I get you anything?"

"Food," grumbled West. His entire body ached from the beating, his head pounded, and he was starving, but he was encouraged now that he had been taken from the cage. West was certain that his presence in the camp was nothing more than a misunderstanding. Despite the brutality of the guards, he considered this to be a prisoner-of-war camp. After all, he was well aware of the brutality inflicted on American POWs in Vietnam. But he believed that he would soon convince the important man across the desk from him that his presence in the camp was a terrible mistake.

"I'm sorry. The kitchen is closed. Cigar? Cigarette?"

West shook his head.

"You are a long way from home, *Amerikanac*. What is your name, please?" Radovan Meakic was always extremely polite, unlike the commandant, who was alternately polite and abusive.

"My name is Samuel West." Despite Jackson's warning as he was being taken from the cage, West reasoned that the purpose of the camp was simply for the Serbs to detain their Muslim and Croat enemies for the duration of the war. From the moment he was dragged from the cage he told anyone who understood English that he was an American. Besides, West didn't speak their language, so he had no hope of convincing them otherwise.

"Well, Mr. West, I cannot help but wonder what brings you out this way. Why do you wish to come into Serbia?" he asked.

"I . . . I thought this was Bosnia."

"Wherever there is a Serb is Serbia. Are you supporting the fanatics in their Islamic insurrection?"

"Of course not," West replied.

"Good. We don't want trouble with the United States. After Bosnia becomes part of Serbia we will do much trade with your country. You're not with the UN, are you?"

"No."

"Well, in that case I am fresh out of ideas on why you would end up at this investigation center. Would you please tell me why you are here in Serbia."

West considered several answers, but each presented a different danger.

"Come now, it is obviously a mistake that you are here," the chief investigator said. "Why would an *Amerikanac* like you help the Turks prepare their rebellion? Just tell me how you got here and I am sure I can arrange transportation to Italy or Germany."

"I'm a cameraman for a television station in the U.S.," West lied, remembering that Jackson's ploy of posing as journalists got them through the roadblock near the coast. "We were doing a story on the effect of the war in small towns, when suddenly we were bombed. I don't know who was bombing the town. It must have been those Muslim fanatics. I got separated from the others I was with. I took a bus out of the town and ended up here."

*I see he is going to be difficult,* the Chief Investigator thought.

*No matter. I will find out everything I need to know tonight.*

He always looked forward to the night. During the day he would defer to the commandant to run the camp. But at night, when Slobodan Princip was in bed with his Muslim woman, Radovan Meakic was the man who gave the orders. He ruled the night.

Unlike most Serbs, Radovan Meakic did not believe the Serb propaganda. He did not use history as a justification for the crimes he was responsible for. He would often recite the sufferings of Serbs from centuries past in order to inspire his men to ever-increasing violence against the Muslims and Croats. But his own hatred of the Muslims was much more personal.

Having failed at psychiatry as a younger man, Radovan Meakic had tried to win acceptance in high social circles. He longed to live among the wealthy and educated. He wanted to marry a society girl. But as he tried to elbow his way into the Sarajevo elite, he always seemed to encounter the same problem: the Muslims.

The Muslims made up much of the educated and land-owning class in Bosnia. That distinction went back for centuries, when the Muslims, since they had converted to Islam during the Ottoman rule, were given privileges over the other Slavs—such as the Serbs—who did not convert. So every time he went to a cocktail party and could hear laughter behind his back, there was invariably a Muslim whispering about him. Every time there was a party that he was not invited to, it always seemed to be a party thrown by a Muslim.

Of course, all the wealthy and well-known Serbs and Croats in Sarajevo avoided him, too. He was a strange man who could be extremely polite and dignified, yet would invariably offend people with off-color jokes, or would be caught in obvious lies when he tried to brag about his accomplishments or his travels and the people he claimed to have met. But since so much of the aristocracy in Sarajevo was Muslim, to him it always seemed to be the Muslims who rejected him.

When the war broke out over the Krajina, Radovan Meakic was trying to make a reputation as a poet. He was failing miserably, so when men were needed to fill positions in the newly formed Bosnian Serb army, which consisted of a few units of the Yugoslav army together with Bosnian Serb militiamen and volunteers from Serbia, Radovan Meakic's education and deep hatred of the Muslims landed him his dream job. As the chief investigator of Omarska, Muslims could not snicker at him behind his back or fail to invite him to their parties or forget his name or criticize his poetry. As chief investigator at Omarska, he was in a position to exact his revenge on the Muslims, and their allies the Croats, and anyone who sympathized with them.

"You are an *Amerikanac*, and my people do not wish to have any differences with your country," the chief investigator said to West. "But I cannot accept these fabrications. I assure you, your only chance of leaving this camp alive is to tell me the truth. If I continue to hear lies, I will have to extract the truth from you."

West shifted uneasily in his chair. "I told you. I'm a cameraman."

"Where are your credentials, please?"

"They should be in my coat, which your guard took from me before I came in."

"Yes, I have your coat right here. There were no credentials."

"They must have got lost."

"Mr. West, you are lying. How could it be that your credentials were lost, but this was not?" Radovan Meakic pulled a white envelope from the inside breast pocket of West's jacket. West went pale. The chief investigator slowly took out a single sheet of paper from the envelope and held it up for West to see. "How do you explain this list, Mr. West?"

West began to say something, then stopped and finally said, "Those were men we were told to try to interview, if possible."

"And the dollar figures next to each name is how much your television station was willing to pay you for each interview?" the chief investigator suggested.

"Yes. That's right."

"Well, I am honored to have such a high station in your company's regard. It seems they were willing to pay you a quarter of a million dollars for an interview with me."

"Those . . . those figures are meant to be in Italian lire. The dollar signs were a mistake—"

"Mr. West, do you think I am a fool? There are forty-six names here, and mine is one of them. The commandant, the commander of the guard, four guards from this center. I know why you are here, Mr. West. And I assure you, you will not leave here alive. But I will give you a choice. I assume you are a soldier, and will accord you with an honorable soldier's death by firing squad if you tell me what I want to know. If, however, you continue to lie to me, you will suffer for many nights to come."

"But I'm telling you the truth. You can check it out with my TV station back home. I'm just a cameraman. All I want is to go home to my wife and kids. I don't know what you're thinking—"

"I don't think you will ever see your family again." The chief investigator turned to the guard. "Please bring this detainee to the white house and strap him in for an interview. He is not to be touched until I get there."

The guard dragged West from the room as West continued to plead innocence, insisting that he was an American and they had no right to hold him. When he was gone, the chief investigator sat back in his chair and thought. He wiped the sweat from his brow and wondered if the *Amerikanac* was acting alone, or if the other English-speaking man was with him.

**23**

———•—◆—•———

**AFTER HIS DINNER WITH** the commandant, Jackson was brought to a huge warehouse next to the administration building. His room was no bigger than a walk-in closet. There was a rickety cot to sleep on. He waited for an hour, listening for the sounds of guards, but all was quiet in the warehouse. He slipped off the cot and pulled on his very own boots, which he had found in an enormous pile the guard had taken him to on the commandant's orders.

He opened the door a millimeter at a time because he had noticed the door had squeaked when he had been brought in. He found it hard to believe they left the door unlocked and unguarded, but it seemed that there were no guards in sight. He made his way down the long corridor and opened the window at the far end, sticking his head out.

There were guards on the other side of the compound, but they wouldn't see him. A few sentries were sleeping with their backs against the rusty shed with the cages. He noticed the flashlight of a sentry who was patrolling the length of the barbed-wire fence behind the warehouse. He waited until the sentry moved along toward the main gate before climbing out of the window.

He ran behind the warehouse, his heart racing as he rested there with his back to the wall. He noticed the sentry turn around and head back his way, so he moved quickly along the back of the warehouse, surveying that side of the camp as he went. When he had put some distance between the sentry and himself, he moved to the wire.

It was a homemade double barbed-wire fence, tightly constructed, buried a foot into the ground. No hope of going under unless he could dig, but that would take too much time. He would not want to try to scale it, either. It was ten feet tall with more than the usual number of sharp barbs. There was the danger of getting hung up on the wire. Beyond the wire were woods, which would provide him with cover if he could get through the fence.

He ran along the wire and noticed a trail that went deep into the woods on the other side. He turned and marked the position of the trail by the number of warehouse windows. The trail beyond the wire was adjacent to the seventh warehouse window from the right.

Then he ran around the far side of the warehouse and came to the rear of the administration building. He leaned his back against it, pausing to look and listen for more sentries. Suddenly he heard noises. He froze in his place.

Jackson soon realized that the noises were coming from inside the administration building. It sounded as if a thousand voices were crying out in the night. He put his ear to a window with a curtain covering it and could hear the Serbs taunting the Muslim and Croat girls. The girls were screaming as other Serbs sang patriotic songs and cheered the rapists on.

Jackson couldn't stand the screams, but what could he do? He was powerless to help them.

He moved along until he came to the red shed. He went along with his back to it, stopping suddenly when he once again heard cries for mercy.

This time it was men screaming in high-pitched screams of terror. There was very little other noise, no taunts or singing that he could tell. Again, the screaming terrified him, particularly since he knew he was one misstep from experiencing the same agony himself. He moved on with an urgency that seemed to grow greater by the second.

He sprinted across an opening between two buildings and ducked behind the white shed. He was directly below a window and could see the light beaming out over his head. Inside this shed he did not hear screams, but rather an engine of some sort. This time he couldn't help but take a look. He stood and peaked through the window for only a few seconds, but that was enough. He would never forget what he saw.

Inside the shed Jackson could see many of the men from the town on the Sana River lying about on the floor, bloody and beaten. Pacing back and forth in front of them was a Chetnik with an electric drill. One Muslim was screaming in terror as he watched a Chetnik holding a chainsaw throw his severed leg into a fire. Directly beneath the window was a large tank filled with water, a net draped across the top. Attached to the net were what looked like electrodes, which were connected to a car battery. Guards to the left were forcing a Muslim and a Croat to have anal intercourse.

In the far corner of the room he saw a man—he did not know it was the chief investigator—standing next to a beautiful woman smoking a cigarette. Just behind her, Jackson could now see West sitting in a chair with leather straps crisscrossing his chest. Jackson's knees buckled and he swallowed hard. He slumped to the ground and covered his mouth with his hands, afraid that he might instinctively cry out. His eyes grew wide as he remembered what Haris had told him about prisoners taken from the cages at night. After catching his breath, Jackson stood and carefully peered through the dirty window again.

The woman was stroking West's face. She whispered something in his ear, and he seemed to mumble a reply. Suddenly, the beautiful Serb woman stuck her cigarette into the side of West's face. Jackson could see West scream as she held it there for several seconds. When she pulled it away, Samuel West began screaming at her. The woman took a deep drag and said something to the chief investigator, who didn't seem to hear her. He had been speaking aloud the entire time, reading from a notepad he held in his hand. If Jackson could have heard him, he would have known that the chief investigator was speaking aloud a poem he'd written about the Serb struggle. It was a very bizarre poem.

Jackson crouched down again. For perhaps a split second the idea of rescuing West crossed his mind, but again he knew there was nothing he could do. It was suicide to even try to help. Once again, he was overcome by guilt, but at the same time, he knew he had to do anything he could to get out of the camp.

*Honestly, I would rather die,* he thought, *than go through what the men in that shed are going through.*

He sat there for another minute considering his options, but in the end he did the only thing he could—he returned to the task at hand.

Jackson made an almost complete round-trip of the perimeter of the camp, surveying the wire, noting the location of the huge open mine pit, where thousands of prisoners were kept, and timing the sentries as they patrolled the wire. He sprinted behind the huge ore-separating facility, which housed hundreds of prisoners. When he came near the main gate, he crawled underneath a truck and waited.

In about a half hour a truck pulled up to the gate. Without stopping or searching the truck, the guards at the gate waved it in. This was promising. Perhaps they also did not search the trucks as they were leaving the camp. The truck came to a stop near the white shed and eight people got out, dressed in civilian clothes. They were Serb men and women from the town who chatted easily with the guards. They walked straight to the red shed. Jackson could hear the high-pitched screams of prisoners as the door opened.

Minutes later, a truck that had been backed up to the loading dock of the red shed pulled out toward the main gate. Unfortunately, as Jackson watched with great interest the truck was searched from top to bottom, even underneath. The driver was made to exit the vehicle and show his papers. Jackson frowned in disappointment.

After watching trucks come and go for over two hours, Jackson circled all the way back around the perimeter of the camp the way he had come, hiding several times as sentries passed. He pulled himself up through the window of the warehouse and fell in silently. Before he had a chance to stand, the door at the end of the hall opened. Silver moonlight from the moon was shining through the window directly upon him. There was nothing he could do. He would be discovered.

As the door opened wide, he saw the white radiance of Sabina's nurse's uniform as she tiptoed through the doorway. She closed the door silently and was about to come down the hall when she stopped short. She could see Jackson clearly, lying on the floor at the end of the hall in front of the open window.

She stood there for what seemed like forever. They stared at each other, Jackson not daring to move. Sabina walked halfway down the hall, paused to look once more at him, then quietly slipped through a doorway, closing the door behind her.

Jackson wasted no time. He got up and closed the window and then went down the hall to stand in front of the door to the room where she had gone. He reached for the knob, but then noticed the word *Bolnica*—Hospital—handwritten on the door in thick black felt-tipped pen. He stood outside the door for a long moment, unsure of what to do, before slowly taking his hand away from the doorknob.

He went back to his room, slipped off his boots, and lay awake for hours, unable to forget the sight of the men in the shed and unable to forget their horrible screams and cries for help. Every time he heard even the slightest sound he would bolt upright with a start, his heart pounding, thinking that they were coming for him. Knowing that he needed another night before even attempting an escape, Jackson could do nothing but wait for the night to end and hope that he could make it through one more day.

He knew that time was running out on his life. How long before they came for him? Was West talking, at that very moment, in the white shed? Had West cracked under torture and implicated Jackson as an accomplice in his mission against the Serbs? If so, this was surely Jackson's last night on earth, but only after he, too, would be subjected to the kinds of horrific tortures he had witnessed in the white shed. Was it really possible that he would die that way? Would he ever see Maria again? Would news of his death ever reach her, or would his corpse simply be thrown into the back of a truck in the middle of the night to be taken from the camp to be buried God knows where?

It did not seem right that he could die such a terrible death, in a place as barbaric as the camp. He was an American. He grew up playing Little League baseball, going to high-school dances, graduating from the University of California. A year ago he had never heard of Bosnia. It was on the other side of the world from where he wanted to be—married to Maria, living in a house somewhere in the mountains of California, raising a family. How could he die in Bosnia? This wasn't even his fight. Why was he being punished? What did he do to deserve to never be able to return home, to never see Maria again? What kind of a cruel God would let this happen to him?

*The same God who allowed defenseless civilians to be slaughtered and teenage girls to be raped,* he thought.

He felt his anger at God rising up inside of him.

"Thanks for your help, God," he whispered angrily, sarcastically. "You've really been good to me, and to all of the prisoners in this camp. What a great, loving God you are."

Suddenly he heard a loud noise, like a door slamming shut down the hall. He froze, petrified, listening to footsteps making their way down the hall. Never before in his life had he experienced the kind of fear he felt now that he was facing the very real terror—the absolute horror—of the kind of tortures he had witnessed taking place in the white shed.

The footsteps stopped outside of his door. Jackson swallowed hard. Was this how it would end for him? There were no windows in his room, nowhere to run or hide. He wouldn't even be able to put up a fight?

Every muscle was tense. His heart was racing and he had to gasp for air. He closed his eyes tightly, almost cringing, expecting to hear the doorknob beginning to turn any second. But instead, now he could hear the footsteps continue down the hall, and as his head began swimming with light-headed relief, he heard another door open and then slam shut.

*It must have been Sabina leaving the hospital,* he thought, still too scared to move, still listening intently. But in a minute he was sure that it had been Sabina. He felt as if he had been granted a stay of execution. *Thank you, God. Thank you for sparing me the—*

He stopped himself. He had been unable to deny his anger at God ever since he had first seen the suffering taking place in Bosnia, and hadn't prayed in months. He could not say with assurance that he even believed in a God any longer, or that he wanted to believe in a God who would allow a place like Omarska to exist. But all alone in his cold, dark corner of the camp, with sunrise still several hours away, Jackson admitted to himself that there was only one thing he could do now.

He slid onto the cold, hard floor and knelt. In spite of himself, he prayed to the God he was no longer sure he believed in. "God," he began, closing his eyes tightly and clasping his hands in front of him on the cot, "I swear I'll do anything if you just get me out of here before they . . . before they. . . ."

*Before they strap me into one of those chairs,* he thought. *Before they tie me down like they did with West, leaving me completely helpless, unable to move, unable to defend myself while the chief investigator or one of his lunatic guards or even that woman who burned West with the cigarette laugh at me as they stand over me with a knife or a chainsaw or an electric drill. . . .*

"God, please don't make me go through that. Please, get me out of here."

## 24

JACKSON WAS SITTING UNCOMFORTABLY *in the belly of a C-130 transport plane, his knees pulled up to his chest, wedged between the large wooden crates.*

*"Lieutenant," a young soldier said, suddenly standing over him. The soldier pointed at the wide cargo hatch in the rear of the plane, which was wide open. "This is where you wanted to get off, sir."*

*Jackson wearily made his way to the door. For the first time, he realized that he was wearing a parachute. "I don't know what to do," he told the soldier.*

*"You'll figure it out," the soldier told him.*

*Jackson leaped from the plane and was free-falling above a lush, green mountain range. Off in the distance he could see the blue expanse of a huge ocean. He enjoyed the peaceful, floating feeling at first, but he soon realized that the ground was fast approaching, so he frantically began pulling at the seemingly endless number of rip cords dangling from the large pack on his back. Over and over he pulled the cords, but he seemed to be gaining speed and he knew that any second his life would be over and there didn't seem to be a thing he could do to prevent it. When there was only one cord remaining he pulled it with all of his strength but still his chute would not open. He stared impotently at the rip cord, noticing now that it was not a rip cord at all, but Emir's silver chain with the Orthodox cross, the crucifix, and the crescent and star medallions. Jackson closed his eyes and began to pray.*

When Jackson opened his eyes he was standing in a field of tall grass wearing his dress blue uniform. In the center of the field was a pink adobe church. As he approached it he could see the congregation streaming into the church. The black-robed priest, who was greeting the parishioners as they entered, noticed Jackson and stabbed a finger toward a white gazebo across the field, where Maria was waiting for him in a long white wedding dress.

Suddenly he was sitting next to Maria on the gazebo. His hands were sweaty with nervousness as he marveled at her, wondering again what he had done to deserve to be so happy. She was stunning, with smooth olive skin, long wavy black hair that reached halfway down her back, and dark blue eyes. She wrapped her hands around his neck and kissed him.

"I'm so lucky," she whispered. "I thank God every night for giving you to me."

"I'm the lucky one," he insisted.

Dark clouds began rolling in over the mountains and the wind picked up. "I wish you'd change your mind," Maria sighed, looking toward the church. "Everything is all arranged."

Jackson took her hand, happy as always to see the engagement ring on her finger. "It's better this way. One year, then I'll be finished with the army. There'll be no more time apart. By the time I get back you'll be done with medical school and we can finally be together. Forever."

"But it sounds awful over there. I've been reading the papers. All of these people killing each other for no apparent reason— Muslims, Serbs, and . . . and . . ."

"And Croats," he finished for her.

"It's dangerous."

"I'll be fine," he told her.

She looked up at him, a single tear on her cheek. "Tell me again, Bobby. Tell me that you'll come back to me."

"I swear it, Maria." he told her. "We'll always be together. I swear to God that I'll love you forever."

Maria frowned. "What, Bobby? What did you say?"

He smiled at her. "I swear to God that I'll love you forever."

She turned her head slightly, her eyes narrowing. "I can't understand you. What are you saying?"

"I said, 'I swear to God that I'll love you forever,' " Jackson repeated, the words sounding perfectly clear to him, but somehow in his dream he now realized that everything he was saying suddenly sounded like gibberish to her.

Maria stood with her hands on her hips, looking down at him. "If you don't stop that I'll—"

"Stop what? Maria, I love you. I'm trying to tell you—"

"That's enough!" She stormed down the steps of the gazebo, heading back to the church, where the congregation was now waiting for her.

Jackson stood and tried to go after her but he could not move his feet. "Maria!" he shouted, but now his words echoed about him and he knew that she couldn't hear him. He tried again to go to her but as hard as he tried he couldn't move. He continued to shout at her to come back, but she didn't respond, and the harder he tried to move his legs, the more he realized that something was terribly wrong. He cried out to her to come back, to give him a chance to explain, but the congregation parted and he watched her walk into the church. He tried shouting to the others, but now a great storm erupted and they could not hear him. Thunder cracked and lightning flashed overhead as the others just turned their backs on him and followed Maria into the church, slamming the church doors shut.

Jackson looked longingly at the church, knowing he had to get there to explain. Bolts of lightning began striking the field all around him, but he could not run for cover because his feet still would not move. It was only a matter of time before he was struck down. He thought of raising his arms to the sky and inviting what he thought was inevitable, but when he realized that if he died he would never see Maria again, he redoubled his efforts to free himself, to run for cover in the church, to try one last time to make Maria understand.

Suddenly Emir appeared, standing in the middle of the field. Jackson shouted, "Emir! Emir, go to them! Tell them what's happening! Explain to Maria what's happening!"

Emir slowly walked toward him, almost gliding across the field. Although it was pouring rain and Jackson was drenched, Emir remained perfectly dry.

Jackson pointed at the church. "Emir! Go to them!"

Emir smiled peacefully, coming up to Jackson. "I made it to the

*mountains of California, Robert," the young shepherd said content-*
*edly.*

*"Emir!" Jackson shouted, and tried to push him toward the*
*church, but his hand went right through Emir, who floated now*
*above the ground like a spirit. "Emir! Emir! Emir!"*

Jackson bolted upright in his cot, sweating and breathing heavily.

"Emir? You must get up. Quickly," he heard a woman's voice
telling him.

"Maria!" Jackson cried out now, not yet completely awake. He
turned and saw Sabina, dressed all in white, her belly slightly protruding, her blond hair tied back in a ponytail. There was sadness
in her eyes, but her mouth was trying to smile.

"I didn't mean to frighten you, Emir," she said, using the name
Jackson had given the commandant at dinner.

"I was dreaming," Jackson explained, running his fingertips
along the three icons dangling from Emir's chain. He wiped the
sweat from his face, still trying to catch his breath. "What time is
it?"

"It is almost sunrise. I wanted to let you sleep as much as you
could, but I'm afraid you must come with me now," she apologized.

"What is it?"

"In a minute. First, there is something I must show you."

Jackson grabbed his boots and followed Sabina down the hall
to the camp hospital, which was merely a small room in the warehouse with three beds, a sink, a dim light, and some medical instruments arranged on a tray.

Sabina stood next to one of the beds and looked down. Jackson
could see that someone was lying under the gray sheets.

"Your *Amerikanac* friend was injured this morning," she told
him. "The chief investigator said to tell you that he regrets that
your friend was involved in . . . in an accident. He ordered that the
man be brought to you."

Jackson came to the side of the bed. Sabina watched him very
closely as she pulled the sheet back, revealing West's naked body.

Jackson quickly turned his eyes and stumbled to a seat, fighting
the urge to be sick.

"Is he going to live?" he asked Sabina in a minute.

"We can discuss it later. The—"

"Tell me!"

Sabina came forward and knelt next to him. "What I tell you now I have not been ordered to tell you. But I tell you, so that you may prepare yourself." She was whispering now, in English. "You have been sent for by the chief investigator of the camp. If you do not go to him directly—"

"What kind of place is this!"

She rubbed his back soothingly. "Emir, listen to me. You must have all your wits about you. I overheard the commandant talking to the chief investigator about this *Amerikanac*. They think he is a very dangerous man. The chief investigator thinks you might be with him so they're coming for you. You have no choice but to go, but you must be very careful about what you say."

Jackson looked at the beautiful woman as she bit her lower lip. She was nervous and clearly putting herself at risk, but she was perfectly levelheaded and calm. It made her seem even more beautiful to him, if that was possible.

"I don't know what to say to him," he whispered to her, not sure why he trusted her, but not regretting it.

"I know. But I believe you will think of something," she said, and patted his hand. "Now stand up and await them. I hear footsteps coming down the hall."


"And you received your medical degree from where?" the chief investigator asked.

"From the University of California," Jackson lied.

"You have an accent. You are *Amerikanac,* or English. You are Catholic. You are a Croat sympathizer. You are a spy."

"I'm not a Catholic," Jackson insisted. He reached into his shirt and felt around with his fingertips for Emir's crescent and star medallion, which the shepherd had lent to him for protection. When he was sure he had it, he pulled it out and held it under his chin. In the quiet of the early morning, a rooster crowed as the sun finally began to rise above the stone peaks of the hills in the distance. "You see, I'm not a spy," Jackson said. "But I have lived in America. I've been told that I picked up a slight accent there."

"It is a very obvious accent. You must have been in the United States for a very long time."

"Yes, I was. It was my father's wish that I become a doctor, so my parents sent me to America for university and for medical school," Jackson lied. "I spent more than eight years there. I returned home to Bosnia when the war started because my town needed a doctor."

"Then you knew this *Amerikanac* in California?"

"No," Jackson replied. He had hesitated just slightly, thinking at first that he should try to help save West, but in the split second that he had to answer, he realized that trying to help West would likely cost him his life. His reply was almost an involuntary reaction, as if some sort of self-protection mechanism suddenly went off inside of him.

"Are you denying that you know him?" the chief investigator asked doubtfully.

"I met him when my town came under attack," Jackson replied, surprising even himself at how easily his story came to him now that he was resigned to the fact that West was a dead man. He could not help but feel guilty for not trying to save West, but at the same time he had to distance himself from West because he was worried that West might have succumbed to the torture in the white shed and confessed his mission. "He said crazy things, about being an *Amerikanac* and having a mission to complete. He said he wanted me to be his interpreter. Of course I knew he was crazy, so I took care of him to keep him from getting hurt when the Chet— when the Serb patriots came to our town. When I opted for the bus out of town, I took him with me."

"What did he tell you about this mission?"

"Only that it could help the Muslims."

"Nothing more?"

"No. Nothing."

"Did he ever say anything about going to Pale? Or Belgrade?" Pale was the newly established Bosnian Serb capital. Belgrade was the capital of Serbia.

"No."

"Did he ever mention Omarska?"

"No."

The chief investigator brought out the white envelope. He took out the single white sheet of paper. "Did the *Amerikanac* ever show this to you?"

Jackson eyed the paper curiously but was too far away to read it. "May I see it?"

The chief investigator jerked it back. "There is no need to see it. Did this man ever show you any papers?"

"Not that I can remember."

The chief investigator fingered his bushy gray eyebrows. His usual troubled frown turned to a tight-lipped snarl as he considered his next move. "The commandant has ordered that I return you to the camp hospital. There, Sabina will be watching you closely. If it is determined that you are not a doctor, you will regret lying to me. In the meantime, I will verify your credentials with this university in America. By tomorrow morning I will know if you have been truthful."

"Yes, sir."

"I don't mind telling you that I hope to discover that you are lying. The *Amerikanac* was wonderful last night. I look forward to questioning him all over again. He proved to be a most stubborn interview. He has great endurance for pain. He brought me much heartache, but also very much pleasure. I am very anxious to find out what it would be like to speak to you, too, on more . . . intimate terms."

Remembering the sight of West's naked body, Jackson unconsciously crossed his legs and folded his hands over his groin.

"Good day, Dr. Bosnic."

# 25

JACKSON HAD BEEN PACING back and forth in the infirmary waiting for an opportunity to speak with Sabina alone. She had been busy tending to sick or injured girls since he returned from his interview.

"Nurse, may I see you please?" he demanded finally.

Sabina was feeding one of the Muslim girls, who was too weak to sit up and couldn't hold a spoon. She put down a bowl of soup, followed Jackson into an adjoining bathroom, and immediately closed the door.

"Listen, I need to ask you—"

"About our patients, Emir?" Sabina interrupted him. "Which one? Kenada? She is having trouble urinating and defecating. Also, the guards were biting her breasts and I think there might be infection."

"I see."

"It is all on their charts, Emir."

"Charts? Yeah, right. The charts. But you see it's my custom to speak with my nurses personally. Charts don't always tell the whole story."

"Very wise," she said. "You will have to pardon my ignorance, Emir. I was only a university student when the war broke out. I would be very interested to hear your diagnosis."

Jackson knew that she had helped him that morning, but now she was challenging him, and he was in no mood for it. "From now on you'll address me as Dr. Bosnic."

"You are no more a doctor than I am a nurse. Do you think I am a fool?" Sabina asked, whispering in English again. "You are an American. You are no doctor who came from a town on the Sana to care for the poor Bosnians in the countryside. You are with the other American."

She sounded so sure, Jackson couldn't insult her by denying it. "Listen, I'd like to help the people of this camp—"

"If you were a real doctor you could do just that."

"If I can escape—"

"Escape is not possible," she interrupted. "Do you think that if escape were possible I would still be here?" She threw back her head. "No one escapes here. It is impossible."

"You saw me last night. I could have gone if I had had a way to get through the wire. Then they'd never catch me."

"You're wrong. In the beginning, before there was the barbed fence, many men got away. But always they were caught. In the morning the Serbs would discover a man was missing. They would get the dogs and within a couple hours they would bring the man back. Even if you made it to the town, it is an all-Serb town now. The townspeople are under penalty of death for helping anyone from the camp. There is nowhere safe that can be reached before the dogs will track you down. One man stayed hidden until morning, in time to make the first train. But when word went forth that there was an escape, all the towns along the line were notified and the man was caught."

"They won't catch me," Jackson told her confidently.

"Yes, they will. They probably did not even lock your door last night because they know it is impossible for you to get away. And after you fail, just for trying to escape they will torture and kill you, and they will also kill five prisoners as a warning to the others not to try to escape."

That caught Jackson by surprise. It was something he had not considered. "Those men are going to die anyway," he reasoned. "If I can get out, thousands could be saved."

Sabina thought for a moment. "The commandant and the chief investigator speak of a mission the other American was sent here for. You know of this mission?"

"Not exactly."

"You mean your friend never told you his mission? Why not? You could have helped him."

"He's not my friend. He's a mercenary, and he never trusted me. All I know is that he was sent by someone who thinks his mission could help end the war."

Sabina's eyes narrowed in interest. "Who sent him?"

"A great man. A Jewish man who survived a Nazi concentration camp. He worked as a lawyer in the war crimes trials of the Nazis after World War II. He made a fortune as a lawyer and a businessman after the war, and became a statesman for the new government of Israel years ago. He gives his time and money to many causes. He works directly with the UN on numerous programs."

"What can one soldier do?" Sabina asked doubtfully.

"Damned if I know. I have a guess, but there's only one way to be sure. The chief investigator has an envelope he took from the other American, who used to guard it with his life."

"If it is important, I will get it."

"Wait a second—"

"I will get it, or I will die trying." Sabina turned suddenly and started to leave.

"Hold on."

"I would gladly risk my life for something worthwhile," Sabina said sincerely. "Sometimes I wonder if I am doing any good here. I nurse the girls back to health and I try to hold them out of the rotation for as long as I can, but they are always thrown back in right away."

"The rotation?"

Sabina's lip curled in disgust. "The Serbs rotate the girls to be raped so they get fresh ones every night. Usually a girl is raped many times a night by different men, then she is given a night off. If she is beaten very badly, she comes to me and sometimes I can get her to miss a night of her rotation."

Jackson closed his eyes, knowing there was nothing he could do or say to change life for her or for the girls. "Look, Sabina, I'm not asking you to risk your life. I'll be honest—I just want to get out of here. If that sounds selfish, you'll have to forgive me, but if I don't get out tonight I'm a dead man—after the chief investigator has his fun with me. Once I'm out, maybe I can get word to someone who can help—the Croat army maybe, or . . ." His words trailed off.

Sabina was silent for a long moment, but finally asked, "What do you need?"

"I'll think of a way to get through the wire. But I need to know where the nearest town is. Are there roads nearby where I might get a ride? Is there a train station? What about rivers? I need a map, Sabina, if you can get me one. And a compass, if possible."

She was shaking her head the entire time. "It is suicide to try to run from this camp. Getting past the wire is the easy part. It is not possible to get far enough away before they track you down. The dogs will find you wherever you hide. The only thing to do is to stay hidden until they give up the search. But where can you hide when they will search every centimeter outside of this camp until they find you?"

Jackson stared back at Sabina. He knew that she had just given him the answer.

"Get me a compass and map," he told her.


Later that day, Jackson sat in the quiet of the hospital, working through a stack of death certificates he was required, as the camp doctor, to fill out. Each blank certificate was attached to a sheet of paper with a name scribbled on it and a cause of death. The causes of death were laughable: sunstroke; allergies; the mumps.

"Jackson," a faint voice called out.

He hurried to West's bedside. "I'm here. Can you hear me?"

Samuel West began feeling about with his right hand until Jackson held it and gently guided it back to West's side.

"Jackson?"

"Yeah."

West was crying now. "My God! I can't see a damn thing! I can't see you, Jackson!"

"I'm here. You're all right—"

"Oh, God, Jackson, he's fucking insane! He . . . he . . . Jackson, don't let him touch me again! Please. . . ."

Jackson had always hated West. He hated the way West constantly made racist remarks. He hated that West thought nothing of killing. He hated that West was only there because he was being paid. But Jackson had never pitied a man so much in his life.

"I'll get the nurse," Jackson told him.

"No, Jackson. I don't want to get better." West tried to sit up, but he did not have the strength. He felt with his hand until he had it on the back of Jackson's head. He tried to pull Jackson down close, but he was so weak his arm fell impotently back to the bed.

Jackson put his ear near West's mouth. "What can I do for you?" he asked West.

"Kill me!" West rasped, and Jackson could feel West's spit in his ear. "Kill me, for Christ's sake!"

Jackson looked down at the person in the bed. He hardly recognized the big, strong man that West had been. Gone were the deep voice and the confidence and the soldier's swagger. Gone were the insults, the demands, and the arrogance.

Jackson pulled a pillow from under West's head.

"Please. Kill me. Kill me. Kill me. . . ."

Jackson readied the pillow again in his hands. They were sweating now.

"I don't want to live. I have no reason to live. Kill me. Kill me. . . ."

Suddenly the doors to the infirmary burst open. Four Serb guards carrying a fifth rushed in and hastily laid him on a table. Sabina was with them, followed by the Vulture—the commander of the guard.

"This man needs help," the commander of the guard barked.

"What happened?"

"He was found passed out in his truck a few miles from here. A Turk must have shot at him from the roadside."

"He has been hit several times, *Doctor!*" Sabina said to Jackson, with a look of panic on her face.

Jackson straightened up and stepped forward, waving at the Serbs. "Clear the room," he demanded. "Nurse, prepare him for—"

"I am staying," the commander of the guard insisted. He was well known for his devotion to his troops, which was partly why they revered him.

"Absolutely not," Jackson said.

The commander of the guard glared at him. "Do you know how the last doctor died?"

Jackson realized it would do no good to argue. "If you insist on staying, get out of my way." He looked down at the bloody Serb. He knew very little about combat wounds, but common sense told him that the man wouldn't live. He'd been shot too close to the heart.

"There's no heartbeat," Sabina said urgently.

"Do something!" the commander of the guard demanded.

Jackson wiped his sweaty palms on the seat of his pants, then began performing CPR. "It's not working," he said after checking for a pulse. "I'm going to try open-heart massage. Give me the Lasorda scissors."

Sabina was shocked. Thinking quickly, she checked the man's pulse again and put her ear to his mouth. "It's too late, Doctor. He has stopped breathing. He's dead."

Jackson knew she was lying. He had felt the man's pulse. It was faint, but the man was still alive.

"Don't just stand there!" the commander of the guard shouted.

Jackson stuck out his right hand. "Give me the damn Lasorda scissors! Give them to me!"

Sabina didn't move, so Jackson lunged across the table and picked through the utensils.

"Where the hell are they!" he shouted angrily.

Sabina just stood there, not knowing what he was talking about.

"Lasorda scissors. Hurry! I have to cut through the rib cage to get at the bullet."

"Hurry!" the commander of the guard shouted at Sabina.

Sabina looked at the implement tray, then looked helplessly at Jackson.

"Give me the Lasorda scissors or this man will die!"

"But . . . but, Doctor . . ."

Jackson hurried around the table to the implement tray. "Where are the Lasorda scissors?"

Sabina looked at him, frightened and confused.

"What's going on!" the commander of the guard demanded.

"If I don't have Lasorda scissors in two minutes, this man will die."

The commander of the guard held up his hands. "I don't know what they are!"

"I need them!" Jackson shouted.

"I don't have them! Do something!" the Vulture insisted.

Jackson pretended to think. "Wire cutters. Get me wire cutters!"

"I don't know—"

"Get them! I need to cut through this man's rib cage to get at his heart."

The commander of the guard stared back at him. Jackson stood over the shorter man and screamed again. "Get me wire cutters or this man will die!"

The commander of the guard glared at him for a long moment, but he suddenly rushed out the door to retrieve the wire cutters personally. The four guards followed. Jackson went to the bathroom to throw up. He felt Sabina's hand on his back.

"I didn't know what to do," she admitted.

"You did fine."

"I am not a real nurse. I've never heard of the instrument you requested."

"Neither have I. I made it up."

He straightened up and walked back to the table, looking at the wounded guard. "He wasn't dead."

"No," Sabina said quietly. "But he was very weak."

"Is he dead now?"

Sabina checked for a pulse. "Yes."

Jackson suddenly craved slivovitz.

He heard the commander of the guard running back down the hall, so he quickly pulled the sheet over the guard's head. The commander of the guard burst in, holding the wire cutters. "Here!" he said, panting.

Jackson took the wire cutters and bowed his head. "I'm sorry. It's too late."

The commander of the guard could hardly speak, he was breathing so heavily. "Too late!" he gasped. "He's dead?"

"The bullet was too close to the heart," Jackson said gently. "Without Lasorda scissors, or at least these wire cutters, there was no way—"

"You let him die?"

"I didn't have the proper instruments."

"You let him die?" The commander of the guard pulled out his pistol and held it just inches from Jackson's face. "You stinking Turk, you let him die!"

"It wasn't my fault!" Jackson pleaded. He held up the wire cutters. "If I had had these he'd be alive. How do you expect me to operate without the basic tools? I didn't let him die. In a real hospital he would be alive now." He waved the wire cutters in the Vulture's face and demanded, "From now on there will always be wire cutters on this tray. Never again will I have one of my patients die because there were inadequate instruments. I'll prepare a list of things I need. For now, these wire cutters will stay here!" He threw the wire cutters on the tray, where they landed with a crash.

The commander of the guard stared at him, shaking as he tried to suppress his rage. He would have killed Jackson, but he and the guards were under strict orders from the commandant not to harm the doctor. Sabina put her hand on the Vulture's hands and guided the pistol down until it pointed at the floor. The commander of the guard stared at Jackson for another tense moment, then turned and stalked out of the camp hospital, followed by the guards.

As soon as they were gone, Jackson fell into a chair in the corner.

"You are a very clever man," Sabina said, watching him thoughtfully. She walked over to the instrument tray and picked up the wire cutters. "I don't have your map and compass yet. But I know where I can get them."

"I'll need enough food and water for five or six days," Jackson said weakly, staring at the guard's blood on his hands. "I'm going out tonight."

"I know," she said, looking at the wire cutters. "Come to the side window of the commandant's quarters at exactly ten o'clock tonight. One way or another, I will have everything you require."

**IT HAD BEEN DARK** for several hours. Jackson was in his room, lying on the cot, his hands clasped behind his head. He stared at the ceiling. Occasionally he could hear the drunken guards in the compound, singing or fighting, or a truck coming or going. With every sound, a tremor would wrack his body. He was not sure if it was fear or adrenaline, but he knew it was natural and was not afraid that it was a bad thing. He was aware of the chance he would soon be taking, and wasn't trying to fool himself. He couldn't expect to have steely nerves. He only wished to get started, because with every minute that he lay there going over his plan, more and more doubt crept into his head. And time seemed to be moving very slowly.

Finally he got dressed and opened the door a crack to make sure there was no one in the hall. Sure that it was safe, he was about to leave when, in spite of himself, Jackson dropped to one knee and, with his hands shaking, slowly and deliberately made the sign of the cross.

He quietly made his way to the camp hospital to pick up the wire cutters. He saw the scalpel, and took that, too. He purposely did not look at West, who he knew was still lying in one of the beds.

He hurried down the hall, opened the window, and climbed out. Staying close to the side of the building, he slipped around to the back and ran down to the far corner, then over to the camp administration building. He found the window Sabina had told him about and looked inside.

Jackson could see Sabina lying on her stomach on top of the dining table, her hands and legs tied. Most of her white nurse's uniform had been torn off. The commandant had his shirt off, and his trousers were unbuttoned. He was waving a sheet of paper in Sabina's face. In his other hand he held his belt. In one violent stroke, he brought the belt down upon the back of her thighs. Jackson could hear the snap from his place outside.

Sabina groaned but did not cry. Jackson looked about nervously, then looked back inside, where the commandant was taking a drink out of a bottle of slivovitz. He was standing over Sabina again, waving the white sheet of paper. He shouted something, then punched her in the back of the head with a closed fist.

Jackson closed his eyes and took a deep breath, running his hands through his hair as he tried to talk himself out of getting involved. But then he heard the commandant shouting again, and made his decision.

His head told him that a compass and a map were not essential, but in his heart he knew he could not leave without Sabina. That was what he had been thinking about all night, and now that he saw her there, at the mercy of the commandant, he knew that he had no choice, even if it made escaping the camp more dangerous.

He pushed gently against the window, but it was locked. He went to the corner of the building and saw a sentry sitting on the stairs. He wiped the sweat from his forehead, composed himself, and rounded the corner of the building. The sentry pulled his gun.

"It's the doctor," Jackson said.

"What are you doing out?" the sentry snapped.

"The commandant sent for me."

"I was not told. Why would he want to see you now?"

"Why do you think?"

"Ah, his Turkish whore. He beat her again. Oh well, it's not the woman that concerns him. She is carrying his baby."

"Yes. He must only care about the baby."

"You better go in," the sentry said.

Jackson brushed past him, then hurried down the hallway until he was outside the door to the room where he had had dinner the night before. He could hear them clearly now.

"Who else knows about the *Amerikanac*'s list?" the commandant shouted. "Don't think I'll protect you anymore! I'll kill you myself if I have to!"

"How many nights have you threatened to kill me, yet always you end up drunk and crying like a baby?" Sabina insulted him through clenched teeth. "Why do you keep me alive? Don't you see that I despise you? What a fool you are to think you could ever make me happy! You're not even a real man! I should know!"

Jackson swallowed hard. He was sure that the commandant would kill her. He opened the door a crack and peered inside. He saw the commandant raise the belt over his head, ready to strike Sabina again. Jackson was about to rush in to stop the blow, but suddenly the commandant dropped to his knees before Sabina, who was still tied to the table. They were eye to eye now. Jackson could hear the commandant sobbing.

"What a big, powerful man you are." Sabina laughed at him.

"You cast a spell on me, you god-cursed Turkish whore!" the commandant cried, burying his face in his hands.

Jackson suddenly burst through the door, catching the commandant by surprise, not giving the commandant time to react or to call for help. Jackson tackled him at the waist like a football player, grabbed the commandant's hair and smashed his head against the floor, then stood and kicked him hard in the groin. The commandant covered up, moaning.

Jackson bent low and whispered in the commandant's ear. "How does it feel, motherfucker!" He could hardly control his rage now that the commandant was at his mercy. Jackson stood and kicked him twice in the ribs. The commandant curled up in a fetal position, groaning. Jackson crouched next to the commandant again and said through clenched teeth, "You fucking little shit! I should beat you to death with my own hands!" He punched the commandant in the face, then again, and then he felt himself losing control. Jackson might have gone on beating him, but he could hear Sabina pleading with him to stop.

He looked to her and was suddenly ashamed of his violence.

"Are you okay?" Jackson asked her, trying hard to control his rage. He began cutting her loose with the scalpel.

"Is he dead? Did you kill him?" Sabina asked as she threw off the ropes that he had cut through.

"He's not dead."

"Good," she said. Sabina searched for the white sheet of paper and found it lying on the floor next to the table. She wiped the blood from her nose, covered her body with her free hand as best she could, and handed him the paper. "Is it helpful?" she asked as she pulled on her nurse's uniform. "Does it tell you what you needed to know?"

"It's a hit list," he told her, his voice trembling, the adrenaline still racing through his body. "A list of close to fifty Serbs and their probable whereabouts. Next to each name is a dollar amount."

"Your friend came here to kill them?"

"Yes. And it looks like he was going to be well paid for it."

"But why?"

Jackson frowned, trying to hide his confusion. "I told you. There's a wealthy man who's sympathetic to the Bosnians. He obviously feels that if some of these men are eliminated, there's a chance for a Bosnian victory, or at least peace."

"How could that be? How could killing a few men end the terror? There will always be another to take his place."

"I know. It doesn't make sense," Jackson admitted.

"And to murder another man. . . ."

"Yes. It surprises me that Mr. Katz would sanction it. But the men on this list are killers, Sabina. If anyone deserves to die, they do." He looked down on the commandant. "And guess who's on the list."

The commandant cowered in fear.

"You mustn't kill him," Sabina pleaded.

"He's on the list."

Sabina pulled Jackson aside and whispered to him. "If you kill him, things will be worse here."

"How could they be?"

"Things were very much worse when I arrived. Back then, I was just another one of the girls who was raped in the red house or the administration building, before the commandant made me his special woman. After he took me for himself, he would rape me and beat me, but at least it was only one man a night, not six or seven. When I became pregnant, instead of throwing me out into the world to have a Serb baby, he kept me here. He told me he fell in love with me."

"So you're in love with him?"

"Don't be crazy. But knowing how he felt about me, I was able to reason with him. Before I became his woman, prisoners starved to death within weeks. Now prisoners get one meal every day. And before, the girls were raped every night until they died or became pregnant. I convinced him to let me set up a camp hospital, and I arranged the rotation so they could rest. Many have lived that would have died."

"Sabina—"

"Without the commandant, do you know who would take over? The chief investigator. Believe me, that man is even more insane."

"You want him to live? After everything he's done to you?"

"Yes," she said, no longer whispering. "I know he will kill me when you're gone. But even if you kill the commandant, the other Serbs will kill me anyway. The chief investigator and the commander of the guard both want me dead. There is much resentment against me here. I will not live through this night. Forget about me. I am already dead."

"Will he really kill you?" Jackson whispered. "You're carrying his baby."

"Do not think of me. But please, you cannot kill him. I am dead already, whether he lives or not. He is better for the camp than the others would be. Just go. I wish you luck, whatever your real name is."

Jackson looked at the list again. "I didn't come here to kill anyone. Maybe I could if . . . if I thought that killing him could change anything, but. . . ."

"It cannot. That is why you should go now. If I am to die tomorrow, I would at least like to see you make it out of the camp alive."

Sabina went into the bedroom and came back with a sheet draped over her shoulders. Jackson tore the sheet into strips. He bound the commandant, gagged him, dragged him into the bedroom, and put him in the closet.

He turned around to see if Sabina was watching. Now that he was alone with the commandant, he thought about Katz. Katz had lived through the Nazi concentration camps. He had been involved with more charitable work, more relief missions, than perhaps any man on the face of the planet.

*Who am I to question such a man's tactics?* he thought. *Even if it doesn't seem right to me to kill the commandant, who am I to question Katz's plan?*

When he was sure she hadn't followed him into the bedroom, Jackson took out the scalpel. He stood over the commandant.

The commandant struggled and tried to call for help, but he was bound and gagged tightly and couldn't move or make a sound. He was defenseless. Jackson dropped to his knees and looked at the commandant.

The commandant leaned as far back as he could and groaned, a high-pitched wail from his throat. Jackson watched without sympathy as the commandant began to weep and plead for his life with his eyes.

"What would your men think of you now," Jackson said finally as the commandant continued to shriek through his gag. "You sound like a pig."

Jackson stood and suddenly slammed the closet door shut. He noticed that his hands were shaking as he carefully slid the scalpel into his pocket.

There was a bottle of slivovitz on a dresser. He took a long drink, coughed for a moment, then had another mouthful. He stumbled back into the dining room with the bottle in his hand, but Sabina wasn't there. He looked about and could see her in the office, rifling through the commandant's desk. He took another drink. When he looked back, she was rolling up a blanket on the commandant's desk. She jumped when she noticed him there, watching her.

She nodded at the blanket. "The nights are getting cold."

"How do you feel?" he asked her from the doorway.

"I am fine. He had only just begun to discipline me."

"No. I mean, do you feel strong enough to travel? What I mean is, I think you should come with me."

She stared back at him, started to say something, stopped, and told him, "But you are a strong man and can get away from here quickly. I would only slow you down."

"It's your decision. It'll be dangerous, of course. But if you want to come, you won't slow me down. My plan doesn't depend on speed. You said yourself the dogs will catch me before I can leave the area. The whole countryside will be looking for me. Especially with the list missing, they'll hunt for me until I'm caught."

"Then how do you propose to escape?"

"You don't know?"

She nodded. "It is a great risk."

He shrugged. "I know. It's your decision. But I think he'll kill you if you stay, and even if he doesn't, what do you expect will happen to your child when it's born? Do you really expect to stay alive in here and care for your child? Eventually he'll kill you. He'll be too drunk some night and beat you too much. Your baby will grow up a Serb, just like its father. It will be taught to hate Muslims. It will never be told of you."

"Please. . . ." She began to cry.

"You're coming with me." He reached for her. She instinctively jerked away from his hand and covered her face.

When she looked back up at him she saw that he was merely holding his hand out to her. Reluctantly, she placed her hand in his. He held it gently and they walked out from behind the desk.

"We'll need a place to hide while they search—" Jackson began.

"I know a place," she interrupted.

"Are you ready to go right now?"

Sabina ran her hand through her long blond hair, wincing when it passed over the back of her head where the commandant had punched her. "I have been ready for a long, long time."

"Good. First, we need food and water for several days."

"I have stored some in the infirmary."

"Okay. Let's go."

# 27

THE GUARD NAMED DUSKO was sitting on the steps to the administration building, cold and bored. He much preferred the warmth of the white house, where he felt useful torturing Muslims and Croats. Even better than the white house was the red house or some of the rooms in the administration building, where he fulfilled his duty to Serbia by impregnating the Turkish whores, although, he had to admit, he did not completely understand how that worked. He knew the Turks had harems and were trying to conquer the Serbs by outbreeding them, but wouldn't a Muslim woman raped by a Serb bear a half-Serb, half-Muslim baby? What use was that? The child would only be half good.

But Dusko didn't question things much. He tried to stifle these doubts. Such as when he wondered about the inexplicable behavior of the commandant, who hated Muslims, tortured Muslims, killed Muslims—yet slept every night with the same Muslim whore. It was as though he cared for her. What Serb other than the commandant slept with the same Turk night after night? Dusko himself had raped dozens, but rarely the same Turk more than a few times. It was once explained to him that the commandant was waiting for the Turkish nurse to have his baby, but that brought him back to the vexing problem of the baby being half-Muslim. What kind of a Serb would want a half-Muslim baby?

He didn't know, so he didn't consider the question any longer. That was what he did when he didn't know the answers. He had a blind faith in his leaders, especially in the chief investigator and the commander of the guard.

*What great leaders of men they are,* he thought. *They are true Serbs. But what of the commandant?* Dusko scratched his head, searching for an answer. *Some of the men say he is half Montenegrin.*

Dusko heard someone coming from inside, so he was instantly on his feet. He stood back as the door swung open, and watched as the Turk doctor helped the Turk nurse down the steps.

"I'm bringing the woman to the hospital," Jackson said to him.

"What do I care?" Dusko grunted.

Sabina spoke in a soft voice. She was holding the rolled blanket under her arm. "The commandant does not wish to be disturbed until the morning."

"I wasn't planning on going in there," Dusko growled.

"And you will let no one else go in, Dusko, or you will suffer the consequences. He is not in a forgiving mood tonight."

Dusko watched her limp away with the help of the Turk doctor.

*I suppose the commandant is a true Serb after all,* he thought, *because though he has taken a single Turkish whore to be his alone, at least he still beats her often. That shows that he is a true Serb.*

Dusko took his seat on the steps. He was still cold, but he was content now that he had come to a conclusion about the commandant's loyalty.

Sabina pointed to the ceiling above the sink in the camp hospital. Jackson jumped up on the sink, pushed aside a panel in the roof, pulled himself up, and found a small pack.

"Go back to sleep," Sabina whispered to one of the girls, who had awakened.

"What's in there?" Jackson asked, handing her the pack. She stuffed the blanket in the pack and threw it over her shoulder.

"Food. Water. A compass and map," Sabina answered.

The Muslim girl tried to sit up in bed. "What are you doing?"

"Nothing. Go to sleep," Jackson said harshly.

The girl's face lit up in astonishment when she saw him. "It's you!"

Jackson jumped off the sink and came over to her. "Martina?"

"Is my brother with you? And my mother and sister? Is JuJu here?"

Her face was bruised and she looked as frail as a living human could look, but Jackson could recognize JuJu's sister. It took him a few seconds to get over the shock of seeing her there. "I . . . I don't know," he lied. He did not know what happened to her mother and sister, but West had told him that the boy was dead. "We got separated after the Chetniks attacked the house."

Martina let her head fall back onto the pillow. Tears ran out of the corners of her eyes, past her ears to the back of her neck. She took several deep breaths before she could speak. "I fear for them so much. Especially Selma. I fear that she will be brought here. I hope she is dead."

"I'm sure she's all right," he said lamely.

Jackson walked over to Sabina and whispered, "How is she?"

"It is very bad for these girls from the small towns. You cannot imagine the things that have been done to her before she arrived here. Being in this camp is probably a relief for her."

"But is she part of the rotation?"

"Yes."

Jackson leaned against the wall to steady himself.

"You mustn't think of her if it troubles you to do so," Sabina said. "You must think now only of escaping. If we are caught, you will end up like your friend. It will be even worse for me."

Jackson looked over at the bed where West was lying. He slowly made his way over to it and opened West's eyelids.

"Yes, he is still alive," Sabina said from behind him. "They often let them recover so they can torture them again. Especially this one, whom the chief investigator feared very much."

Jackson gently lifted West's head and slid the pillow out. He looked at Sabina, who returned his gaze without blinking. He carefully put the pillow over West's face. A few seconds later, West's head began to thrash from side to side. Startled, Jackson pulled the pillow up.

"Give it to me," Sabina demanded. Jackson looked at her in astonishment. "I have done it before," she told him, taking the pillow.

Jackson turned his back and walked to the far end of the room. He heard West's bed shake for a full minute. When there was silence, Sabina walked up behind him.

"We must go now," she said softly.

Jackson swallowed hard and nodded. *So that's it?* he thought. *It's as simple as that? No medals for West, no soldier's burial? A life has just ended here in this room, the life of a man I knew. He wasn't a friend—I didn't even like him. But I knew him and I guess I was even responsible for seeing him safely through Bosnia. Maybe I should go to him, say something, or do something other than just leaving without even looking at him one last time. Was West religious? Should I say a prayer for him?*

"*Amerikanac,*" he heard Martina call out, interrupting his thoughts.

He cleared his throat. "What about the girl? Can she travel?" he whispered to Sabina.

"She cannot even walk."

He had to clear his throat again. "I can carry her."

"We are not taking her."

"But—"

"She's not well enough," Sabina told him plainly.

"We can't leave her here—"

"There's nothing you can do," she insisted.

"*Amerikanac.*" Martina called for him again.

Jackson walked slowly back to Martina's bed. He held her hand and looked at her in the eye. He started to say something but soon began to weep. "If there was anything I could do . . . ," he managed finally. He put his face into her sheets and sobbed. When he finally looked up, he couldn't look at the girl.

"You are escaping. Am I right?" she asked. Jackson did not answer. "I won't betray you," she promised.

"Lie back, Martina," Sabina said. "It is as we discussed last night," Sabina whispered in the girl's ear. She stood and winked, patting the pack.

"Will you ask the *Amerikanac* air force to bomb this camp?" Martina asked Jackson.

He dropped to his knees, putting his arms around the girl and resting his head against her. His body was shaking and heaving with emotion.

"I'm so sorry," he sobbed. "I'm so sorry. I'm so sorry."

Sabina put her arms around him and tried to lift him, but he stayed there, crying into the sheets. "There is nothing to be sorry about," Sabina told him. "The girl will be fine. Won't you, Martina?"

"Yes," Martina said after a pause. Then she turned Jackson's head so she could see his face. "You must see Sabina to safety. By helping her, you will be helping all of us."

He looked at the girl, at her smooth skin, like a baby's, at the bright eyes, the white teeth smiling at him.

"Listen to her," Sabina said. "I need you. I am relying on you to get us out of here. Think what will happen to both of us if we're caught."

Jackson was kneeling at the bedside, looking at the girl. Neither Sabina nor Martina spoke for a long moment. Finally he stood and took a deep breath, wiping his eyes on his shirtsleeves. For the second time that night, he had felt ashamed in front of Sabina, this time for being weak. He reached for the girl's hand and said, "Good-bye, Martina."

"May Allah protect you," Martina said, taking his hand.

Jackson turned abruptly and walked out of the camp hospital.

Sabina hugged the girl, tears welling up in her eyes now. "Remember what we talked about last night. Do not give up, Martina," Sabina said, then rushed out of the room.

Jackson followed Sabina down the corridor.

"The place I told you about is upstairs," she said flatly, all business now that they were on the move. "The upper floors of the warehouse are no longer used. There is a small room where nobody ever goes. I have the only key."

They took the stairs to the third floor, then all the way to the end of the long corridor. She took out the key and opened the door. Once inside, Jackson was overpowered by the stench.

"What is this place?" he asked her.

"This is where the commandant used to have his women. This is where I met him the first time."

"What's that smell?"

"There are bodies in the closet."

"What?"

"Don't worry. He has all but forgotten about this place. They use the sheds and the administration building now for their rapes and murders and torture. They tired of climbing the stairs."

"Why are there bodies in the closet?"

"He used to save them."

"The commandant?" Jackson gasped.

"Don't think of that. You must go now. I will wait here."

"Can you . . . Will you be all right here? Isn't there another room to wait in?"

"This is the safest place. Please, go. Hurry."

He bent and tore off a piece of the bottom of her nurse's uniform, stuck it in his pocket, and went to the door. "If I don't make it back, I don't know what you'll do."

Sabina shrugged. "If you are not back before sunup, I am throwing myself out that window."

Jackson nodded.

"Godspeed, Emir."

"Robert. My name is Robert Jackson."

Sabina smiled weakly. "It is a good American name," she said in English. "Many nights I have prayed for America to come and save my people."

"I better go."

"Godspeed, Robert."

## 28

**JACKSON JUMPED OUT THE WINDOW** at the end of the first-floor hallway and ran to the back of the warehouse. He counted down the windows until he reached the seventh. He looked for a sentry's light, but saw none. He dashed for the wire and hit the ground.

He took out the wire cutters and hastily began cutting the double barbed wire while kneeling in the dirt. Each time he cut the wire, it made a click that in the quiet and tenseness of the night sounded extremely loud to him. He was just about through when he heard a voice from behind.

"Vasily? Is that you?"

Jackson lay flat on the ground and rolled away from the wire.

Dusko reached for his flashlight and shined it along the length of the wire, passing over the section Jackson had begun cutting through. He did not notice anything, so he continued to shine his light up and down. Dusko was almost up to Jackson, whom he could not see in the darkness. Then the light swept back and stopped on the cut wire. Dusko halted. He took a few steps closer. Jackson stood now, directly behind him. Just as Dusko was taking a deep breath to let out a call for help, Jackson had his arm around his throat in a choke hold.

Dusko hit the ground with Jackson on top of him. The guard pulled out a pistol and aimed it over his shoulder at Jackson. Jackson quickly grabbed Dusko's wrist and forced the muzzle of the pistol into the back of Dusko's head.

If a shot rang out, Jackson knew he would be caught. But he knew the guard could not fire as long as he had the gun to the guard's head.

Dusko was already suffocating, but Jackson squeezed even more tightly. At first he thought that he would kill Dusko because, if he didn't, the guard might jeopardize the escape. That meant not only his life, it also meant Sabina's. But as he felt Dusko's grasp on the pistol begin to weaken, Jackson was not so sure anymore.

*He's a man,* Jackson thought. *A soldier. He was probably drafted and hates it here. He probably has a wife and kids at home. How can I kill such a man? I know he's a Serb and that he's a guard at this hell on earth, but he's probably a good man and wishes he wasn't here.*

In a minute, Dusko let go of the gun and then Jackson had it. He was sitting on Dusko's back now as Dusko gasped for air. Jackson took the gun and slammed it down on the back of Dusko's head once, then again. He felt Dusko's body go limp.

He dragged Dusko to the fence, finished cutting through the wire, pulled Dusko through and carried him part of the way down the trail. He searched Dusko's pockets but found nothing of use. He pocketed the pistol and the flashlight, went back to the wire, and stuck the torn piece of Sabina's dress on one of the barbs. He returned to Dusko, dragged him into some bushes, and made sure he was still unconscious.

When Jackson saw Dusko's face again, he noticed that it was the guard who had tortured the prisoners outside of the cages. He was suddenly overcome with anger, and an intense hatred rose up inside of him, causing him to grip the barrel of the pistol and raise it over his head, ready to repeatedly slam the handle into Dusko's skull.

But Jackson had never killed a man before. As angry as he was, as much as he despised Dusko and wished him dead, Dusko was unconscious, defenseless. With an effort, Jackson shoved the pistol in his belt behind his back. Although he was a soldier and Dusko was the enemy, Jackson refused to become a murderer.

*If there is a God, he'll be punished,* Jackson said to himself as he ran down the path into the welcome cover of the dense forest.

After ten minutes of running, the trail ended. He was on the road now. After checking the map, he set off alternately running and walking down the road. He hid in the trees every time a truck from the camp passed by. An hour later, he could see the lights of the town so he stayed in the woods and hiked parallel to the road. Once in town, he stayed in the shadows of the moonlight until he found the train station.

He walked down the tracks in both directions, scouting out the lay of the land. He finally found a spot a half mile from the station where there was a small bridge safely out of view of the station.

*The train will have to go slowly until it passes over the bridge,* he said to himself.

He headed back through the town, taking only dark and empty streets. As he was walking through a dark alley, four guards from the camp came flying out a back door of a tavern, stinking drunk. He ducked into the shadows and waited for them to stumble up the alley.

Jackson found a bicycle chained to a fence nearby. He used his wire cutters to cut the chain, then set off on the bicycle back toward the camp. When he knew he was close, he ditched the bicycle deep in the woods. He searched in the moonlight until he found a small fallen pine tree. He dragged it to the road and left it there.

He waited for another two hours, but not one vehicle passed. He was beginning to get worried. The night before, when he had scouted out the main gate, there had been many trucks coming and going. Now, much to his dismay, not a single truck was heading for the camp. He couldn't go back through the wire because he would leave footprints back to the warehouse. He began working on a contingency plan, but before he came up with anything, the fatigue of the past several days finally caught up to him and he fell asleep.

A few hours later, just before sunup, Jackson awoke with a start. He was lying in the woods a few feet from the road. He could see the first hint of light in the east, and could hear shouts and whistles coming from inside the camp. The Serbs must have found the hole in the wire.

Thoughts whirred so quickly in his head that he became dizzy and had to put his head back down for a moment. Panic set in.

*This isn't the way it was supposed to happen!*

Two motorcycles from the camp went flying down the road.

There were more and more shouts from the camp. He looked through the branches and over the treetops in the distance, noticing that the sky was growing red. He could hear an alarm sounding now from the camp.

Hearing another truck coming, he lay flat on the leaves and pine needles. He watched and waited, wondering in which direction the truck was going. Then he saw it, heading for the camp, and pulled himself to his knees. Just when it passed him, it screeched to a halt. He crawled to the side of the road. He saw a guard get out of the passenger's-side door to remove the pine tree.

Jackson ran, crouching low, and climbed into the back of the covered army truck. When it was moving again, he felt around with his hands. He could detect nothing in the darkness other than the stickiness of the floor, but he knew that was nothing for him to fear. It was only half-dried blood from the corpses removed from the camp in the night.

The truck slowed and stopped at the gate. "What's going on, Milan?" the driver asked the guard.

"There's been an escape."

"All of this because there has been an escape?" the driver asked, waving at the guards assembling in the compound. He began to laugh. "These prisoners are such fools. It's impossible to escape."

"The commander of the guard seems particularly upset this time."

"I would bet a month's pay the prisoner is returned by noon."

"Dead or alive?" the guard joked.

"Who cares?" the driver said, laughing as the truck pulled away.

The truck pulled into the compound. In a minute it slowed to stop, so Jackson quickly looked out, jumped, and ran behind the cover of the white shed. He was still dressed in the black shirt and olive green pants and his black army boots. Even if every guard had already been instructed that he was wearing their uniform, the last place they would expect to see him was inside the compound. He ran into the courtyard and joined dozens of Chetniks and guards who were running frantically in every direction, trying to organize search teams. He ran right for the warehouse, through the door, up the three flights of stairs, and down the long corridor. He knocked on the door furiously, but oddly, Sabina did not answer.

He put his ear to the door and could hear Sabina inside the room, pulling open the window.

He pounded on the door again and shouted, "It's Robert!"

He put his ear to the door again. Now there was silence.

He pounded on the door.

"It's Robert Jackson. I'm alone. Sabina? Open the door!"

He heard the key go into the lock. Soon it clicked open and she was there, holding the door open for him. He slid by her and immediately slumped to the floor, out of breath.

"I was beginning to think you wouldn't make it," she said. Jackson could see the window was open and the sun was a red ball on the horizon.

"You can close the window," he told her. "Now we wait."


After resting for a few minutes, Jackson went to the window and watched the guards running about as the hue and cry went out that there had been an escape. The commander of the guard was inspecting the cut fence in his bare feet, holding the torn piece of Sabina's nurse's uniform.

The commander of the guard hurried down the trail, disappearing into the woods. He returned a minute later with a guard who was carrying Dusko over his shoulder. The commander of the guard appeared to be in a rage.

A minute later, the chief investigator stormed out of the administration building, closely followed by the commandant. The two men stood there shouting and pointing at each other.

For the rest of the day, Jackson watched with pleasure as almost every guard was sent out in jeeps and trucks and motorcycles. A pack of dogs was gathered and set loose to follow their tracks from the cut wire in the fence.

After a couple hours, Jackson tired of watching. He sat down, feeling confident that everything was working as planned. The dogs would follow his scent to the train tracks. If the Serbs did not conclude that he had gotten out on the train, the dogs would follow his scent back to the town. From there he had set out on the bicycle. The dogs couldn't track him on a bicycle, so they'd search all the surrounding towns. They would watch the trains. Then, after a few days, they would have to give up. He and Sabina would have all the time in the world to make their real escape, with no concerns about being tracked down by anyone.

# 29

---

JACKSON SPENT MOST OF THE first day of his escape sleeping on the floor, his head resting on Sabina's pack, trying to recover from his night on the run.

"Are you hungry?" Sabina asked when he finally awoke.

"A little. But I can wait. We'll be here for a few more days. If you're hungry, you should eat."

Sabina shook her head. "I can wait. Is there anything I can do for you?"

"No, Sabina. You don't have to worry about me. I'm sorry about last night, with the girl. I'm all right now."

Sabina let it pass, as if she didn't know what he was talking about. "Are you certain you don't want me to prepare you something to eat? It will be a long wait."

"It seems like a long wait. But it's a very short wait when you think of the payoff."

"I don't mean to complain. But are you sure there is nothing I can do for you?"

"I don't need anything."

He watched Sabina rubbing her belly absentmindedly, her pregnancy just beginning to show.

"Did you sleep at all?" he asked her.

"I slept very well."

"You don't look like you slept."

"Oh? I slept very well. Do I look tired?"

"Yes. But you still look beautiful."

She looked down, crossed her arms, and turned away from him.

Soon they heard a disturbance outside. Jackson motioned to her to stay down, then went to the window. There were five men lined up outside the white shed. To his right he could see a group of prisoners brought out to watch. One from the cages, one from the ore-separating building, one from the open mine pit, and two from the field. That way they would go back and tell all the other prisoners in the camp.

Jackson went white when he noticed that Haris was one of the five prisoners ordered to stand against the white shed.

"What is it?" Sabina asked.

He went to her and sat next to her and looked at her directly in the eyes. "It's the five men they're going to kill because of . . . because of us."

Sabina gasped.

"Don't listen to it, Sabina. It'll be over soon."

"I don't want to hear it," she cried, and he could see that whatever it was that had kept her going for those months with the commandant, whatever it was that had allowed her to care for the girls in the camp and save so many of their lives, to pull him together last night, was gone, and the tears began streaming down her cheeks, her eyes red and her chin quivering, lips trembling.

She pulled the blanket over herself and huddled next to him.

"Sing to me," she said.

"What? Sing?"

"Yes. Sing to me."

"I . . . I don't sing."

"Talk about something then."

Before he had a chance to open his mouth, the first shot rang out. Sabina jumped at the sound. She looked at Jackson pleadingly.

He swallowed hard.

"Please talk to me!" Sabina said urgently. "I do not want to hear the shots."

"Talk about what?"

"Talk to me about anything. Talk to me about America."

He didn't want to talk about America. How could he think of anything but the five men that were about to die because he was trying to save his own life? But Sabina insisted, so he found himself saying, "I was from California."

"Go on. Keep talking. Is it warm there?"

"Yes," he said, and when he paused they heard the second shot. Sabina put her arm around him and held him tightly.

"Yes, in many parts it's warm," he said, and now he was talking fast because he wanted to be talking when the next shots were fired. "In other places it can be cold. There are mountains that rise from the sea. It can be very warm at the beaches and snowing in the mountains at the same time."

He remembered that it was only days ago that he had told Emir about the beaches and the mountains, and how Emir had wanted to learn much more, and had wanted a promise from Jackson that they would go there together.

"They make movies in California," he told her. "In Los Angeles, there are movie stars everywhere. When I was your age I'd drive down there with some friends to go to the clubs"—the third shot rang out—"and I'd see movie stars and rock stars and sometimes I'd crash parties in Beverly Hills, where all the people are very wealthy. But I got tired of that, and went to college near San Francisco, which is a more beautiful city than L.A. There are lots of pretty houses and cable cars, and less than an hour away is the wine country, which is beautiful to ride through, particularly if you have a convertible—or a Jeep, like I had. Then there's Lake Tahoe, which is great because there's skiing in the winter and boating in the summer. I worked up there for a couple of summers, in a casino, dealing blackjack. It was a lot of fun for a while, but then college was over and I had to join the army. I was sent to Georgia, which is a southern state, in the old Confederacy, if you know anything about the Civil War—"

"I only counted four shots," Sabina said, interrupting him.

Jackson listened to the silence for a moment. He walked to the window and could see that, although four others were lying dead at his feet, Haris was still standing. Jackson was hoping that meant that Haris was to be spared, but soon a fat guard with a goatee walked toward him holding a long wooden spear with a sharp metal spike atop it. The fat man with the goatee greased the spear with lard, dropped it next to Haris, and took out a bowie knife.

Turning away, Jackson hurried back to Sabina.

"Listen to me, Sabina. Listen to me only. I'll talk to you about America. Let me tell you where I'll take you when we get out of here. There are so many things to see there. Listen to me now, only me, very closely. I'll tell you how great it will be in America. Promise you'll only listen to me and nothing else. I'll talk to you about America all day if I have to. . . ."

# 30

FOUR DAYS LATER THE CAMP had returned to normal—or as normal as it had been before the escape. The Serbs had stopped sending men out to search. The compound was now quiet, especially during the day, when many of the guards were sleeping off hangovers. Jackson and Sabina continued to wait in the darkness of their room high up in the warehouse.

"There are three more crackers," she said to him just after midnight.

"You eat them." Jackson went over to the window.

"Are you sure?"

"You eat them. But not right now. It's time."

Sabina looked up at him with little expression. "Could you help me up?"

That was not a good sign. The first night of their escape she had been very clever and strong. But since then, she had become more and more withdrawn, weaker and more frightened, with each passing day. He could hardly blame her. For the first day or two he had been the one who almost cracked, first over Martina, then over what they did to Haris. Then it was the difficulty of the waiting that got to him, but he had had to pull himself together because Sabina seemed practically helpless now without him.

He helped her to her feet and held her by the shoulders, pulling her close to make sure she was listening to him. "You must promise not to speak anymore," he said sternly. "Don't talk again until we're miles from the camp. And when I say to do something, or if I point somewhere, you will go immediately, with no hesitation."

She nodded her head.

He used her key to unlock the door. The sentry's pistol was in his hand. They sneaked down the hallway and down the stairs to the door because he thought it would be too difficult for her to make it out the window in her condition. He waited for a sentry to pass, then they hurried behind the warehouse and hid in the shadows of the moonlight underneath the seventh window from the right.

After a few seconds he sprinted to the fence. In a few minutes he cut through the wire where it had been repaired and he came back for her. They rushed to the fence, climbed through the wire, and he directed her down the path. He fixed the wire the best he could to ensure that the sentry wouldn't notice that it had been cut through again. Holding her arm, they walked quickly away from the camp. They didn't speak until they were on the road.

"If a car comes, we hide in the woods. If it stops, don't make a sound."

She nodded but he could not see her.

For close to two hours they walked down the road, being forced to hide in the forest several times. Eventually they reached the town, where he was careful not to be seen by even the most harmless-looking peasant. He thought the townspeople might still be looking for a pregnant woman with a man. There were few people about in the early morning and he was very careful, so they did not run into anyone. They walked along the tracks until they came to the bridge, then they lay down on the fallen leaves in the woods along the tracks.

"In the morning a train will come," Jackson said to her. "It will be traveling slowly until it passes over the bridge. We'll go out there when it approaches. Then I'll run toward the train and climb on. When you see me coming back on the train, start running. When I come to you I'll grab you and pull you up. You have to run as fast as you can in the direction the train is traveling, and you have to help me pull you up. Do you understand?"

She nodded her head.

•    •    •

The train set out at eight-fifteen in the morning. Jackson watched from his place in the woods to make sure there was nobody watching, then sprinted and easily hopped onto a cattle car. He pulled the door open and quickly got into position, hanging off the car by one arm. He readied his free arm to grab hold of Sabina. She was ahead now, running as fast as she could, occasionally holding her small, round belly with one hand.

When Jackson called to her she looked over her shoulder and held up an arm. He grabbed it and held on as hard as he could. Sabina swung behind initially as he swept her off her feet. He pulled her up and she made a nimble move to get her foot on the train. She put her arms around him and, in so doing, knocked the pistol out of his belt where he had stuffed it behind his back. It fell to the tracks rushing beneath them. They tumbled inside the cattle car, where they were immediately overcome by the odor of dung and perspiration.

"The gun! I'm so sorry!" Sabina cried right away.

"It's not your fault," Jackson assured her. "I shouldn't have put it there. Hopefully, we won't need it." In truth, losing the gun upset him very much, but he knew it was important not to upset her.

Scattered all along the wooden floor was trampled human waste, and discarded clothes lay in the corners. Jackson picked up a tattered copy of the Koran before Sabina noticed it. He held it behind his back and went to the door, tossing it out when he thought she was not looking. He slid the heavy door shut, cutting off the sound of a cock crowing at a nearby farm.

"You don't have to hide things from me," Sabina said. "I am well aware of the use the Serbs are making of these trains."

He wasn't going to ask her what she knew, but as she sat on the dirty wooden floor she told him matter-of-factly that she had been brought to Omarska by train. After Jackson sat down in a spot she brushed clean for him, she began the story of how it had happened in her town. It was very similar to Haris's story, and to what happened at the town on the Sana River.

"The town leaders were beaten, taken out back, and lined up

in front of a ditch, where they were shot in the head. They toppled over into the ditch, which was then filled in. The Serbs played soccer over the mass grave the next day," Sabina went on in a monotone voice as she stared at the walls of the cattle car. "They kept the women in the school gym and raped us. I was a virgin before that day, and so were many others. The ones who were beyond childbearing years were killed or driven away. Many Serbs didn't want to rape us, but they said they were under orders."

"Orders?" Jackson asked. "Rapes occurred in the town I was in, and they happened in the town of one of the prisoners I met in the camp. Now your town, too. Who could give such orders? Who has such authority over all the Serbs in Bosnia?"

"They are certainly being ordered," Sabina insisted. "Two times I have been in a room with Serbs who did not want to rape me. They told me to shout and yell like I am being raped. They ripped off my clothes, but they did not touch me. However, they told me I must tell the others they raped me, or else they said they would kill me." She looked at him now. "Do you not like hearing this? Should I be ashamed?"

"Of course not. But if you don't want to talk about it, you don't have to tell me."

She looked away, at the walls of the cattle car. "They picked certain girls and brought us to the trains several days later. We were all packed into one car. There was no food and no toilet. There was also no water and it was very hot. Many passed out. In every town along the way they stopped and picked up more people, men or women, and filled the rest of the cars. We came to the station in Omarska, where we were loaded into trucks and brought to the camp."

Jackson was astounded at the extent of the Serbs' terror. Northern Bosnia must have been 90 percent Muslim before the war. The Serbs were trying to relocate almost the entire population.

He went to put his arm around her to hold her, but she slid out from under it and moved away from him.

"I'm sorry," he said. "I didn't mean anything. I thought it would make you feel better."

She didn't look at him.

"It's cold in here," he said after an awkward moment.

Sabina took the blanket out of the pack and wrapped it around herself. "I'm fine," she said, though he could see she was shivering.

"This train could be going to your town," he said, hoping that whatever he did wrong could be forgotten.

"Perhaps. But it could go in several directions."

"If you watch outside, will you be able to tell if we're headed to your town?"

"Before the war, I rode the train often to visit my sister."

"I want you to sit here, next to the door. You can just see out, right here through this crack. I want you to keep watch, to see where we're going."

She sat where he told her to as he went to the opposite side of the cattle car. He jumped and grabbed hold of the ledge of the small window in the top of the car, which was used to provide air to the cattle.

"What are you doing?" she asked him.

He pulled himself up and looked about, then dropped to the floor of the car. "I'm going to keep an eye on the sun and the shadows so I can tell what direction we're going. What direction is your town?"

"Why don't you use the compass?" she asked, taking it out of the pack and handing it to him. "My town is north, and a little bit west. Are we going there?"

"Is there anyone there who can help us?"

"I have many friends," Sabina said, after pausing to think. "But most are probably dead or gone. I had some Serb friends, though, who should still be there. I am sure they would help us."

"How sure?" he asked.

"They are very good friends," Sabina said, but then corrected herself, "I mean, they *were* good friends."

"We'll see. We have to get off somewhere fairly soon. I don't want to be on this train when they start loading it up for a return trip to Omarska. We'll have to jump eventually. Can you do it?"

"Will the train be going slowly, like at the bridge?"

"I'll try to make it a place where the train is going slowly."

"Then yes, I can do it. Especially if you go first and catch me."

"What about your baby?"

"Don't worry about that," she told him.

The train rattled on. Sabina stared out of the crack by the door at the countryside rolling by. Every fifteen or twenty minutes, even though he had the compass, Jackson pulled himself up to the windows high up in the car. He saw the green rolling hills, so much like Switzerland. He saw the green-gray, rocky mountaintops, like those in Italy. The sky was blue, the air was clean and cool, and the sun warmed his face through the small window.

## 31

SABINA AND JACKSON WERE BOTH looking through the crack by the cattle-car door. Jackson saw a town—at least, he knew there was a town because he could see a church spire and a minaret rising side by side from behind the huge oak trees.

"Is it your town?" Jackson asked Sabina.

"No. It is my sister's town."

"Where are we?"

She pointed to the town on the map. "Here. Near Banja Luka."

Jackson stood and prepared himself to open the door. "We're getting out."

"Here? Or when the train stops?"

"Look, if you can't do it, we can try to slip out at the station. But it would be much safer to jump now. There might be soldiers—or Chetniks—at the station."

"We better jump now," Sabina agreed.

Jackson looked at her protruding belly and reconsidered. "No, it's too dangerous for you. We'll wait."

"Open the door," she insisted. "You go first."

"Are you sure?"

"You better hurry," Sabina told him quickly.

He pulled the heavy door open and waited for a stretch of even terrain, then jumped, rolled, and popped right up. He sprinted after the train, which was slowing as it neared the station. Sabina was sticking her head out of the car, looking back at him.

Jackson had almost caught up to her when suddenly Sabina threw herself from the cattle car. She hit the ground hard and tumbled several times. He knelt beside her, rolling her gently onto her back and brushing the blond hair out of her eyes.

She looked up at him and forced a smile. "I think I am all right," she groaned. "But may I lay here for a moment?"

"No. We might be seen."

He lifted Sabina into his arms and carried her across the road that paralleled the train tracks, where there was a wheat field they could hide in while she rested. When he laid her down she inched away from him and pushed his hands away. He backed away and knelt there, watching her.

She insisted that she was fine, but he could tell that she was in pain. "My sister's house is on the other side of the town," Sabina told him, grimacing as a sharp pain shot through her belly.

Jackson looked up at the bullet-riddled minaret. "All right, but let's walk around the outskirts of the town," he suggested, trying to hide his concern.

"Help me up," she asked.

"It's all right to rest here longer."

"I will rest at Tina's house." Sabina tried to get up but could not. "Can you help me?"

"I'll have to put my arm around you."

Sabina nodded that it was all right. He put his arm around her shoulder and helped her to her feet. She pushed his hands away and insisted on walking without assistance through the wheat field, then down a dirt road where they passed a white stucco farmhouse. They slowly made their way down quiet tree-lined streets until they neared a cluster of whitewashed houses with red-tiled roofs. Sabina picked up the pace as they approached her sister's house.

Jackson was going to advise caution, but the house was in perfect shape, the front lawn and garden immaculate. Three children on bicycles pedaled past them, laughing as they went. A man down the street was contentedly painting his house, while across the street a boy was mowing the lawn. Jackson finally allowed himself to relax. The neighborhood appeared perfectly safe.

When they were nearly in the yard, Sabina tried to run but immediately bent over in pain, holding her belly. Jackson tried to help her, but she pushed him away and suddenly reached into her pack, pulling out a gun. She aimed it at his head.

"Don't touch me again!" Sabina screamed through clenched teeth. Jackson stood still with his hands raised as she slowly backed away until she was in her sister's yard, turning and struggling to make it to the front door. He saw her knock on the door weakly before bending over again, dropping the gun and holding on to her stomach. Jackson ran to her, but just before he reached her, the front door opened and he froze.

"Yes?" a hard-looking woman asked testily. She was wearing a housecoat and a red scarf around her head. She held a broom in her hands.

"Where is Tina?" Sabina asked urgently.

"You have the wrong house."

"No. I'm sure this is it."

"There is no Tina here," the woman insisted, sizing them both up. "Go away."

The woman tried to close the door, but Jackson held it open. Sabina was startled to see him standing behind her.

"We mean you no harm, woman," Jackson assured her. "This is Sabina, Tina's sister."

Suddenly the woman looked happy to see them. "Oh! Please, please, come in." When the woman was not looking, Jackson picked up the gun and stuffed it in his belt behind his back. "I am Anna Radja. Come right this way, I am so happy you're here."

Anna led them directly to the kitchen. She leaned the broom against the counter and stood next to the dishwasher.

"How do you work it?" Anna asked Sabina.

Sabina didn't understand the question.

"The dishwasher," Anna explained. "We have been trying to figure it out, but can't get it to work. You must know how to work it."

Sabina glared at her. "Who are you?" she cried. "Where is Tina?"

"Don't waste our time, woman," Jackson said. "Can't you see she's not well?"

"Where is my sister?" Sabina demanded. "And her family? What happened to them?"

"Leave me alone," Anna warned them, realizing that she had made a very big mistake by letting them in the house. "I'll call the militia. Get out of my house!"

"Your house?" Sabina cried. "How dare you call this your house!"

Anna reached for the telephone but Jackson ripped it out of the wall. "I can't let you do that," he explained coldly.

"What happened to the family that lived here?"

Anna was clearly scared now. "I have no idea."

"Tell us!" Jackson demanded.

"I swear I don't know. I came here to Novi Belgrade after it was liberated from the Muslims—"

"Novi Belgrade?" Sabina repeated. "That's not the name of this town."

"It is now."

Jackson closed his eyes and swore under his breath. "Where are all the Muslims?" he asked, realizing now what had happened in the town.

"Some Muslims fled to Jajce, where they kill Serb babies and feed them to the animals in the zoo—"

"Save the propaganda," Jackson said. "Have any Muslims remained?"

"No. There is not one Muslim left in this town." Anna clasped her hands in front of her face. "Please, don't kill me. My husband and I didn't come here until after the liberation. We didn't harm any Muslims. We came from Šabac, in Serbia. We were promised our own home, and jobs, and free transportation. How could we say no? We were told we would have a dishwasher. In Serbia, we had no jobs. We lived in a one-room apartment—"

"What happened to the Muslim women?" Jackson interrupted.

Anna instinctively lowered her voice. "It is something that is not talked about in the town. By the time my husband and I arrived, there was little trace of the fighting that had taken place. But still, I have heard things—bad things—including what happened to the women. Some were sent off on the train. Many are said to have disappeared. But Jajce is where to look if they are alive. That is the closest Muslim-controlled city."

"How long ago?" Jackson asked.

"About a month. Please, don't kill me."

"How far is Jajce?"

"It's too far to walk," Sabina said weakly. "Where is my sister's car?"

"It . . . it's in the garage. I—"

"Give me the keys," Jackson insisted.

"Excuse me, but you won't get far," Anna said, the initial concern for her life now turning to sympathy for Sabina and her family. "The army has roadblocks all along the road to Jajce. They will ask you for papers."

"We'll take our chances."

"There is a better way," Anna said. "I will drive you. You can both hide in the trunk."

Jackson considered it, then shook his head. "You'll turn us in at the first roadblock."

Anna went to a drawer and pulled out a pistol. Jackson had not even considered that she could be reaching for a gun. He cursed his own stupidity, then tried to decide whether to disarm her or to pull the gun that was behind his back.

"Remember the way it was before the war, when Serbs and Muslims and Croats lived together in the same towns, worked in the same shops, married each other, and trusted each other?" Anna asked, handing the pistol to him. "There. I will trust you. Will you trust me?"

Jackson looked over at Sabina. Suddenly she was sweating and her face was gray. He saw her eyelids flutter momentarily. Then she fainted into Jackson's arms.

## 32

JACKSON SAT IN A metal folding chair at the side of the bed. Sabina was lying under the quilt her mother had made for Tina, her sister. She had stirred several times in the day, rolling her head from side to side and repeating over and over, "Shut the window. Shut the window." But she had not yet opened her eyes.

He still wore the black shirt and olive-colored pants he had been given at the camp. His army boots were at the foot of the bed, along with two empty bottles of Italian *grappa*. Sabina's pistol—a Russian model, Jackson had noticed, probably stolen from the commandant—was stuck barrel-down in one of his boots. He had given the Serb woman, Anna, her pistol back. He had slept very little since Sabina had lost consciousness, and he had eaten almost nothing.

When the door opened, Jackson saw the Serb doctor come in.

"She has not awakened?" the doctor asked. He was in his sixties, completely bald with a gray beard. His bifocals hung from a silver chain around his neck and rested on his chest. He tilted his head back and looked down his crooked nose at Sabina.

"No. She's having the same nightmare," Jackson told him.

"It is no wonder."

"Are you sure she's not in a coma?"

"Yes, although I expected her to regain consciousness by now. But her body has suffered a great trauma, not to mention the mental and emotional shock."

"You can't give her anything?"

"You must be patient."

"It's hard to be patient in this town," Jackson said.

The doctor nodded solemnly and looked over at Jackson. "But you must not blame the entire town. It was a curious thing that happened here. I have not yet come to terms with it. But I know these people, and I know that what they did here is not a reflection of their true selves."

"How can you say that? How many innocent people were murdered here? How many rapes, how many homes stolen—"

"You don't have to remind me what happened in my own town. But let me tell you something. If I tell you, you might choose to hate me. But I would like to tell you because it is the only thing I know about what happened here."

"You're helping us. I won't hate you."

"You might," the doctor said, sighing. He sat on the corner of the bed and began to straighten the quilt. "When the army first surrounded the town, they bombed us for days. Many people were injured. My office was turned into an emergency room. The other doctors in the town were likewise up to their arms in wounded. The wounded were Serb, Muslim, and Croat alike. We couldn't keep up with the injuries, but we did our best, taking the most seriously wounded first, stabilizing them, and moving on to the next most seriously wounded, and so on. Many times, people died while they waited. I slept maybe an hour a night for a week. But I saved many people. I received much help from my neighbors, who also worked around the clock to help me the best they could. If you were here then you would have been very proud of the people of this town. I had Muslims and Serbs and Croats helping me. It didn't matter to any of us whether a wounded was Serb or Muslim or Croat. As I said, the most seriously wounded were treated first."

"You see," Jackson said, "I knew you were a good man."

"But that was before the Chetniks came," the doctor told him. "You have told me about the town on the Sana River, so I do not have to tell you what happened here. It is the same story. When they came and targeted the Muslims and Croats, we Serbs were also very frightened of the Chetniks. What if they mistook us for Muslims and Croats? Many of us began wearing the black shirts and black pants and black gloves of the Chetniks. Many others painted Serb slogans on their houses, so that the Chetniks would not blow them up. To say you are a Serb is one thing, but there was still the possibility that you were a Muslim or Croat sympathizer. Serbs began pointing out fellow Serbs they hated, calling them traitors. My neighbor, a Serb, was killed along with the Muslims because a coworker of his wished to have his job. He told the Chetniks that my neighbor had been hiding Muslims. It wasn't true, but the Chetniks locked him and his family in his basement and burned his house to the ground."

"There was nothing you could do about that," Jackson whispered.

"Of course not. But one night, a Muslim man came by with his two sons. One of them was lying on his back, tied to a board. The boy was only six years old. His back had been broken after he'd been thrown out of a second-floor window by a Chetnik. The father came to me for help. I turned him away. Not only that, but I called the police, which was now run by the Chetniks. They found him and took him away. I don't know what they did to him. I don't want to know. I do know, however, that his son died."

Jackson was leaning forward now, listening intently to the old doctor.

"From then on, I would not treat Muslims or Croats. I have an old German Luger that my father took from a dead Nazi in the Second Great War, which I used to turn Muslims and Croats away from my door at gunpoint."

"How could you do that?" Jackson asked, not attempting to hide his disappointment.

"I was afraid."

Jackson regarded the doctor for a moment. "I can't hate you," he said finally. "I might have done the same thing. I don't like to think I would have, but how can I know?"

"I don't dislike Muslims or Croats," the old doctor said. "I have three daughters. One married a Serb. Another married a Croat, and the third married a Muslim. I love all of my sons-in-law equally. They are all good men. But you have seen what the Chetniks are capable of. I was afraid for my family. I was afraid to die."

Jackson nodded in understanding. "You're at risk now, aren't you?"

"If you were discovered here, yes, I would be in great danger. But if you had done the things that I did when the town was under attack, you would realize that I embrace this opportunity to make amends. I am sick with shame."

"What about Anna and her husband?" Jackson asked. "They've been patient with us, but I sense that their willingness to help is diminishing."

"They are afraid as well. They've heard the stories of the attack, of the executions of Serb traitors. But you have nothing to fear from them. They don't hate *Amerikanacs*. They don't even hate Muslims. They'll let you stay here until this girl is better."

"They'll be happy when we're gone," Jackson said.

"Yes. And so will I. But only because that will mean that the girl is better, and you are on your way to safety." The doctor stood. "When your wife awakens, have Anna come for me."

"She's not my wife."

"Is she your sweetheart?"

"No"

"Who is she?"

"She's a woman I met," Jackson said simply.

The doctor glanced at Sabina. "She's just a girl," he said.


Jackson was sleeping in the folding chair. His hands were clasped on the bed beside Sabina and his head was lying in his outstretched arms. He awoke with a start and saw her smiling at him. Her hand was on top of his. When she saw that he was awake she took back her hand and rested it on her stomach.

"Were you praying for me?" she asked.

"I must have fallen asleep," Jackson said.

"You have been sleeping for quite some time."

"I wanted to be here when you woke up."

"You're not ashamed of me?" she asked, rubbing her stomach.

He was shaking his head. "I'm very proud of you. Look where we are. We made it out."

Sabina smiled wearily but shook her head. "Please, don't avoid the subject. I did a bad thing. You are the only one who knows I did it purposely. If I cannot confess to you. . . ."

"There's nothing to confess. You were never pregnant."

"Yes, I was," Sabina insisted. "It was the commandant's baby."

"No. You're still a virgin—"

"Don't!" she cried, turning away.

Jackson wanted to hold her, but instead he just crouched close to her and whispered, "You never willingly gave yourself to a man, so that makes you a virgin. Since you're a virgin, it's not possible that you were ever pregnant."

She looked back at him, a tear still on her cheek. She brushed it away with her fingertips. "Am I damaged?"

"It's too early to tell."

"You're a bad liar. It is a wonder you fooled the commandant."

"I don't know who you're talking about."

She smiled at him. "How long have we been here?"

"Three days."

"You waited. I would not have thought that you would wait for me."

"Of course I waited."

"I have a confession to tell you—"

"There have been enough confessions today," Jackson interrupted.

"This one is different. It is something I did against you."

"You didn't do anything."

"I want to explain about the gun."

"You don't have to explain."

"I want to tell you why—"

"Tell me later," Jackson cut her off again. "You need to rest. I should send for the doctor."

"No. Sit down in your chair and watch me, the way you have been watching me for three whole days."

Jackson smiled. "I never left your side."

"How can I thank you?"

"You can get better."

"And then, where will we go?" Sabina asked sadly. "There is nowhere safe for us anymore. What will we do?"

"We'll go to America," he said, smiling at her.

"To America? Is it possible?"

"Sure," he told her.

"And live in California?"

"We'll live wherever you want."

"I would like you to decide where we will live. I don't know your country. You have been many more places than I have. It would be wise to let you decide."

"No," Jackson said, shaking his head and smiling. "I want you to decide. I'll tell you more about America. I'll tell you about New York City and the skyscrapers there and Central Park and the blues clubs in the Village. And I'll tell you about Vermont and the green hills. I'll describe the Florida Keys to you, and I know a little about the great plains and the deserts of Arizona."

"What about Washington? It's your capital."

"I've been there, so I'll tell you about Washington, too."

"Is it romantic there? I have seen pictures and it looks romantic."

Jackson had to clear his throat. "No. San Francisco is romantic. I know San Francisco very well."

"Tell me again about the mountains of California. I would like to ski with you. I have done it before, near Sarajevo. There is good skiing there. We had the Olympics once."

"I'll take you to Squaw Valley, where the Olympics have also been held. There's a bowl there that's very steep—"

"No, I am not good enough for that," Sabina said, smiling.

"There are other runs we can go down together."

"But you like the steep ones. You can ski the steep slopes while I practice on the easier ones until I am good enough to ski where you ski."

"No. I'll ski behind you on the slopes you like, and I'll watch you all the way down the mountain."

"You will make me blush doing that." She laughed. "Besides, I will want to watch *you*."

"On sunny days I'll ski very close behind you, so you can see my shadow beside you."

"I would rather have *you* right beside me."

"I'll be behind you, admiring you."

She sat up a little. She looked happy.

"But you will wish to go fast," she said.

"At the end of the run I'll pull beside you, and we'll both smile because you'll still be blushing, and then I'll go ahead and show off for you."

"And for the other girls."

"What other girls?"

Sabina was blushing now. It was good to see the color back in her face. She was not so pale now, not so helpless-looking. Jackson did not want the spell to be broken. "After skiing, we'll go to the casinos. But first, we'll buy you the prettiest dress in town—"

"And you will wear a tie?"

"I won't wear a tie. But I'll wear a jacket and a nice shirt and slacks, and shiny black shoes with silver tips. We'll go straight to the fifty-dollar blackjack tables, where the high rollers play. We'll walk up to the table and everyone will stop to look at you—and at me, to see who is so lucky as to be with you."

"No. They will be looking at you."

Jackson shook his head. "They'll be looking at you because you're so beautiful. And you're also brave."

She was still smiling with her mouth, but in her eyes he could see that she was suddenly somewhere else.

"I'll tell you more about San Francisco," he said. "But not right now. I need to save some stories. If I tell you everything now, you'll become bored with me."

She smiled, and now it was a smile with the eyes again as well. "Never."

"Even when I'm working all day, when I come home tired and want to watch the football games?"

"I played football for my school," Sabina said proudly.

"I'm talking about American football."

Sabina shrugged. "No matter. You can teach me about American football. What kind of work will you do?"

"I'll start my own company. That way, I can be the boss, and I won't get so tired at work, so I won't be boring to you when I come home."

"And what about me? Will I work?"

"If you want to."

"I will work, but not a hard job, because I don't want to be boring when I come home to you. Or, if you don't think you will grow tired of me, I can work at your company so we are always together. Tell me you want us to always be together."

"I want us to always be together," Jackson told her.

# 33

---

**THE SERB SOLDIERS OF** the mountain battery spent the early morning hours trying to find their range. There were five of them huddled around the 120 mm truck-mounted mortar. They argued ceaselessly about targets, then about coordinates, then about who would drop the mortar. There was no chain of command. They had not seen an officer for two weeks. They were entrenched in the hills surrounding the Bosnian city of Jajce, where Tito had been named marshal of Yugoslavia fifty years earlier, after the Serb, Croat, and Muslim partisans had fought together to free Yugoslavia from the Nazis.

That morning the soldiers had begun drinking early. The people of the city below would suffer because of it.

"Look, there," one of them cried, pointing a crooked finger at the city below. "It is a hospital. That corner over there has not been hit. That is what we will target."

"Go suck your father's penis, you son of a Turkish whore. The hotel. That is what we will hit. The hotel with the satellite on top."

"That satellite has been hit a dozen times. It's nothing more than a clothesline now."

"What do you know, you fool? It's your fault we hit the brewery. What a fool to hit the brewery. We will want a brewery when the city is ours."

"I thought it was a mosque."

"A mosque! Does a mosque look like a brewery?"

"I thought the smokestack was a minaret. How can I tell what is what without my glasses? It's your fault. You're the one who smashed them."

"You should not have insulted me."

"I was drunk. You could have let me take them off my face before you belted me."

"I could use a belt. Where's the Gypsy?"

"I have him below, digging a trench."

"Below? Aren't we close enough? Can't we read the license plates of the Red Cross trucks from here?"

"He volunteered. He said there was a spot below, near the cemetery on the hill, underneath a beech, that would be perfect for a man with a shoulder-fired rocket. He said there would be shade and a good angle to the market."

"It's too close. Even the Muslims with their popguns might be able to hit a man down here. Get him up here. I'm thirsty."

One of the Serb soldiers walked down through the tall grass of the mountain pasture as far as he dared and called for the Gypsy. When there was no reply, he aimed his rifle and shot away the dirt next to the Gypsy's head as he stood in his hole, digging. The Gypsy reflexively hit the ground, looked up, and saw a soldier waving for him to come up.

The Gypsy looked back down at the city nervously, then climbed out of his hole and sprinted up the hill to the Serb soldiers. A few shots rang out from the quiet city below, but with their weapons, they could not hit him from that distance.

"Yes, Duke," Zarko said to no one in particular, using the traditional Chetnik title of Duke, knowing these Serbs liked to be called that when they were drunk, which was most of the time.

"More slivovitz, Gypsy."

"Yes. Is that all?" Zarko asked deferentially.

"And bring food."

"I will try, Duke."

One of the soldiers slapped him. "Don't try. Do it!"

Zarko's eyes settled on his old carbine. The Serbs were using the butt of the rifle to crack walnut shells. He turned back to the

Serb soldier who had slapped him and smiled. "Forgive me, but they don't always give me food. They think I will eat it myself. They don't believe it is for you soldiers."

"Somebody write him a note."

They all looked at each other. None knew how to write.

"Just get the slivovitz, Gypsy, and any food you can get."

Zarko bowed to them like a court jester. A soldier kicked him in the ass to send him on his way, laughing at him. Zarko went off with a cracked-tooth smile on his face.

But when he was away from them he did not smile. He had been there for five days, ever since he was picked up trying to get into Jajce after escaping from the town on the Sana River. He had met up with two Muslims also trying to find their way into the city, but soon they were captured by a Yugoslav army patrol. Just for fun, the soldiers forced them to march single file through a mine-field. Since he was only a Gypsy, the soldiers let him be third in line. The two Muslims were blown to pieces right before Zarko's eyes, but he was fortunate enough to make it the rest of the way through the minefield.

The soldiers brought Zarko to the mountains overlooking Jajce to dig trenches for the Serb gunners. Most Muslim and Croat conscripts did not last more than a day or two. Drunken soldiers usually shot them or beat them to death. But Zarko had endeared himself to the soldiers and was constantly offering to help, so he had already survived much longer than most.

He hiked unmolested to the top of the mountain. The soldiers knew his face and his story well enough by now. He would parade by smiling, and if they asked him to, he danced, or told them a joke, or fetched water for them. At the supply tent he picked up the slivovitz and enough food for five soldiers. He ate as much as he could on the walk back. He threw the rest of the food away.

"This was all they would give me," Zarko told the gunners when he returned. "Only the slivovitz."

"Pour the drinks, Gypsy. And have one for yourself."

"Don't give any to him," a soldier insisted.

"Why not? He's all right," another said.

"He is just a digger."

"But he's not a Croat or Muslim. Hey, Gypsy. Tell us again about your politics."

"A Gypsy knows only about the politics of love," Zarko said.

They laughed at him. "So you're a ladies' man, Gypsy?"

"Yes. In my town, I broke many hearts."

They laughed some more. "I broke many bones in my town, Gypsy," a drunken soldier said.

Zarko forced himself to laugh along with the soldiers. "What will it be today, Duke? Perhaps that apartment building beyond the cemetery?" he asked, knowing the apartment building was abandoned.

"What a fool you are. That building has been empty for weeks."

"Beg your pardon, but from below I had a very good view. There were many Muslims and Croats going in and out of that building."

"You're a fool. It's empty."

Just then they all could see a banner unfurled out of the top floor of a six-story, prefabricated apartment building, one of the tallest buildings in the city. Even the soldier without his glasses could see that it was a huge Red Cross banner. They could just make out a group of twenty or thirty people standing together on the street corner below.

They all laughed upon seeing the huge Red Cross banner. "I think we have our target!"

"They might as well have painted a bull's-eye!"

"Let's hurry, before another battery gets it first."

"Let's bomb that group of Turks first, then the Red Cross."

They all stumbled over to the mortar and began fighting over who would operate it.

"I wish to tell you that it's a trick," Zarko insisted. "It is the apartment building you should bomb." Zarko continued to plead with them to listen until one of the soldiers kicked him in the groin.

He doubled over in pain and found himself staring straight down at his old carbine, which was lying in the mud. He knew he had no more bullets for the old gun, but as he looked at it he thought that if he was quick enough he could fall upon the soldier who had kicked him and could crack his skull with the butt of the rifle before the others could stop him.

"Look," the soldier called out to the others. "Look how he covets the gun. I think he has finally decided it's time to die. Go ahead, Gypsy. Arm yourself!"

Zarko didn't look up. He kept staring at the old carbine.

"Don't be stupid, Gypsy," one of the other Serbs told him. "We like you. Behave yourself. You have it good here."

The Serb that had kicked him picked up the old wooden rifle and broke it in half over his knee. He laughed when he saw the shock on Zarko's face, and soon the others laughed as Zarko tried to rush the soldier. They easily held him back and finally pushed him backward down the hill.

"Dig us some holes, Gypsy!" the Serb who had kicked him shouted, after Zarko stopped tumbling down the slope. He threw the two halves of the carbine down the slope to the Gypsy. "But keep low. It's time for target practice."

He began shooting at Zarko with a howitzer.

Mounds of dirt flew all around him as he crawled into one of his own trenches, between the Serb gun emplacements and the Bosnian defenses. He was sick with anger at the Serb who had desecrated his uncle's gun and he was still in pain at being kicked, but he wasn't concerned about being shot at. He felt safe in the trench he had built. Besides, the soldier was too drunk to hit him and probably wouldn't even remember the incident when he woke the next day with a hangover. Zarko knew he would be called up soon to collect the mounds of spent shells. He would climb back up the slope as if nothing ever happened and he'd get them slivovitz and sing them songs and tell them jokes.

But now, alone in the trench he had built, he was furious as he tried in vain to fit the two halves of the carbine together. "I can escape you fools anytime I want!" he screamed aloud in a fit of anger just as a light rain began to fall. He knew they couldn't hear him over the sounds of their guns and mortars. "I will play the fool for a while, and I'll dig you the deepest, most beautiful trenches. You won't notice that every trench is dug right next to a tree, or a big rock, or at the top of a goat pasture. You won't know that every time I volunteer to get you more slivovitz, I'll be memorizing the gun emplacements on this hill. When you're dug in and comfortable and drunk, I'll escape to the city defenses and I'll tell them all that I have learned.

"I'll point out the foxhole I dug by the beech up the hill, the one with the trunk split down the middle so that it looks like the peace sign. And I'll tell them about the trenches I dug by the boulder in the tall grass, and the others by the cluster of cherry trees. I'll tell the Muslims and Croats in Jajce exactly where to bomb for maximum effect. And from the city below, I will have the pleasure of watching you and your comrades die from the Bosnian shells. Then I will allow myself to be recaptured. I'll be sent to another hill and I'll do it all over again until you're bombed out of all of these hills!

"I will be your undoing! Me, Zarko, the false Gypsy, will be a hero to the people of Jajce. And when this war is over I'll settle down in Jajce. Maybe then I will tell the people the truth. That I am a Serb! That I am a Serb who was so ashamed of my people during this war that I claimed to be a Gypsy. I will become known as Zarko the Good Serb, hero of the siege of Jajce!"

## 34

**FROM THE DARK CLOUDS** over the city of Jajce, a raindrop—clean, pure, life-sustaining—fell for thousands of meters.

The raindrop landed on top of a building littered with the torn asphalt that remained after Serb bombings. It united with many other raindrops to form a puddle, then spilled over into a crater in the roof. The water landed on a broken table in the abandoned apartment below. It spilled over the edge of the table onto the floor, where it ran by the skull of an old, forgotten Croat woman. Then it went down the lopsided kitchen floor, over the fallen plaster from the ceiling down to the end of the room, out the side of the building where the wall had been blown apart. Hanging from the side of the building was a large Red Cross banner.

The water dropped and landed on an outcropping—a metal beam twisted outward from the bombing—and ran down this beam until it fell and was caught by a gutter. It flowed past the rats that were living there, down to where the gutter had been shattered near the street. The thin stream of water landed in a tin cup held by a little girl with dirt on her face standing by the corner of the building. She held her little tin cup there until it was filled. Then she made room for her younger brother, who was next in line at the water queue. While she waited, she allowed herself a sip of the water, savoring the feel of it against her lips, on her tongue, and sliding down her throat. The rest she would bring to her mother, who was very ill.

Jajce was a small city in a narrow valley at the junction of the Vrbas and Pliva Rivers. It was not a sprawling city—rather, it was packed tightly within the hills that for centuries had provided protection from foreign invaders. The Serbs now bombed the city from those very same hills.

Jackson and Sabina had to be patient to find a way through the Serb lines. It was three days since Sabina had regained consciousness after losing her baby. She ate very little and hardly slept. There were black circles under her eyes and she almost always looked to be on the verge of crying, though she never shed a tear. The only time she was happy was when she was alone with Jackson, talking about how their life would be in America.

After Anna dropped them off a few miles from Jajce, they slipped into the city in the early morning, as the Serb soldiers were sleeping off their hangovers. They noticed the Red Cross banner immediately and headed straight for it. It was a logical place to begin to look for Sabina's sister. Jackson was also anxious to ask around for news of Aleksandar, who was very well known in Jajce. Aleksandar had been a local hero as an exceptional basketball player in secondary school. Then, a few years later, his rock band played all the clubs before the war broke out. If Aleksandar was alive and in Jajce, he would be easy to find.

They walked past the water queue without noticing it. Suddenly they heard the whistle of a mortar overhead. They dived to the ground as the mortar landed with a frightening crack, scattering dust and debris and flying glass everywhere. They waited for more mortars, but none came right away. They ran, unable to see through the thick cloud of black smoke that the mortar had landed in the middle of the water queue.

They rushed into the bottom floor of the building, which the Red Cross had turned into a shelter. Volunteers were running out to help the victims of the water queue bombing.

They searched the melting pot of faces found in the shelter, Muslims, Croats, and Serbs who had elected to stay in their city rather than surrender it to the soldiers in the hills. Along the far wall were six survivors of a mortar attack that had taken place during a cease-fire several days before. In the maternity ward—which was just a corner of the room where a dozen expectant moth-

ers were forced to flee after the city's maternity clinic was shelled—
the faces of scared mothers could barely be seen in the faint firelight cast from the small pile of burning twigs. A radio tuned to the
only station still operating was broadcasting a warning to the people
of Jajce on the dangers of eating pigeons.

They were directed around the corner to a hospital without
power, anesthetic, antibiotics, or plasma. The hospital doubled as
a children's shelter, where a tireless young woman conducted
school, teaching the children about life in Bosnia before the war.
That day she was showing them pictures from her life before the
war. There she was in the picture, a Muslim in a bikini by a pool
with a group of friends, many of whom were Serbs and Croats. The
teacher, who was not a real teacher, had spent the first twenty
minutes of her morning maintaining a punk hairdo and slipping into
a tight leather miniskirt, even though she was a Muslim and the
Serb propaganda would have her wearing a chador.

Sitting apart from the group of children surrounding the
teacher was a boy who had not spoken for months. He just sat and
stared at the stump where his leg used to be. On the wall behind
him was a faded picture of Mickey Mouse. Many other injured
children lay unconscious on the soiled sheets of the hospital. Half
the head of a little girl was shaved where shrapnel had been removed from her skull. The children subsisted on dandelions and
dog food.

Not finding whom they were looking for, Jackson and Sabina
followed a trail of blood to the exit of the hospital. They were told
they should leave now because visiting hours were close at hand.
The Serbs often bombed the hospital during visiting hours because
it was most crowded then. Outside, an architect concerned about
the stability of the old building charted direct hits. On this side of
the building alone he had counted seventeen.

They came to a break in the wall where someone had painted
the words "This way to heaven." Jackson was about to step through
the narrow opening when he noticed two men sprinting toward him.
Shots from snipers cracked and echoed in the hills as the men
pushed Jackson out of the way, diving for cover behind the wall
next to him. Four women on the porch next to the entrance to
sniper alley applauded the men who made the sprint, offering high

fives as the men caught their breath. Jackson looked out and saw a body in the open space where someone had not been so lucky.

"Why the hell didn't you warn us!" Jackson shouted at the women.

"We were talking," one of them replied simply. "We didn't see you."

"This is crazy!" Jackson was furious. "There should be a warning posted!"

"There was," the woman told him. "An old man used to come by and draw a skull and crossbones there by the entrance and the word *Snajper!* in chalk. When the rain washed it away he would come by and draw it again. Yesterday he waved good-bye to us, walked out, and just stood there, waiting, until they shot him."

Jackson looked at the body he had noticed in the open space. It was an old man. "Maybe you women should take over and write the warning," he suggested, no longer shouting at them.

The woman shrugged. "The old man took the chalk with him. It's still in his pocket. Why don't you go get it for us?" The women on the porch laughed at Jackson, and were still laughing as he and Sabina walked away.

A boy wearing sweatpants and high-tops and bouncing a soccer ball on his head offered to take Jackson and Sabina around the back way to the other side of the alley. Of course, he would have to be paid. Jackson searched his pockets but he had nothing to give. Without saying a word, Sabina offered him a wild apple she had picked on the way into Jajce. The boy jumped at the offer.

They followed the boy, who told them to step exactly where he stepped. Everywhere the boy took them they could hear the sounds of the waterfall at the foot of the old castle, which had brought in tourists by the tens of thousands before the war. The boy cautioned them about drinking the water from the waterfall. The Serbs had intentionally contaminated it.

The boy wound through back alleys, careful of which side of the street he was walking on. Being on the wrong side could expose them to sniper fire. He taught Jackson to pay attention to clothes hanging on clotheslines outside of apartment windows. If clothes were hanging, it was safe to walk on that side of the street, because people in the line of fire would obviously not go to their windows to hang clothes. If there were no clothes hanging on that side of the street, you did not walk that way. The drapes would be closed, for fear of snipers.

They passed windows with sandbags in them, children collecting twigs for fire, a store that sold "toilet paper, cheap booze, and condoms." The mosques and Catholic churches were always empty, and there were no prayer meetings or masses. Prayer meetings and Catholic masses drew crowds of Muslims and Croats. Muslims and Croats drew fire from the Serbs in the hills.

Children set up make-believe roadblocks in the narrow, cobblestone streets of the old town within the castle walls, while others atop the ancient walls of the Banja Luka Gate pretended to be snipers.

A Serb MiG roared by, flying low, drawing the attention of a woman standing outside the Franciscan monastery. She had turned to prostitution to make money to feed her babies. Behind her in a cemetery were bulges of dirt where the newly dead were buried next to victims of the Inquisition and the Nazi invasion.

The boy took Jackson and Sabina through a barber shop, receiving a friendly greeting from the barber, who watched depressing news reports from a television hooked up to an old car battery. The barber had stopped charging for haircuts, because money had no value anymore, and people would not trade food for haircuts. He stayed open just to pass the time.

They went into the barber's basement, where the boy led them down an old tunnel built in the late 1960s in anticipation of an invasion by the Soviets. The tunnels were now used to shelter the homeless. They walked between rows of people sitting up against the walls with their knees drawn to their chests to allow others to pass. Occasionally they would hear a Serb shell or rocket explode overhead. Dirt would fall from the ceiling.

The tunnel brought them up into another makeshift hospital, where a man who was kept waiting for hours died in the hallway as overworked doctors and nurses stepped over him. Outside the hospital was a bus stop to take men to the front—the Muslim and Croat defenses around the city, dugouts where men with World War II weapons tried to keep the Serbs from overrunning their homes.

They checked the ancient catacombs, where elderly people came to avoid freezing to death in the night. Then back on the street, where a homeless Muslim girl fed her grandmother a mush made from rice and cereal. The old grandmother had hepatitis. It was not the only disease becoming epidemic.

Suddenly a Muslim-launched mortar was heard screaming into the hills, causing the people of Jajce to scramble for cover. They were well aware by now that for every Muslim and Croat mortar fired, the heavily armed and well-supplied Serbs would send down a hundred. There were so many people crammed into the city that almost every Serb shell found a victim. Blood flowed in the gutters as bodies were cleaned for burial.

Jackson noticed the small city zoo, long ago bombed out by the Serbs so that the Muslims and Croats could not eat the animals.

*So much for the Muslims feeding Serb children to the animals in the zoo,* Jackson thought.

The Serbs began playing loud music in the hills. Not Serb propaganda songs; it was rock music, played to remind the people of the city that the Serbs in the hills had electricity. The roar of another airplane momentarily drowned out the music. Jackson recognized it as an American C-130 transport plane. Parachutes opened in the sky and crates of food and medical supplies floated down into the cemetery. Muslims and Croats rushed out to get the crates, but as soon as they were in the open, Serb gunners opened fire. Not one person made it back alive. Not one crate was retrieved. The Serbs knew it was coming. American planes had dropped leaflets days before, explaining the mission. Of course, many leaflets blew into the hills, so the Serbs knew exactly where and when they were coming and had gunners in position, ready for the massacre.

Jackson spent the entire day wandering the city in a daze, seeing the many horrors and cataloging them but not really appreciating the hell that Jajce had become. There was too much suffering. He couldn't truly put himself in any one person's place, to feel the hunger and the cold and the desperation, not the way the people of Jajce had felt it every day for months, with no end in sight, with no hope of having their lives ever return to the way it used to be. He could look upon them sympathetically, could look into the hills and shake his head in disgust at the men causing such suffering, but he could not truly begin to understand just how miserable life had become for the innocent people of the city.

Back over by the Red Cross building, the trickle of rainwater was dripping into a pool of blood. Seven civilians had been killed and ten wounded in that morning's mortar attack on the water queue. In two days, the Serbs would bomb the funeral.

# 35

AFTER SEARCHING EVERY HOSPITAL, every shelter, and every tunnel in Jajce the boy showed them, Jackson and Sabina could find neither Aleksandar nor Sabina's sister. Jackson knew they couldn't stay in the doomed city with Sabina in her condition. Jajce was a death trap—it couldn't hold out much longer. Besides, he knew he simply couldn't stand to be there one more day. They would stay the night and leave at first light.

The Serbs, who hoped to make Jajce part of an ethnically pure republic, allowed Muslims and Croats one route out of Jajce—a treacherous mountain journey to the city of Travnik. The departure point was the bus station on the edge of town. Jackson received directions from the boy, who told them that weapons were not permitted on the journey. He handed the boy Sabina's pistol. The boy coolly snapped the cartridge out, saw that it was loaded, and slammed the cartridge back in place. He waved good-bye happily and scurried back into the ravaged city center.

Since it was already dark, they had to wait until morning to set out. A hard rain was falling and the auto tunnel leading to the edge of town where the bus station was located was packed with others hoping to get out the next morning. There was no room for Jackson and Sabina in the tunnel, so they spent the night in a stable behind a tavern.

"I like sleeping here, with the animals," Sabina said, lying on a bed of hay, her eyes closed and her head resting on a leather saddle.

"You should have a bed of roses," Jackson said. He was sitting on the ground next to her, his back up against the stable door.

"But I like tulips."

"When we make it to Italy, I'll bring you tulips every morning while we wait to go to America. Will you get bored with tulips every day?"

"No. I would like that. But we will not be able to afford them every day. We will need money to get to America."

"We shouldn't hurry to get to America. While we're in Italy we should have a look around. Have you ever been there?"

"No. But I have been to Prague. And I went to Vienna when I was a little girl."

"You'll like Italy. We'll start in Venice. Have you seen pictures of Venice?"

"Oh, yes. It looks very romantic. Is it as romantic as San Francisco?"

"Even more romantic. But I get sick of it after a while, so we won't stay there too long."

"Where will we go?"

"To a small town I know of on the east coast, called Barletta. There are people there who can help us get to America. I can work for them until we have enough money."

"I am anxious to meet these friends of yours who will help us."

"No. I wouldn't want you to meet them. They're not really friends. But they'll help us."

"What will I do while you work for them?"

"You can shop," he said, smiling.

"Shop for what? There is nothing that I need."

"You'll need lots of new clothes for America."

"I watch movies. I know how Americans dress. I can pick out things that will make me look like the women in America, so you will not be ashamed of me."

He lay close to her and propped his head up with one arm. "I don't want to change the way you look. You're more beautiful than any woman in America."

"You only think that because you are . . ." Her words trailed off.

"Because I'm what?"

She laughed at him but did not answer.

"Because I'm what?" he repeated.

"Nothing," she said, still laughing at him, her eyes still closed.

"Were you going to say because I'm in love with you?"

She opened her eyes. Her face looked happy. "How could you say such things to me if you were not in love with me?"

He looked at her lying there, her green eyes moist from the emotion of talking to a man about love for the first time. She was no longer wearing the nurse's uniform—she had on gray corduroy pants and a blue denim shirt and a brown wool peasant's coat belonging to Anna. It was too big for her, and her hands didn't extend past the sleeves. She had washed off the dirt from their escape and combed her hair and tied it back in a white bow Anna had given her, but she had slipped it off a minute ago and let her long blond hair fall over the black saddle where she lay.

"I'd like to touch you," Jackson said. She looked away and he saw her shudder. "Not in any way other than to hold you, and to rub your neck and to brush your hair out of your eyes when it falls in front of your face."

Sabina thought for a moment, and with her eyes closed, she told him, "I want you to touch me. I am sorry for making you feel otherwise. It is just that, when you do it without asking, I feel like . . . when *he* touched me."

"I didn't mean to—"

"I know."

"I care for you," Jackson whispered.

"Yes. I know."

"When you were unconscious, I was very concerned for you."

"I know. You never left my side."

"No. Not for a minute. And I heard you speak while you were sleeping, as if you were having a nightmare. You kept saying, 'Shut the window,' over and over."

He saw her close her eyes more tightly at the memory. Then she explained in a hollow voice, "When I was first taken by a man, when the Chetniks came to my town, one of them took me in my own room. As he was doing it, I looked at my window. I thought I saw my father there, watching the Chetnik do the things to me. I know it could not have been him, because my father had already been killed. Also, it was a second-floor window. It would not be possible that anyone was watching. But still, I could see my father there, watching it. Then I saw my mother, and two of my friends, and a boy I grew up with. They were all at the window, watching. Or at least I imagined them to be there, watching me, ashamed of me."

"Nobody was watching you," Jackson insisted quietly. "Nothing ever happened. Nobody ever touched you."

"I know," Sabina said.

"I'll never mention those things again. How can I? How can I mention something that never happened?"

Sabina curled up beside him. "Will you hold me, Robert, and touch my hair?"

Jackson put his right arm behind her neck and let his hand rest on her shoulder. He was careful not to let his hand fall too close to her breast. She huddled closer and held his left hand, guiding it to the top of her head. He began to brush her hair with his fingertips, gently, resisting the temptation to kiss her ear.

As he was doing it, he thought that the way he was touching her was more tender and more meaningful than any time he had even been with any woman other than Maria.

He concentrated on Sabina. He admired her face, so peaceful-looking now, at her long lashes, her eyes closed and relaxed. Her full lips were pulled back in a slight, contented smile. She began to turn her head when she wanted him to brush one side or the other, and when she ducked her chin to her chest he knew she wanted him to rub the back of her neck.

"In the camp—" Sabina began.

"What camp?" Jackson cut her off.

"No, it is all right. This is not a bad thing." She closed her eyes as she began. "In the camp, he often locked me in the closet when he was not happy with me. I liked it very much. I liked the loneliness. I slept best there, away from the commandant. Often, I would do things to displease him just so he would lock me in the closet for the night. That is where I had good dreams. I would sit there and imagine I was in a forest with no people. It was only me and the animals. They came and sat beside me as the birds perched on my shoulders and sang for me and the bears brushed my hair."

She was smiling at the memory.

"Am I just a bear to you?" Jackson asked playfully.

"No," she laughed.

"You're like a cat," he told her.

"If I could purr, you would know that I am very happy."

"I'm glad."

"Are you happy?" she asked, concerned for him. "Even after the things we saw today?"

"Let's not think about that."

"Talk to me about America then."

"How about Italy?" Jackson said, brightening, realizing that he was letting his concern over tomorrow's journey show. "Let me talk about Italy for a while. Then maybe Germany and Switzerland. We can go there, too, before we go to America."

"If you would like to. But let's not stay for too long. I want to go to America and ski with you."

Sabina took his hand now in hers and rested them both on his chest. She fell asleep with her head on his shoulder. Jackson could hear her breathing, and could feel her breast barely touch his side with every breath she took. He did not fall asleep for a long time.

## 36

**THEY STAYED IN THE STABLE** until the sun came up. Then, as more and more of the city's residents began to gather near the tunnel, Jackson woke Sabina.

"Did you sleep well?" she asked.

"Sure," he said. "What about you?"

"I had a good dream," she told him. She was smiling and talked excitedly, the words coming out in a rush. "I dreamed that I was in the woods. It was very beautiful and the sun was shining and everywhere I looked there were tulips. I was very happy."

"I'm glad you had good dreams. Was I in your dreams?"

"Maybe," she teased him.

"Tell me."

She shook her head, smiling, and looked away to hide her face.

"Then I won't tell you my dreams," he teased.

"Please tell me. Did you dream about me?"

"Maybe," he said.

"Now you're teasing me."

"I really did dream of you. We were in San Francisco, in our apartment, and I was cooking you dinner."

"You? What a strange dream. Of course, I will do the cooking. Were there children in our house?"

"Sure there were," he said, but only after a slight hesitation.

Sabina suddenly stood up and he watched her walk to the far

end of the stable. She began stuffing straw into her pack, then she turned her back to him. When she turned around again, the pack was stuffed inside her shirt. She looked nine months pregnant.

She walked by him without saying a word.

They pushed through the masses crowded about at the bus station. Those lucky enough to have a hundred deutsche marks could buy a place on a bus to take them to the plateau atop Mt. Vlašić. All others prepared to walk unless they had their own transportation.

A Muslim wearing green fatigues with a Bosnian patch on one arm went about trying to convince people to leave all belongings except for small bundles. People with cars were asked to leave their things behind in order to make room for the sick or elderly or pregnant. Young girls were urged to cut their hair and bind their breasts to keep from being raped on the road. Guns were indeed prohibited. Sabina was offered a ride by a Muslim family, but she declined, giving the space to a man who walked with a cane.

Finally the three buses took the lead, followed by a line of cars. Then came people on tractors, wagons, cart horses, and wheelbarrows. Recent floods had left the road covered with an inch of mud. The columns of people who trailed behind were told to walk in the middle of the muddy road—to avoid land mines. There was very little talking. The men always walked with their heads down in shame. Women stared hopefully into the distance. Little boys and girls carried packs close to their own body weight.

As they left the city and passed through the Serb lines, soldiers yelled, "Butcher them! Butcher the pigs!" and threw rocks into the columns of people. A young mother-to-be saw a body on the side of the road and became hysterical, soothed only by Sabina, who put her arm around the pregnant girl and helped her along. Soon there were many more gray-faced bodies alongside the trail. Nobody bothered to pick up the bodies, and they could not be buried because land mines lined the road.

By late afternoon they were struggling up the steepest climb. The road was littered with suitcases and children's toys the weak had dropped by the roadside. People offered to lay the dying on hoods of their cars in hopes of getting them to Travnik, while the dead were rolled to the side of the road to make way for those who still had a chance. One woman handed out acorns for people to eat. Jackson gratefully accepted and ate his.

After an agonizingly slow and exhausting climb to the top of Mt. Vlašić, they came to the plateau, where Chetniks wearing dark sunglasses confiscated all cars. Even a Red Cross car was confiscated. The three buses were emptied and returned to Jajce. Now the entire procession would have to descend Mt. Vlašić on foot.

It was getting dark. The climb had taken its toll on everyone, even the strong. Many more bodies lay on the sides of the roads. Every hundred meters a Serb irregular with sunglasses would be standing by, occasionally shooting his gun into the air to hurry the refugees along. When someone fell, the Serbs kicked them until they either struggled to their feet or were helped up by other refugees.

Before beginning the descent, Jackson looked back over his shoulder. In the last light of the day he could make out a line of refugees stretching across the entire plateau. It looked to him like some biblical scene depicting masses of ancient people being driven from their homeland. Ahead now was the long, steep descent, with even more Serb irregulars lining the road, which had no guardrail.

In a little while there was a pack of Serb irregulars just off the trail gathered around a fire. Jackson could see a Muslim girl standing by the fire. He had noticed her when they first set out, a particularly beautiful girl with long black hair and blue eyes. She reminded him of Maria.

He thought of Maria now, in medical school at Cal. He thought of her long, tanned legs and her Latin accent and the way she called him Bobby. He remembered how much fun they had together, always joking and smiling and never serious. Their life together was always a whirlwind of activity, skiing, hiking, biking, parties. They could lie in bed for hours talking and touching and joking. He remembered being very happy with her.

Then he remembered the last telephone call he had made to her from Venice. Maria had cried and had begged him to tell her that the allegations about him were not true, but he couldn't. He had had to admit to her that he had stolen the guns and given them to Muslims. She had been so upset she could barely speak, and had soon hung up on him.

*It's not her fault,* he told himself for the thousandth time. *She just doesn't understand. I didn't understand, either, until I received my education from Aleksandar.*

It would have been natural for him to doubt Maria, to doubt that she loved him. But he knew that she loved him as much as he loved her. They had grown up together. They had been apart for months at a time during college and while he was on assignment for the army and then when she started medical school. But never in all that time had either strayed, and there was never a doubt that they would marry and raise a family together. They wanted all of the same things. More than anything, they wanted each other. So even though Maria had no right to doubt that he was doing the right thing because she knew what kind of person he was, he could not blame her for being reluctant to believe him and to join him. Unlike him, Maria had never sat in a café that was chosen as a target for a mortar attack precisely because it was filled with innocent civilians. She had never seen children starving in caves after being driven from their homes. She hadn't spoken with men like Aleksandar who took the time to explain the complex situation in Bosnia. She hadn't been in the town on the Sana River, or in the camp, or in Jajce. And she wasn't there now, to witness the exodus of thousands of pitiful-looking people. How could he expect Maria to understand?

*If she understood, she'd come,* he told himself for the thousandth time. *She'd come because she loves me, and she'd come to help because it's the right thing to do. Maybe we'd move the smuggling operation to the coastal city of Split, which is safe from the war and has an excellent port so I could continue to smuggle arms. She could work in the refugee centers tending to the sick and dying. She's practically a doctor; she'd be invaluable there.*

But now, seeing the suffering of the thousands of people trying to make it over the mountain, he couldn't deny the magnitude of the horror and he realized, finally, that it had been selfish to expect Maria to come to him. He knew now that he had no right to ask her to come. It was one thing for him to stay, because he had nowhere to go. He was a deserter, with no country and no career. Maria, however, had a family and a home and, most importantly, she had a dream to help the Mexican-American migrant workers who lived in California in conditions worse than those of some third-world nations. Maria had grown up one of them, and even though her parents had struggled to ensure her a proper education so she could escape that hard life, she always swore she would return to help her people.

*Yes, it was selfish to ask her to come to me,* Jackson thought.

But, still, he wished she would come to him.

Jackson looked back at the black-haired Muslim girl who reminded him of Maria. She was nearly naked now and was being dragged into the woods by a Chetnik. He could hear her screams accompanied by the grunts and insults of the Chetniks. Not one other person in the procession looked up. There was nothing the defenseless Muslims and Croats could do about it. They walked on impotently, pretending not to hear the girl's screams. Jackson walked on with them.

A Serb paramilitary with a gang from Belgrade who called themselves the White Wolves suddenly came out of the shadows and ripped a pack off of a young man's back. The young man resisted just a little and was kicked in the groin. The Serb dumped the belongings and, not finding anything of value, threw the pack over the cliff. The paramilitary reached out and ripped a gold earring out of the young man's earlobe. The young man screamed and cried out, holding his bloody ear.

Then the paramilitary grabbed Jackson.

He ordered Jackson to strip naked. Many other men and woman were being told to do the same. When he tried to resist he was punched in the face, so he took off all of his clothes as the Chetnik examined the chain around his neck. The Chetnik didn't know what to make of it, but he knew it wasn't valuable so he ignored it and searched the pockets of Jackson's pants.

Sabina had stopped to watch Jackson's fate. He noticed her and jerked his head at her, signaling for her to go on, but she didn't move. The procession moved past her as the paramilitary held up Jackson's clothes to see if they would fit. When the Chetnik noticed Jackson watching him he kicked Jackson and shouted at him to rejoin the others trudging down the mountain. Jackson resumed walking, glancing back to see the paramilitary wearing the olive pants and the black shirt he had been given at Omarska.

A few hours after sundown they neared the bottom of the mountain. Many more men and women had been stripped naked and were walking barefoot. All were exhausted. The Serbs beat anyone who did not keep moving. There were more and more bodies on the side of the road, more and more girls being taken aside. Jackson was walking behind Sabina. She looked strong again, helping the pregnant Muslim girl. He realized that if she had not stuffed her pack with hay and used it to make herself look pregnant, she might have been taken aside and raped. Jackson grinned in admiration for her.

*Maybe she hasn't cracked after all,* he thought.

After passing a ski lodge gutted by fire, they could see the many small campfires just outside of Travnik. People redoubled their efforts and helped those who were struggling. Jackson carried a young girl over his shoulder. He was too tired to think of his nakedness anymore. The pregnant girl leaned on Sabina to keep from falling over.

Then finally, as if from out of nowhere, with the city just a few hundred meters away, the first Bosnian patch was seen on the arm of a soldier. A woman ran up to the soldier and kissed the patch.

The young Bosnian stood straight and tall and announced in a clear, strong voice that they had made it, that there were tents up ahead where they could rest and receive water. He was handsome and strong, a symbol of the best of Bosnia. He was surely chosen to be stationed there to give the people hope. He was wearing a green beret and was giving the Bosnian salute—the right hand held out showing a full palm with all five fingers splayed. Behind him was the Bosnian flag—six lilies against a blue background divided by a diagonal white stripe.

Suddenly the young Bosnian limped forward and grabbed Jackson by the arm.

"Robert? Robert! What are you doing here?"

Jackson was too tired and hungry to have noticed him at first. "Adem?" He was suddenly very ashamed of his nakedness.

Adem pulled him aside. Jackson called for Sabina, who kissed the pregnant girl good-bye before finding someone else to help her. She was very aware that he was naked, and did not look at him. The father of the girl Jackson carried thanked him, shaking his hand weakly.

"What are you doing here?" Adem repeated.

He was so weary and surprised to see Adem that he did not know what to say.

"I'm so glad to see you again," Adem said finally. "I heard that things have gone very badly in Dubrovnik."

"How badly?" Jackson asked.

"Street-to-street fighting. The Croats have fought the Serbs back to the hills, but they're still being bombed. How did you get out?"

"I left when they started bombing the city walls," Jackson replied, thinking that it seemed like a lifetime ago. "Have you seen Aleksandar?"

Adem shook his head sadly. "No. But come along to my house. I will tell you everything I know."

# 37

ADEM HAD CONSTRUCTED A SMALL wooden shack on top of an apartment building in Travnik with wood scrounged from Jajce. He had lined the ceiling and walls with Muslim prayer rugs from bombed-out mosques. He drove a supply bus to Jajce three times a week along a five-hundred-meter corridor the Muslims and Croats kept open, at great loss to men and ammunition, in order to keep Jajce going. On the roof of his shack were old shingles also scavenged from Jajce. Adem's girlfriend, a Serb named Sonja, was stirring a pot of beans with a wooden spoon.

"I heard about Sarajevo," Jackson said. Adem had given him a pair of Levi's, a gray sweatshirt, and an old pair of tennis shoes. "Emir said you were shot at the airport, and that only Aleksandar made it through."

"Ah, then Emir made it!" Adem said happily. "Yes, I was shot. The damned UN spotlights lit us up for the Serb guns. We were trapped in the middle of the runway at the airport. I was wounded in the leg. I thought for sure I was going to die. Finally, with Emir gone back and Aleksandar gone forward, the UN spotlight went out. I could hear a UN truck coming for me. But then I heard Aleksandar calling my name.

"I yelled to him to leave me, but he followed my voice and threw me over his shoulder and carried me through the Serb lines. He didn't stop until morning. I was unconscious most of the time. He left me with some Muslim refugees he found on the road. Aleksandar didn't tell them where he was going. I thought he would return to Jajce, but I have inquired and he has not been there."

"How did you get back here?"

"The refugees were heading to Split, but I was not as badly wounded as I had thought and I could walk on my own, so I told them I was leaving. They wouldn't let me go; they said I was too weak. But I wanted to come back home for Sonja and my family, so I snuck out in the night and wandered here. It took me a week, but I made it and found Sonja."

"I knew he would be back," Sonja said with a smile. She was extremely thin and pale, quite ordinary-looking but always upbeat, with a sincere smile. "My family left for Split, but I knew Adem would come for me. When he returned, I was here, waiting for him."

Adem put his hand on hers. "We used to have our own flat in this building, but Sonja had taken in so many refugees by the time I returned, there was no room for us. So I joined the Krajina Brigade and built this. Every time I go to Jajce I come back with more rugs from the mosques to nail to the walls, because winter is coming."

Sonja laughed as she waved her hand at the walls. "Every time Adem adds more prayer rugs, it gets smaller and smaller in here, but warmer, as well."

Jackson could understand why Adem had to build his little home on the top of a building. It seemed every square inch of the city was accounted for by the refugees pouring in from Jajce and so many other cities and towns. Homeless people were huddled under every canopy and doorway, trying to stay out of the rain. All the schools and gymnasiums were bursting with people, every apartment had been opened to friends and family who had come from all over northern and central Bosnia after being run out of their homes. Turkish viziers had once ruled Bosnia from Travnik. The once proud city had now become a Muslim and Croat ghetto.

"I like it. It's very comfortable," Sabina said to Sonja. Sabina no longer bothered with the burlap sack, and she seemed to have gained strength walking over Mt. Vlašić, helping the pregnant girl make it to Travnik.

"What's this about a brigade?" Jackson asked. "Do the Muslims have an army now?"

"Army? No, no, I would not call it that. We have these patches and we put them on military-looking shirts and jackets. But we have few weapons. What kind of army has no weapons? No, most of us are just the unfortunate ones who have been run out of our towns. The Serbs keep pushing people to the population centers, like Jajce and Travnik. They come here from all over northern and central Bosnia, from Sanski Most, Banja Luka, and all the smaller towns in between. Then the Serbs surround us and bomb us until we move to the next place. When Jajce falls—which it soon will—the Serbs will surround us here, and we will be forced to move somewhere else, probably Zenica or Sarajevo."

Jackson frowned. "Why do you say Jajce will fall?"

"The Croats have begun pulling out of Jajce," Adem explained. "Soon it will be almost defenseless. I have heard rumors that the Croats have struck a deal with the Serbs. In return for the Croat retreat, the Serbs will give them some territory in the south."

Jackson could hardly believe what he was hearing. His Muslim men had warned him months ago that this day would come, but he hadn't believed them.

"What will you do now?" Jackson asked Adem.

"Travnik will become the front line, and they will bomb us here. Then we will flee to Zenica or Sarajevo."

"And then? Soon you'll run out of places to run to."

"At some point the West must help us," Adem said. "They must supply us with arms. When we can defend ourselves, the Serbs will stop fighting."

"Imagine what we could do if we had our own aircraft," Sonja said dreamily. "We could bomb the Serb positions in the hills. We could cut the Serb supply lines to Belgrade. We could blow up the train tracks. With air support and weapons for our people who desperately want to fight back, we could instill fear in the Serbs. The Serbs are cowards. They only fight us because we are helpless. As soon as we can defend ourselves, the fighting will stop. The Serbs will be ready for peace." Though she was an ethnic Serb, Sonja had always considered herself a Bosnian, and therefore thought nothing about addressing her enemies as Serbs.

"What about you, Robert?" Adem asked. "What will you do now? You are welcome to stay here with Sonja and me. You can drive a bus like me and help those in Jajce."

"We're going to America," Sabina said, smiling.

Adem looked at Jackson.

"Perhaps you should try to make it to Sarajevo," Sonja suggested.

"Sarajevo is no worse than most cities in Bosnia now, despite all the attention they get there," Adem told them. "The Serbs are drawing attention to Sarajevo to keep the world from focusing on places like Jajce and Bihać and Tuzla, and from their death squads and concentration camps. It is very bad though, yes. But it is still better off than Jajce. However, Sonja, they cannot expect to fly out of there, if that is what you are thinking."

"We have to get to the coast," Sabina said.

"Split is not very bad," Adem suggested. "Not very bad at all. They have seen little fighting. And I think I can get you there."

"How?" Jackson asked. "Not with the peacekeepers?"

"No. Not those fools. There is a British Battalion group only ten miles from here, but they're useless. However, I happen to know of a group of Italians leaving here tomorrow morning. They are going to Split. You can go with them, if you are sure you are well enough."

"I am," Sabina said. "Thank you. We will go with these Italians."

"Robert?"

"I guess so," he said.

"Will you come with us?" Sabina asked excitedly.

Adem and Sonja both shook their heads. "We're needed here," Adem said. "We did good work running guns, Robert, but it was too little. What are a few rifles and grenades against Serb tanks and planes and rockets? Here, I feel I can help my people much more."

"I understand. You're a good man, Adem," Jackson said.

"So are you," Sabina said to Jackson, rubbing his hand.

LATER THAT NIGHT, ADEM had gone out to drive one of the buses back to Jajce under the cover of darkness. Sonja went to the bus station with him, where she helped load the buses with whatever provisions the people of Travnik could spare for their brothers and sisters in Jajce.

Jackson and Sabina were alone in the shack atop the rooftop overlooking Travnik.

Jackson had gone out and scavenged for wood, which he now placed in the makeshift fireplace in the center of the room and built a fire. Sabina unrolled the thick blanket Sonja had pointed out to her and made a bed on top of the prayer rugs that lined the floor. She threw several more blankets on top and pulled them down at one corner, placing the single pillow at that end. When she was done, she knelt there, inspecting the bed.

"You must be tired," Jackson said, coming up and kneeling next to her.

"I am. Are you tired?"

"Yes. May I help you off with your shoes?"

She spun around and sat on the bed and put her feet in front of him. He untied the laces and began to pull her shoes off. He noticed her wince, so he was very careful and slowly guided her feet out of them.

"It's the blisters," Jackson said. "I have them, too."

"My feet cramped walking over the hill."

Jackson looked at Sabina's tiny feet, at the blisters on the tips of each of her toes and on her heels. He gently placed her feet in his hands and began to rub them slowly and tenderly, careful to avoid the blisters.

"Don't," she told him. "You don't have to—"

"I want to," he said. "Just lie back and let me do it."

"You don't. . . ."

"Be quiet. Just relax."

Sabina closed her eyes. He watched the expression on her face. He saw how she tilted her head back, moving it from side to side, how her lips quivered, and how she was breathing deeply and rapidly. He found it oddly sexual, this reaction to the way he touched her feet, and it made him more determined to please her with every touch. He gently ran his fingers down the middle of her foot, almost tickling her, but not wanting to make her laugh, wanting only for her to enjoy, to feel his admiration for her emanating through his fingertips.

When he was done, he began unbuttoning his shirt. He saw Sabina sitting on the blankets, watching him.

"It'll get cold in here after we fall asleep and the fire burns out," Jackson said to her, buttoning his shirt back up. "We should leave our clothes on to sleep. To stay warm."

He could almost see the relief wash over Sabina's face. She got under the covers, then held them up for him to slide under. He lay on his back, looking up at the prayer rugs nailed to the roof. In a minute she came closer, resting her head on his chest.

"Will you brush my hair?" she asked him.

"I love to brush your hair," he said, and began to run his fingers through the long strands, red in the light cast by the fire. "I'll do this every night. We'll make it a tradition."

"But some night, we may wish to do other things," she said.

He swallowed hard. "But we'll start like this. Or we'll end like this. Every night, I promise, I'll brush your hair."

"When we make it to Italy, we will have money so we can buy a brush."

"Yes. And clothes, and makeup if you want it—though I would prefer you without it—and anything else you need. But even when we have a brush, I'll brush your hair every night with my fingers."

"And in the morning, I will use the brush to try to look appealing to you," Sabina told him.

"You don't need to worry about that. But if you want to brush your hair in the morning, you should do it."

"I will. And when we get to America, I will have my hair cut short like the women in the fashion magazines."

"I like your hair the way it is."

"But I want to look American for you," she insisted.

"I like the way you look now."

She sighed. "I wish I could sit in a tub for a week."

"When we get to Italy," he promised.

"Yes."

"I like to brush your hair," he said. He was beginning to drift off.

"I like it, too."

"And I liked rubbing your feet."

There was a pause. "Robert? Can I tell you something?"

"Anything."

"I did not like the rubbing of the feet."

Suddenly he was wide awake. He sat up and put her head on the pillow and looked down at her.

"I am sorry," she said, trying not to cry. "I am so difficult."

"What is it? Did I hurt you?"

"No. But you gave me no choice. I felt you were...."

"I didn't mean it in that way," Jackson explained. "I just wanted to make you feel better."

"I asked you not to. And still, you insisted."

"I thought you meant that I didn't have to if I didn't want to. But I wanted to. I thought you wanted me to."

"I felt you were ordering me."

He made a move to hug her, or to brush the hair out of her face, but he caught himself.

"I will never force you to do anything, Sabina," he promised. "If you don't want me to brush your hair, you can tell me and I'll stop. If you don't like it when I hold you, I won't hold you—"

Sabina sat up and moved close to him. "I like it when you hold me. But I don't like it when you hold me too tightly, so that I can't move, and I don't like to feel that I can't get away. And I don't like it when you tell me what to do."

Jackson wanted to shout at her, to grab her by the shoulders and shake her, to make her realize that he would never harm her. At first he told himself that women are too emotional, so confusing, irrational. But then he remembered this was Sabina, and though he didn't think he could fully imagine what she had been through, he knew he had to try to learn, because only by learning could he understand. And he suddenly wanted very badly to understand.

"I'm sorry, Sabina. I'll never make that mistake again."

"It's not your fault," she sighed, her voice cracking with emotion. "You shouldn't have to put up with the problems I have. I am ruined for any man. Who could love a person who lives with my shame?"

Jackson was shaking his head. "Any man would love you."

Sabina was about to cry.

"I've fallen for you, Sabina."

"I do not understand this of the falling."

"I love you."

Sabina did not say anything for a long time. She looked at him, at his black wavy hair still damp from the light rain when he went out for the firewood. She looked at his brown eyes and put her hand on his cheek.

"You have said that to women before."

"To one other," he admitted.

"I have never been in love before," she told him. "What happened to your other love? Is she dead?"

Jackson lay down again and stared at the prayer rugs on the ceiling. "No."

They lay there silently for a full minute. He felt Sabina sit up, then she was pulling him up to a sitting position to face her. She took his hand and placed it on her breast. "Will you take care of my heart, now that I have put it in your hands."

He looked at his hand, and her hand on top of it. She squeezed his hand and he looked at her. "I'll hold it gently in the palms of my hands, and then I'll swallow it and it will beat inside of me, and I'll protect it and care for it as I care for my own heart."

"There will be no difference between us that way," Sabina said.

"There is no difference between us. Except that I love you more than I love myself."

"No," she whispered. "You must love yourself in the same way that you love me. Only in that way is there no difference between us."

"Then that's how I'll love you."

"And I will love you in the same way."

She slowly leaned over and kissed his cheek tenderly. A cold gust of wind blew through the wooden planks and prayer rugs. Jackson could feel the coldness now on his cheek where she had kissed him.

"It's cold," he said. "Lie down and let me cover you with the blankets."

"Will you do something for me?" Sabina asked him. "Will you let me brush your hair, the way you do for me?"

"I'd rather brush your hair."

"But I would like to do things for you, too," she explained. "I don't like it when it is always you who is doing things for me. That way I don't feel that we are equal."

"I have a lot to learn about you."

"I know I am difficult now. But you will learn, because I'll tell you everything."

"Only the things that aren't too hard for you to talk about," he said.

"In time I will tell you everything." Sabina smiled slightly now. "How else will you know how to care for my heart?"

"You're right. I want to know everything. In time."

"We will have plenty of time in America," she said happily.

Sabina lay down with her head on the pillow and invited Jackson to rest his head on her chest. Then she began stroking his hair. He felt the sensations shooting down his spine and throughout his entire body. He lay there until her hand stopped moving and he heard her breathing regularly. He got up and put more wood on the fire and lay next to Sabina, looking at her lovely face glowing in the firelight.

## 39

**EARLY THE NEXT MORNING,** Adem brought Jackson and Sabina to a clearing in the forest just south of the city. The Italians were middle-aged men who, unlike the Italians Jackson knew from his smuggling experiences, were not Mafia, just concerned men with good intentions. They also seemed to share a lust for danger and were eager to embark on what they considered an adventure through the war-torn country. Each was wearing expensive hiking boots and colorful ski parkas. They were unpacking crates and stuffing supplies into packs for the journey to the coast.

Jackson became anxious when they were delayed for an hour. His mood didn't change when he saw what they were waiting for.

"How fast can that thing walk?" he asked angrily. He pointed at a baby elephant no taller than he.

The leader of the expedition, a handsome Italian with blow-dried gray hair and a thin black beard, glared at Jackson. "If you don't like it, go without us," he said in English.

"Why do you come all the way here to save an elephant?" Sabina asked.

"We heard about this baby elephant in Bosnia who lived through the bombing but was starving to death. We put on a carnival in Assisi to raise the money to rescue it and ship it back to Italy, where we can care for her."

"What are you going to feed it?" Adem asked the Italian, whose name was Francisco Cippolini.

"Oh, we have brought plenty of food for her," Cippolini replied.

Jackson began cursing and walked away, considering his options but knowing he really had none.

"There's no need to worry. We have been guaranteed safe passage by the government of Croatia, as well as the Bosnian-Serb government," Cippolini said confidently. "I have it in writing. We will not be disturbed."

Jackson shook hands with Adem and said good-bye after making Adem promise to return to Medjugorje once Travnik came under attack. Adem went to hug Sabina but settled for gently shaking the hand she stretched out between them.

They set off at a slow pace. To be safe from highwaymen they took less-traveled roads. They stopped frequently to feed and water the elephant. There were twelve Italians, all weighted down with food and water. Also, a huge pack was thrown over the elephant, which was filled with more food and water.

They camped well off the road the first night. They had encountered only a few Yugoslav army units and were not harassed. They passed many refugees, who looked at them suspiciously. Rarely did the Italians acknowledge the refugees. The Italians were not unhappy to be there, however. They were filled with good cheer and camaraderie at their unselfish undertaking.

On the second day they made good time and didn't stop until noon. They halted at the side of the road and passed food around. They offered Jackson and Sabina some bread and water, but the other food, they explained, was needed for the elephant.

As they were eating and resting, Jackson noticed several black crows in the tree over his head fly off, calling loudly to each other. He sat up, concerned. Hearing the sound of jeeps coming toward them, he squinted down the road. The Italians didn't seem to notice anything, but Sabina was watching the road intently as well.

"Trouble coming," Jackson said. He grabbed Sabina's arm and pulled her up.

Cippolini talked as he ate. "No trouble, Roberto. We have safe-passage letters. Sit down. You need the rest."

Jackson and Sabina walked to the edge of the forest on the side of the road. They could see the jeeps speeding toward them.

Soon the long beards of the Chetniks could be seen through the dust kicked up along the road.

"I'm telling you, these guys are trouble," Jackson said again, looking back at the woods, considering a dash. But the Chetniks could see them now. It was too late.

The Italians were still sitting when the Chetniks pulled up. The Serbs, wearing all black with long black beards, laughed and jumped out of their jeeps to get a better look at the elephant.

"What is this? Another pregnant Turk?" one of them joked.

"It doesn't stink enough to be a Turk," another snorted.

Francisco Cippolini stood and stepped forward, smiling and speaking Italian. "Good afternoon, gentlemen. My name is—"

"Shut up, Turk!" the Chetnik leader demanded, slapping him across the face. The blow knocked down Cippolini. From his place in the back, Jackson moved Sabina behind him.

Cippolini stood again and shouted an Italian insult directed at the Chetnik, then reached into his breast pocket to pull out the safe-passage letters. As soon as he put his hand in his shirt, the leader of the Chetniks leveled a Kalashnikov at him.

"He's only reaching for papers!" Jackson suddenly cried out, knowing the Italians did not speak Serbo-Croatian so it was up to him to explain before Cippolini was shot. He pushed Sabina back as he came forward with his hands up. "We have no weapons!"

"He is reaching for a gun," barked the lead Chetnik, who wore a black wool cap with the Serb double-headed eagle medallion pinned on the front.

"No, no! Look in his pocket! We have the blessing of your government!"

The Chetnik in the wool cap pushed the attending Italians out of his way and reached into Cippolini's pockets.

"I cannot read these," the Chetnik said angrily, handing them to Jackson.

Jackson saw that they were written in Italian, which he did not understand, either.

"Look, here," Jackson said, pointing out the red-and-white checkered crest of Croatia on the letterhead of one, and the insignia of the newly created Bosnian-Serb government in Pale on the other. "One is from the government of Croatia and one from the Bosnian-

Serb government. They're safe-passage letters for us and this animal."

"I see nothing from Belgrade," the Chetnik in the wool cap growled.

"But the Bosnian-Serb government in Pale—" Jackson began.

"We take no orders from Pale," the Chetnik scoffed. "Only from Belgrade."

Jackson was about to protest, but then he remembered something Aleksandar had once explained to him: the new Bosnian-Serb government established in Pale was only for appearances. Belgrade, the capital of Serbia and the seat of the Yugoslav government, was really calling the shots for the Bosnian Serbs.

The Chetniks began searching the Italians' packs. They took all the food, including the elephant's food, and stored it in their jeeps.

Francisco Cippolini pleaded with Jackson to reason with the Chetnik in the wool cap.

"Please, sir, don't take our provisions," Jackson said as respectfully as he could. "How will we get the elephant out of the country without food or water?"

The Chetniks laughed at him. "I see your problem," the one in the wool cap said. He motioned to a Chetnik behind him, who took aim at the elephant with his machine gun. Two Italians jumped in front of the elephant. The Chetniks laughed even harder and pointed at them. "If you wish to die with your animal, it makes no difference to us!"

Jackson turned to the two Italians and warned them in English, "Get back! Don't be fools! They'll kill you and laugh about it later!"

The Italians stood there with their arms crossed defiantly.

Jackson was sure the Chetnik in the black wool cap was about to order them shot along with the elephant, when suddenly there was noise from down the road. A group of men leading several mules came into view around the bend. All of the travelers' worldly belongings were lashed onto the back of the mules. Their metal pots and pans clanged rhythmically.

"It is only Gypsies," a Chetnik said.

"Put away your guns," the Chetnik in the wool cap said casually. "We will wait for them to pass, then deal with these foreigners."

When the Gypsies came close they could be heard singing softly, a lazy but upbeat Gypsy song. The Gypsies, dark-skinned men wearing tattered clothes and straw hats, nodded to the Chetniks, who let them pass undisturbed, as Gypsies were no threat to the Serb aim of a Greater Serbia, populated exclusively by Serbs. Gypsies come and go, the Serbs reasoned. They do not threaten Serb claims to land.

The Gypsies moved along, begging as they went. A Chetnik threw some coins on the road so they would keep moving. One of the Gypsies, whom Jackson was staring at, discreetly flashed him the peace sign.

As soon as the Gypsies passed by with their pots and pans banging against each other on the backs of the mules, the Chetnik in the wool cap turned his attention once more to the Italians and Jackson. "Do you question my authority? Is this not my homeland? What right do you have to come onto my soil and give me orders? I should kill you all!"

His proclamation was met by an eerie silence. So eerie, in fact, that all of the men—including the Chetniks—looked up the road toward the Gypsies. The metal clanging of their cooking pots had ceased. Jackson turned and ran for Sabina.

Suddenly there was a prolonged burst of machine-gun fire. Jackson grabbed Sabina and hit the ground, pulling her down and covering her with his own body. Only a couple Chetniks had time to fire back. There was a great deal of screaming. Soon Sabina was shouting at Jackson to get off of her, but he stayed on top of her and covered her head with his arms.

Then, just as suddenly as the fight had begun, it was over and Jackson heard the sound of running feet. He looked up to see a Gypsy standing over him.

"Elephants were of great use to Hannibal against the Romans, Robert, but they will do little against Serb tanks."

The so-called Gypsy removed his straw hat and the scarf around his face, revealing a rugged sun- and wind-burned face. He had the same lean, athletic build as Jackson, but he was younger and two inches taller.

"Aleksandar!"

The handsome young Muslim hugged Jackson and then turned to the other men dressed as Gypsies and shouted in English, their common language, "Brothers, this is Robert Jackson, the man I have told you about! He is a gunrunner extraordinaire! Robert Jackson, these are my brothers."

Jackson turned to the other men, who he was shocked to see were finishing off the wounded Chetniks with long Turkish hook-bladed knives. When they were finished and were wiping the blood from their knives, he was introduced to them. They all had Middle Eastern names. They removed their Gypsy clothes and began tying checkered Arab scarves around their heads and pulling on long white robes.

"Look at you," Jackson said happily, relieved that his friend was safe and feeling sure that, with Aleksandar to lead them, he and Sabina would make it to the coast. "How many costumes do you guys have?"

Aleksandar suddenly lost his good humor. "Much has happened since we last saw each other, my friend, and for that I will let your insult go because you could not know. But I warn you not to joke about my faith. My brothers have showed me the one true way. Now I carry on the jihad in Bosnia, for the glory of Allah."

*This was the man who only weeks ago worshipped Bruce Springsteen,* Jackson thought. "I'm sorry, Aleksandar," he said in a less familiar tone. "As you said, I couldn't have known. And I thank your brothers who saved us. What are you doing here, if I may ask?" he said to their leader, Fadi bin Laden, a tall, dark-skinned Arab with a neatly trimmed black beard.

"We have offered our lives to our Bosnian friends," Fadi said in a deep, confident voice. He smiled at Jackson. "Such as yourself."

The most heavily armed of the men, Abdullah Abdul Akbar, a short, thick man with a scraggly beard, was more specific. "We have come to this land to kill the infidel Serbs who invade and rob this Muslim nation!"

"You're real Muslims?" Jackson asked.

Abdullah raised an AK-47 into the air defiantly. "We come from Iran and Libya and Syria, if that is what you mean. We come to fight for the glory of Allah, or die in the struggle and go directly to paradise. We have vowed to give our lives for this cause. You do not believe in us because we are America's enemy—"

"Look, I didn't mean—"

"—but we fight for what is right. The Bosnian people have turned to us because the Western world to which they were seduced for decades has turned its back on them. But we come. We will liberate Bosnia, or we will die trying."

"You are mujahideen," Jackson said.

"And they do more for Bosnia than America, Britain, France, and Germany combined," Aleksandar told him.

Jackson bowed slightly. He said with great formality, "I thank you, Fadi bin Laden, and Aleksandar my friend, and all of your brothers. You've saved us from these Serb animals."

Francisco Cippolini spoke up in a frightened voice. "I thank you, too, Mr. Fadi—"

"What is this?" Abdullah interrupted, nodding at the elephant.

"It is an elephant," Cippolini said.

"I know it's an elephant, you fool! What is it doing here?"

Cippolini came forward. "We have come from Italy to save it. We heard that it was starving, so we raised money to bring it to Italy."

Without warning, the Iranian fired his entire clip into the side and the head of the baby elephant. Blood poured out of it. The elephant wobbled, dropped to its front knees, and collapsed on the side of the road.

Abdullah turned on the Italians. "How many orphaned children have you passed on the roads? How many starving women? How many guns could you have purchased for the defenseless Muslims of Bosnia? But you come here to rescue that thing? That animal! When there are *people* dying every day!"

The Italians were again frightened for their lives. "Please, don't kill us—"

"Get out of my sight," Fadi said softly, but sternly. He wanted them gone immediately, because he knew Abdullah was capable of killing them all without warning when he was in such a rage.

The Italians quickly collected their things and watched over their shoulders fearfully as they hurried down the road, westward, toward Croatia.

"No! That way!" Abdullah ordered, pointing to the east, back into the heart of Bosnia. "You need an education!"

Aleksandar winked at Jackson. "He gets a little excited sometimes," Aleksandar whispered. He turned his attention to Sabina and smiled his most charming smile. "Who is this beautiful girl?" he asked Jackson in English, thinking she wouldn't understand.

"I am Sabina," she told him, smiling at him.

"We escaped together from a Serb camp," Jackson explained.

"A prisoner-of-war camp?"

"Worse."

"A concentration camp?" Aleksandar exclaimed. "I cannot believe it."

"I can prove it to you," Sabina said flatly.

"There is no need to prove anything, beautiful girl," Aleksandar said, smiling. "I would believe anything you told me."

Jackson saw Sabina blush.

Fadi came up to them. "We would all like to hear of this camp, but now is not the time. First, we will dispose of these Chetnik bodies, then take the jeeps and the food back to our base. I would very much like to hear all the girl has to say later. And I would very much like to know more about you, Mr. Robert Jackson."

## 40

THE MUJAHIDEEN BASE WAS A small, deserted roadside café at the junction of two highways in western Bosnia, near the Croatian border. In front was a dirt parking lot and a faded sign advertising Turkish coffee and sweet rolls. There were several tents set up behind the café. Beyond the tents were densely forested green hills.

That evening, most of the twelve mujahideen were assembled around a fire by the tents. Their mules were tied to a tree near a patch of grass. The jeeps they took from the Chetniks were parked next to the tents behind the café. Jackson, Sabina, Aleksandar, Fadi, and Abdullah were in the small café, sitting at a round table. The night was quiet and they could hear the mockingbirds singing in the hills.

They were all very interested and appalled as Sabina told her entire story. Jackson could tell they all wanted to ask her questions, but they didn't, and he was glad they didn't.

"After I left Adem with the refugees, I tried to get back to Dubrovnik," Aleksandar explained to Jackson. "I was unarmed and alone so I stayed away from the roads. There are many bandits on the roads these days. But before I got to Medjugorje, I came across a group of Chetniks in the hills about to raid a town.

"There were about a hundred of them. They were drinking late at night in a clearing. I crawled close and listened to their plans. They were going to kill or deport the men and older women. The girls and younger women were to be raped so they would have Serb babies, and also to instill fear into them, and into their fathers and husbands as well, so they would all leave the town and never dare to return. I heard them read off a list of names of the Muslim leaders of the town, who were to be taken to the reservoir and executed.

"The Chetniks had already bombed the town into submission, but it was their experience that that alone would not drive the Muslims out. The Muslims always expect it to be like any other war, where the town is merely occupied by the invaders. But the Serbs do not want to occupy. They want sole possession, so that Serbs from Serbia can be brought in to settle the town and make the town Serb. They are trying to redraw the maps of Serbia and Bosnia. It sounds unbelievable, but I swear it is true."

"I don't doubt it," Jackson said.

"There was nothing I could do for the town. I am only one man. Even if I could have convinced the people of the town what was to come, they had no weapons to defend themselves. So I took off running, hoping to make it to Mostar to get support. On the way, I heard gunfire, so I checked it out. It was Fadi bin Laden and his men ambushing a Serb patrol.

"When the shooting stopped I came to them and told them what I had overheard. They were only twenty men, but they set out at once. They gave me ammunition, since I had run out days before. In the early morning, as the Chetniks slept off their hangovers, they moved in and silently began slitting the Chetniks' throats. I must admit, it was very difficult for me to watch them killing in cold blood. But as I watched Fadi and his men I began to understand the jihad, which Abdullah had explained to me on the hike back to that town. Do you know about the jihad, Robert?"

Jackson nodded. "The holy war. Islam versus infidels. Yes, I know of it."

"Oh, but it is so much more. Did you know that any believer in the Islamic faith who dies while fighting for Allah will go directly to paradise? Abdullah explained to me that they are the martyrs of Islam. It is the greatest honor to die while fighting for the faith, which is why so many Muslims in the Middle East fight on against the Jews and the decadent West."

"You were never much interested in religion before," Jackson muttered.

"Oh, but that night as I watched my new brothers slitting the throats of the Chetniks, I felt the power of Allah sweeping through me. Never before, in all of our work together, Robert, had I ever felt that I did more for my people. After that, Abdullah began teaching me the ways of Allah. I am now prepared to give my life for the glory of Allah to carry out the holy war against the Serb aggression."

Aleksandar began looking to Jackson like a fanatic, the way the Serbs described Muslims in their propaganda—bloodthirsty lunatics; ready to die for Allah, prepared to kill all infidels. The Aleksandar he had known—as well as every other Bosnian Muslim he had ever met—was nothing like that. Jackson felt as though he had lost a dear friend.

"Did you save the town?" Sabina asked.

"As my new brothers were slitting the Chetniks' throats, a Chetnik awoke and began shooting. Soon it was a firefight. We were all packed together in a small clearing in the woods, amongst the Chetniks. You had to be very careful who you were shooting at. The fight lasted an entire minute. Every Chetnik was killed. We lost half our men, but have since picked up two boys from Jablanica."

"The Yugoslav army moved in," Fadi continued. He spoke English with an upper-class British accent. "We were forced to retreat. The town was attacked two days later, but we couldn't fight the army."

"We rely on ambush," Abdullah said harshly in his Arabic-accented English. "In this war, as in any war, it is better to attack by stealth, be brutal, and be decisive."

Fadi changed the subject. "We have heard Sabina tell of the camp and how she got there, but what about you, Robert Jackson? How did you end up there?"

Jackson told his story. They questioned him at length about Samuel West and his mission. All agreed that assassinating members of the Serb high command, as they referred to the Serb and Bosnian-Serb leadership, would have little affect on the war.

Abdullah looked at Sabina critically. "Perhaps your experience would make you more conscientious about following the ways of your religion. I urge you to surrender to the will of Allah, girl. Surely now you must be ready to embrace the sacred scriptures."

"On the contrary," Sabina said. "It is because your Allah permitted all this to happen that I renounce religion even more than ever." She sounded very strong and sure.

Abdullah folded his arms. "That is a mistake. I would be very pleased to introduce you to the teachings of Muhammad the prophet. And I could equip you with the chador."

"The chador? Are you joking?" Sabina said. "This is Europe, not Iran. I am Bosnian, not Arab."

Abdullah glared at her. "You should talk to Aleksandar. When we met him he talked of rock-and-roll music and parties with alcohol and women. Now he is a holy warrior. He will tell you the way to paradise, of the one true path. I sense a strength in you, girl. You should be bearing Muslim boys who will be the next generation of holy warriors."

Sabina was about to reply when suddenly grenades exploded behind the café. They heard massive machine-gun fire outside. Everyone hit the floor. Fadi, Abdullah, and Aleksandar grabbed their weapons and went to the windows. Jackson pushed Sabina under the table and kept low.

"I thought you said there were no Serb units in the area!" Jackson called out.

"There are none!" Abdullah shouted back.

"Some Serbs must have found the Chetniks we ambushed and followed us here!" Fadi shouted as he tried to look out the window.

"Serbs would not come this far!" Abdullah replied.

The café was splintering away. There was so much machine-gun fire the men could barely get their heads up to look. Fadi bin Laden finally raised his head to the window. He jerked it back down in a hurry.

"They are Croats!" Fadi called out incredulously.

"Croats?" Aleksandar repeated. "Impossible! Why would they fire on us? We're their allies!"

"I can see their flag! They are Croats!" Fadi insisted.

Abdullah began yelling to the Croats over the sound of the gunfire. He shouted that they were not Serbs, they were Muslims.

He kept repeating, "Allies! Allies!" over and over. But nothing could be heard over the firestorm outside.

Jackson was spread low on the floor next to Sabina, who crawled over to Fadi. She tried to take his red-and-white checkerboard turban. Fadi glared at her and would not let her have it. She crawled over to Aleksandar and he gave her his turban, then his M16 when she asked for it. She tied the turban to the barrel and stuck it out the window. Aleksandar understood what she was doing now and took it from her and held it up higher.

Soon the shots diminished, then stopped altogether. When they did, Abdullah began calling out again, "Allies! Allies!"

A harsh voice from the hills told them to come out of the café.

Abdullah led the way, followed by Fadi, Jackson, and Sabina. Sabina was carrying her pack over her shoulder. They stood in the middle of the encampment, surrounded by the bloody corpses of the mujahideen who had been sitting at the campfire.

"Holy shit," Jackson muttered, looking at the corpses.

"They are in paradise now," Abdullah said confidently, looking at his slain comrades' white-robed bodies.

Fadi was furious. "Fools! Look what you've done! Look at my men!"

"You are not Croats! Identify yourselves!" the voice from the woods called out.

"We are Fadi bin Laden and Abdullah Abdul Akbar, here to fight alongside our Muslim brothers and Croat allies!"

Soon the Croat paramilitaries—the Ustasha—came out of the woods with their guns trained on their prisoners. Like the Chetniks, the Ustasha wore black uniforms. On several of their black shirts was the swastika. Many of the Ustasha had shaved heads, and still more had spiderweb tattoos on the backs of their necks. One held the Croatian flag: blue, white, and red stripes, with a shield in the center.

On the shield was a red-and-white checkerboard design—like the Arab turban that Aleksandar had given to Sabina. The red-and-white checkerboard shield—the *sahavnica*—was the symbol of the Croat Ustasha government during World War II. The *sahavnica* is to a Serb or a Bosnian Muslim what the swastika is to a Jew. Tito had outlawed the display of the *sahavnica*. The new Croatian government brought it back, using it as the symbol of the new Croatia.

The leader of the Ustasha stepped forward wearing black riding boots that came up to his knees. By the light of the campfire, Jackson could see that his black uniform pants were tucked neatly into the boots.

"I am Captain Mirko Pavelic of the Mostar Guard. You are on Croatian soil. You are hereby sentenced to death. Get down on the ground."

"But we are your allies—" Fadi began.

"Silence! We don't ally with mujahideen or Turks!" Captain Pavelic shouted.

"But—"

"Get on your knees! Hands behind your backs!" The Croat captain walked forward now with a pistol in his hand. The other Croats—there were about ten—gathered around to watch.

"Wait!" one of the Ustasha shouted. When he came forward he walked up to Jackson. "I know this man," he said as Jackson looked back at him, recognizing him instantly. He was a forty-two-year-old former salesman from Dubrovnik. He had been a quite handsome bachelor before the war, with a pencil-thin mustache and slicked-back hair. But when the Serbs bombed the café in Dubrovnik, he had been badly burned in the fire. The skin on the right side of his face was now a grotesque blackish purple.

"This is the *Amerikanac* I told you about, who runs guns to the Turks. I pretended to help him, but always I told Admiral Skopjak when his shipments were coming, so our Croat brothers could intercept him and demand a percentage. This is the man who left me to die during the Serb offensive on Dubrovnik," Franjo said harshly to his comrades. "Hello again, Robert Jackson." Franjo lashed out violently and punched Jackson in the face. The blow caught Jackson off guard and made his knees buckle, sending him to the ground.

Jackson wiped the blood from his split lip. "Hello, Two Faces," he said to Franjo, calling him by the nickname that Zarko and some of the others had used many times, but Jackson had never used before.

"Captain Pavelic, I request that this man be given special treatment," Franjo said. "I have a score to settle with him."

"I saved your life once," Jackson pointed out. "We were friends."

"Were we friends when you left me for dead and went off with the Turks? You like pigs so much? You choose to be with pigs? Good. Now you will die like a pig."

Captain Pavelic considered Jackson closely. "He is an *Amerikanac*. He is an interloper. He has no business being here, helping the Turks in their insurrection. You may give him special treatment."

"I know him well, my captain," Franjo said. "I know that it would bring him great pain to watch his friends die like pigs as well."

"Yes, that can be done. But we don't have all night, and it may take some time to kill this *Amerikanac* properly. So we will shoot his friends quickly and proceed with the special treatment."

"Not the woman!" a Croat cried from behind.

"Do you desire her?" Captain Pavelic asked without turning around.

"Yes!" several called back immediately.

"Never has any of us had such a beautiful woman!" another Croat insisted.

"We don't have time," the captain said.

"We were promised women, Captain!"

The captain wasn't happy about it, but he put his pistol back in its holster. "Very well. We will make the others watch," he said. "Then we'll kill the two Turks before beginning with the *Amerikanac*. Who will be first with the woman?"

Several Croats came forward and pulled Sabina to her feet. They all began shouting and insulting her and cheering each other on. They tore at her clothes until she was standing nearly naked next to the campfire.

Jackson had leaped to his feet but was immediately kicked back to the ground. He tried again to get up, but Franjo and two others held him and wrestled him back down. Franjo held Jackson's head up to make him watch what was happening to Sabina. She was struggling with them as they tried to pin her to the ground.

Suddenly shots rang out from behind them. Jackson strained

to see Aleksandar atop the café, the full moon directly behind him, his mujahideen robe blowing in the wind. He was holding up his right hand, showing the Ustasha that he had a grenade. In his left hand was his M16.

"I've pulled the pin!" Aleksandar warned. "I'll kill you all if you don't put down your weapons right now!"

"You'll kill your friends, too!" Captain Pavelic shouted back.

"You're going to kill them anyway. I want you to drop your weapons. When my friends are safely away, I will let you go."

"You'll kill us anyway, because if you don't, you fear that we'll come after you."

"It is a deal that I am prepared to make with you," Aleksandar said simply, then added, "It is a promise."

"Do you promise before Allah, Turk?"

"Yes, before Allah," Aleksandar promised. "If I lie, may Allah strike me down, and may I never see paradise."

Captain Pavelic looked at his men, standing in a packed crowd around Sabina. None were in a position to fire. "Two of your friends will be permitted to take one of your jeeps," he finally offered. "You may go with them. The other two will remain here until you are away and we have secured the area. When I'm satisfied that you are gone and there have been no tricks, the other two will be given a jeep and allowed to go as well. You have my oath before God."

"No!" Aleksandar replied, after considering the offer. "You'll let them all go! Then I'll surrender myself to you!"

The captain took out his pistol and put it to Fadi's head. A lieutenant put the muzzle of his AK-47 on Abdullah's temple.

"They will die in five seconds if you don't agree," Captain Pavelic told him. "It is a fair deal. I need assurance you won't throw the grenade. If I let them all go now, we'll be at your mercy. You must see that. Be reasonable."

Aleksandar hesitated, then shouted, "All right! I agree!"

Jackson knew that this was the end. Aleksandar was not the same man he had known only a few weeks before. He would choose his new mujahideen brothers, or perhaps Sabina and one of the mujahideen. But Jackson would be left to die, and he knew it. As soon as Aleksandar and the other two were gone, the Croats would kill him and the other, then try to catch Aleksandar. He had to gasp for breath, realizing that once Aleksandar was gone he would endure a horrible death at the hands of Franjo and the others.

Captain Pavelic and the lieutenant pointed their guns in the air. Fadi and Abdullah scrambled to their feet, cursing the Croats. "Go," Captain Pavelic ordered. "Hurry up and go."

"No! I choose the girl!" Aleksandar shouted suddenly, pointing his M16 at Sabina. "And that one!"

From the top of the café, Jackson could see that Aleksandar was pointing his M16 directly at him.

"No!" Franjo cried out. He pleaded with Captain Pavelic. "Not this one! He is for me! It is my right!"

"Shut up, Two Faces!" Aleksandar shouted at him. He aimed the M16 directly at Franjo. "I'll kill you right now if you say one more word. I want the girl and the *Amerikanac*," Aleksandar repeated.

"Up!" Captain Pavelic ordered Jackson and Sabina. "Take one jeep and go!"

Jackson stood on unsteady legs. He went to Sabina, who also stood on her own power, but with difficulty. She covered herself with her torn clothes and her pack. Jackson helped her to a jeep and started the engine. He looked up at Aleksandar on top of the café.

"Go!" Aleksandar shouted. He still had the grenade in his right hand, the M16 in his left.

"Come on!" Sabina shouted back.

"Go now!" Aleksandar insisted.

Jackson drove out of the clearing behind the café and around to the front. He stopped just before pulling onto the highway.

"Stop!" she cried. "Wait here."

"I know," Jackson said.

They both looked up at the top of the café. They could just make out the figure of Aleksandar, standing defiantly in the silver moonlight. From behind the café, they could hear Captain Pavelic shouting something at him.

Sabina reached over and beeped the horn. "Blow up the jeeps!" she shouted.

Aleksandar hesitated for only a second before throwing the grenade in the direction of the jeeps and opening fire with the M16.

Jackson and Sabina could hear the Ustasha screaming, running for cover. They watched Aleksandar fire the rest of his clip. They heard the grenade explode, then Aleksandar slid down the red-tiled roof of the café. He ran and jumped into the back of their jeep.

"What about your friends?" Jackson asked, meaning Fadi and Abdullah. "Where are they?"

"They're on their way to paradise," Aleksandar replied, rolling his eyes.

Jackson sped off. In a few seconds they were on the highway racing south, around a curve which led to a long straightaway. Aleksandar told him to stop, but Jackson kept his foot on the accelerator.

"They have more jeeps!" Aleksandar shouted over the noise of the jeep and the rushing wind. "I could see them from the top of the café, parked just down the highway. They'll be coming for us. Pull over now!"

"The hell I will!"

"Trust me, Robert!"

Jackson looked in the rearview mirror. There was no sign of the Ustasha, but he could see Aleksandar looking him in the eye. They stared at each other for a long moment.

"Trust me, Robert," Aleksandar said again, still looking Jackson in the eye.

Jackson clenched his teeth and suddenly stood on the brake pedal. The jeep skidded to a stop.

"Run into the woods!" Aleksandar ordered. Sabina did so, then Jackson reluctantly followed, only after seeing Aleksandar wedge his M16 between the front of the driver's seat and the gas pedal. Then Aleksandar threw the car into drive and made sure it was going straight. He jumped out and ran into the woods, watching the red brake lights disappear down the highway.

"Go! As fast as you can, deep into the woods!" Aleksandar shouted. He waited for a minute at the edge of the woods, until he heard the surviving members of the Ustasha speed by in their black jeeps.

Jackson and Sabina stopped running and waited for Aleksandar. When he caught up to them, Aleksandar took off his mujahideen robe and gave it to Sabina to wear. Underneath his robe, Aleksandar had been wearing blue jeans and a San Francisco 49ers football jersey that had been a gift from Jackson.

## 41

AFTER HIKING THROUGH THE WOODS for over two hours, Jackson, Sabina, and Aleksandar sat and rested with their backs against three oak trees. Aleksandar was looking at Sabina as she rested her head on Jackson's shoulder and he stroked her hair. When she opened her eyes, Aleksandar smiled at her.

"Are you Robert's girl now?" Aleksandar asked her.

"Never mind that," Jackson told him. "What the hell were you doing with mujahideen? You were supposed to guide someone for Mr. Katz. Are your new *brothers* more important to you than Mr. Katz?"

Aleksandar was shaking his head. "Oh, come on, Robert, you know I'm no religious fanatic."

"Yes, but—" Jackson began.

"Robert, I heard about the offensive against Dubrovnik. I didn't even know if you were alive, and I certainly never dreamed that you'd try to take Katz's man north without me. I was planning to return to Medjugorje, but the mujahideen were killing Serbs and buying weapons for Muslims, so I decided to stay with them awhile to help."

"But—"

"Now that that's settled, I think we should move on," Aleksandar said, making it clear that it was the last word on the subject. "We should make as much progress as possible in the darkness."

"I'm sorry for those men who helped our people," Sabina said to Aleksandar, referring to the mujahideen.

"They wanted to die fighting in the jihad," he replied, shrugging. "They should be very happy now."

They walked on through the woods until they ran into a river. The rushing mountain water sparkled in the moonlight.

"Hold on, Sabina," Jackson said. "I want the compass." He tried to reach into the pack that Sabina insisted on carrying herself, but she would not let him.

"I'll get it," she told him.

Aleksandar was eyeing the backpack. "Yes, I noticed this pack. What else do you carry?"

"A map, a compass," Jackson answered for her. "We used to have some food and water, but it's gone."

"What else?"

Jackson shrugged.

Sabina knelt and took off the pack, unzipped it, and searched with her hand until she found the compass. She pulled out the flashlight as well and offered them both to Jackson.

Aleksandar suddenly reached out and snatched the pack from her hands. Sabina jumped to her feet and tried to take it back, but he would not let her.

"Give it to me!" she demanded.

"Keep your voice down," Jackson warned her. Then he said to Aleksandar, "What the hell are you doing? Give her the pack."

"Give me the flashlight," Aleksandar said to Jackson.

Sabina was nearly hysterical. "Give me the pack! Give it to me!"

"Aleks," Jackson said, and now he stood in front of his friend and balled his fists. "Give her the pack."

"Don't threaten me, Robert. You should have checked the pack a long time ago."

Jackson realized that his friend was probably right. He remembered that Sabina had kept the gun a secret from him, so now he, too, wanted to know what else she was carrying. He shined the light on the pack, where his friend was taking out two notebooks.

"What are these?" Aleksandar asked.

Sabina looked alternately at both of them. Realizing that they would make her explain, she came forward and took the notebooks, then sat on the ground and motioned for them both to join her. They sat on either side of her. Jackson shined the light on the books, which Sabina lay open now in her lap.

"I was in the camp for close to six months," she said, lowering her voice so that they could barely hear her. "Every day, if I could, I would record the name of every man or woman brought to the camp. I would record every beating. Every rape. Every castration, every torture, every impaling. Every time a prisoner was made to have sex with a pig, I recorded it. I have signed statements from every girl who was raped in that camp, and from every prisoner who ended up in the hospital. I would sneak into the hospital at night to take their statements. This I intend to deliver to the governments of the West.

"When the Western world hears of these horrors, how can they turn a blind eye to Bosnia any longer? How can they not demand the shutdown of the camps, even if it means using their military? These notebooks will lead to the closing of the camps, an end to the torture and rape and murder."

"They'll think you made it up," Aleksandar said. "They'll think that you made up the notebooks, that they aren't real."

"They will believe."

"Why?"

"Because nobody could make this up," Sabina told him.

Jackson began flipping through the notebooks. He held them close and squinted in the yellow light. He could see her neat handwriting in red ink.

"These notebooks are extremely important," Sabina went on. "The Nazis kept excellent records in their camps, but the Serbs keep no records. These are the only records of what is happening."

"The books could be important," Jackson conceded. "But you could have trusted me. I could have left you in the camp. I could have left you in Novi Belgrade or Jajce."

"Oh Robert, please don't be angry with me. From the first time I saw you, standing with the others in the compound, I wanted to love you. I knew right then you were different. You looked so strong, so healthy. Your teeth were straight and white, your posture upright and rigid, like a soldier's. Later, when I saw the boots on your feet, I knew that you must be a soldier. Never have I seen such boots except on the feet of the Blue Helmets. You made me weak in the legs, and I still get weak in the legs when you touch me. But you have to understand what the Chetniks and soldiers had been doing to me. And it is not as though America has done anything to help us. Why should I have trusted you? But you have to understand that now—since my sister's house, when you stayed with me—I have given you my heart, and I trust you with my life and I will go with you to America and love you always."

Jackson kept looking at the notebooks. He flipped through the pages until he saw the last entry. It was a sworn affidavit, detailing the things that had been done to a girl from a small town. He started to read it, but it was brutally detailed so he only skimmed it. At the bottom of the page, in barely legible handwriting, he could see the signature of Martina Feric.

"I saw how you were with the girl in the camp hospital," Sabina went on as he stared at the signature. "I couldn't let you get that way again. You care so much. If you read what was in these notebooks, I was afraid of how it would affect you. But most importantly, if I had told you what was in my pack, you would have insisted on carrying it, the way you carry my heart with you now. You would have known that if the Chetniks found the notebooks, whoever was carrying them would die a terrible death. I would rather die myself than to see any harm come to you."

Jackson looked at her and swallowed hard, unable to reply.

Satisfied now, Aleksandar stood. "I know it must be heavy going, carrying the girl's heart as well as your own, but it will be light out soon. We should make as much progress as possible in the dark."

They set out again and crossed a shallow stream and were again headed due west. Sabina took Jackson's hand as they resumed hiking through the forest.

# 42

ZARKO BEGAN RUNNING WHEN he heard the sound of the river. He had his hands out in front of him to protect his face and eyes from the branches as he rushed through the trees. When he reached the river, he slid down the bank and put his hands into the cold water. He scooped some out and threw it into the air.

"The Sana!" he exclaimed happily.

Zarko had been hiking through the mountains since escaping from the Serbs in the hills overlooking Jajce. He had learned that an attack was close at hand, and had planned to inform the Muslim and Croat defenses, but it was too late. The Croat defense force had pulled out of the city already. Rather than joining the exodus of thousands of Muslims and Croats from Jajce to Travnik, Zarko set out on his own to try to make it back to Medjugorje. At first he had carried the two pieces of his broken carbine, which he had nailed back together the best he could, but eventually he carved his initials into his uncle's old rifle and left it on a mountaintop.

"You have served my family well," Zarko had said aloud to the carbine. "But now it is time for me to obtain a tank."

He was scooping water into his dry mouth when he suddenly picked himself up off the river's edge, hearing something above him. He hurried up the muddy slope and heard it again, coming from the underbrush. He pulled aside the branches until he found a boy no older than five or six. The boy's face was gray and he was shivering from the cold. Zarko picked him up and carried him down to the river's edge, where he could see the boy more clearly in the moonlight.

"There is no need to be afraid, child," Zarko said, holding the boy in his arms. "What are you doing here?"

The boy's lips trembled when he spoke. "A mosque," he groaned.

"A mosque?"

"I must find a mosque."

"Why must you find a mosque?"

"The old man told me to," the boy replied simply.

"Where is this old man?"

"By the river."

Zarko looked about. "Where?"

"Far from here. I have been to many towns since the old man told me to find a mosque. But in every town, there are no longer any mosques."

"Tell me, boy," Zarko said softly, trying to be gentle with him. "Did the men with beards come to your town?"

The boy nodded.

"I, too, am looking for a town with a mosque," Zarko said. "Would you like to come with me?"

The boy hesitated, then nodded.

"In that case I will tell you something that will be of use to you. When we walk down the river and come to a town, we will tell the people there that we are Gypsies."

"Why will we tell them we are Gypsies?"

Zarko wanted to say, Because a Gypsy doesn't concern himself with politics. A Gypsy doesn't have to fight for his homeland because a Gypsy has no homeland. Most importantly, Gypsies have no leader who can manipulate them and feed them propaganda and convince them to kill Serbs or Croats or Muslims.

Instead, Zarko simply said, "You've never pretended to be a Gypsy before? You should try it. I do it all the time. It's fun to pretend to be a Gypsy."

"But my brother says Gypsies are bad."

"No, no. Gypsies are very good. I wish we were all Gypsies," Zarko told him truthfully. "What's your name, boy?"

"Jakobin."

"I will call you Jaka. It will make a good Gypsy name." He took the boy's hand. "Now, let's not waste any more time, my little friend. It is not easy to find a town in the north with a mosque."

Zarko and the boy walked downriver. They walked all day and much of the night. When the boy became tired, Zarko carried him, and when the boy was thirsty, they stopped and drank from the river. When the boy was hungry, Zarko told him they would soon find a town and would eat there.

When the sun came up, they could see a minaret rising above the treetops.

There was no evidence of any fighting in the town so they made their way to the four-hundred-year-old mosque. The white marble was wind- and rain-weathered, the dome a faded powder blue, and the minaret was leaning to the left, held up by scaffolding. Zarko pulled open the heavy iron doors and stepped inside.

The mosque was filled with men, women, and children. Many had Muslim prayer rugs pulled closely around them because it was cold inside. There was no heat. The hydroelectric plant that supplied electricity to the town had been destroyed months before.

Many of the people turned and stared at Zarko and the boy. The imam of the mosque came forward and welcomed them. When he saw the boy had been wounded, the imam took the boy to the doctor.

"We will do what we can for the boy," the imam said when he came back.

He gave Zarko a prayer rug and brought him close to the fire in the center of the mosque, where many people were huddled. Zarko could see that it was not wood that was burning and giving them warmth, but a pile of teddy bears.

"Where did you get such toys?" Zarko asked the imam.

"They were a gift from the people of America for the poor children of Bosnia."

"The boy will need antibiotics. Was any medicine sent with these toys?"

The imam shook his head sadly. "No. But I am afraid even antibiotics might not save his arm now. It has rotted."

"You can't take his arm! He's just a boy!"

"This isn't a hospital. We will do our best for him."

Zarko cursed the Serbs and would have gone on swearing but he remembered he was in the presence of a holy man.

"You're welcome to stay here as long as you wish," the imam said, forcing a smile. "But it is going to be a long winter."

Zarko looked out again across the great room, at the people packed together with prayer rugs pulled over their shoulders.

"I will stay the night," Zarko said. "But in the morning I must leave, to find my friends. We have important work to do."

"And the boy? Perhaps you can get him to a hospital."

"I have to leave him with you," Zarko said regretfully. "Where I am going, it is no place for a child."

"As I said, we will do our best for him," the imam said. "But it would be better if you could get him to the coast. This place, too, is no place for a child."

# 43

JACKSON, SABINA, AND ALEKSANDAR were walking westward through a dense forest. They came upon a clearing where the moon was clearly visible in the blue-black sky. Jackson was looking up at the stars, then suddenly he stepped into nothingness and was falling. He hit the ground shoulder first, knocking the wind out of him.

"Robert?" Aleksandar called down to him. "Robert!"

Aleksandar dropped down into the hole, which was only about five feet deep. Jackson was on his back, struggling for air. When he could breathe again, he looked up and was blinded by a bright light.

He thought he had died.

*Have I gone to heaven?* he wondered.

"Who's there?" he heard an unfamiliar voice ask. It was a man with an English accent. "Are you all right? Do you understand English? Or French?"

"Yes, yes," Aleksandar said. "I speak English, and I'm with an American."

The Englishman shined the light on the side of the hole so that Aleksandar could help Jackson out. Jackson walked hunched over as the pain in his shoulder began to set in.

Aleksandar helped him to a tent as the Englishman lit his campfire stove. He was in his midthirties, with gold-rimmed glasses and blond hair nearly to his shoulders. He wore khaki pants and a khaki flannel shirt. He was looking at them as if they were ghosts.

"Please forgive me; you must be wondering who the devil I am. Colin Cathcarte. I'm with the UN Genocide Convention investigation team. What in bloody hell are you doing here?"

Jackson introduced himself, Sabina, and Aleksandar, and explained that they were trying to make it to Split from Jajce. He asked the Englishman why he was there.

"It will be easier to show you in the morning," Cathcarte said. "For now, I suggest that you all lie down exactly where you are. This whole field is filled with land mines. I'll explain tomorrow." Cathcarte patted him on the back. "Get some rest. We can talk in the morning and I can offer you breakfast. It will be light soon."

"Can you help us get to Split?" Sabina asked.

"There's a UN base not far from here. I can see you that far. They can arrange for transport to Split."

"What is that smell?" Aleksandar asked.

"We can talk in the morning," Cathcarte said nicely. "You'll be quite safe here. Not to worry."

Cathcarte gave them blankets and they all went to sleep. In the morning, Jackson was the first to wake. He couldn't believe what he saw.

He was in a clearing the size of a football field. Within the boundaries of the field were a half dozen holes like the one he had fallen into the night before. Next to each hole were rows of rotting corpses.

At the far end of the field he could see the Englishman, taller and older than he had originally thought, pushing a long steel pipe into the ground. Next to him was another man, smaller and heavyset, with curly black hair. Jackson waved to them to see if it was safe to walk through the field to them. Cathcarte signaled him to come along.

"Good morning," Cathcarte said. "Actually, it's afternoon, but we thought we'd let you sleep. You all looked like you could use it."

"We're safe from land mines here?" Jackson asked.

"Yes. This is Simo. He runs the land mine detection equipment. We've cleared the entire field. Most of the land mines were buried in the graves. The perimeter is still a bit risky, I might add, but we're fine here. Just stay with us; you'll be all right."

Jackson shook Simo's hand. "You're Muslim?"

"Croat," the man said.

Jackson was immediately on guard. "What are you doing with that?" he asked Cathcarte.

Cathcarte motioned to him to watch. He twisted the long metal rod several feet into the ground. Then he sniffed the top of the hollow rod and nodded to Simo. He signaled Jackson to do the same. Jackson inhaled deeply through the end of the rod and immediately threw his head back and dropped to his knees, wanting to vomit.

"It's a mass grave," Cathcarte said. "As you can see, we've already dug up several of them here. This is how we find them. It's a little tough on the nose, but it's effective." He pulled the steel rod up from the ground and tossed it aside. Simo began digging.

"Why are you here?" Jackson asked.

Cathcarte wiped the sweat from his brow. "Spy satellites pinpointed these graves. We've known about them for months, but it wasn't until recently that we could get some men out here to investigate."

"No, I mean, why are you investigating? I don't understand."

"It's just your basic intelligence gathering. The satellites spotted the graves before the grass grew over them. Of course, we had no idea who committed the murders, so that's why we're here. It's for the war crimes investigation."

"War crimes?"

"I'm a forensic doctor," Cathcarte explained. "I'm here to gather evidence for the war crimes tribunal."

"You mean like Nuremberg?"

"Yes, of course. With a name like Robert Jackson, you must know all about Nuremberg."

Jackson didn't understand.

"As I'm sure you know, the UN has already handed down the indictments."

Jackson got back on his feet. "So, what's the verdict?"

"A few still had identification in their pockets. They're Muslims, all right," Cathcarte said, sweeping his hand at the stacked corpses lying in the field. "Can't be sure yet who killed them. Might be Serbs, because we found Russian bullets in the bones. Also, we've learned from other excavations that the Serbs tend to bury their victims all curled up so they don't have to dig such large holes, which is what was done here. But we're so close to Croatia, we haven't ruled out the Croats."

"Why are Croats killing Muslims now?" Jackson asked. "They're allies."

Cathcarte laughed. "Not for long. The Croats are sure the Serbs will soon overrun the country, so they're making their own land grab now. The Croatian government hasn't exactly condoned it, but Ustasha units have already been 'cleansing' some Muslim towns near the Croatian border."

Simo spat loudly and cursed. It was clear he was disgusted at his countrymen's recent actions.

"We've learned of a Croatian concentration camp near Dretelj," Cathcarte continued. "And after Franjo Tudjman's dinner in London, who knows?"

"Dinner in London?"

"You haven't heard? No, how could you. The president of Croatia was having dinner with other statesmen in London when he was asked how he thinks Bosnia will look in ten years. So President Tudjman drew a map on his cocktail napkin."

Cathcarte dropped to his knees and drew in the dirt. He drew the borders of Bosnia, then a line diagonally across the middle of the country. On one side he wrote, "To Serbia." On the other, he wrote, "To Croatia."

"But where's Bosnia?" Jackson asked.

"That's exactly the point. Tudjman envisions there will be no Bosnia. I don't know how he intends to pull that off unless Croatia turns on the Muslims, which judging by troop movements we've seen, could be any day now."

"What will the Muslims do? How will they survive without Croatia's help?"

"Oh, they can't. It would simply not be possible." Cathcarte shrugged, then dropped his instrument. "But there's nothing you and I can do about it, is there? Come on, I see your friends are up. Let me get you some food."

They passed by a stack of bodies crawling with maggots. "They all look like civilians," Jackson noted.

"That's because they are. It's insanity. We have several investigators in Bosnia checking out what our spy satellites show us. So far we estimate that eighty-five percent of the dead are civilians. In most wars, civilian casualties are closer to fifteen percent. It's remarkable. Look at these bodies here. Quite extraordinary. See how I've arranged them? Their feet are lined up in a perfect line, as if they were standing next to each other on level ground. Now, if you come down here very close, you can see the bullet wounds. The line the bullet wounds make is perfectly straight across all of the bodies, as if someone just lined them up and ran a machine gun back and forth across them in the back."

They walked a little further, then Cathcarte stopped once again next to a row of corpses. "See here? Their hands are tied with wire. Why kill all of these people when they're obviously helpless prisoners?"

In a minute they rejoined Sabina and Aleksandar, who were just waking. Cathcarte gave them army rations, which they ate despite the lack of taste and the disagreeable texture. The Englishman caught them up on news of the war.

"It sounds hopeless," Sabina said after he told them of the diplomats' most recent attempt to end the war.

"They claim progress is being made," Cathcarte told them. He drew another map of Bosnia in the dirt and divided it into ten sectors. "This is roughly the Vance-Owen peace plan. The Americans are quite keen on it. Under this proposal, Bosnia would be divided into ten territories: three for the Serbs, three for the Muslims, three for the Croats. The tenth is Sarajevo, which will be a divided city—or a united city, depending on how cynical you are. Each ethnic group's territories may or may not border another. For example, to get from one Muslim territory to another, you would have to fly. It's really pretty silly, but if it stops the fighting, I say full speed ahead."

Jackson studied the map for a minute. "It's unbelievable. How can they think that will work in the Balkans?"

"It's better than the latest Serb offer. The Serbs would get half of Bosnia, the Croats a third, and the Muslims two little pockets, one around Sarajevo, the other at Bihać."

"How could we ever agree to this?" Aleksandar asked incredulously. "It rewards the Serbs for their aggression."

"Not completely," Cathcarte disagreed. "It appears that the Serbs have been targeting Muslim and Croat civilians because they're trying to drive them—or scare them—away from their homes and towns. That way the areas can be repopulated with Serbs, possibly in the hopes that these Serb areas in Bosnia can eventually be absorbed by Serbia, creating, in effect, a Greater Serbia. Under this plan, even though each ethnic group effectively controls its own territory, the territories themselves will remain a part of Bosnia—that is, Bosnia won't be partitioned and the Serb territories won't be permitted to become a part of Serbia." Cathcarte shrugged. "In any case, at least it will end the war."

"Under this plan, who would get Prijedor?" Sabina asked. Sabina's town was near Prijedor.

"I think the Serbs would get Prijedor," Cathcarte said.

"Who would get Jajce?" Aleksandar asked.

"The Croats, I think."

Aleksandar was furious. "And what about the men responsible for this?" Aleksandar asked, waving at the grave sites in the field. "At least they will be punished, yes?"

"Well, that would be nearly impossible. It could have been any soldier with a machine gun and a shovel," Cathcarte explained. "But every bit of evidence helps. You see, the key in these war crimes trials, we believe, will be to produce evidence of a widespread plan to commit these atrocities. That way we can go after the leaders, the men who must have been responsible for the orders to do such things."

"Do you believe you will be able to?" Sabina asked.

Cathcarte shrugged. "From what I know now, I can tell you with all confidence that there was definitely a widespread plan. Very systematic. It certainly must have come from the top. But proving it is the easy part."

"I don't understand," Aleksandar said. "If proof is the easy part, what's the problem?"

"Well, you can't very well have a trial without an accused, can you?" Cathcarte pointed out. "The only reason we had the Nuremberg and Tokyo war crimes trials after World War II was because the Allies won and Germany and Japan were occupied. We rounded up the suspects and invented the idea of a war crimes tribunal. It was the first and last time such a thing has taken place, until now, if—"

"If you have the suspects," Jackson finished for Cathcarte.

"Yes. But of the forty-six indicted men, forty-three are Serb and three are Croat. Neither side has lost the war, and neither side is going to hand over their own men to be displayed to the world as war criminals."

"Then how will there be trials?" Aleksandar asked.

"That's not my department," Cathcarte said. "If you want my opinion, there's a good chance there will never be a trial. The UN has no power to come into a country to extradite accused war criminals. So they may never get the men responsible."

Suddenly Jackson jumped to his feet. "How many men did you say were indicted?"

"Forty-six."

Sabina also realized the significance of the number forty-six. She reached into her pack and handed Jackson a single sheet of paper. "I made a copy of your friend's list for myself," she explained when she saw the surprise on his face. Jackson had lost West's original list when he was stripped naked on Mt. Vlašić. "In case it was important."

Jackson eagerly handed it to Cathcarte. "Are these the men who've been indicted?"

"Why, yes. Yes, they are." Cathcarte looked up at him, puzzled by the dollar signs.

"You clever old man," Jackson said, almost to himself. "Katz, you clever old bastard."

"What is it, Robert?" Aleksandar asked.

Jackson looked up, realizing that the others were staring at him. He started to reply, then smiled and asked Cathcarte, "Look, about going to Split—"

"Yes, well, I debated whether to wake you, but I elected to let you sleep," Cathcarte interrupted. "I'm afraid it's a little late to set off for the UN camp now, but I sent word to them over the radio. There'll be someone here in the morning to escort you." He stood up. "You seem very interested in this war crimes business. With a name like Robert Jackson, I can certainly see why."

"Why do you say that?" Aleksandar asked.

"You mean you don't know who Justice Robert Jackson was? No, I suppose you don't."

"Who was he?" Jackson asked.

"An American Supreme Court justice. He was also the chief prosecutor for the Allies at Nuremberg. I must admit that I didn't know of him, either, not until I took this assignment and studied up on my history. But since you share his name, I assumed you must know something about him." The Englishman smiled at Jackson. "I guess we all need a history refresher course now and again, don't we?"

## 44

**IN THE EARLY MORNING HOURS,** long after the campfire had died out, Jackson slid out from under Sabina's arm, out from under their blanket, and crawled over to Aleksandar. Jackson shook him awake and signaled for him to follow. They walked off together as quietly as they could toward the trees.

"What is it?" Aleksandar asked when Jackson stopped at the edge of the woods. Jackson had a queer look on his face, one that worried Aleksandar. "Is there something wrong?"

Jackson was grinning, his white teeth and the whites of his eyes the only thing Aleksandar could make out in the darkness. "Everything's going to be fine. But I have to leave."

"What do you mean? We're leaving tomorrow. Everything has been arranged; it'll be easy. The UN camp in the morning and Split before nightfall."

"You know I can't go to the peacekeepers."

"You can give them a different name, Robert. There are no U.S. soldiers at this UN camp. They won't know who you are or that you deserted. You could tell them anything, they—"

"That's not it." Jackson smiled, then reached into his pocket and pulled out a slip of paper. He stuffed it into Aleksandar's pocket. "I'm giving you an address in Venice. It's an intermediary who can put you in touch with Mr. Katz. I'm sure he'll help you and Sabina get to America once Sabina shows him the notebooks and tells him about the camps. Tell him I'm coming, soon, with one of the men from the list."

"What?" Aleksandar exclaimed.

"I'm going back to Omarska," Jackson told him.

Aleksandar stared back at him.

Jackson put his hands on his friend's shoulders and stood very close to him. "Mr. Katz sent West to Bosnia on a mission he thought could end the war. It sounds crazy, but I think there's a shred of hope in the plan. West's mission was to kidnap one of the indicted war criminals and bring him back to stand trial. Mr. Katz has access to intelligence from the spy satellites. He knew about the concentration camps, about the towns being overrun and the girls being raped and the Muslims being slaughtered, but he knew the Western governments weren't about to go public with the information, therefore nothing would be done.

"Mr. Katz knew that the best way to show the world the horrors was to broadcast it as the 'trial of the century.' Imagine the attention the first international war crimes trial since Nuremberg would get with today's communications technology! News stations would carry the trial live. Networks would be falling over themselves bringing stories of the trial night after night. It would make the cover of every magazine and newspaper in America. Workers would watch the trial during their lunch hour. The whole world would stand still when the verdict was read."

"And all this will end the war?" Aleksandar asked doubtfully.

"It might, because once the world learns what's happening here, how can they not put a stop to it? Besides, Aleks, it's important for the world to learn what's going on, because we can never allow what's happening here to be repeated."

"That's a noble thought." Aleksandar frowned. "But in the meantime, my people are being butchered."

"Aleks, your only hope is help from the West, especially America, but Americans don't understand what's going on here. How can the president send American boys to die for Muslims in a place called Bosnia, a place they never knew existed?"

"I don't want Americans to fight for me," Aleksandar insisted. "I'm prepared to fight the Serbs, and so are many others. We just want guns so we can defend ourselves."

"And you'll have them, as soon as the Western world understands what's happening here, and as soon as they learn that the Muslims are the victims in this war. It's hard for Americans to look at Muslims as the good guys, because they don't understand the situation here. But when the people of America and Europe find out the true story, they'll demand that we do something."

"I'm not so hopeful."

"I am, Aleks. Think about it! After a few weeks of U.S. warplanes bombing their positions, the Serbs will back off, especially once the U.S. arms the Muslims. How tough will those Chetniks bastards be once they have to face armed resistance rather than defenseless civilians? I'm telling you, Mr. Katz had it all figured out."

The Muslim now clapped his hands onto Jackson's shoulders and pulled him close so that their noses were only an inch apart. "I will go to Omarska, Robert."

"No, Aleks. You need to take care of Sabina. She's very . . . she's very valuable."

"She loves *you*."

"She needs to get to America."

"She needs to be with you," Aleksandar disagreed, "whether it's in America or Italy or wherever you decide to go."

"Trust me."

Aleksandar was shaking his head. "Forgive me for saying this, Robert. I don't mean it as an insult. But I would have a better chance at Omarska than you. I think you know that."

Jackson shook his head. "I've been there. I know the town. I've seen guards leaving the bars in town, drunk and defenseless. It won't be as difficult as you think. I even know one of the guards whose name is on the list."

"I think you overestimate the importance of this mission. Let's go back to the coast, where we can continue to smuggle guns to my people."

"I plan to, Aleks, but not the way we used to do it. That was small-time. After I return from Omarska, Mr. Katz will owe me. With his backing, I'll turn our two-bit smuggling operation into a private Bosnian defense department!"

"If that's possible, then I'll go with you to Omarska, and together we'll use Mr. Katz's money to arm my defenseless people. Why must I go to America with Sabina, who you say you love?"

"I love her enough to want her to be safe in America. There's only one man I can trust to get her there. That's you, my friend."

Aleksandar shook his head violently. "This is insanity! This is my country, Robert. I cannot desert my country!"

"You're forgetting something. Getting Sabina and the notebooks to America could do more for Bosnia than all the guns you could ever hope to deliver yourself. A war crimes trial will take time, Aleks. But if her stories of the camps and the rapes of the defenseless towns get coverage in America, the people will insist that we put a stop to it. I can't take Sabina to America. You're the man who has to get her there, Aleks. I can't trust anyone but you with such a responsibility."

Jackson and Aleksandar stood there in the dark, not speaking.

"Should I get her for you?" Aleksandar finally asked.

"In a minute. First, I have a few things to tell you about her."

"What things?"

"You have to be gentle with her," Jackson began. "She doesn't like to be touched unless she invites you—"

"I wouldn't lay a finger on the girl!" Aleksandar cried.

"Shut up and listen. You haven't been told half of what she's been through, Aleks. She has to learn to trust men again. She's a very special woman. It would be a shame if she were ruined for any man. You have to do more than get her to America. You have another responsibility to her which is just as important."

"Tell me what I need to know." Aleksandar sighed.

"She doesn't like to be touched—even if you only mean to put your arm around her to comfort her—unless she first gives you her permission. She likes to talk about the future, about how her life will be in America. Most importantly, avoid talking about children, at least until she tells you everything that happened to her."

"Is there anything else?"

Jackson thought for moment about how special he thought both Sabina and Aleksandar were, then added, "Buy her fresh tulips every day once you get to Venice."

Aleksandar took a deep breath and let it out. "For a while I thought Sabina had made you forget about your Maria."

"Sabina is special. But nobody can replace Maria."

Aleksandar's eyes narrowed. "I would be very interested in meeting your Maria when I reach America."

"Don't even think about it—we're still engaged," Jackson said, trying to laugh. Then he added seriously, "Just take care of yourself and Sabina."

Aleksandar was shaking his head doubtfully. "Sabina's not going to want to leave you."

"I'll make her go," Jackson said plainly.

"What will you tell her?"

"Whatever it takes."

"It won't be easy," Aleksandar told him, but he knew his friend's mind was made up.

Jackson took off Emir's chain and held it out to his friend.

"You keep it," Aleksandar told him. "I won't need it where I'm going—you will."

"Emir looked up to you," Jackson said. "He'd want you to have it."

"He looked up to you, too, Robert."

"But he loved you like a brother," Jackson insisted, pulling the chain over Aleksandar's head. "I also love you like a brother."

Without taking his eyes off of Jackson, Aleksandar touched Emir's chain, then in turn brushed his fingertips over the cross, the crucifix, and the crescent and star medallions that had once protected the young shepherd.

"The chain is yours," Aleksandar said, offering a compromise. "But I'll accept it as a loan, to protect me and the girl. Then I'll send it back to you when I reach America."

Aleksandar offered his hand, and Jackson shook it. Aleksandar started to speak, then stopped suddenly. He kissed Jackson on both cheeks.

"May you live a hundred years, brother," Aleksandar said formally.

Jackson knew that, for the first time, he had truly earned the respect of Aleksandar, whom Jackson respected more than any man he had ever met. They regarded each other in silence again, looking at each other for the first time as equals.

"I won't disturb you when the girl comes," Aleksandar told him as he turned to go.

"No. Come back in a few minutes."

Jackson waited at the edge of the woods for Sabina. He heard her whispering his name as she ran toward him.

"I'm here," he said.

"Robert, what is it?" Sabina cried. "Is there danger? Are you not well?"

"I'm leaving," he said flat out.

"No!" she said, coming right up to him.

"Do you understand about the list?"

There was another pause, then Sabina held him and rested her face on his chest. He stood there with his hands at his sides.

"You don't want to hold me one last time?"

"I'll hold you again soon," he whispered.

"Hold me now," she told him.

He put his arms around her and they held each other closely.

"Why do *you* have to go? Send Aleksandar."

"It has to be me. I've been there already."

Sabina was crying into his shirt. "Say nice things to me."

"Let me brush your hair," Jackson said.

She clung to him and turned her head slightly from side to side as he stroked her hair.

"You're so much like a cat," he said.

"Can you hear me purring?"

"I can feel your heart beating."

"Yes," she said, and put her hand over his heart. "I can feel your heart as well as mine. They are inseparable. Especially when we're this close."

"No matter how far apart we are, our hearts are inseparable."

"I believe it, too."

He held her at arm's length now, brushing the hair out of her eyes. "Soon you'll be safe. You'll be far from here and won't have to worry about a thing. You'll begin to remember how great life can be."

"When will I see you again?"

Jackson frowned, so Sabina put her fingertips on his mouth. "At least end it with something nice," she told him.

He reached down and held her hands gently.

"Aleksandar is taking you to Venice," he said.

"How will you find me?"

"Aleksandar will find you a place to stay," Jackson said after a slight hesitation. "He'll take me to you."

"And what if Aleksandar doesn't live to show you where I am?"

"Don't talk that way."

"You're right. But what if it did happen that way?" she asked through her sobs. "I'll never see you again."

He held her close again and she looked up at him. He could see the tears, her eyes puffy, her chin quivering. He had forgotten how very young she was.

"What if *you* die?" she said through her tears.

Jackson smiled. "I won't die, because then you'll die, too, since I have your heart. That's why I'll guard my life like never before. Do you think that I'd ever let anyone harm you?"

Sabina shook her head.

"Then you can see now why I'll return to you?"

Sabina looked into his eyes, then smiled and nodded. "Yes, I see it now."

They heard Aleksandar coming back.

She tried to fix her hair. "I wish I didn't look so ugly. I don't want you to remember me like this."

"You're beautiful. And when you get to Venice, Aleksandar will buy you new clothes and earrings."

"And a brush. I will try to look beautiful for you when you come."

Aleksandar walked up to them. "I have food and water for you, Robert," he said.

Jackson took the bundle before looking at Sabina one last time. "I admire you very much, Sabina."

"Ciao, Robert," she said softly.

After a moment, Jackson turned and ran off into the woods.

—————•◦•—————

## 45

**IT WAS THE FIRST SNOW** of winter. The people of Medjugorje looked to the sky and had faith that it was a gift from heaven, a whiteness to cover the ground, the restaurants, the hotels and the souvenir shops along the main strip. It was Sunday and the sun was beginning to set. There were few religious pilgrims in the town in the dead of winter, but the masses and the rosary services went on, played over the loudspeaker, though now the streets were empty and there were few people there to hear any of it. And in the church choir every evening, the Virgin Mary continued to appear to the six visionaries to give her message of peace.

On the way to Apparition Hill, a lone figure leaned into the wind, trudging through the snow-covered road. The fur-lined hood of his parka covered his face. His hands were in his pocket and he was walking slowly in the twilight, past the family farms and the playground, then to the base of the hill where the gift shops were boarded up for the winter.

He walked up the hill carefully, mindful of the loose stones under the snow. He paused briefly at each of the fourteen bronze tablets on the way to the top. Finally, when he reached the spot where the Virgin Mary had appeared, he brushed the snow away and sat on a rock. He sat waiting with his elbows on his knees and his hands clasped under his chin, staring up at the cross. His bare hands were trembling from the cold.

"All right," Jackson said aloud. "I'm ready."

He had been coming to the hill every night since returning to Medjugorje a month before. *Fifteen minutes isn't enough time,* he had told himself, remembering that he had once told Zarko he would give her fifteen minutes to appear to him on the hill. Now he realized that he might have been a little unrealistic.

*Miracles take time,* he told himself. *Now I'll give her fifteen minutes every day.*

When he had first begun returning to the hill night after night he simply did it to have some time alone, to work out his troubles, to think about Maria. In time he found himself speaking aloud, and realizing that talking to oneself is a sure sign of insanity, he decided it would be better to talk to the great crucifix mounted at the top of the hill. Soon he wasn't talking to the crucifix, he was talking to God, finding a small measure of comfort in their one-sided conversations. Now Jackson was trying to do most of his talking in the form of prayer.

"God, thank you for giving me this moment," Jackson began, his eyes closed tightly. "Thank you for my health and for my life. Thank you for having faith in me even though I've been finding it so difficult to have faith in you. Thank you for watching over me even when I spoke against you."

*Do you really believe in God?* he asked himself as he prayed.

*I'm trying,* he told himself, and tried to focus on his prayers.

"Thank you, especially, for Abram Katz. Thank you for his generosity, and please protect him, keep him healthy and safe, so that we can continue our work here."

Jackson always made sure to pray for Katz because it was his money that had turned Jackson's small-time smuggling operation into a miracle—a real-life miracle—for the Bosnians. Instead of one boat, one guide, one group of men taking guns into the heart of Bosnia, now he had seven boats. Katz also supplied him with a barge, which Jackson used to smuggle trucks, jeeps, and, if his latest deal went through, a tank into the port of Ploče, and then into Bosnia. He had twenty men he could count on to guide the weapons in-country, and dozens of others to go along for protection and to drive the cars, buses, and trucks.

*Yes, you better watch over Mr. Katz, God,* Jackson thought as his mind wandered, as it often did, when he talked to God on the hill. It had troubled him at first that he couldn't focus on praying alone, and very often thoughts popped into his head while he was praying that were not the things he wanted God to hear. But then he realized that God must understand. Besides, at least he was praying now.

"Thank you, God, for Zarko. Thank you for giving me a right-hand man that I can trust and can rely on. Thank you and please watch over him and Zinna and Jaka."

*Without the Gypsy, none of this would have been possible,* he told himself. It was JuJu's emerald—which Zarko had held on to and had given to Jackson as soon as Jackson had returned from Omarska—that had paid their considerable expenses to smuggle Dusko out of the country and deliver him to Katz, which earned Katz's gratitude and support. And it was Zarko who had volunteered to go north, to bring back men like Adem and so many of his friends in the Krajina Brigade with their buses and their knowledge and their determination. Without Zarko—and without Zinna's black-market connections—it wouldn't be possible for him to be capable of delivering so many guns, rockets, jeeps, and possibly even tanks to Bosnia. But just as importantly, Zarko and Zinna—who lived together now along with the Gypsy boy who had almost lost his arm—gave Jackson something that he had been afraid he might never have. They were his family now. He lived with them in Zinna's hotel, which they urged Jackson to make his home.

But Jackson knew that he would soon return to Dubrovnik. The bombing had stopped and the Serbs had been driven from the mountains. Jackson longed to return to the most beautiful city he had ever seen. He had made a lot of friends there before the siege and, despite missing Maria and despite the war, he had genuinely enjoyed the nights in the cafés, the afternoons learning to play soccer from the children next door, and the early morning jogs through the ancient fortress-city. He couldn't wait to walk down the Placa again and have the people wave to him, calling him *simpatican* and buying him drinks, inviting him to their homes not only because they thought he was a powerful arms merchant, but because they wanted to thank him for coming to their country to help. He loved the people in Dubrovnik and that was where he planned to make his home.

*All right. Back to your prayers,* he thought. *You'll be in Dubrovnik soon enough.*

"Please, God, protect Aleksandar and Sabina," he continued, his eyes still closed, the snow beginning to accumulate on his hood and on his shoulders. "Please let them make it to America, and please help Sabina grow strong again, as strong as she was when she orchestrated our escape from the camp."

He laughed now, shaking his head in admiration at her cleverness, when he thought about it. He should have known the night they escaped. She had told him to come to the commandant's window in the night, to pick up the map and compass. But she had hidden the food and water, the maps and the compass, in her pack in the ceiling of the camp hospital. There was never any need for him to go to the commandant's window. She could have given him those things when he first asked for them, but she didn't give them to him then because she wanted him at the window that night. She was counting on him to rescue her.

Jackson had had over a month to think about their escape, and he had finally come to the realization that she had set him up all along, had used him to get her and the notebooks out of the camp. She must have known that first night that he wasn't a typical prisoner. She saw him crawling through the window after surveying the camp, and she knew that he was with West, a man the commandant and the chief investigator had feared very much. She probably guessed that, like West, he was an American. She even admitted to him once that she recognized his army boots. She must have decided that he was her best chance to escape. There was only one problem—why would he want to help her? What was in it for him?

*As all Bosnians know,* Jackson thought, *Americans only do what's in our best interests.*

After thinking about it over and over, he concluded that Sabina had intentionally let the commandant catch her stealing West's list, knowing the commandant would begin beating her just as Jackson was coming for the map and compass. She knew Jackson needed her help. She knew he had to escape that night, before the chief investigator confirmed that he wasn't a real doctor. She knew that he would have to save her from the commandant because he needed the food, water, maps, and most importantly, a place to hide inside the camp until the search was called off.

*You had it all figured out, Sabina,* he thought. *Even a selfish American couldn't leave you to face certain death as punishment for helping him. You knew I'd take you with me.*

Jackson didn't blame her for not giving him the benefit of the doubt, especially not after what she'd been through. But her mistrust of him had caused her to knock the gun out of the back of his pants as he was pulling her aboard the train, which could have proved a costly mistake.

*That was a dangerous move, Sabina. If you were here now and we were honest about all this I'd tell you that I might have needed that gun.*

But he also realized that Sabina never would have knocked his pistol away if she didn't have another one stashed safely in her pack. She knocked Jackson's pistol away on the train and didn't tell him about the one in her pack because, after everything she had been through, she wanted control of their only gun in case she needed protection from him. She wasn't about to trust any man, not even after he helped her escape from the camp. She pulled the commandant's pistol on him as soon as she saw her sister's house and thought that she no longer needed him.

Sabina had tried to confess those things to Jackson after he had earned her trust by staying with her at her sister's house. But he hadn't given her the chance. There was no need for her to ask for his forgiveness, although he wished now that he could ask for hers.

*Have you realized that I never really loved you?* Jackson wondered. *I was wildly attracted to you, and I needed you and, yes, I admired you so much. But I didn't fall in love with you, Sabina. I hope you forgive me for making you think that I did, just as I hope you forgive me for using you to save Aleksandar.*

Aleksandar was the bravest man Jackson had ever known, but he was also reckless, and he wouldn't have lived much longer during the war. So Jackson lied to Aleksandar, telling him that he must see Sabina safely to America to deliver the notebooks that Jackson said were invaluable, even though Jackson knew it wasn't true. He knew the notebooks would be, at best, a headline for a day or two in the newspapers, but they wouldn't change a thing. The killing of defenseless civilians was no secret. The mass graves were no secret. The thousands of refugees desperately trying to gain entry to Italy, Austria, Germany, and dozens of other countries, including America, were no secret. Just as he had always doubted that a war crimes tribunal would do much to make a difference—despite what he had said to Aleksandar and despite delivering Dusko to Katz, which he did solely to earn Katz's favor—Jackson knew that Sabina's story of the camps would change nothing. He had only told Aleksandar that Sabina and the notebooks were important because he wanted Aleksandar to get them both safely to America.

*I could see he was taken with you, Sabina, as any man would be, as long as that man wasn't already in love with another, as I am. I hope he buys you tulips every day in Venice, and I hope you give him a chance. I think he's deserving of you—I think you're both very deserving of the other.*

Jackson doubted that he would ever know if they would stay together, but he was sure that Aleksandar would get them both safely to America.

*That's enough about them,* Jackson thought. *Pray for Maria now.*

"God, please please please let Maria be happy. Please let her have everything she wants in life. Please help her finish school and become a doctor. Please help her to help those who need it most, as she's always wanted to do, and please let her find a good man who will make her happy and give her the family she's always wanted."

*Do you really mean that?* he asked himself.

*No, I don't mean that,* he told himself truthfully. *I shouldn't lie. I still want her. I'll always want her.*

*Then why haven't you tried to reach her again?*

He had decided that he had to let Maria go. He couldn't ask her to leave America, to live with him in the hell on earth that his new home had become. Even the coastal cities of Split and Dubrovnik, which were now safe from attack, were filling with refugees. He couldn't ask Maria to drop out of medical school and leave her family for the kind of life he could offer her. He realized that, despite the great loss he felt and knew he would always feel, he couldn't be so selfish. He loved Maria too much to ask her to give up so much for him.

*Don't get yourself thinking about her again,* he ordered himself, knowing that he didn't miss her any less since making his decision to let her go. *It's too damn cold up here tonight.*

He resumed his prayers. "Please, let the people here learn to live in peace. Not just for four years or even forty, but forever. Please make this goddamned war end."

*Oh, that's a good one,* he told himself. *Swearing while you're praying.*

Sometimes he considered not even praying for peace, because he doubted it would ever come. He feared that peace might be impossible in the Balkans. They had enjoyed over forty years of peace since the end of World War II, but almost out of the blue they had started killing each other just like they'd been killing each other for centuries. He didn't see how it would ever stop because every time they slaughtered each other nobody took the blame. The Serbs and Croats had been arguing for decades over how many tens of thousands the Ustasha were responsible for killing in World War II, but nobody ever took so much as a first step toward binding up the nation's wounds. In the Balkans they merely pretended to forget or they simply denied the bloodshed, but Jackson believed that crimes of the magnitude that were taking place there couldn't be forgotten, so the hatred and distrust would simmer and grow and be passed on from generation to generation.

To Jackson the rape of Bosnia was like the rape of the girls in the camp. If they survived, their physical wounds might heal and they might marry and raise a family and maybe they could even live the rest of their lives without ever appearing to be affected. Similarly, Sarajevo and Jajce and all of the cities and towns would be rebuilt, and someday a Balkan country might even put on another successful Olympic Games and the world would applaud them again for moving past their troubles. But just as the thousands of girls like Sabina who were raped would carry emotional scars with them for the rest of their lives, a country that was raped like Bosnia had been raped couldn't forget, which was tragic because nations, Jackson thought, weren't as strong as people. A nation could all too easily be manipulated by a leader willing to use the past to stir up long-suppressed feelings of fear and hate.

Then Jackson thought about the rapist, who is usually punished before being given the opportunity to be rehabilitated and to rejoin the community. How does a country rehabilitate itself? And who is going to see that punishment is meted out? Before that can even happen, somebody has to stop it.

*I know I can't stop it,* he admitted. *But I'll stay here and fight for what I think is right for as long as it takes. I swear to God I will.*

*You did it again,* he told himself. *Swearing while praying. Taking the Lord's name in vain.*

He asked himself again, as he often did when he prayed, *Do I really believe in God?*

*Probably,* he thought. *Well, I know I want to believe. I'm sure as hell trying, even though it isn't always easy.*

Then he wondered despite himself, as he often did while he tried to pray, why a loving, merciful God wouldn't put a stop to the war.

*That's enough,* he ordered himself. *Nobody can answer that one. Don't even bother to try. It's too cold for this tonight.*

But he desperately wanted to know why God would let so many helpless people be slaughtered.

*I can't expect miracles,* he told himself finally. *There's no such thing as miracles. All I can do is try to do the right thing, as often as I can, the best that I can. That's all I can do, and I can't expect miracles and I can't worry about things I can't control.*

That's why, when he prayed for himself, he only asked for one thing.

"God, please give me the courage to always do what my heart tells me is the right thing."

Before he could finish the rest of his prayers, he heard someone coming up the hill over the many loose stones, so he quickly crossed himself. He still wasn't completely comfortable among the religious pilgrims who sometimes came to the hill at night, even during the winter, to pray. They always assumed he was like them—a true believer who had made the long pilgrimage to pray at the spot where the Virgin Mary had appeared. Often they tried to befriend him and invited him to prayer groups or special services at the church in town. He wasn't ready for all that. He knew he had a long way to go before he'd set foot in a church again.

He opened his eyes and stood, burying his cold hands deep in the pockets of his parka as he turned to go.

That was when he saw her.

She was standing just above him, in front of the great crucifix. Her long, curly black hair fell down her back. The sun was setting and the sky was crimson behind her and the lights from the town looked like stars surrounding her. The snowflakes seemed to dance about her. She smiled at him, her face glowing now. Tears fell from her bright eyes, dark blue like the Adriatic at night.

He dropped to his knees.

She walked up to him. He could see the cross, the crucifix, and the crescent and star medallions dangling from Emir's silver chain around her neck. He embraced her, holding her tightly around the waist, and he wept, his tears streaming off his cheeks and into the snowy ground.

"Maria."

# EPILOGUE

**THE TREASURED STARI MOST BRIDGE** stood in Mostar for over four hundred years. In November 1993, four years to the day after the Berlin Wall came down, signaling the beginning of a New World Order, the Stari Most collapsed into the Neretva River under Croatian shelling.

By March 1994, the Muslims and Croats had ended one year of hostilities against each other and once again fought together against the Serbs. In November 1995—after Serb ambitions were checked by six weeks of NATO air strikes and a Muslim-Croat offensive—the United States helped broker the Dayton accord, which set up a loose federation of Muslim and Croat territories in Bosnia on the one hand, with a Serb republic made up of "ethnically cleansed" Bosnian territories on the other. The Bosnian Serbs, who made up just 34 percent of the population in Bosnia before the war, were given control of over 49 percent of Bosnia.

The International Criminal Tribunal for the Former Yugoslavia, the first international war crimes court since Nuremberg, was established by the UN Security Council in February 1993. By November 1996, the tribunal had announced the indictments of seventy-five suspected war criminals—three Bosnian Muslims, eighteen Bosnian Croats, fifty-one Bosnian Serbs, and three Serb officers of the former Yugoslav People's Army. However, because the Dayton accord provides no process by which war criminals are compelled to be handed over for trial, many indictees may never be arrested.

Dusan Tadic, a Bosnian Serb, became the first international war criminal to stand trial since the end of World War II. In 1993, after being indicted for "the collection and mistreatment, including killing and rape, of civilians within and outside the Omarska camp," Tadic moved to Germany on a Muslim prisoner's passport, where he was recognized by displaced Muslims living in Germany. Tadic was arrested and extradited to the Netherlands to stand trial at The Hague. On May 7, 1997, Tadic was convicted of committing "crimes against humanity." In one case, Tadic beat three prisoners unconscious and then forced a fourth to bite off the others' testicles.

Dusan Tadic's trial was largely ignored in America and around the world.

The two men indicted as the overseers of Serb "ethnic cleansing"—former Bosnian-Serb president Radovan Karadzic, and Ratko Mladic, the commander of the Bosnian-Serb army—are living free in Bosnia. Although Yugoslav president Slobodan Milosevic is widely recognized as the mastermind of the "ethnic cleansing" campaigns against non-Serbs in Bosnia and Croatia, he was never indicted for his role in the Bosnian War. Instead, after signing the Dayton accord, Milosevic was applauded for agreeing to bring peace to the Balkans.

More than two hundred thousand people were killed during Milosevic's campaign of "ethnic cleansing" during the Bosnian War. Over two million people were forced from their homes.

In his zeal to create a Greater Serbia, Milosevic next turned his full attention to the predominantly Albanian province of Kosovo, where his nationalistic policies had been stirring up ethnic tensions that had lain dormant for years. Because 90 percent of Kosovo's population are of Albanian descent, the province had enjoyed a great deal of autonomy before Milosevic came to power in the late 1980s. However, in 1989, Milosevic revoked Kosovo's autonomy, causing a nearly decade-long attempt by the Albanian majority to peacefully restore their rights. Eventually the Kosovo Liberation Army (KLA) took up arms and was able to establish control over portions of Kosovo, but in 1997 Milosevic sent Serb troops to engage in a systematic campaign of destruction and terror, looting and pillaging property belonging to Kosovo Albanians, who were forced from their homes. The government-sponsored violence against Albanian civilians inevitably led to an escalation of the crisis.

In February 1999, using the threat of military pressure, NATO demanded that both sides meet in France to sign a peace agreement. The KLA accepted the plan in mid-March, but instead of agreeing to the peace plan, Milosevic escalated the conflict once again by launching another large-scale offensive in Kosovo. Over the next several months Milosevic's forces engaged in a widespread and systematic plan resulting in the murder of thousands of men, women, and children, and forcing the deportation of more than 740,000 Kosovo Albanian civilians.

On March 24, 1999, after months of unsuccessful attempts at restoring peace, NATO launched an air campaign against Serbia and Milosevic's forces in Kosovo. Milosevic agreed to a UN-approved peace agreement seventy-eight days later.

In May 1999, Milosevic was indicted by the UN war crimes tribunal for crimes against humanity for ordering the campaign of terror and violence directed at Kosovo Albanian civilians. The United States has offered a bounty of up to five million dollars for his capture.

15- 1/07/03
16 = 6/13/05